GULLIVER TRAVELS

by Justin Luke Zirilli

For Mom
I'll never let you read this, but it's still dedicated to you.

ROUND I

CHAPTER I

My plane touches down on the tarmac of John F. Kennedy International Airport roughly, screeching and squealing and throwing me forward against my tightened seatbelt. The ground outside flips from diagonal to horizontal.

I should be excited.

I am terrified.

The first thing I think as I step off the Boeing, traipsing my way through the scuffed carpeted passageway, is: wow. So I'm actually here.

My second thought is: if I change my mind, the very plane I just stepped off of is headed back to LA in an hour.

Third? I would kill for a cigarette.

(And a lighter.)

Perched atop his "throne" (a stool half the size of his big ass), the power-tripping Hispanic security guard confiscated my fire back at LAX — because a skinny twenty-something with bleached-blonde hair blaring Robyn through his earbuds just MIGHT be on the terrorist watch list, one "Praise Allah" short of setting the plane ablaze mid-flight. I liked that lighter, too. It was stamped with the symbol for Sagittarius and produced a flame taller than a crack lighter's.

My legs are still half-asleep, my body jittering from nicotine withdrawal. I'm blindly following my fellow flyers, figuring at least one of them must know where they're going. All around me families are reuniting and hugging, helping each other with hefty carry-ons and sprinting for the street outside. Boyfriends and girlfriends and boyfriends and boyfriends lock in teary-eyed embraces. College sweethearts? Lovers no longer at a distance? Whatever. Just get me to the street.

The crowd leads me to a main concourse, but none of the little stores I find along the way sell lighters. With each disappointed cashier's glance, my skin itches more, my head hurts more. I am pulled in a throng of people who are walking far too fast for my comfort.

I give up searching for smoking paraphernalia when I reach the baggage claim and then the busy sidewalk outside the terminal, protected by a massive cement overhang. I take a deep breath, filling my lungs with car exhaust as my ears try to make sense of the cacophony of honks, screams, and squeaking luggage carts assaulting me from every angle. Someone thunders past me, almost knocking me over my wheeled suitcase, screaming into his cell phone: "FUCK that! Tell him my flight was late. I'll be there in an hour!" A mother with three little children looks up at the source of the spewed profanity, then at her kids, wondering if permanent damage has been done. I wonder: what was she expecting? Welcome to New York, lady.

And welcome to New York, me.

The wait in the cab line takes twenty excruciating, cigarette-less minutes. I find myself picking at the skin of my fingers fanatically while nibbling bits of flesh off my lips. Luckily the cab driver — a heavyish guy in a turban with wild black and gray facial hair — becomes the first saintly New Yorker I meet by offering me one of his own cigarettes from a crinkled soft pack, along with a push-button blue lighter. Either he's psychic or my anguish is emblazoned all over my face. Regardless, I rip the treasure out of his hand through the bulletproof partition between us. All he asks is that I hold my ciggie below the cab window, since smoking in cabs is illegal and he doesn't want to lose his license. Fair enough. At this point, I would smoke on the roof of the cab, hanging on for dear life with my one free hand as we sped along the highway.

Outside the airport is a pretzel-like labyrinth of knotted three-lane roads, choked to suffocation with other cabs and cars, buses and trucks. My driver hunches forward, growls under his breath, and steps on the gas, swerving this way and that to get us out to the highway. All the while he holds a heated conversation in a foreign tongue on the Bluetooth earpiece he keeps jammed into his ear with a hairy, chubby finger.

Meanwhile, a small touch-screen television on the back of the driver's seat blazes to life, drowning out my driver's foreign bitch session with tinny stereo music. It tells me to see *The Lion King* on Broadway, presenting a shot of Times Square and a full cast of singing animals covered in tribal face paint for maximum enticement. It urges me to try out a new tapas place somewhere near Jamaica, which I thought was an island but is apparently also in Queens. (Where is Queens? In the city?) And finally the TV sweet-talks me, hoping I will consider buying a triplex co-op in some neighborhood called Gramercy that costs (*cheap! going quick!*) a mere seven million dollars.

This cigarette hasn't helped as much as I hoped. These are pure, unadulterated nerves I'm dealing with. I should be overjoyed — I've arrived at the next chapter in my up-until-now unremarkable life. Gulliver takes Manhattan! An epic journey into uncharted territory! But I am too busy trying to unpack the explosive bundle of nerves that has taken up residence in the center of my gut, and before I know it, I am sucking on the filter and we've barely even moved from the terminal.

Discouraging voices in my head ask if this was all worth it. Leaving Los Angeles for a city I've never seen except in movies, where it is usually being ravaged by a monster or natural disaster of some kind. Then again, it's not like there's anything worth sticking around for back there. This isn't me pressing the reset button on my life so much as kicking the shit out of it and trading up for a completely new one.

And this train of thought reminds me I have yet to turn on my cell phone since landing in this city. Such an oversight is so unlike me, but this is a brand new Gulliver, after all. Moments after I power on, my iPhone chimes, vibrates, and pings for my attention as the voicemails and text messages begin to stack up.

Voicemail takes priority. First message is Mom, cheery yet clearly worried because I didn't call her the second I got off the plane (she knows the exact minute it landed). Of course she doesn't admit that she's worried, but her voice gives it away.

"My sweetie! Are you landed yet? Hope the flight went well. Did you get any sleep? Did you remember to not put liquids in your carry-on? Hope your luggage made it with you! What time is Todd picking you up? Call me soon, okay? Just a quick ring for your Mommy. Love you!"

Dad is next. His relaxed voice is weighed down only slightly by his annoyance. I picture him at his desk at work, stacks of paper teetering around him, his office phone ringing off the hook.

"Hey, Gulliver. It's Dad. Hope you landed safely. Listen, please call your mother; it's hard for me to make any calls, or honestly, get ANYTHING done when she keeps beeping through every five minutes. I told her you probably forgot to turn your phone back on, but of course she's expecting nothing short of a shoe bomber sending your plane plummeting into Lake Erie engulfed by flames. Okay, kid? Miss you already. If you need anything, just shoot me an email. Love you."

The third message is from Graham. Just hearing his voice twists my already anxious stomach into an even tighter knot. I sneer at my iPhone and consider deleting the message before it's through as, in his cautious, oh-so-delicate voice, he asks if maybe I'm caught in traffic on La Cienega, because he really, really needs to talk to me about everything that happened five months ago. He's had a revelation! Things don't have to be like this! And thanks so much for texting him that I'd be willing to see him and let him speak his mind and heart!

Oh, and he's been waiting for me at the Starbucks on Santa Monica, exactly where I told him I'd be as I was settling into my seat on a 747 prepped to take me across the continent — roughly three thousand miles away. He's even got my iced venti quad soy caramel macchiato awaiting my arrival.

"Hurry, before it gets watery! See you soon, baby!"

Baby? Fuck you.

Goodbye Graham, hello New York.

The fourth, fifth, and sixth message are also Graham, and promptly deleted. One voicemail remains, the first I'm excited to hear. I'm overcome by raucous laughter, attracting the attention (and concern) of my driver, who breaks from his dramatic Bluetooth exchange just to check in on me.

It's Todd, my former big from Sig Ep at UCLA and soon-to-be-roommate, who is roaring into the phone.

"Gully! Get. In. My. City. NOW, BITCH! You find some hot piece of ass on your way up the damn street? Join the mile-high club and get locked in the bathroom mid-flight? I will COCK BLOCK YOU! Call me, you whore."

Anger: gone. Excitement: rapidly flooding in to replace it. To hell with Graham; thank God for Todd. There's no way I'd be making this trip if it weren't for him. (Well, both of them, technically.) First because he tortured me every week on our cross-continental phone calls, saying if I ever felt like California was becoming a bit of a yawn, why not join him in the city that never sleeps? And second, because I would never, ever pick up and move to a city where I knew no one, no matter how bad things got in Cali.

And now to respond. Mom and Dad get the same text: *"Don't worry, I'm alive, plane was delayed, will call you later. Love you!"*

Graham gets: *"Sorry BABY, must've slipped my mind! Can we try for the same time tomorrow?"*

Cruel? Maybe. But don't think for a second the asshole doesn't deserve it.

Then I call Todd. The phone doesn't even have a chance to ring before his deep, should-be-hetero voice blasts out of the receiver.

"Oh my GOD, I cannot BELIEVE you're actually here!"

The cabbie turns to see where this booming voice is coming from and I shrug, pointing at my phone before shrinking into the corner between my seat and the door.

"About that. I'm not actually in New York, I decided it was too risky to move out of LA in this recession. Plus, all that drama? Gone! Graham and I are back together, we're moving in together and we're engaged! You'll come to the wedding, right?"

There is a moment of silence, broken only by Todd's deep breaths.

"You fucking smart ass, when will you be in my city."

"Well." I peer between the driver and passenger seats. "I see a lot of big, tall buildings up ahead, and we're not stuck in gridlock so… soon?"

At 10 PM the East Coast is dark but for bouncing red taillights and the trailing white blurs of streetlights on whatever highway my driver has selected to take me to my new home. My body thinks it's 7 PM and wonders where my glorious western purple sky has gone. Beyond this light show, I can make out the expansive skyline of Manhattan with its many-shaped silhouettes dotted with yellow and white lights, stabbing the sky and getting taller then shorter, taller then shorter. I am breathless at the sight. Even downtown Los Angeles, with its skyscrapers visible from the freeways, has nothing on this.

"Listen Brobraham, I hooked us up with some sweet reservations at this place here in Hell's Kitchen. Burgers. Big fuckin' burgers. You're not vegan or any shit like that, right?"

"What if I am? New city, new diet…"

Todd doesn't stop to respond. "After that, I got us on a couple of lists for parties in HK, Chelsea, FiDi. Some new ones, some old. There's one where the dancers swing over the crowd on fabrics and cables. Or at least that's what I'm hearing."

Originally from Long Island and now back on his native East Coast after a four-year educational stint at UCLA, Todd speaks at the speed of light on speed. He has a way of forcing you into silence because your brain is too busy trying to catch and process every word he flings at you. Sometimes you even wonder if he's speaking English because his brain produces language too quickly for his mouth and vocal cords to keep up. Even after living with him for three years at UCLA, I still find my head racing to catch every word and assemble it properly so he doesn't have to.

"Well, I was thinking about a quiet night in, actually. Flights always drain me. Ooh! Can we go antiquing instead?"

"Smart. Ass. Listen I have to clean this place up before you bust in. Had some boys over last night, fucking disaster area. Plates. Cups. Condoms. A moose eating out of my trashcan."

"You serious? Well, minus the moose, I mean."

"You know it. Call when you're downstairs. You remember the address, right?"

I don't, but I scribbled it on a piece of paper, which I am now pulling from my pocket. "Forty-seventh and ninth?"

"Yuppo. Apartment 14N. Like nipple. Or nuts. I once bagged a dude with three nuts. Did I ever tell you 'bout that? Totally hot, in a weird way. Tell the doorman you're here for me and he'll let you up. See you soon, bro!" And he's gone.

Doorman? Did Todd ever tell me he had a doorman? If so, maybe he just said it too fast. Then again, Todd is also the kind of guy who rarely, if ever, talks about himself. Back in college, he shot his way up the ladder of our fraternity by being the guy who asked questions and only talked about himself when you asked first, then quickly set his sights back on you. He was endlessly interested in what YOU were doing, what YOU had to say. Maybe he never thought the doorman was important enough to mention on our weekly phone conversations. But now that I'll be living here, I'm certainly intrigued.

Another yellow cab swerves in front of mine. My driver slams on the brakes, screaming foreign profanities out the window before apologizing profusely to me. I shake my head and inform him that he can make up for my first New York City near-death experience with another cigarette, which he flips behind him and I catch in my left hand. Then the world's most generous cab driver returns once more to the fight on his Bluetooth, leaving me to look out the window, blowing smoke at the passing cars and lights.

My mind wanders to reality (stupid, stupid thing!). The facts are thus: I have moved to New York with nothing. No job. No friends, except for Todd. Three suitcases. A nice injection into my savings courtesy of Mom and Dad, despite their initial insistence that they would never fund my fanciful flight across the United States. And that's it. Most of my things are still at home (out of my old apartment and back in the basement of my parents' house in LA). Of course, I need to find work — fast. The money in my savings won't last long. In LA there was no work to be had but at least I had a home, and friends, and a car.

Then again, my old place was a ramshackle one-bedroom shared with a desk monkey at Paramount who left dishes in the sink for weeks until they crusted over and congealed into a food-coated tumor. It was cheap, which made it easy to pay the rent with freelance design gigs here and there — a poster for a local band, a brochure for a law firm or advertising agency, a mockup of a website for some Silicon Valley startup — but I sure won't miss it.

And the friends I called my own in Los Angeles were frenemies at best. Half of them were buddies of Graham also, ones who knew but never bothered to tell me that my beloved boyfriend of five years was cheating on me. The other half wanted to sleep with me (either for the first time or a repeat). Either way, endless drama. Enough to push me onto that plane and out of LA.

And my poor car Rufus, three joy rides away from an overheating engine and ultimate vehicular demise. We had some good times, but if I didn't abandon him first he was bound to leave me — stranded on the side of the 10 freeway. It was high time to move on.

So I may have come from basically nothing, but it's still scary. There's nothing to fall back on here. If I can't make it, I'll have to beg Mom and Dad to fly me home, carting an extra suitcase just to contain my shame. Todd said I can stay rent-free until I find a steady source of income. That should be comforting, but it's one thing to speak so generously, another entirely different thing to keep this offer on the table when it's month four and I've contributed nothing besides an extra body to occupy the bathroom. Todd has assured me time after time this will not be the case: "Trust me, bro. We lived together before, it worked then. It'll be like old times, but without the closeted housemates and at least fifty percent less puke. Better beer, too." But still. Warnings from Los Angeles echo in my ears, twisting my already-knotted stomach.

"It's too expensive there, even the Starbucks costs more."

"During a recession? Are you insane? You'll end up working in porn before you land a legit job."

"You don't live in New York City, you struggle to stay alive as it slowly kills you."

"My sweetie, please be careful. And remember, if it gets too hard out there, you can come stay with Daddy and me for a while, save up, and then start over out here."

With a deep breath and my eyes shut tight, I forcibly shove them all out of my mind. Despite all this, my fleeting conversation with Todd has lifted the wall of anxiety that's been plaguing me since my ride to LAX. Fuck reality. At least for today. Tonight will be a riot — eating and drinking and hopping from bar to bar with Todd. He told me before I left this morning he had cute friends I need to meet: a blonde with a killer six-pack and a job at an advertising firm, an up-and-coming go-go boy who somehow climbed the ranks of gay New York City nightlife in record time and now sits at the right hand of one of the scene's top promoters. And others, whose descriptions are equally impressive. (And equally intimidating.) I can hardly wait to see what the night — not to mention the rest of my life — has in store.

When I look back up, Manhattan has snuck up on me. I don't recall going through a tunnel or crossing a bridge, but here I am. Those skyscrapers, so small and slender from my vantage point on the highway, now loom like giants. I am looking out the window, upward, following floors and floors of chrome, brick, and glass.

Everywhere are traffic lights no one pays attention to — cabs and trucks and SUVs blatantly run red lights, honking at each other as though they're entitled to. Pedestrians scurry in front of those red light-runners. Well-dressed twenty-somethings in Armani and Kenneth Cole pour out of every opening on the sidewalk on their way to God knows where. Every block has a Starbucks, and every Starbucks has a line (a comforting similarity to home I cling to immediately). A party bus bounces by, bass blasting inside, shaking the windows of the taxi.

Then the dark, closed stores in the vicinity of Penn Station beget the neon explosion of Times Square, which looks just as it did in New Year's Eve shows I've seen since my childhood. My driver is cursing again, this time because the mayor apparently shut down half of the roads going through this major thoroughfare to make things better for pedestrians. Around us thousands of people are flooding out of shows, Playbills clutched in one hand, Jamba Juices or lattes sloshing in the other. Men are selling crib notes displaying "100 Sex Positions" for a dollar. Someone else is waving a sign advertising: "Obama Condoms! Palin Condoms!" There are shabby looking Mickey and Minnie Mouses and a six-foot-tall walking Statue of Liberty wearing Happy 2011 sunglasses, selling photo ops. I look at it all and tell myself: this is now mine.

New York, I've come for you. Please be gentle.

I catch sight of a street sign and deduce we're only a few blocks from Todd's place. I thank the fuming driver, tip him a lot more than I need to, and grab my luggage out of the trunk. I sling two bags over my shoulders and drag the third behind me.

Instantly I realize I should have stayed in the car. The Times Square crowds are beyond obnoxious (as Todd forewarned). I'm constantly dragging my suitcase over people's shoes or turning to my side so those too stubborn to alter their path can get by without crashing into my stuff. I earn sneers and swears. I am apologizing, wondering if any will pull a gun or knife on me.

But then the crowds are gone almost instantaneously. I look behind me and still see the surging sidewalk masses of Times Square, but here on this side street there are pockets of air between groups of people. I'm no longer shoulder-to-shoulder with tourists speaking forty different languages. On top of that, everywhere I look, I see gay. Two men holding hands. A cute blonde ten feet ahead of me doing an (impressive) impression of Wendy Williams.

"Chase, you spend too much time watching that crap!" his friend in a side-ways-cocked blue visor laughs.

"Whatever, you're just jealous," the impressive impersonator says as they turn the corner and are swallowed by the river of people walking along what a sign tells me is 9th avenue. It's shorts weather, but so many of my new neighbors have opted to wear skintight jeans. I won't fault them because I'm sure I'll be sporting the same when I go out tonight.

I finally reach the corner of 47th street and 9th avenue. I adjust the bags on my shoulder and walk into the building, unsure of what to do next.

"What floor?" asks the doorman, busy watching a telenovela on a small TV hidden behind his desk.

"I'm here to see Todd DiTempto?"

This earns a sigh of frustration as the man bends down and produces a book that he plops on the desk and flips through furiously. "Floor fourteen. Elevators around the corner. Sign here."

I ride up in a plush elevator all by myself, my eyes drawn to another of those small televisions, this one installed above the twenty-five buttons (the word of the day is "vacillate"). The doors open up to reveal a carpeted hallway with light blue walls and framed pictures hanging every ten feet. Under the doors I can hear televisions, laughter, glasses clinking. I find 14N and knock.

The tall wall of muscle that answers is my fraternity brother and now-roommate. He has a drink in hand, smiling that douchey dumb jock grin, revealing dimples as deep as keyholes and perfect teeth.

"BRO!"

I am lifted into the air as my bags fall to the floor, and then the sweetest words I've heard in ages:

"Welcome HOME!"

CHAPTER 2

I feel like Little Orphan Annie as I step into the "little two bedroom" I now realize Todd never adequately described. High ceilings. Crown moldings. The walls painted in a warm taupe. The whole thing looks like a spread torn from a Crate & Barrel catalogue. Candles flicker all around the apartment, hidden on every shelf and in every corner. I wonder if Todd takes time to light these every night, or if he has only done so now in my honor.

"Holy shit! 'Little two-bedroom?' Who in God's name did you sleep with to get this place? And where did you bury his body?"

"Someday I will tell you the story of this apartment. Rest assured it has a lot to do with rent stabilization, a long line of relatives stemming down from an old woman who owned this place in the 20's, and a lot of names on the lease that are neither mine nor yours."

Todd takes me on a tour of my new place: the chef's kitchen, complete with island counter, tall oak cabinets, a double oven, and a dishwasher — a definite departure from the kitchen at my old place, which featured a sometimes-functional hot water faucet and a shiny but solely decorative cold water handle.

"Only three suitcases?" he shouts from the hallway as I check out his living room, complete with a TV larger than a stained glass window. "You shipping the rest tomorrow in a dozen steamer trunks?"

"Start fresh, you said." I step in front of a full-body mirror and survey the havoc wreaked on my hair from the open cab window, nodding in approval at the result.

Todd comes out of nowhere, his arm wrapping around me, and gives me a loud peck on the cheek. "Since when do you actually listen to me?"

"Since I listened to your insane suggestion to move here and now my survival depends on it?"

Just so we're clear: Todd DiTempto is a good 6'1". He looks like a giant beside me, despite the fact that I'm almost 5'10" myself. His face is blanketed in stubble and his eyes are set deep in his face, creating dark circles that complement his angular face perfectly. His hair is as black as those circles — professionally short and perfectly trim — which I guess it has to be if you still somehow kept a job in the financial sector during the whole recession thing.

Next on the tour is my new room. A queen-sized bed. A window looking out over 9th avenue and the masses below. The walls are the lightest of blues, trying to pass as white. There's a desk, a standing six-drawer dresser, a walk-in closet. The floors are shiny wood. The walls are empty except for two photos — Todd and me on the day he graduated, my face doing all it can to keep from crying. And then next to it, me and Todd on my own graduation day a year later, where I'm just recovering from crying because the prick surprised me by showing up all the way from New York. Sounds from the street below seep in through the window — all pitches and patterns of honking, so much laughing and screeching, the scraping of tires on gravel, an ice cream truck's singing bells, the *squeeeeak* of the door to the taco place underneath us — all of this riding a slightly chilled breeze that smells like laundromats and hamburgers.

"Unfortunately, there's only one bathroom," Todd says from the door.

"Oh, what a dump," I mumble, too overwhelmed to be convincingly sarcastic. I turn to him, my eyes stinging and moist. "Todd… this is. I. Thank you. I don't even know how."

And I'm hugging him again, squeezing with all my strength. He shouts, "Up up up!" and lifts me above him like I'm a twenty-pound barbell at the gym. I screech and slap at his head, mussing up his hair, sending flakes of gel flying in all directions. I yell at him to let me down. Todd releases me from his inhuman grasp, throwing me across the room onto my bed — is that memory foam? I look up at the not-actually-white ceiling and catch my breath, still laughing.

"Get dressed, get pretty. Unpacking and all can wait. We've got burgers in twenty, then we're getting schwasted at Industry, Therapy, Barrage, Vlada, The Ritz, Posh, and Bar-tini."

"That's it? Sounds pretty uneventful." I smile, faking a yawn. "Are there any bars in this city we won't be hitting up?"

"I won't be satisfied until you have no memory of your first night living in this city, you dig?"

"Consider it dug."

Todd gives me thirty minutes to get ready even though we're already running late. I throw my stuff on the bed and set to work prettifying myself.

"So what if we're tardy for the party, bro?" he says as I pick out a blue and white striped polo and a pair of distressed, indigo-dyed jeans. "We always arrive 'gay late.' If you get there on time, you pay by having to wait twenty minutes for the rest of the crew to show."

After a healthy spritz of one of Todd's twenty colognes (the one I picked, from Diesel, is shaped like a clenched fist), we are in the elevator, then on the street, walking down 9th avenue through the evening throng. Traffic on the street is gridlocked and totally pissed about it, but on the sidewalk, groups of gays en route to kick off the night's festivities are moving at a healthy clip. It takes twenty minutes to reach the restaurant (which is only a few blocks away) because Todd recognizes someone every twenty-five feet and has to stop for obligatory hugs and chatter. I am introduced then forgotten, too busy nodding and smiling politely to take in anything that's being said. Then we're off again, and stopped again, until we reach the restaurant.

A small gaggle of gays screams: "Her Majesty finally arrives!" There are hugs, kisses (both single and Euro-double), then we enter the establishment, where a table awaits us near the center of the dim dining area.

This night wastes no time becoming a blur. Every time I blink, minutes fly by and empty martini glasses stack up next to me like a crystalline pyramid. Some taste like apple and caramel. Others like chocolate and more still like pomegranate, lychee, melon, Tobasco — baskets full of citrus fruits, blindingly neon in their liquored liquid form. I shoot them back, each so sweet in its own way. The room spins. I am giddy. My Italian turkey burger has been ignored — sparing stomach space for vodka and gin and whatever they might be mixed with.

It is during this blurry meal that I meet Rowan, Servando, Brayden, and Shane — Todd's core crew. A roll call of the gay devils:

Rowan is tight and toned with a buzzed head of probably-blonde hair. He has an eyebrow stud and a penchant for saying, "Bitch, please!" He's wearing a skimpy wifebeater that hangs off him, exposing a pert nipple whenever he reaches over to steal ("Borrow," he says, with a wink) one of my french fries.

Servando is tall and skinny with a head of moppy black hair. His high-pitched laugh is infectious, as is his cherubic smile — seasoned with just a bit of sex appeal conveyed by deep blue eyes that pierce straight through you and devour.

Brayden has dark, hard spiked hair highlighted with a deep grape-purple dye — a veritable hairy explosion with its blast center atop his head. It's wholly capable of popping a balloon if you smacked it into his forehead hard enough; in a fight, he need do nothing more than lower his head like a bull and charge. He has mastered the five o'clock shadow in such a way that he deserves a feature in *GQ* — so the rest of us hirsute fellows can learn his secrets. He wears a pair of impossibly tight skinny jeans that still somehow hang low and a V-neck tee that probably came from the Californian sweat shops of American Apparel.

Shane is wide-shouldered and has muscles to rival Todd's. His hair is similar to mine — swept down across his forehead in a Nike-esque swoop that keeps falling in front of his eyes before he wipes it away. His shirt asks me if I'd like to FCUK him (my unspoken answer is: "Yes, please"). When he smiles, deep rivets of dimples emerge.

My eyes are falling out of my head. My dick doesn't know which way to point. I settle on imbibing as much liquor as my mouth agrees to pass along to my body, answering their many questions via giggles and slurs. They are all smiles and jokes and fleeting touches of my hand from across the table as I tell them about La La Land.

"I went there once," says Rowan. "My ex-boyfriend brought me, we went to the bars in Weho. Fiesta Cantina. The Abbey. Um, East West or something like that?"

And with each passing bar name I am transported back there, surrounded by the smiling frenemies I hastily abandoned, dissipating in my memory like so much gay dust. The dark stone walls of Abbey, the flickering heated torches in the open-air courtyard. The crowded second floor at Fiesta, cheap drinks and a deck overlooking the strip. The "we wish we were all that" faux-class of East West, with its Pier 1 wannabe decor and frantic gobo lighting.

And in each and every one of them, my ex-boyfriend.

I nod and smile like this rolling list of booze-serving locales brings back the fondest of memories. It's okay — I've left that all behind. And with each drink it gets further behind still, until LA is just a tiny speck surrounded by darkness, like the end of a *Looney Tunes* cartoon. That's all, folks! Now it's my turn to ask the questions.

I serve them up fast and furiously. Where do they work? Where do they live? Where are they from originally? Only Todd is from this state. The rest came to chase a dream, whether a photo spread in a magazine, their own line of high-fashion menswear, or making headlines in the *Wall Street Journal* daily. We are all transplants, finding permanent residence in America's greatest, wildest, gayest city (we hope). The answers to my questions, of course, go forgotten between cocktails. Luckily, I imagine the others are drunk enough to forget mine, too, so we can always ask again at a later, more sober date.

Some time later, Todd is pulling me by the hand and we're laughing and skipping up 8th or 9th or 10th avenue. I've surrendered any notion of where we are or where we're going to my new roomie. In a brief second of privacy on the street — with the boys from dinner ten feet ahead, pulling out their IDs to flash at a bouncer, Todd proudly informs me that each and every one of his pals would sleep with me.

"Are they all single?"

Todd shrugs. "Single enough."

I bite my lip and he laughs, saying that as long as I keep it down so he can sleep, he doesn't care who I bring back or what I do when I get them there. He dangles a key in front of me, then slips it (with some effort) into my tight pocket.

Now I'm thinking about the boys. In my head they stand underneath signs displaying their names in neon lights. The problem is they're dancing around each other in circles like cups in a game of Find the Coin. Was Shane the one with the crew cut? Or was that Rowan? I'm almost positive the one with the spiked purple hair explosion is Brayden. At least I think…

There's a slight problem at the door of Therapy when the bouncer — a blonde straight man with a shoulder span that rivals his impressive height — flips my ID in five different directions and asks me twice when my birthday is (even though California licenses boldly state the date the license-bearer is of legal drinking age). It probably doesn't help that I stutter as I try to remember the date and year I was born.

But Todd swings his head out the door and says, "Teddy, he's with me, and he's new from California. Let's show him a good time in the city, okay?"

Teddy laughs a hearty hetero laugh and suddenly gives me a hug and kiss on the cheek. "Anyone who's friends with this stud is all right by me." He spanks my ass hard enough to hurt as I walk past him and into the dimly lit, hard-wood-accented bar.

Therapy welcomes me with a dramatic wooden staircase over a rock garden. My eyes wander up to a skylight that attempts to show the stars above, though they're dimmed by the brighter blaze of New York's still-lit windows. Warm lighting, hot boys, hotter waiters, and a unisex bathroom with two guys conspicuously jerking off at the urinals. So this is gay New York, huh? Keeping my distance, I relieve myself and meet Todd and the boys at a long mirror over a trough sink. We primp and preen before pushing our way through swinging steel doors, heading into the fray.

Todd leads us upstairs. The moment we reach the second floor, I become aware of a forest of disembodied eyes peering out of the darkness long before I can make out any faces. They're sizing me up. A wooden railing surrounding the staircase is home to at least a hundred men shrouded in shadow — leaning, watching. Waiting to pounce?

"Don't worry, bro," Todd claps my shoulder. "They rarely if ever move. This is an S&M bar."

"I should have worn my harness!" Rowan chirps.

"Stand and model," Brayden explains, having witnessed my terror. "Look but don't touch. Usually."

We settle in a reasonably quiet corner. Drinks find their way to us before we've had a chance to situate ourselves. There's a hand on my leg. I lean forward to engage in whatever is being talked about as I reach under the table and move the hand between my legs, give it a good push deeper in. Oh drunken Gully, you brave little slut! I survey the faces around me in hopes of figuring out if the adventurous digits belong to the same body that is stroking my ankle with a deliberate foot, but no eyebrow lifts significantly. Anyway, it's a moot point: any one of their appendages is more than welcome to caress any part of my body it chooses.

Suddenly, the dim lights get dimmer still and a spotlight hits the stage. Everyone else's attention turns toward it, so mine does too.

"Hey, boys! Let's hear it for tonight's hostess. You may know her from any one of her forty-five weekly parties here, on Fire Island, or up in Provincetown. She's New York's next hottest queen, even if RuPaul and her panel of judges don't know it — yet! Give up your virginities for Demanda Tension!"

I try to clap and knock over my glass. No worries, because it's empty, and the waiter with an ear gauge I could stick my thumb through is already setting a martini glass rimmed with Sweet'N Low down in front of me.

Demanda takes the stage clad in a small dress of striped pastels and a floppy straw hat. Her long brown hair is gorgeous, her makeup impeccable.

"Good evening, you silly queers," she says. "Do you like my outfit? I felt it was time for something a little more… summery."

"You get it, bitch!" screams Servando, clapping like a seal.

Demanda yells, "Hit it!" and escorts us through a rendition of "Poker Face," re-christened "Poke His Face." She deserves a world of credit for turning a plenty-sexual song into something that pulls a blush from my cheeks. I've never heard such a catchy song about face-fucking.

Then the song is over. The hand between my legs has slipped into my fly and is stroking. The bar is spinning. I am drinking someone else's drink. When I look up, I realize the crew is staring at me.

"What?"

A hand is on my shoulder. I turn around and feel Demanda's hot breath on my face. "Get up here, boy!" And I am dragged from my seat. Todd and the guys are laughing and pushing me. At this level of intoxication, resistance is futile (and damn near impossible). I am now onstage, the spotlight blinding my drunk eyes.

"And who is this cute little thing?" She's playing with my shirt, lifting it up. I pull away and try to bat it back down again.

"Go, Gulliver!" Todd yells, raising his glass with the rest of the table. Is any one of these boys staring harder than the others? Whose hand was in my nether-regions? Whose foot was on my ankle?

"Gulliver? Like in *Gulliver's Travels*?"

I nod and step backwards a bit too far, catching myself against the brick wall behind me.

"Careful, Gulliver dear," she says, taking me by the forearm and straightening me up. "We don't want you traveling to the emergency room this evening, do we?" I shake my head emphatically. "*Gulliver's Travels*," Demanda repeats, her lips pursed. "Hmm. I've never read it." Then she shoves her wireless microphone at my face. "Do any cute twinks get fucked in it?"

For what seems like an hour, my mouth is agape. Finally I manage a shrug. "I've never read it either!" I giggle.

From below: "He just moved here from LA!"

Thanks, Todd.

"Oh, boy. That explains it," Demanda grumbles. Several boys in the crowd clap at the obligatory LA dig. I do what I hope is a sexy pout. "Fresh meat on a Friday night in Hell's Kitchen? Boys, who wants to take our little Gulliver home and show him how welcoming we New Yorkers can be?"

More hoots, cheers, and laughs. The spotlight is so bright; all I see is white and rippling shadows spanning to the back of the bar. Everything is spinning. I blink hard to straighten out my view, realizing three things in the following order: it's cold; my nipples are rocks; my shirt is off. Wait, when did that happen? Demanda is swinging it over her head, then throws it in the direction of my table. "Top or bottom, Gulliver?" She unbuttons my jeans. One. Two. Three. Four. Thank God I put on my favorite new briefs, the ones that cling to my thighs and make my package look like a pair of rolled up socks. My jeans fall around my ankles. I flex my legs, making sure every last bit of curvature that's there shows itself proudly.

"Bottom!" screams Todd — thanks again, buddy. I shake my head, laughing. I'm saying no, no, I'm not, but my face is redder than a vodka cranberry.

"Oh, they're gonna love you here, baby." Demanda gestures to me like I'm a prize in the final round of *The Price is Right*. "Am I right, tops?"

The roar that meets Demanda's question more than affirms it. She grabs my dick and squeezes. "Come and get your fresh meat, boys. Be gentle, though. Don't want to wear him out on his first week in town!"

Then, before I know it, my first official bout of New York mortification is complete. Demanda shoves me back to my seat, demanding I give her room to do her next number. I am more than happy to oblige, especially since yet another drink is awaiting my return to the table. The boys congratulate me as I button my jeans and pull my polo back over my head sheepishly.

"No, keep it off," Rowan grins.

"Seriously," Servando adds.

"I'm not drunk enough. Yet," I say, though I can't imagine being much drunker without a stomach pump cameo later in the evening.

I blink and we're on the street again. Todd says something about how our evening crawl has only begun. It takes some time for my body to remember how walking happens.

A cabbie honks and Shane flips him two triumphant middle fingers. "Fuck you, bitches! I'm walkin' here!" In the headlights he looks like a rock star onstage at Staples Center. Rowan and Servando are pulling me, Todd just in front, saying if I'm in the mood to dance, Therapy isn't the place. (Apparently I jumped out of my chair and started rocking out to Demanda's closing number — whoops!) So we're going to Posh now, which is conveniently located around the block.

More brick, more hardwood floors, but far smaller. Posh is just one story. Where Therapy had tables and couches, Posh has a few stools at the bar and a wide span of floor tightly packed with sloppy dancers. We grab drinks then dive in, surrounding an island DJ booth. "4 Minutes" is playing, and I choose to lip sync to Madge's part while the other boys take on JT.

Shoving! Pushy! There's not enough room on this floor. I'm wearing half my drink as a gorgeous black man with dreads pulled back in a ponytail shoulders his way past me, grabbing my ass and apologizing as he does so. I down the rest of my whatever-it-is to avoid the problem. A dumb move, because Todd is there with another to replace it. I shrug and dump half of it on my shirt, which is apparently hilarious to the crew.

And then we are dancing. To the shitty new Christina Aguilera single. To Black Eyed Peas and Kylie and David Guetta and Adam Lambert. I am moving and the club is spinning. Rowan and Servando have me surrounded, Rowan behind and Servando in front. My eyes are open then closed, my mouth smiling then singing. Then Rowan's mouth is on my neck and I'm kissing Servando, our vodka breath and cacophony of colognes fighting back the smell of sweat enveloping us. The bass is hard and I'm sweating. My shirt is, once again, off. A hand is between my legs. My dick grows to meet it. Rowan? Servando?

Doesn't matter, because now we are all three making out.

It's the first time I've ever kissed more than one person at the exact same time. My booze-ridden brain is wondering how the hell it's possible that three mouths can meet without noses broken as a result. They lock together perfectly. But how? It's like I just discovered a cool new app on my iPhone that's been there the whole time.

I'm so hard. I'm so drunk. Either Rowan or Servando has a tongue ring; it clicks delicately on my teeth every once in a while. I lick at it for the temporary metallic chill it provides. It's like we're flipping in the air, the lights around us flashing, the bass throbbing, our hands rubbing, grabbing, caressing. I look beyond our locked mouths and see Todd, who's dancing up on someone I don't recognize. We meet eyes and he laughs, nods, and flashes me a thumbs up, mouthing: "Get it."

Beyond him I see faces. Hundreds. Then thousands. Now millions. Not clearly — no. They are blurs of eyes and jawbones and messy hair cascading over tanned foreheads, all bathed in shifting colored lights — now raspberry, now blue raspberry, now pink flamingo, now cherry red. And they are watching. I'd be watching too, if I weren't already a part of this peculiar makeout session. Is this a rare and hot occurrence at Posh, or a standard display? I don't know. I don't care. Rowan or Servando's hand is down the back of my jeans, caressing my ass cheek. Servando or Rowan's hand is down the front, jerking me off.

I blink and now we're in a cab. SUV, not a car. The TV tells us about *Lion King* and tapas and the triplex which still hasn't sold. Brayden yells at the screen to shut the fuck up and kicks it, somehow turning it off. He is my hero and I kiss him thank you. He pokes his tongue out and I let him in my mouth to explore. Servando or Rowan is still jerking me off under my jeans. The windows are open and I am gulping the chilly New York air as it invades the cab.

The road turns bumpy and for a second I feel my many drinks and bite of burger come up as my body hovers off the seat. But a quick swallow takes care of that.

When we tumble out of the cab I scream, "Bye-bye, LA!" and triumphantly fling my iPhone onto the seat, slam the door, and watch it speed away. On it is a text message from Graham calling me a fucking piece of shit; he hopes I get AIDS in New York and die falling in front of a subway. There's pain in me somewhere, but the booze cuts through it, separating us.

Todd takes off after the cab and stops it just before it disappears. He grabs my phone, tips the driver again for his troubles, and pockets it as he jogs back up to us. "I'll just hold on to this for ya, Gully."

"Whatever," I shrug, flashing my Mastercard to the bouncer of a club in Chelsea called Purgatory. He takes a long hard look at me, fishes my ID out of my wallet, and hands me back my credit card, rolling his eyes but allowing me access to the bar.

Purgatory is dark at first, and then, past the coat check, flashing lights of red, blue, green. A bar runs the full length of the right side of the dance floor and, at the back, a DJ (DJ Mikey Make-Out, Todd clues me in) is spinning Ke$ha. I'm dancing and drinking. Drinking and dancing. Strangers come and go, ask me where I'm from, if I know how cute I am, if I think they're cute. I nod. I kiss. I let them touch me and buy me drinks, only sometimes in that order. The new Britney plays. Then some old, old Spice Girls. Then still more Ke$ha. Different songs, but the bass is one continuous pattern of vivacious vibrations. Yes. Yes. Yes. New divas. New songs. New York. A new me. And the kissing.

At one point I turn around and everyone is gone. I'm alone. I imagine the club vacant; I have no idea where I am or how to get home. My waking nightmare is opening my eyes and finding myself face-down in an alley somewhere in a pool of my own vomit and/or blood, crying because I don't know how I got there or why my ass is sore.

And then I blink and Servando and Rowan are back and we're kissing again. The same tongues with the same tongue ring and it's just as fun as before. I can make out with them for hours. Days. All week. I'll look for jobs while we make out. I'll show up for my first day in a new jacket and tie, making out with them as I emerge from the elevator. I'll cash my first paycheck with both of their tongues down my throat.

Todd appears out of nowhere, emerging from the crowd like a gay nightlife Moses, parting the Pink Sea. He's accompanied by an attractive guy with short black hair and a tight shirt that reveals slight hints of musculature.

"Gully!" he yells, interrupting my makeout session. "This is my boss, Mikey Dolan. He created GuyTime. We run four parties a week in the city, plus a ton of events in every other city too."

"Hi!" My arms wrap around him and I give him a kiss on his cheek.

"And who's this sexy boy?" Mikey asks, patting me on the back like we're best friends while handing me a drink ticket with the other.

"My buddy Gulliver from LA," Todd says, holding me up as I almost pitch forward, reaching for the ticket. "Just arrived tonight."

"Your roomie is a nightlife superstar," Mikey tells me before turning to Todd, who's already in full blush. "And Gulliver's a cutie, mind if I take a picture?"

Servando, Rowan, and I, all shirtless and sweaty, oblige, stepping back carefully and smiling as sexily as we can in our drunken state. The flash is blinding, white everywhere. Mikey snaps a second one for good luck, and for this one, a cute blonde boy joins us. I am too dizzy to actually nail down any of his features. We are all blurs in a world of blurs. He introduces himself as Chad or Chase or Dave. Maybe I give him my name, or maybe I just mouth it assuming my voice will follow the movement of my lips. He declares or asks me something, his beautiful lips flapping, but his voice is no match for the glorious bass.

Mikey's camera flashes fade away. The walls and floors of Purgatory crumble and become the near-barren walls of my bedroom; the floor spins and becomes the ceiling above my queen-sized bed. How'd I get here?

Rowan is here, too. His legs are open and my head is between them. Servando is also here, behind me and inside me, his hands anchoring me to the mattress. I wonder where that guy went — or is he here with us? Everything is spinning. Flipping. Cartwheeling. If Servando lets go we'll all fall because somehow the bed is upside down, hanging from the ceiling. We are Cirque du Soleil and the boys from Therapy are back to cheer us on. This fresh meat bottom from La La Land with the nice legs and trimmed chest hair. Welcome, they're shouting. Take it off, they cheer.

Servando kisses my back. Rowan scoops me up by the chin and sticks his tongue down my throat. I moan. The bed is flipping, flipping, flipping. On the wall I am watched by Mortar Boarded Todd and Me, next to Mortar Boarded Me and Todd. I'm on my back. I'm on my side. Servando is in front of me. Behind me. Rowan's on both sides. They are under me and I am under them. They are inside me and I am inside of them.

We're laughing, we're wrestling, we're flinging condom after condom on the floor. And then we're sleeping. And then we're at it again. And then I'm in the bathroom. Hello, bite of turkey burger! Been awhile. How ya been? Servando is standing above me, pulling me up from the bathroom floor. And then we are asleep again. Much like how our mouths fit so well together, our bodies are intertwined in a way that allows us all to comfortably fit on the bed just so.

Outside there is honking and screeching, screaming and laughing. We're dead to the world, and New York is still so fucking alive.

CHAPTER 3

The job search is shit. It's like I forgot we're in the stormy center of a global financial crisis. Of course Todd is amazing — between his day job managing the finances of corporate institutions and his night gig as a promoter, he says he is pulling in more than enough to keep me going as long as it takes until I find gainful employment.

But that doesn't do much for my own sense of self-worth. Life in Los Angeles may have sucked, but at least I could say I was paying for my own rent, car, utilities, and alcohol — most of the time. Every once in a while, Mom or Dad left a little surprise in my bank account when things got shitty. But even that still left me feeling more or less autonomous. Presently I'm feeling like a freeloader — or, worse, a kept boy who's not even putting out to his generous sponsor. But Todd just gets pissed whenever I mention this, so I suffer in silence.

It's been two weeks and there is a glaring imbalance between the number of resumes I've sent out and the responses in my inbox. I'm now officially nauseated by the sight of my own damn cover letter:

"Dear Sir or Madam, my name is Gulliver Leverenz and I found your job listing on Craigslist / Media Bistro / Creative Hotlist. I am writing to you in regards to your posted position of assistant designer / assistant to the designer / designer's assistant / junior designer / design intern. Please find attached a link to my web portfolio, I am confident that you will find I have ample / respectable / deep experience in web / print / package design. I am excited / thrilled / enlivened by the opportunity to work for your company /

agency / shop / organization and look forward to speaking to / meeting with / getting to know you in the near future."

Copy, paste, send. Copy, paste, send. Wait. Wait. Wait. Refresh email. Scowl. Do it all over again. Why do so many employers bother posting for jobs if they're not going to seriously consider the applicants? I'm not some unqualified hack, okay? I know my way around Photoshop, Illustrator, even Fireworks, for God's sake. My portfolio is an impressive collection of work ranging from websites to business cards to full-on branding campaigns. But no one seems to care.

So I go back to the listings, feeling even more worthless than before. Wondering if the bravado with which I departed home for this new city was more of a fever dream than an actual visit by the legendary Manhattan Muse. I mean, what good is New York, with all its glowing lights and tall buildings and other such promising iconography, if it won't let a bright-eyed newcomer assimilate into its bustling streets?

It's even worse when, days later, I see the same company re-post the same call for professional help on Monster or HotJobs. I've taken to sending more dramatic queries to some of those re-posters, just to see what (if anything) will get their attention.

In these queries are a handful of exclamation points and declarative statements that border on manic. *"JOB ME NOW!!!!"* is actually the subject of my most recent correspondence with a small integrated marketing agency based on Wall Street. (Is it still "correspondence" if they ignore you like a corporate leper?) In them I am swearing my allegiance to everything from pharmaceutical design (*"I LOVE creating logos for erectile dysfunction medications!!"*) to nonprofit flyer creation (*"I totally sympathize with the plight of families in third world countries that need sustainable LED lamps to replace the environmentally destructive kerosene ones they currently use"*). Send. Read. Copy. Paste. Send.

But whenever my Gmail chirps, all that awaits is a Facebook comment or email that slipped past my spam filter claiming that some vague, insatiable "she" wants me to add three inches to my penis in order to please her properly. Those Facebook comments are becoming faster and more furious now since word spread that I gave my relationship with Graham the ultimate snuff — leaving him rotting at a cruisy Starbucks in Weho while I flew cross-country to start a new life. My destination? A city as strange and wondrous as any make-believe world to my friends who will never, ever leave Los Angeles.

"You moved to NYC? Are you serious!?"

"Gulliver! We're so excited for you! Knock 'em dead out there!"

"We're coming to visit, bitch! Better get us into all the hotspots VIP style, girl."

I'm trying to make a clean break from LA, but they make it complicated. They call me, and of course I'm going to answer and update them on my adventures. Thankfully, my present situation looks positively stellar on paper. I just skirt around the small detail of unemployment, that whole "worthless slug" thing. They don't want to hear it anyway. They're satisfied with stories of the clubs and bars Todd takes me to. I'm so lucky, they say. LA is plunging into economic ruin and here I am living an A-list life courtesy of Mr. Todd DiTempto.

As if I needed the reminder. I may be lucky, but I don't feel that way at all.

My only company during my daily dig for employment is Señor, Todd's Scottish terrier. I've taken on the responsibility of caring for the pup as my method of rent payment. This involves filling his *Hello, Dolly!* water bowl, buying puppy chow at the nearby Food Emporium, rubbing his tummy, bathing him, and taking him out whenever he gets antsy and starts barking at the front door. On our walks we usually venture up 8th avenue, toward the shops at Columbus Circle where people who make one hundred times more than the starting salaries I'm vying for eat their organic, grain-fed, cage-free lunches in the food court of the Whole Foods or on the benches of Central Park.

I've also become conscious of the rewards of not only being cute myself, but also being tethered to a cute dog. In one week's time I've received five phone numbers, had three coffees bought for me (my rule: never turn down a free drink — alcoholic, caffeinated, or otherwise), and been otherwise stopped at least seven times. I'd like to say it's all me, but this is a team effort. Señor hooks the fellas and I reel 'em in. It's an easy icebreaker to drop down and coo, lavishing the terrier with adoration, affection, and far too much attention. And the way Señor all but falls on his back like one of those fainting goats profiled on *Mythbusters*, legs in the air and head hanging back on the sidewalk, it's easy to tell he's more used to this than even I am. Fucking adorable slut that he is.

The sad truth? Señor and I have a lot more in common than I'd like to admit. We both eat, drink, and live on Todd's dime. We wait for him to come home with baited breath, tails wagging. But Señor can actually do a backflip on command; I'd probably end up with a concussion. And when you come to realize you're on the same level as a dog, and even that dog is better at its job than you... well, that's just a fantastic shot to your ego, isn't it?

Today Todd comes home with a treat for both Señor and I. Señor gets a new chew toy from the pet store down the block — a pig in a blanket with a smiley face on top of the hot dog, which Señor drags away to a dark corner to defile and drool all over. Over the soundtrack of slobber and mastication, Todd delivers my good news: he's found a job for me. Suddenly, I'm all but drooling, too.

"It's not design or any of that shit you like to do," Todd cautions me first.

"Whatever. So long as it's money."

"And you still have to interview, and train, and all of that — you sure you want to do this?"

No.

I don't WANT to do it. I'd love to sit around with Señor all day and enjoy the fruits of Todd's labor. I wish I didn't have a conscience that forced me to wallow in guilt instead of taking full advantage of my leisure and luxury. I'd much rather park myself on the couch and play Wii every day, step out for a mid-day cocktail and try to scare up a cutie for a date. But I just can't. The knowledge that I am freeloading off of my best (and only) friend sits on my chest like a sumo wrestler, making every moment I am not gainfully employed a psychologically suffocating experience.

"It's fine. I'll do whatever it takes. What is it?"

"How do you look in green, bro?" Todd asks, holding out an apron.

CHAPTER 4

Getting hired at Starbucks wasn't exactly the cake walk Todd made it seem. Turns out that apron was borrowed for dramatic effect. Not mine yet. Not nearly.

The problem was that his "hookup" to the manager wasn't powered by a business or personal relationship, as I initially assumed. (Most of Todd's connections come from actual friendships or business partnerships, whether with owners of clubs, colleagues at his financial firm, bartenders, or fellow promoters.) He just happens to know the manager of the Starbucks around the corner from our apartment because he's there all the time, guzzling caffeine to fuel him as he barrels through his insane daily schedule like a live flame dropped on a gasoline spill trickling out of an oil tanker. I wish I had known in advance, because then I might have shown up for what turned out to be the first of three interviews a little more prepared. Or prepared at all, for that matter. After so much had already come so easily thanks to my blessed roommate, I expected an immediate hire; I got a pile of forms to fill out instead. What I imagined would be my first day of work turned out to be the first step in a weeklong gauntlet of interviews and challenges, the likes of which might make any epic literary hero go pale and give up.

And there was fierce competition: apparently a job pulling shots and steaming milk in the middle of Hell's Kitchen was a much-coveted position. Of the hundreds of Starbucks in Manhattan, this one had high traffic with high incomes and fewer customers likely to smear their feces all over the walls. Because of the many out-of-work actors and formerly employed corporate citizens who had kids to feed, I would have to prove my hunger for the job — and my steadfast passion for coffee, tea, and marble loaf — to even stand a chance.

And I thought sending cover letters to unresponsive HR departments was demeaning.

Instead of pledging my allegiance to company causes, varying clients, and design methodologies and programs, I now had to show my potential new boss — a stringy, coffee-stained forty-year-old named Patty with hair the color of the Italian Roast — that I was willing to die for a perfect shot of espresso or correctly steamed soy. That I would do anything in my power to ensure a customer had the optimal cappuccino, the most sublime Starbucks experience imaginable.

To the very end, it was a total nail-biter. But when the smoke cleared, the job was mine. For now. My hire was tentative, based on how quickly I learned everything about the sultry mermaid-siren and her strong and bitter wares. Coffee tastings during which we sniffed, sucked, and spat like we were sampling fine wine, not a morning pick-me-up sold in paper cups on corners in every city in the world. Hour-long sessions behind the steam wands and espresso spigots. Textbooks I had to lug home in order to study the distinct differences between Ethiopia Sidamo, Sumatra, Caffe Verona, and Pike Place Roast. The problem was that Starbucks doesn't sell flavored coffee — they all taste the same to me: bitter, ball-shrinking, and sorta burned. Half my effort during this time was arranging my face so as not to give away the torment unleashed on my taste buds and stomach as I downed tiny cup after tiny cup of the bastard brew.

Again, I survived. I learned how to pour the ideal shot, steam the proper milk, mix muddy mocha syrup, and free imprisoned Frappuccino murk from its cardboard holding pen with a razor. So here I am behind the counter of a corporate behemoth, stretching my legs as they fall asleep from eight hours of quasi-exertion, trying to keep from showing obvious annoyance or anger when yet another customer busts in through the door to add to the never-ending line of businessmen and women that stretches from the biscotti to the pound bags of coffee across the store.

I came home the night I got the job to find Todd rolling around on the floor with Señor. He took one look at my face and said, "Oh shit, bro. You didn't get the job?"

"Actually, I did get it." I flopped down on the sofa like a rag doll, and with about as much strength to spare. After a moment, Todd crawled up and sat next to me, with Señor following suit.

"Dude, you know you can hold out 'til something else comes along, I told you," he said, prying open Señor's mouth to stare at his teeth. "Or — think of this as a badge of honor. Everyone who moves here takes some shitty job to get by at first. And truthfully, I've heard some horror stories. It could be a lot worse than slinging Frappuccinos."

"Then sling I shall," I said, punching the air weakly like a superhero smothered by clinical depression.

So sling I do. The paycheck is meager. My colleagues are energetic and friendly, maybe a bit too much of each. The customers are gay and never-ending. I come home smelling like day-old espresso. The stench takes two thorough showers to dissipate, only to waft back over me the minute I show up for my next shift.

If someone told me my New York experience would be this, would I still have come? Once Todd convinced me to take the plunge, I succumbed to all sorts of ridiculous dreams of this city. Not only were we partying non-stop (the one part of that dream that's come true), I was also working at a respectable design firm, climbing up that ladder *Mad Men*-style, designing campaigns for huge clients around the world. Dressed in smart suits I had the money to custom tailor to show off my ass just so. Instead, here I am in a forest green apron with coffee grinds caked beneath my fingernails and scone sugar crusting up my sleeves. Bright lights, big city, venti caramel macchiato. That's how my dream turned out.

Now my free time is evenly split between drunken debauchery with Todd and the boys and applying for more respectable work. During my break, I am close enough to the apartment to run home and send out a barrage of resumes to the unlucky saps in HR who probably have my name memorized and have alerted security not to let me in the building under any circumstances.

In reply, I've received nothing but spam offers so my "sexy girlsfriend will better prefer the bedding down with me," so Señor and I head out for a walk. I take him to an expansive courtyard a few blocks from Todd's place. It's

Señor's favorite because of the smell of meat wafting over from a Mexican restaurant and burger bistro that frame the space on either side; it's my favorite because every cute guy in Hell's Kitchen comes here to stare at every other cute guy in Hell's Kitchen. Kind of the human equivalent of sniffing each other's butts.

"What's his name?" asks a man in very skinny pale blue jeans and a pale blue and purple striped cotton shirt I saw on a mannequin at Express earlier this week. His brown hair is brushed past his ears and swept across his face, each blade pointing at apple green eyes.

I'm looking at him, but he's eyeing the dog. "Señor," I say.

On cue, Señor looks up, sees the man, and down he goes, legs in invisible stirrups, tongue lolling simultaneously with a wagging tail.

"Someone wants to be scratched!" And the man is on his knees. I wonder if I could lie on my back and get him on his knees just as quickly?

"And his owner, what's his name?"

"Gulliver." I smile as our eyes meet for the first time.

"That's cute," he laughs. "What's your real name?"

"Gulliver." I smile wider.

"Oh! Well, I guess it makes sense that a traveling man like Gulliver would name his dog in a foreign tongue."

"He's not my dog, actually. He belongs to my roommate. I'm just walking him while he's at work." He nods vaguely. "And you are?"

"Stanford."

"That sounds faker than my name," I say. "Were Princeton and Harvard just a little too prestigious for you? Berkeley a little too hippie?"

There's a triple-beep and Stanford rips a Blackberry from his impossibly-tight jeans pocket, scrolls down the screen, and attacks the keypad with vigor. Then he looks up. "Agents. Assholes. Listen, I'm just killing time before a meeting, do you want to grab a coffee?"

I would rather grab a bucket full of battery acid and drown my face in it. But he's cute and I'm lonely as hell, and there are still twenty minutes left of my break.

We find our way to some chairs right by the fountain after Stanford grabs me an iced Americano (I don't tell him that, as an employee of the chain, I get a "partner discount"). Just beyond us is the outdoor patio of the Mexican restaurant where people sip large frosty margaritas with tiny bottles of beer sticking out their tops. In the other direction is the stone fountain Señor has fallen in puppy love with, sparkling water shooting and splashing in all directions. We're close enough to be cooled by the mist without actually getting wet. Señor is leashed to the underside of the table, yipping and skipping from my legs to Stanford's before trying to make a run for the fountain, dropping to his stomach, and enjoying the mist.

It turns out Stanford is a recent transplant to New York as well, only he hasn't traveled out of his time zone. He's from Boston, another city I've never been to, which he describes as "cold — really, REALLY cold," visibly shivering as he recalls the winters there. His company, a talent agency, sent him to Manhattan to open a satellite office. Which, he assures me, is nothing impressive. "A hole in the wall would be a deceitfully positive review," he laughs, wiping the perspiration off his iced quad venti nonfat latte with sugar free vanilla syrup. (Did I mention I hate working at Starbucks?)

"I've never really understood actors," I say, taking a drag of my cigarette, blowing smoke into the air above us. "I knew a few in LA. They're so self-centered and oblivious to anyone but themselves."

(Of course I don't mention my ex is a wannabe movie star who's just "making some cash between gigs" at Hollister while he waits for his agent to ever return one of his calls. This only marginally affects my opinion, I assure you.)

"You're not alone in thinking that," he laughs. "But my guys and girls are very nice. Talented. Though I must admit I'm more comfortable with you now, knowing you're not about to shove a headshot in my face."

"Yikes. Does that happen a lot?"

"You'd be surprised how shameless an out-of-work actor can be when they smell agent blood in the water."

"Well, my best dance move involves looking like a slutty cowboy on an invisible horse, and I could kill plants with my high notes, so you're safe around me."

"Noted," Stanford laughs again.

I'm far more interested in his story than in sharing any tidbit of mine. Every time he asks about my life, I quickly answer before turning it back around on him — using the Todd DiTempto methodology. He sips his iced latte to the bottom, then removes the top to pluck out ice cubes, chewing them down one by one as he tells me about the actors he represents.

"Nobody huge," he admits. "Just a few recent college grads who are touring with *Wicked* or *The Wedding Singer* or *Dora the Explorer*. Recent hires like me get saddled with fresh talent, a way of showing what we're made of. There's no skill required to place top tier clients. Someday I'll have that cake walk. Until then, my stable is a riot. Hard workers. Fun to talk to. Hungry. And the money is good, even though their take-home, and therefore my take-home, are far smaller. But the fact that they sent me as the pilgrim to New York says I'm gaining the confidence of my higher-ups."

"What does someone so 'far down the ladder' do every day?"

"A lot of running around. Meetings with referrals and sitting through a handful of talent showcases put on by various schools on a weekly basis. You know, fun stuff." He shrugs and pops another ice cube into his mouth. "I really do try to keep a low profile, though. The second boys around here catch wise to the fact that I might be even slightly connected to someone who could somehow maybe get them on stage, even as an understudy, suddenly I'm everyone's best friend. If anyone's ever super-excited to nab a date with me, I know they'll come to dinner with a resume."

"That sounds fun." I'm slowly sipping my iced Americano, not even halfway done. "You're like a celebrity!"

"It gets old fast. And what about you? What are you doing in New York on this leg of your travels?"

I roll my eyes. "Every guy gets one of those corny remarks. You already used yours."

"Can I earn another?"

"Well, you did buy me coffee. And to answer your question, I'm not really doing much right now. I sort of just picked up and moved here." He nods and chews another cube. "Things got out of hand in LA. I ended a long relationship. Not worth going into details." Stanford grits his teeth. I briefly wonder why the hell I am even telling him — to date the only one who knows all this is Todd (and maybe Señor). "I was having trouble finding work there, too. So after a lot of persuading, my fraternity brother, owner of the slut-pup beneath you, finally got me out here. I dropped everything. Packed my stuff, shipped it to my parents, ravaged my savings to pay for the flight, and *voila*."

"Well," Stanford laughs, "I meant what are you doing for work, but thanks for the life story."

"Ah," I nod. "I'm slaving away for minimum wage at Starbucks. Recessions, right? Who needs 'em?"

"Cheers to that!" He raises his empty cup and pretends to drink. "But what are you looking to do?"

"At this point, anything that won't jeopardize a future run for political office. I wanted to do design at one of the big ad agencies. Leo Burnett. Saatchi. Ogilvy. Anything. But despite the fact that they're always posting want ads, they don't seem interested in actually filling them. Hey, didn't you have a meeting?"

"Well, it was an interview, actually…" he checks his watch. "And it should have happened fifteen minutes ago."

I then realize I should have been back at Starbucks by now also. "Oh, shit! I'm so sorry…"

But something tells me not to scurry off just yet. I'm panicking but trying to keep my cool. If Stanford asks me on a date, it might be worth the scolding back at the store…

"No, it's fine. I mean, to be honest, I'm ready to offer the job to you.

Consider this your informal but official interview for the position of my assistant."

Wow. That was unexpected. For a long moment, I'm totally speechless. Then I laugh a little. "You're joking. Right?" But his expression says otherwise. He doesn't crack a smile. Now I'm really confused. "Why?"

"Why not? It's nothing glamorous."

"But you're offering me a job in a field where I have absolutely no experience. Did someone spike your latte or what?"

Stanford winks at me and examines his cup. "If they did, it's more than welcome. Listen, I already told you the office is a subpar hole in a dilapidated wall. Pay is pennies for now until I land a few clients. But I'll start you out slow. I'd rather have untouched clay to work with than someone already doing all the wrong things. Let's do it! Are you in?" He stretches out his hand, those green eyes taking stock of my own.

But before I can shake his hand, Stanford yanks it back and says: "Just so we're clear, this is a trial arrangement. If we don't work out, we split. Easily. Amicably. No hard feelings. No drama. I reserve the right to drop you at any time and you can leave me with a two-week warning. That way, if my crazy idea is too crazy, we both leave looking good. Deal?"

I still don't believe him. I probably won't until my first paycheck is in my hands. But this offer is too good.

"Deal, you crazy bastard."

"Ahem. That's Mr. Crazy Bastard to you."

CHAPTER 5

It is 8:30 in the morning when I show up at the address Stanford gave me last week. He insisted I show up after nine, but my mom's weekend-long nag-blitz had me convinced that the subway would go off the tracks or the five alarms I set on my phone would all turn themselves off or the streets in front of Todd's apartment would crack wide open and demons with pitchforks would emerge and make it impossible for me to cross — thereby getting me to work late, thereby getting me fired, thereby ensuring that I never have a job ever again, thereby ruining my life for the remainder of all eternity.

So now I'm early. My eyes are burning, my stomach churns with a sour sensation only undersleep can produce. And Stanford isn't answering the buzzer in the rusty panel beside the cracked glass door at the front of this nondescript building on 1st avenue and 35th street. My back is to the East River and the 35th street pier where a boat called the *Zephyr* is at port, rocking back and forth in the surging surf. The day has decided to begin on a cold note; my nipples are hard as rocks, threatening to tear gashes through the bright, solid blue button-up shirt I picked up at Express on Sunday.

I try to peer through a dusty window to the left of the door, past a yellowing sign that says, *"Offices for Rent! Cheap! Monthly. Weekly. Whatever!"* — only to find the rusty slats of a set of horizontal blinds. A subpar hole in a dilapidated wall, as Stanford referred to it, may have been too generous a statement. But hey, it's work. At least I won't feel like some freeloader waiting for Todd to bring home the bacon. Plus, Señor is probably elated to return to Doggie Day Care (as a thank you, I told Todd I'd gladly walk him there every morning on my way to the office).

With time to kill, I lean up against the brick wall, light a cigarette, and look out at the East River. It's a great chance to catch a breath — maybe the first time I've done so since moving here. Ever since I set foot inside Todd's apartment I have been on a booze-powered roller coaster through New York's clubs, bars, restaurants, beds (and floors), parks, and streets. With no job this metropolis had begun to feel like a theme park. Oh that this were the case.

Now back to the work-a-day world I go — even if the work is nothing at all related to what I majored in during college. Or, really, anything I have experience in. Cars speed by mere feet in front of me, sometimes honking, sometimes blaring morning talk radio out open windows. The smell of exhaust is strong and sweet. I step out from under a scaffold and let the sun kiss my skin.

I miss Rufus, my old car. Yeah, he was a piece of shit, but he was MY piece of shit. And he was named after my favorite modern-day crooner, His Excellency Rufus Wainwright, so there's emotional attachment there, too. Watching these cars and SUVs speed by makes me pine for his busted air conditioning, making more noise than an airplane engine without producing a single puff of cool air; his passenger seat that wouldn't recline unless you punched it right above the cushion; the piles of text books and Coffee Bean bags in the back. Now Roof is serving my brother Leo, who uses him in my stead to pick up girls and wow them with his sweet-ass set of wheels. I can only imagine what he's done to my poor baby (and in my poor baby...).

"Good morning, employee!" I drop my cigarette as I am wrenched out of my head. Stanford is standing beside me, smoking a cigarette of his own and looking out over the water. "Pretty great view, so long as you don't turn around and see where you'll be spending your day, right?"

"I'm sure it's fine," I laugh. "I hope I'm dressed up enough..."

Stanford's loud guffaw echoes down the empty sidewalk. He is in a pair of shorts and a tight T-shirt that allows a tuft of chest hair to peek out of the deep V-neck. "Overdressed. You don't have to look this good even when you're meeting clients. I hope you didn't blow your first two paychecks prematurely on a new wardrobe."

"No, I would never," I say, wondering if I kept receipts for the other outfits.

Stanford turns and produces a large keychain from his pocket. It seems a bit much until I discover that there are no less than five doors between the outside world and his inner sanctum, each with its own lock. The hallways we walk through feature cracked and stained tiles, walls that probably haven't been painted since the building was first erected, and busted safety mirrors wrapped in cobwebs up in the corners, showing a shattered and fragmented world behind us as we walk.

Well, Stanford doesn't walk so much as sprint. His long legs cover twice as much ground as mine. I find myself panting to keep up with him, desperate to stop and rest. He does this while talking over his shoulder at me AND typing on his Blackberry.

"For the first month I thought this place was abandoned. Turns out most people just use it for storage instead of office space. But there are a few small design shops and agencies. The rent is so disgustingly cheap — and with good reason, considering the state of the building, distance from public transportation, and generous amounts of outside noise from the highway. Almost there!"

We walk up four flights of stairs (he hops up two steps at a time, sometimes three). I can feel the wetness growing under my arms when we finally reach the office, which still has a sign that reads: "Greengrove PR International."

"They went out of business," he says. "I'm working on getting the sign taken down. Not that I'll ever want anyone to see this place. My goal is to be fully moved into a better place, even one of those rental office spaces closer to Grand Central, by the time any client or superior needs to visit."

"A fair goal," I nod, sipping my coffee and helping Stanford wrench open the door to my new place of work.

Despite how much he put the place down and how terrible I imagined it to be, I am still shocked by the actual state of the office. It is one room. Stained tile floors have been replaced by carpet that would bring shame even to a dollar motel on the side of the freeway ("I'm going to have that ripped up as soon as we land our first client"). There is a teetering stack of empty liquor store boxes in the corner ("Those should be getting picked up later this week"). And one desk ("Yours will be here by tomorrow, or so Office Depot promised").

Stanford throws a bottle of juice and a brown paper bag into a squat fridge (the kind I had in my college dorm) and goes over to his desk. He pulls a folding metal chair out from underneath and, with much groaning and squeaking (from both he and the chair) sets it up so it is facing him.

"Come." He slaps the metal seat, sending the echo around the empty space. "First company meeting!"

Stanford, in his chair, seems so out of place amongst his surroundings. He is so much bigger than this rental hovel, but his eyes are happy, childlike. He looks around as if already seeing beyond it — to the massive office he'll have in a small number of months, complete with a waiting area filled with plasma TVs showing footage of the actors he represents and a wall decked out in signed and framed Playbills.

"As I said," he starts. "This isn't much. Hell, it isn't anything. Well, it is one thing: a start. It won't be easy, but we'll make it fun. Since you know nothing, I can teach you anything. Maybe you'll even have ideas I never thought of, coming at my business with your unique outside perspective."

I'm smiling like an idiot and nodding. "Thanks again for the chance. I'll give you the best I can."

"That's all I can ask for. And now, day one of training. Here we go."

I should have brought a tape recorder or a video camera, because Stanford flies into a 600-word-per-minute monologue, taking me through how his day goes and where I will fit into it. I am in charge of scheduling, so I need to learn how to use Microsoft Outlook, allowing me to ensure that he is never double-booked for lunches, meetings, auditions, and phone calls.

I am also in charge of the "slush pile" — a never-ending box of resumes he keeps next to his desk. General office maintenance is also on my list of duties; that stack of boxes I admired upon entering is my first responsibility of the day. We are both in charge of keeping the refrigerator stocked and clean. I answer the phone and take messages, and I need to be responsive at any time, day or night, because we'll never know when we might get a shot at representing the next Gavin Creel or Jonathan Groff or Sutton Foster.

I tell him I have an iPhone and he says he'll set it up so I receive forwarded calls from the office as well as forwarded emails from our joint account. I will not be writing as his assistant, he says. I will be responding as him. Flattering, that he's willing to trust me with representing him as a person, even if just in a digital sense.

Stanford is interrupted at least once every five minutes by a *Beep!, Ding!,* or *Wow-wow!* from his Blackberry. Some are calls, and he answers those, putting up a finger and making an apologetic face, sometimes spinning his finger in a circular pattern if he feels the call is going on too long. Some are emails he is able to respond to with rapid keystrokes while continuing the day's training. Others are text messages he ignores, saying, "No time for a personal life. You'd think these horny, dream-filled actors would understand that."

I, meanwhile, have had to pee since we got in the office. I couldn't locate a bathroom but am too afraid to interrupt the stream of words pouring forth. So instead I cross my legs, squeeze tight, and continue my attempt to scribble words as quickly as he verbalizes them. I am failing, and when I look down at my notepad I find it hard to make sense of anything I've jotted down. A silent countdown to my inevitable firing begins.

Minutes become hours. My head is spinning by the time Stanford takes his first breath since opening his mouth and says, "Okay, that's it for now. Lunch?"

I nod, closing my notebook. "Exhausted" doesn't do the dull buzzing in my head justice.

"Good! Pizza sound okay?"

I don't have the opportunity to say yes (or no) before Stanford hops up from his chair and sprints to the door. If this were a cartoon, he'd have left a Stanford-shaped puff of smoke in his wake, with me blinking and blankly staring after.

Lunch is NOT a break. It is merely a change of scenery. We sit in a pizzeria a few avenues closer to civilization. It is corporate lunch time and we are surrounded by long tables filled with men and women in business casual who are chomping on mixed greens and calamari, joking about absent co-workers and bitching about meetings where wasted time was the only outcome. Cute waiters in tight black pants run from table to table, placing metal trays of treacherously thin-crusted pizzas on table stands.

A large pie is suspended between Stanford and I, covered in gobs of fresh mozzarella and deep green basil leaves. Empty plates lie before us, and he continues to tell me all that's involved in creating a satellite agency from the ground up. The funniest part, he informs me, is that this is all before we're managing any big stars. When we land one of those, the real craziness begins. Fear of failure surges in me every five seconds.

What am I doing? This is not my skill set. This is not what I want to do. I want to be buried in a multi-foldered Photoshop file. I want to play with masks and create logo guides and branding resources. I want to superimpose club names on the dimpled bubble butt of a porn star to get New Yorkers to attend the newest, hottest party in Chelsea. THAT is what I'm good at — what I studied late into the evenings and through all-nighters in the frat house at UCLA, with Todd bugging the crap out of me to go drinking. I don't even know what Outlook is!

But I also want to make money. To not feel like a leech on the verge of being booted from Todd's apartment like a castaway on *Survivor*, forced to return to Los Angeles where the naysayers and frenemies will be waiting with gloriously colorful banners proclaiming: *"We Told You So!"* and *"That's What You Get!"*

So I'll hit this with my best shot. Worse comes to worse, Stanford will give me the axe and I'll drown my sense of failure in a trough of vodka — and between Rowan and Servando's legs.

I bravely reach in front of me and tear a slice of pizza from the tray. Stanford's eyes widen, his brows lifting, and he laughs. "Oh, yeah, humans are supposed to eat, right?"

Cheese is hanging from my mouth as I nod and desperately feed myself. "Always a good idea, boss."

"Good call. I guess your final responsibility is to make sure I keep myself alive."

"I'll add it to the checklist," I say with my mouth full.

Stanford picks up the bill, my first official work perk — free lunch! Already things are looking up. We each smoke a cigarette outside, listening to the mix of chirping birds, screaming kids on recess at a schoolyard across the street, and the omnipresent angry honking of cars on every avenue and street in our vicinity. With a cigarette in hand, Stanford switches to responding to emails with his thumb, allowing him to simultaneously forward his career while killing himself with lung cancer. I'm impressed.

"Shit. Okay. I gotta run, Gulliver. It's too nice of a day to sit in that dusty asshole of an office, don't you think?"

I'm not sure what the right answer to this question is, so I just keep my mouth shut. Luckily, he doesn't wait for me to speak. "So I'll take the hit and head back to the office. I just shot you an email of a bunch of things I'd like you to do. Okay?"

"Sure thing, boss."

And then once again Stanford is gone. I swear, I blink once and he's already forty feet away from me. By the third blink he has rounded the corner and is probably already back at the office. Insane.

My first afternoon is spent running errands, which allows me to smoke half a pack of cigarettes as I run from place to place. I also have plenty of time to call Mom and Dad and Leo. Mom I speak to on my way to Kinko's, where I make copies of various completely unintelligible legal-looking documents. She is all congratulations and reminders to "do more than what is expected of you."

I leave a voicemail for Dad while wandering the aisles of Staples in search of staples. I let him know that I am living the dream of a corporate life because Stanford gave me his corporate credit card and said I could buy the fancy pens if I so choose. (And I do.)

Then I have the standard two-minute conversation with Leo, rushing between classes as I similarly jog to the soon-to-close post office to ship the stuff I copied at Kinko's to what I guess is the main office of Stanford's firm in Cambridge. Leo's dating two girls and still has enough time to secure himself a leading role in a college production of *The Full Monty*. I tell him there's no way in hell I'll attend any event that involves me seeing him anywhere near naked. He calls me gay, tells me he loves me, and then hangs up.

Stanford is very good about keeping me busy, shooting me texts or emails with my next instructions. The hours blaze by and I am astounded when I glance at the clock to discover it is already 7:30 PM.

Stanford texts: *"Okay Gully. That's it for Day 1. Good job. Good hustle. Now go home and have a cocktail."*

Me: *"K boss. You callin' it quits too?"*

He: *"LOL. What's quits? CYA in the morning. — S."*

My legs are tired. My eyes force themselves closed despite my need for them to stop me from getting hit by rush hour traffic. My iPhone is a text message away from dying. My head, which was fuzzy all afternoon long, now feels like a sponge that somebody wrung out and left to dry. But despite all this, I'm smiling as I walk past Grand Central Station, heading back to Todd's mansion with Señor in tow. Not a bad day. Not a bad boss.

Thanks to Doggy Day Care, Señor looks exhausted too, far from his normal yipping, skipping self. When we get home, he drags himself to the corner and drops like a sack into his cushy bed. I swear he begins snoring mid-fall.

"Amen, boy." I kick off my pants, fling my shirt across the living room towards my bedroom, and crash on the couch, eager to join my puppy pal in dreamland.

CHAPTER 6

We can't find Rowan. Todd, Servando, Shane, Brayden, and I are outside of Socket, standing in a smog of cigarette smoke in front of the two-floor cavernous club at a luxury hotel somewhere in New York's west 50's. The night is unseasonably cool so we're shivering, trying to remember when we last saw him, and we're not too happy about it.

Socket is a party I've quickly come to hate. One where the crowds are so dense that you are sucked into the throng the second you walk through the door. This surging mass of gay humanity draws you in like a rubber ball flung into a stream. You are dragged, pulled, and pushed to the very depths of the club — the back bar on the top floor where drinks are laughably overpriced, served in plastic cups that make the Dixie variety look like mason jars by comparison. You are then given a brief respite before the crowd decides it's over you and begins to pull and push you back the way you came in. During this exodus you are bumping constant shoulders and feeling the repeated chilled sloshing of spilled drinks on your new shirt. You finally end up back outside of the club, drenched, robbed of ten dollars, without the opportunity to drink whatever it was you bought, your hand stamped for effortless reentry.

If you do somehow fight the tide trying to eject you like an unwelcome transplant, you must drink with your elbows pulled in to your stomach and dance in the three centimeters of quasi-personal space you are allotted. And always around you people are walking. Where are they going? There are lines for coat check. Lines for the bar. Lines for the lines. Socket is ADD to say the least. No one can stand still for a minute before someone in your party proposes picking up and moving across the dance floor or downstairs to the VIP area. We aren't partying, we're just continuously relocating ourselves and spilling drinks on each other.

And yet this is the fourth week in a row we've been. Because the boys are cute. Because it's the place to be seen. And I am here because there's no way in hell I will separate from my posse and tackle one of New York's gay bars all by myself. Maybe others are this brave; I am not one of those select few. I go where my boys go. I am slightly thankful for Rowan's disappearance — it's given us a new and unexpected adventure to deal with on a night that would otherwise be a carbon-copy of the many nights at Socket before it.

We take a vote to see if either we all go back in to brave the well-dressed and well-liquored crowds to locate our friend, or send the boldest of our group back inside to rescue him, or sacrifice him to the party and pray that he texts us later for an inebriated reunion at Vlada or Ritz or Posh. Making any decision either takes ten minutes or just feels that way because of how drunk we are.

"Guys, I'm right here."

It's Rowan. Right beside me.

Rowan takes a drag on his cigarette, lifts his chin, and blows it toward the towering floors of hotel room windows above us. He leans his head back too much and stumbles a little, almost throwing me off-balance as well.

"How long have you been here?" I ask.

"I was right behind you," he hiccups. "We held hands on our way out. You, me, and Servy."

"Oh yeah!" Servando laughs loudly, his voice echoing on the walls and windows around us. A bouncer flashes an angry glare. I grab Rowan's cigarette and take a drag, warming my insides.

"Next stop?" Todd asks.

Collective shrugs establish him as the leader — which is nothing new. Wherever the liquor is as plentiful as the eye candy will do just fine. And so we're walking down 8th avenue heading to Barrage hoping that Shane can seduce the bartender into giving us the midnight happy hour deal even though it's at least three o'clock in the morning.

Servando, Rowan, and I hold hands again, occasionally grabbing at each other, threatening to push each other into traffic. I wonder if we'll sleep together again tonight. We haven't reprised our tryst from my first night yet, but I don't mind. In LA, sleeping with someone was a death sentence. Either they want to be your boyfriend the next day or your exes hear about what went down and immediately set to work on further tearing apart your reputation. But with Rowan and Servando, it's perfect. We're not ignoring the fact that it happened — in fact, it often finds its way into dinner or drinks conversation. Tonight seems promising, though. And I'm game if they are.

At Barrage, Shane succeeds beyond our wildest expectations and we end up drinking for free. Barrage, like every other bar in Hell's Kitchen, is dark, barely illuminated by warm lighting that emanates from overhead or behind couches. The walls are a savage red color and there is an oversized print on the wall of the bathroom showing two muscular guys looking down at the urinals. One looks shocked, holding an extended tape measure; the other looks unhappy, a magnifying glass held to one eye. Oh, and it's probably called Barrage because it has garage doors up front that look out onto the street. Which is cute.

A DJ spins Miley Cyrus' "Party in the USA" in one corner, holding one half of a pair of headphones to his ears. We're throwing back Manhattans in the opposite corner, perched on an L-shaped set up of couches and tables surrounding three short stools and a squat table.

The music here is gracefully lower — only slightly ear-splitting. We are able to actually speak. We go round-robin style, updating the crew on our lives. When it's my turn, I tell the boys about my new gig working for Stanford. None of them know him, which in and of itself is a wonder. Everyone seems to have met (read: slept with) everyone else in this city. That's nothing new to me — in fact, it's a piece of LA that is all too familiar. And yet, somehow, Stanford has ducked beneath the radar. I make a fleeting mental note to ask my boss where he drinks when he goes out at night, to see if maybe we just frequent a different set of establishments (assuming he goes out at all).

"And check this out!" I say, pulling out my wallet and producing from it my new business card. On a thick and textured piece of bone-white paper it says:

Gulliver Leverenz
Senior Casting Associate
Diedrick, Kemnitz & Hobbs Casting, International

"Whoa. Big boy over here!" Brayden says, grabbing the card and holding it up to the light.

"The title is beyond glorified," I counter.

"Is it?" Servando asks. "Last time I checked, everywhere we went tonight, you've been stopped by cute strangers trying to get all up on your junk."

(In my defense, it only actually happened twice.)

"Well, I mostly answer phones and carve through the resume slush pile of waiters, temps, and Aldo shoe representatives that Stanford gets. But he's also put me in the crosshairs of the starving actors of Manhattan. He said with everyone bugging the hell out of me instead of him, he can actually get his work done."

"So how do I get your job?" Brayden asks. "I'll kill you if I have to."

"Please, it's really not that great."

"Sure, bro," Todd says. "Because that gang of boys over in the corner pointing and whispering and trying to get your attention for the past half hour is SUCH an annoyance."

"How do you know they're not looking at you? You're the superstar promoter working some of the hottest parties N-Y-C has to offer."

Laughter. "How many times have you heard Todd say that on the phone since you moved here?" Brayden asks.

"Enough times to memorize it," I wink. "Okay, so the few times I get noticed are nice. But the job is a lot of grunt work and not a lot of money. Stanford says he'll give me a cut of his take for every actor I help him take on and then get cast. So we'll see. And now that I know how many actors are surging above, under, and through this city, it fascinates me that not a single one of you boys is pursuing a theatrical career. Talk about potentially awkward."

"Says who?" Brayden yells, jumping on my lap. "I'm ready for my cum shot, Mr. DeMille!" He is straddling me. He thrusts into my lap and tries to kiss me and I'm laughing and pulling away from his amorous attempts. His spiky now-orange hair threatens to gouge my eyes out, his fiercely curled eyelashes flutter with dogged determination.

"Down boy! Don't make me throw my drink on you."

"He'll just squeeze his shirt off and drink it!" Servando says.

"What the fuck?" Brayden growls, stopping his horsey ride short. We quit our laughing and follow his furious gaze across the bar, toward the DJ.

"What is it?" I ask. All I can see are the many faceless heads of the Barrage clientele, none of which I particularly recognize.

"Asshole," Brayden mutters. He hops off of me and stares hard at whoever caught his attention.

That's when I see the subject of his anger: at the bar, a tanned boy in a red hoodie who looks almost exactly like Brayden orders a drink, his arm wrapped possessively around a shorter, dyed-blonde twink who might as well have been me a few years ago. It's like peering into an alternate reality. My drunken brain tries to reconcile what it's taking in.

"It's not worth it," Todd says, his hand slowly venturing out for Brayden's shoulder. "Let me get you another drink, yeah?"

"Fucking asshole." Brayden shrugs away Todd's hand. "No. FUCK him!"

The sensation that I'm missing out on a boatload of context is overpowering. The cautious faces of the crew, the rage bubbling over within Brayden. I'd ask someone to fill me in, but now's definitely not the right moment.

"Brayden, the bitch doesn't deserve a second of your precious attention. Drop him, girl. Mmkay?" Rowan stands up and wraps his arms around Brayden's waist, planting a loud kiss on his cheek. "You're hotter than that twink bitch. Downgrade central. Ya dig?"

The rage in Brayden seems to dissipate, his squared shoulders slumping, his eyes softening. Rowan, sensing this, removes his grip and returns to his seat.

"You're right." Brayden is now grinning, reaching for his drink. "He doesn't deserve a second of my time..."

I'm still clueless as hell, but I join in the posse's chorus of, "Exactly."

"—Right after THIS."

Before any of us have a chance to restrain him, Brayden is stomping across the floor, shoving guys out of his way and upsetting the happy-go-drunk flow of the party. I lose sight of him in the crowd and we are on our feet in desperate pursuit.

Rowan and Todd are yelling, "Brayden! No! Come back!" Servando and Shane sprint even quicker, trying to dance around the crowd.

"YOU FUCKING ASSHOLE!"

Brayden's voice breaks above the din of conversation and bass. I get through the crowd just in time to see his cosmopolitan mid-air, a slow-motion torrent of tasty liquor that flies in a million directions after splashing directly into the epicenter of Red Hoodie's face.

With Red Hoodie dazed and drenched, Brayden spins on his twinky date, wrapping his hands around the kid's throat. I am too stunned to move. I watch them fall to the floor, observe the crowd clear around them like they are a suspicious package left sitting in Times Square. I never would have expected this sort of rage from Brayden. But Todd is taking control, yelling for me to help break them up.

Fists are flying. Brayden and Twink are rolling around in an awkward, poorly choreographed drunken fist exchange. And then Red Hoodie is on top of the dervish. I can't tell if anything is connecting, if bones are being broken and faces are being irreparably scarred. I bounce around the perimeter of the fight, as though my jockeying this way and that is actually accomplishing anything. At least I'm not the only one passively observing — the entire crowd has taken a page out of the "Fist Fight in a High School Cafeteria" manual and also merely look on, as though a hall monitor or principal will break in at any time.

It feels like an hour, but it's actually all of fifteen seconds before two large black blurs — bouncers in dark pants and muscle tees — descend on the trio, plucking them up separately and flinging them out of the bar.

Todd, Servando, Shane, Rowan, and I rush out the door where Brayden is pulling himself free of his own private bouncer. "Let me the fuck go, you fucking ASSHOLE!" He's kicking at the air and yanking, pulling, screaming.

"You fucking crazy bitch!" Red Hoodie wipes blood from his ballooning lower lip.

The twink is bawling.

A crowd gathers on two sides — those inside of Barrage looking out through the glass doors, and those on the street who suddenly are thinking: hey, maybe this is the place to be tonight.

Brayden shrieks. "YOU FUCKING SLUT! DID YOU TELL HIM WE HAD A DATE TOMORROW NIGHT?!"

Red Hoodie lunges, perhaps for a shot at Brayden in return for the sneak attack. The bouncer is on him instantaneously. So Red Hoodie spins and throws a punch at the bouncer. Bad move. The bouncer ducks before Red Hoodie's fist leaves his side and drives a forearm into his exposed abdomen. Wind rushes from between his teeth and he drops like a martini glass, spilling out onto the sidewalk.

The twink, meanwhile, has removed himself from the altercation and is a few feet from the bar's entrance, a cigarette dangling from his mouth, tears pouring down his face, red handprints on his throat. Red Hoodie, heaving, beaten, bleeding, pulls himself to his feet and limps towards his crying date. They are homeward bound without another word.

Brayden, however, is still entangled in the other bouncer's grasp, screeching a list of names, each with a hyphenated "fuck" attached at either beginning or end. Todd apologizes profusely to the bouncer, assuring him that of course he doesn't usually bring drama, and of course he'll get Brayden out of here and get him sober. Todd drags Brayden away from the bar, the rest of us following closely.

That is the end of our night. No diner stop, as Rowan and Shane take it upon themselves to escort Brayden to a cab. He'll be staying with them tonight, they pledge, as Brayden continues howling at the moon and spitting on the street; there are red flecks amidst the phlegm. Red Hoodie now has a name — Marty, a name Brayden shouted over and over again as he was escorted into the cab by his two new caretakers.

Todd and I return home to a chorus of honking horns in standstill traffic on 9th avenue. He sighs audibly and shakes his head. "Drama. No fun, Gully. No fun."

"Is he going to be okay?"

"Who the hell knows. They broke up almost a year ago. Sometimes I worry that B's permanently unhinged."

"What happened?"

"The douche bag cheated on Brayden and then dumped him."

"But really? A year later? Come on."

"Apparently, they were on the mend. Marty's been trying to convince him to give him another chance for weeks now. They had a date tomorrow night. And then, well, there you go. Same old Marty. Guess we can consider the door closed on that asshole, then." I shrug in agreement. "But you didn't hear that from me. Swear it. Last thing Brayden wants is to have the story go on any longer than it needs to."

"I swear."

Todd opens his arms and I fall into them. He gives me a squeeze and lifts me in the air. "Night, bro."

In my room, I stay up for hours. I can hear Todd snoring from across the apartment. The sounds of the street are suddenly so goddamn loud I can't shut them out. Every time I think I'm about to fall asleep my eyes shoot open and there I am staring at the ceiling again. Outside someone is screaming. Crazy homeless person? Another gay, drunken fight?

I think of Brayden. His eyes filled with rage, pushing tears out like unwanted invaders. Cheated on. Dumped. Lied to. Led on. I hear him screaming. I see the cosmo flying through the air, spiraling. And I am recalling the night I found out about Graham, learning that the boyfriend I never suspected of even looking at another boy had been fucking one for months behind my back — his old college roommate. Who he'd always had a crush on. Who he'd thought, back then, was straight. Who I, too, thought was straight, all the while he and Graham were spending time together. Or else I might have balked at the late nights they were out together, or that time Graham called to say he was crashing at Kevin's because he was "too drunk" (and apparently, too horny) to get back home safely. Of course I never questioned this. In retrospect, I was pretty stupid.

Right then was when I had my own Brayden moment, except I threw myself at my about-to-be-ex instead of a drink. And it was in the privacy of my own home. Graham was stronger, able to push me into a wall with such force that I crumpled to my apartment floor. The rage was so deep, like Pandora's box opened wide, fears and worries I never knew I had spewing out all around me. Was I at risk for an STD? How many others had he slept with? When someone you trust does something like that, suddenly you trust nobody. How can you trust a stranger when you can't trust the person you thought you knew best?

And then I cry. From what? Pity? Mourning? Memory? I'm too busy heaving and shaking to care.

When sleep comes, I dream and it's no better. Behind my eyelids I'm flying back to California as fast as I possibly can. Leaving New York City shrinking into foggy oblivion behind me. I am not on a plane, but rather, using my arms like wings. I flap so hard and fast, like the city might be chasing me, gaining ground, trying to swallow me whole and then spit me back onto its busy streets. And with each frantic flap, I'm still crying, because there's nothing for me here, but what's back in California is no more promising.

I thought I'd left these feelings back in LA. That I was no more likely to run across them here than I was a palm tree, a Coffee Bean and Tea Leaf, a star on the Walk of Fame.

I guess I was wrong.

CHAPTER 7

Brayden is on his tenth cigarette. We're sitting out in Sheep Meadow, Central Park's very own meat market. We are surrounded by hundreds of New Yorkers enjoying this perfectly manicured piece of lawn, this painstakingly designed oasis of nature amidst skyscrapers. Our shirts are off, our bathing suits scandalously small. Here, I learned from Todd as we got dressed this morning, is where the gays go to ogle each other and maybe pick up a quick post-brunch hookup the old-fashioned way (because satellite signals are so stressed in the area that it's impossible to even fire up Grindr properly).

My eyes, meanwhile, are falling out of my head. You couldn't swing a dildo without knocking over a supermodel from heaven. Muscles seem to be a prerequisite for entry to this patch of grass. I am trying to make sense of abs and pecs that put what I've got to shame while trying to remain unaroused enough not to pop out of the tiny swimsuit I bought with Todd at some boutique in Chelsea. Some faces I recognize. Others I want to recognize. Someone, somewhere, is blasting Sara Bareilles' "Love Song."

In the distance, the rest of the crew is disappearing over a hill. Their destination: a carnival that apparently crops up on Central Park's ice rink during the summer. I planned on joining them until Brayden said he wasn't in the mood; I broke the awkward silence that followed by saying, quite convincingly, that I was too comfortable to move my body in any way more arduous than spinning over on my stomach to even out my color. Furthermore, now that I'd seen the wonder of the Central Park meat market, I wasn't going to give it up so fast. Todd flashed me a glance that said "thank you," and then they were off.

Brayden has been a zombie since brunch. Over mimosas he just sat there, his eyes following the conversation silently at times, other times just staring into his uneaten Eggs Florentine. This had an obvious effect on the rest of the guys, who were trying their best to ignore the elephant sitting in our booth despite the fact that it was swinging its trunk dangerously in each of our directions.

Now alone, Brayden and I sit in silence. I look at his face — stubbly. His roots are showing through his dye job. I can't see his eyes through the pair of aviators he's wearing. Do I mention last night? Or do I act as though nothing happened, following the modus operandi of the rest of the guys? And in that case, what the fuck DO I talk about?

"Thanks for hanging back with me," he says, nubbing out his cigarette with one hand while drawing cigarette number eleven with the other.

"No problem. I have little to no interest in paying four bucks to skid down a slide on a burlap sack. I'll just use that cash to buy a drink and trip down a flight of stairs for free."

Brayden chuckles, the first time I've heard him laugh all day. Then he falls back into silence. Across from us, a group of twelve muscle daddies and bears are laying out a blanket, removing boxes of Popeye's fried chicken and cases of cupcakes from a plastic bag. I finish my vodka lemonade and refresh it accordingly. When the glass is overflowing, I hold up the container.

"Refill?"

He just looks over at me, quiet for a long moment. Then, mercifully, breaks the ice.

"So you saw me at my worst last night. Sorry about that."

"Okay, no refill. Please. Your scene's got nothing on what I witnessed in LA."

"Oh yeah? You had your fair share of drama out in La La Land?"

My stomach has had enough cigarettes. I am starting to feel nauseous, which inspires me to close my pack and put it back in the shoulder bag I volunteered to carry, transporting the sheet we are sitting on and the vodka lemonade we are drinking.

"Who, me? Nope. I've always been practically perfect in every way."

Brayden laughs again. He lifts his sunglasses and stares at me. His eyes have deep, dark rings around them. The lids are puffy. "You're pretty funny this morning, Mrs. Poppins."

"Credit's yours. I'm sure none of the other guys would have caught a Disney reference if I threw it to them underhand."

"Credit taken."

"But sure. I had a boyfriend back in LA that cheated on me. If you ever end up over there, just ask about me. You'll hear stories. I've been on both sides of some pretty epic scenes. Seriously epic." Translation: Graham had the pleasure of wearing at least three of my drinks over the course of the five months after I broke up with him.

Brayden lies back, his hairless toned abs expanding and swelling, drinking in every last ray of sunlight. "How much did Todd tell you about the situation?"

"Nothing. We sorta stumbled home and at some point I guess I crashed into bed, since I woke up there this morning with my shoes on. What is the situation?"

The story Brayden tells me is a slightly more detailed version of what Todd related the night before. I nod silently, sipping my lemonade, squinting through the sunlight.

"I just wanted to say I'm really sorry about it all. I know where you're coming from. I know what that feels like."

"Please. Don't get wrapped up in it. Marty's a piece of shit. The guys told me that over and over again. This is completely my own fault. I let him back in. Gave him another chance. Granted, I still want to tear out that little twink's throat..."

"Yeah, I'd still kill the guy my boyfriend slept with, too. But, take this for what it's worth: you'll learn to direct your anger entirely at Marty soon. You made a mistake giving him another chance, but never forget that he's the ass-hole."

"Yeah. Thanks, Gully. Change of topic?"

There's so much more I want to say, despite Brayden cutting me off. But this chat foretells more to come just like it. If I ever see Marty again, I resolve to give him a vicarious piece of my mind for two-timing my new buddy (the way I wish friends of mine would berate Graham every time they see him so he never has a good time without being reminded of what a dick he was to me).

"Oh shit, check out that guy. Orange bathing suit."

I follow Brayden's eyes. Twenty feet away, a wide-shouldered blonde catches a football. He has broken the teeny bikini rule, forsaking something more revealing for a pair of checkered board shorts with a drawstring left untied. It works.

"Top or bottom?" he asks.

"I mean, isn't it obvious?"

"You're right. Total bottom."

I almost spit-take my vodka lemonade. "Very funny."

"No, I'm serious." Brayden sits up and spins around, facing me. A wide grin is on his face. "He's a total bottom."

"You are so full of shit. Look at him!"

We do look, and he is looking back at us, the football clenched in his hands.

"Ah, Gully, looks can be deceiving. Gawker blogged about this last year. New York City has significantly more bottoms than tops."

"He's not one of them."

"Want to bet?"

"Sure. Ten bucks."

We haven't completed our official handshake when Brayden breaks the grip and raises his hand, giving an ecstatic wave in the blonde's general direction. The blonde waves back and blows an over-dramatic kiss, one of his legs bending behind him effeminately.

"I'll let you keep your cash. His name is Teddy. I've slept with him. I can confirm that he is the biggest power bottom in Central Park today."

"One, you're a cheater. Two, that's ridiculous."

"Servando and Rowan have, too."

I roll my eyes. "Of course they have."

"Anyway, maybe we should catch up to those little sluts. What do you say?"

"Sure," I say, gathering up our things.

I take one last look at the meat market — the lunching bears, the Frisbee-throwing bottom, the hundreds of bodies laying out and chatting and blasting Lady Gaga, drinking from plastic bottles holding anything but what their innocent labels claim.

And then, in silence, Brayden and I leave it all behind us for the path that will take us back to our buddies, and whatever else the day has in store.

CHAPTER 8

Today's talent showcase is being held in a small audition room in the Actor's Equity building in Times Square. Considering the very nature of theater, it's ironic that the building that stands as a representation of the craft is so unassuming. Before I started working for Stanford, I would pass by without a second glance, none the wiser that inside, dreams were being reached or kicked forever out of reach at the rate that people die from hunger in third world countries.

The school is one I've never heard of — which is saying a lot. The actors were trained in some relatively new theater concentration that's part of a private school in Allentown, Pennsylvania. Stanford warned me that I would be treated to an afternoon of flat standards and wilting monologues (if I was lucky). Judging from the tiny handful of agents commiserating in far too many folding chairs in the back of the wood-floored, white-plastered, demimirrored dance studio, most agencies shared in my boss' wisdom.

The school was kind enough to splurge on a table of refreshments — sandwiches and wraps from Cosi and an iced tub of white zinfandel. Stanford said I should feel free to drink myself into a stupor so long as I didn't come back with a recommendation to represent a coat hanger I'd mistaken for a six-foot-tall baritone.

I introduce myself to the other agents while we wait for the showcase to begin. As we sip our wine and nosh on chicken caesar and greek salad wraps, we trade war stories. The other representatives are also from smaller agencies, or interns and trainees from larger ones. We're all in our twenties, young and not-yet-weary for the most part. But some are worn thin — they have dark bags under their eyes and chew on Tums between sips of white zin. Of course they are the interns from the larger agencies, veritable slave ships of talent representation. They tell stories of nights that turn into mornings and talent that treats them like they're gas station attendants. I tell them about Stanford — no one has heard of him. But when I mention the agency they are all agape, saying, "Oh, I didn't know they had an office here!"

I put a finger to my nose, warm with excitement that I am delivering this brand new information, and say, "We're the pioneers."

A pianist enters and takes his seat at a splintered, dusty upright piano stashed in the corner. It is time. Here we go. I reach into my shoulder bag and pull out a notebook and pen, resting my wine and plate of food under the folding chair. I switch over to professional mode, telling my ears to pay attention, setting my eyes on detail-scan. I am on star patrol.

The actors are a rag-tag bunch, all wide-eyed gay boys and long-haired straight girls, plus the occasional ample-shouldered straight guy — guaranteed to be laid consecutively every night of every run because not only is he dreamy looking, he's heterosexual, and thus Broadway's equivalent of a unicorn. Now someone is singing Sondheim — a choice I learned quickly is a bad one. The sheet music is too complex. Stephen Sondheim never really cared for the mental or physical health of anyone involved in his productions. For him, it's all about the audience. The resulting songs are so complex they cause finger cramps in pianists and vocal strain in actors who try their best to do the musical theater god's work justice. Predictably, the pianist can't keep up, and it's obvious from the first note that he's not going out of his way to — he isn't getting paid enough. (Or possibly, at all.)

My phone vibrates. It's Stanford, asking for an update. I text him that there are two promising performers so far. One is a boy named Steven Tylor O'Connor, a skinny twink of a thing with twinkling eyes. He has definite male lead quality and there are at least three equity tours I can see him easily slipping into as a chorus member or understudy. Then there's Chantelle Warren — a bombastic black girl who almost knocked me out of my seat when she belted "You're Gonna Love Me" from *Dreamgirls*. Predictable choice? Maybe. But the voice made up for it and then some. Stanford instructs me to take down their information and get back to him with any other possibilities.

The Sondheim boy ends his song and leaves, clearly regretting his decision to disregard what friends and professors told him about choosing "Marry Me a Little" for his one shot at representation. He is replaced by the director of the school's theater program, a short, heavy man with an infectious smile and wispy gray hair that looks like it has recently been snacked on by a camel.

"Thank you, Sean. Again, I'd like to thank all of you for coming out today. Our academy appreciates the work you do, and we are so grateful you take time out of your day to come and hear our graduates. Our next actor is the last one we have for you this semester. For awhile we feared we lost this one to early stardom. He left our program for a semester to perform as an understudy in the national tour of *Jersey Boys*. But luckily, he came back and gave up his summer so he could graduate on time with his class. He will be singing for us today 'Lost in the Wilderness' from Stephen Schwartz's *Children of Eden*. Come on up, Marty!"

I'm jotting down notes on the past two performers feverishly when the boy begins. The first three notes grab my attention, halting my pen mid-scrawl. His is the kind of voice you'd hear on a Broadway cast recording. If you were lucky. The kind that goes beyond good training, beyond the masses you can kindly compliment and place in a touring chorus or respectable regional theater. This is God-given, naturally-blessed talent.

I look up and lock eyes with Brayden's evil twin.

His face no longer puffy from the pot shots, he pushes out deep, resonating note after deep, resonating note. His eyes are no longer filled with anger, instead lost in the brain of Cain, contemplating how he and his brother, now in exodus from God's heavenly garden, need to make a life for themselves.

Aside from the wonder I imagine all the agents are experiencing, mine is fourteen feet deeper. Because, as I watch him, I remember Friday night, the bits before and after hazy but a few choice moments vividly crystal clear. There he is on the floor of Barrage being throttled by his furious ex who — very much so, I now notice — is his doppelganger. And despite all that, here stands Marty, singing me into a different universe.

I hear Brayden screaming, "ASK HIM, YOU TWINKY SLUT!" But, as Marty hits the final high notes: "Lost in the wilderness, finally we'll be found," Brayden's voice becomes a squeak, a car horn severed with a switchblade, and then nothing.

The agent pool erupts in applause — thoroughly unprofessional, I am fully aware — but I am applauding, too. My hands are on autopilot, smashing together frantically as if he's floating away to the magical land he came from and each *clap-clap-clap* is keeping him on the ground for one second more. Stanford would do the same — that is, if not actually leaping from his chair, elbowing the other agents out of the way, and producing a rappelling hook from a hidden utility belt, which he would hook to Marty just before they flew up out through the skylight together and on to instant stardom.

Marty suppresses a blush and does a little bow before skipping back to the door he emerged from. We're still clapping and the director tells us thank you again for coming and if there are any actors we'd like to schedule follow-up meetings with, they will be in town for the remainder of the week before trucking back to Allentown for graduation. After that, of course, they are all more than willing to move back to the city if they earn representation.

I've already forgotten the names of the other two actors on my sheet — what's-her-name and the boy who may or may not have had a face. Everything is Marty, the asshole I dressed down to his ex-boyfriend not even a week ago. We agents politely say goodbye to one another, but there is deceit in our eyes. If the director of the program came into the room and unlocked a cabinet full of the weapons from *Clue* we'd be on each other, slicing, bludgeoning, strangling, and shooting to make sure no one beyond our very selves was aware that a man named Marty Perry was alive on this earth.

I send a text to Stanford, who, in no uncertain terms, coaches me to slip out through a side door and wait by the elevator bank on the street level for Marty to emerge. I am praying he doesn't remember me from Friday night and flee at the sight of me, thinking I have come with unholy intentions and Servando, Shane, Rowan, Todd and — God save the kid — Brayden are right around the corner, ready to attack.

Nearly an hour later, the actors trickle out of the Equity building. Marty does seem to remember me — but not exactly. His eyes open for a half second. He looks me up and down. How DOES he know me? Did I hit on him? Did we pass on the street? Maybe I look like someone else he knows. I beckon him over with a quick nod. He says something to his friends and heads in my direction.

"Hey!" he says. "What'd you think? Was I okay?"

"Okay?" I hand him my card. "What I think is you and I need to grab a drink and discuss your future. Maybe our future."

Somewhere inside of me, a voice nags that this isn't right — I should have left Marty to be eaten alive by the other agents and gone home. But this is professional, right? In the auditions I've been privy to, I've never heard a voice anywhere near Marty's caliber. If I let my personal shit get in the way of this acquisition, Stanford might as well fire me right out. I owe it to him to bring Marty into our fold.

So long as I don't tell Brayden, what's the harm?

"Sure. I can do that. Where do you want to go?"

I let Marty suggest our watering hole, as I still don't really know my way around. My only request is that we stay out of Hell's Kitchen. The reason I give is the crowds — the real reason being I don't want to chance crashing into Brayden (and I doubt Marty does either). We end up at a place called BlueBar — a shotgun narrow drinking establishment in Chelsea that is (surprise, surprise) dim, featuring loud music and a few places to sit with more room to stand.

When first I heard of the sheer amount of gay bars in Manhattan, I wondered at the number of options available to a boy who wanted to go out and get sloshed. But now that I'm here, it's funny how they all just blur together. Whether one floor, two floors, or three, they're all basically the same. You begin to differentiate them based on the clientele — the impeccably dressed Hell's Kitchen professionals; the stubbly, artsy guys of the East Village; the muscle-kissed, meatheaded Chelsea Boys who have now, for the most part, gracefully transitioned into Chelsea Men — or by which drag queens hold court, hosting bombastic shows where they lip-sync to pop music and dole out free shots to audience members brave enough to humiliate themselves for a swig of well gin.

Marty and I find our way to a corner. We're drinking and talking. He tells me about college, how he can't wait to move here. I talk about moving from LA, working for Stanford, getting the hang of the more aggressive speed in New York City. He's originally from a small town in New Jersey and quips that even Pennsylvania was lightning compared to his hometown. At no point as we drink does he mention his altercation on Friday night. And I'm not about to bring it up. I am, however, wondering how he and Brayden ever came to meet each other.

He's so glad I loved his performance and tells me how, when he was kicked out of his house for being gay and had to move in with his older sister, he really connected to this song, used to listen to it over and over. I tell him his voice is gorgeous — and so is he.

Whoops. I didn't mean to say that. Marty blinks as we find ourselves standing at the precipice between professional drinks and something neither of us was planning on. But we're three drinks and four shots in the hole, thanks to the omnipresent shot boy wearing nothing but a pair of Andrew Christian underwear styled to look like a pair of denim jean cutoffs.

What am I doing? He's just so attractive! And it's been weeks since my night with Servando and Rowan. I'm drunk and horny and even though there's a voice asking over and over how stupid can I possibly be, my dick is screaming louder. Plus, who's to say he'd even take the bait? All he has to say is no and then there's nothing to worry about.

"You're pretty cute yourself, Gully," he winks.

Then we're in the bathroom and the door is locked. Our pants are around our ankles and we take turns dropping to our knees. I lick his thighs, cut in all the right places, I know, from the modern dance classes he's taking. He moans and runs his hands through my hair before pulling me up for a kiss, then drops to his knees to return the favor. We end up against the wall, jerking off, orgasming simultaneously. It is only then that we realize someone is banging on the door. We leave the bathroom, blushing from booze and sex.

He's staying at the Four Points Soho Hotel; I am more than happy with a change in scenery. We jerk each other off for kicks since we're the only ones in the elevator. We stumble down the carpeted hallway, taking breaks to pin each other to the wall for more kissing, licking, rubbing. I see Brayden's face over and over again. Guilt piles up in me like the stack of phone books in the entryway to Todd's apartment building. But I can't stop. Or I won't stop. Whatever, I'm not stopping. Not when I'm this close. I am constantly spinning the situation in my head.

It's just one time. What Brayden doesn't know won't hurt him — he's never going after Marty again, anyway. He and I are just collections of bones and organs about to smash into each other for one night, then go our separate ways come morning. Guilt and morality are but mere human inventions, why should I give in to them?

Marty fumbles for his key card and we fall into the room, me on top of him with our feet holding the door open. We keep kissing, in full view of anyone who might happen to pass by (sadly, no one does). I kiss him harder, as if that'll push the guilt away. It doesn't help that he looks like Brayden's fucking brother. But if Graham can cheat on me, if Marty can cheat on Brayden, if anyone can cheat on anyone, why can't I do this? Just this one time?

"I have a bed." He points behind him, arching his head back and pointing his chin up in an effort to make sure that that's true. I take advantage of the opportunity to go to town on his neck, licking the source of the hypnotizing notes that fucked me in their own way a few hours earlier. The notes that practically sang me here like a siren's song. Who am I to resist?

"We should go there, then," I say and jump up, pulling him into my arms, the door slamming behind us. We race for the bed, screaming the first one to get there tops — and I win.

Well, we both win.

We fuck drunkenly on the king size bed, the curtains open wide so our performance can be enjoyed, admired, even envied by the audience that is New York City. When I'm inside him, he moans inaudibly and I lean forward so I can hear. I kiss his mouth as he gasps again, "I love you, Gulliver."

I pause, look down at him. The moonlight illuminates his face in all the right ways, making him even more beautiful. And it's fine. I'm inside him. We're drunk. People who are drunk and beautiful and fucking say meaningless things like this. And I'm not about to leave the poor guy hanging. He's too talented. Too hot. Too something. And God, it's been so long since I heard those three words.

Especially from someone I'm so attracted to, someone I clicked so easily and immediately with. It's been years, of course, because the last time—

I stop thinking.

Instead I smile, then let that smile slip into a full shit-eating ear-to-ear grin. Then slowly — very, very slowly — I take the time to lean forward, bite his ear, and whisper, "I love you too, Marty."

CHAPTER 9

Back at UCLA, I would call my mom twice a day — once in the morning and again at night. Mentioning this often garnered a reaction that bordered on uneasy. Was I some sort of unapologetic Mama's Boy?

In a way, maybe I was. It always surprised me that my peers DIDN'T call their parents often (if at all). Some had good reason, whether that be sour relationships, parents that couldn't handle the fact that they were gay, or whatever. But so many didn't call home because they just didn't feel like it. That, to me, was the worst reason of all.

So call I did. These calls were rarely, if ever, longer than ten minutes apiece – more of a check-in or check-up than anything. "Are you getting enough to eat out there? You need to get a PO Box so Daddy and I can send you a care package, Gully." But it was good to hear Mom and Dad's voices. College was the first time I was ever so far away from my family — even if only a few hours by car. I never did the sleepaway camp thing growing up, or a road trip or wild spring break with friends. Then, all of a sudden, there I was at college, being forced ever-so-slowly into adulthood without an adult I knew in sight.

Now that I am in New York, the calls have become longer and more frequent. I find that if I forget to text Mom when I first wake up, as well as a few times throughout day, she tends to jump to the conclusion that a piano dropped out of a skyscraper and crushed me to death. It's not that I mind having to be accountable to her, sending those "Hey, I'm still alive, I swear" messages. It's just that sometimes I forget and all of a sudden my phone is exploding with texts that increase in both urgency and gloom with every character.

Today is one of those days.

Marty and I awaken with our legs intertwined, the afternoon sun baking our bodies. We lay in bed and count our blessings that, somehow, the hangover fairy passed us over and went on to the next unfortunate gay coupling that had too much sex after too much to drink. To celebrate, we order room service and are able to go two more times before the cart arrives. We share oatmeal and egg whites and fresh-squeezed orange juice, naked, watching cartoons until I remember to turn my phone back on. That's when it explodes, dancing off the end table and hitting the floor, seizing with every text message, which comes out to more than ten.

"Somebody's popular," Marty says.

"Yeah, with my mom." I kiss Marty on the mouth, tasting the OJ, and tell him I should get going anyway.

Marty pouts, huffs, and crosses his arms, forcing me to tackle him on the bed, where we wrestle for ten more minutes and have sex one last time. When my phone vibrates yet again, I tell him that if I don't get in contact with my mom, there'll be police helicopters patrolling the entire city in search of me within the hour.

We exchange numbers (and a hundred more kisses) and I'm off, heading down in the elevator and then out to the street.

When I emerge, the sun is high enough that its painful rays are obstructed by the SoHo skyscrapers, thank God. I am instantly overcome by the chirping of birds mixed with angry taxi honking and the laughter of teenage girls. Even the garbage bags outside Starbucks seem to glisten in the light. The weather is so beautiful I decide to walk the four or so miles up from the hotel in SoHo to Todd's place, giving me time to call Mom and assuage her fear that I've been eaten by a lion that escaped from the Central Park Zoo.

But Mom is in full-on nag mode this morning. First it's about my drinking — I'm doing too much of it. Then it's about sleeping in too late. I tell her I'm working and deserve to sleep in on the occasional Saturday morning. She then switches her tactic to say I'm working too hard and should find a better work-life balance. I know that if I countered it by saying I go out plenty with the boys in Hell's Kitchen, she would then turn it back around and accuse me of going out too much, which might be negatively affecting my job performance. I love my mom for this reason. She plays both sides against the middle and, I am convinced, uses nerves and anxiety to keep her heart pumping and her blood circulating. The day that nothing is worrisome is the day she'll drop dead. It means our conversations are never dull — they are strategic tugs of war with more reversals than the Super Bowl.

When she's finally been defused (with her favorite fall-back: "Well, Gully, it's not like you'll listen to your old mother, anyway,") I ask her how everything is going in California. She promptly bemoans the state of the economy. My younger brother's college tuition at UCLA has become positively unbearable and will, no doubt, get even worse in the coming years. But family finances are good — Dad has found unexpected luck in a bunch of stocks no one ever thought to look at through the lens of a global recession. While the free world plunges into the depths of poverty and chaos, the Leverenz family is making money hand over fist. This inverse fortune has filled Mom with about ten tons of excess guilt, and so to counterbalance feeling like Marie Antoinette carelessly swimming in riches while her subjects starve and die, she is getting herself involved in a lot of charity work. She's been organizing dinners for the homeless of California, doing grassroots stuff to help those without healthcare. Because she doesn't just worry about me, she worries about everyone.

As we chit-chat I pass countless cafes, restaurants, pubs, fusion places; it's probably two o'clock or so but the city's Saturday brunch is still in full effect. All have set up their patio seating areas where New Yorkers sit and uphold one of the finest metropolitan traditions. The most popular ones, of course, are those that offer unlimited mimosas or screwdrivers. New York's the city that never sleeps — so they get drunk during their day of rest to make up for it, drowning their hangover in the hair of the dog and a gallon of hollandaise.

To many (including me, when I first arrived), New York seemed like a grimy haven for a population with a collective drinking problem. In LA we drank less and less often. But in my time here I've come to discover the one reason New Yorkers probably drink more than most: cabs. No need for designated drivers — New Yorkers can always stumble to the curb with their hands flung in the air to summon an angel taxi to take them back to their bed (assuming their mouth can communicate where to take them). And if a cab isn't available (or they've spent too much money on mimosas) there's always the option of a hot and bumpy subway ride or even a walk, like the one I'm embarking upon presently.

After another few minutes of talking about my job, Stanford, and how Todd is doing, Mom hands the phone over to Dad, who's in a cheery mood. He's been out on the hammock in the backyard, reading the newspaper and bird-watching. It's good to hear from him. While I talk to Mom all the time, Dad I speak to much less frequently. It's not that we don't have plenty to talk about — it's that we have absolutely nothing to talk about. He's speaking in his famous monotone about stocks I've never heard of and will never care to hear of, and the Dodgers, a team that plays some sport I've forgotten.

I find my mind wandering to my night with Marty. I remember what his skin felt like pressed against mine, how his voice sounded as we rolled around the bed in the moonlight. The taste of our drinks mixing in our mouths. I am also pleased to discover that the leaning tower of guilt surrounding the fact that I spent all night with Brayden's ex seemed to lighten significantly around the third time we had sex. I am happily lost somewhere between Marty's legs in my mind, not at all processing what Dad is saying...

Until I hear Graham's name.

"Wait, what about Graham?"

"He came by the house the other day, looking for you. Did you not tell him you were moving to New York?"

I go from zero to furious in half a second.

"Oh, I told him, alright."

The asshole knew I was in New York; everyone does by now. What was he doing at my house? Not only on the Leverenz turf, now he's appearing in my head, too — smiling at me, wearing one of those sleeveless tanks he was so fond of (always solids, never stripes) and a pair of board shorts (always checked, never khaki). A surfer. A snowboarder. A total dude. But also a math nerd who led his high school mathletes team to the national championships. It always looked like he never bothered to do his hair, but that was the secret. It actually took twenty minutes to give it that just-walked-through-a-touch-free-car-wash look. Asshole asshole asshole. Get OUT of my brain.

"Huh. That's strange. He had flowers for you and everything. When we told him, he looked so hurt. Maybe you should call him?"

"I'm not calling Graham. He knows I'm in New York, now he's playing fast and cheap. Going after your sympathy. If he comes back around just slam the door in his face."

I'm trying to create the scene in my head: Graham standing on my porch with flowers he knew would never actually get to me. What did he say? How long did the conversation go? Did he ask to be let in? Was he? I want to know these answers, yet I don't. I can't tell which is worse: knowing what happened or just imagining what might have. And on top of it all, I wonder if this is the first step in some scheme of his, what he might do next.

"You were together for five years. It's not that easy to just cut him off…"

"It IS that easy," I snap. "I did, didn't I?"

There is silence on the other end of the line. I imagine my father holding the phone away from his face like it suddenly grew a full set of teeth and tried to nip him. I don't remember the last time I raised my voice to him like that.

"Listen, Dad, I have to go. Tell Mom I love her. I'll talk to you soon, okay? Go back to your hammock."

"Okay, honey," Dad says.

"I love you, my sweetie!" Mom yells from the background.

"Bye." I hang up and jam my phone in my pocket, silently cursing Graham. What the fuck? One minute he's telling me he hopes I die, now he's showing up at my house with flowers, pretending he doesn't know I left? Why is this so complicated for him to understand? We are O. V. E. R.

Graham cheated on me. Often. With the same guy. Just because he admitted it months after the fact doesn't mean all's forgiven. Too little, too late. Maybe he should have thought of how much he loved me before the first time they fucked. Or the twelfth. A mistake is forgivable. An undercover second rela-tionship is not. Even calling it "a mistake" enrages me all the more. The asshole. The insane, fuck-crazy asshole.

Graham BEGGED me to take him back. And at times, I seriously considered it. After being with someone for five years, being single was a strange world I quickly realized I didn't want to be a part of. Suddenly I had all this free time. My phone bill dropped by fifty percent. I found myself sitting at home wondering: what did I ever do to fill up all of these minutes and hours every day? On days off from work it was even worse. I deleted and re-added his number to my phone at least a dozen times. I laid in bed and cried and screamed and bitched to any friends that would hear me out, apologizing as I did so because I knew I was repeating myself day in and out.

And he never called. Never texted. Every day I assumed he was out with Kevin — or in with Kevin, even worse. I imagined words he used with me being repurposed for his brand new relationship. I grew to hate him more and more while my stubborn love for what we had held on. Wouldn't let go.

But then things changed.

I began to see friends I had hardly spoken to in years. I got invited out more. My life, which had apparently been on hold for five years, came pouring back over me. I could only reject invites for so long before I finally gave in. And then the fun started. For the first time in months I felt attractive. No, fuck attractive — I felt gorgeous. If I found someone cute, all I had to do was go up and say hi. I re-discovered the excitement of sex with a new person — having to discover their ticks and hot spots. With that came the occasional awkward hookup, sure — every now and again I had a terrible night and wound up back at my apartment in tears, wondering why I even bothered trying again after that asshole broke my trust. But on the whole, I realized the single life was an adventure in and of itself.

That was when Graham started to chase me. First it was Facebook. Then texts. Then voicemails. From one a week to one a day in record time. The new friends I met out in Single Land, audience to my rants about Asshole-Graham, were the ones who commandeered my iPhone to delete his messages and pleas. But still Graham promised. Things would be different. Better next time. I thought if I ignored him he'd go away, but then he began showing up at parties I RSVPed to. Or at my apartment. And every time he did I left in hysterics, because despite how badly I wanted to hire an assassin to shoot him dead, there was still some stubborn part of me that thought: maybe it's worth another shot? Lord knows you can't trust anyone else. And with trust out of the equation, why not be with the one guy with whom it all worked otherwise?

So I packed my bags and told only a few people outside of my bloodline what my plans were. Todd made it all happen, so excited for our frat-brother-and-best-friend reunion. The friends I had before were all Graham's friends (or long gone, pissed at me for ditching them for Graham in the first place). My new friends were new enough to not really care if I was leaving. It was easy. There was so much to do, so much to worry about, that I didn't have a spare second to look back. Only forward.

It's only now, when things have settled down some, that I find myself still idly thinking back, wondering if maybe I was too hasty to throw it all away...

A car honks loudly, startling me out of my rage and pulling me back to the sun-baked street. It suddenly stinks of overheated garbage. I don't know how many blocks I've walked, have no memory of crossing streets or avenues or even waiting for traffic to cease. It's like I was dropped in the center of the sidewalk blindfolded and only now allowed to take in my surroundings.

It's obvious what Graham wants — a call. An angry text. Or an IM, an email. Some sort of engagement. A sliver of proof that he's captured my attention.

Well, sucks for him.

I want to. My finger shakes, ready to type his memorized phone number into my keypad; my mouth quivers, ready to scream despite the pedestrians speeding by in both directions.

But no. I will hold steady, because I know that'll hurt him most of all. He's probably got his phone set to vibrate as he works his shift at Hollister. He's been practicing for days what to say, how to twist each sentence to keep me on the phone longer. To plead his case once again.

But every vibration will be from someone else. He'll rip the phone out of his pocket, growing increasingly desperate each time. His face will register only the slightest trace of disappointment as he reads the promotional text message for this week's party at TigerHeat. Updates from Facebook. Missed calls from his parents. Invitations to go out with my frenemies. But never a word from me.

I wonder if this is just the beginning, if the silence I've enjoyed since my cab ride from JFK is about to come to a sudden, noisy end. Was this a desperate last chance, or the warning shot before an onslaught? I need to prepare for either. Fuck him for making me.

But all this makes me smile. I know this will kill him, and I want it to. Because no suffering he'll ever experience will equal what I went through. Every day I can inflict pain on him is a day I'll live happier.

Like a crying child ignored by his parents so he learns to sleep the whole night through, Graham will slowly but surely learn that I am gone from his life. For good.

CHAPTER 10

I warned Marty about the office on our way there. "Listen, it doesn't look like much, but just trust me when I say things are going to get a lot better soon."

I've been running defense for our hole in the wall all week long. How could I not? I'm as ashamed of the space as Stanford is (and tells me constantly). We're stuck in a destructive cycle: our office is shabby enough to scare away any prospective actor, but we need to sign a few good actors in order to earn the capital to buy a new space and better furniture. I guess I figured the more I talked to Marty in advance, the more I might blunt his first opinion of the agency, Stanford — and by extension, myself.

Marty was too busy nervously humming scales under his breath to hear my four thousandth warning. He almost fell down a subway entrance, knocked some guy off a curb and into the street, and tripped over a garbage can on the way here. The day was disgustingly hot, a soupy humidity that left his hair frizzy, which in turn left him panicking while lip-syncing a monologue I heard him recite at least a dozen times in his hotel room this morning (where I once again spent the night).

But now he is taking in the dusty vacant wonder that is the New York City satellite office of Diedrick, Kemnitz & Hobbs Casting. In the past month, Stanford has slowly been adding to the office small little flourishes funded exclusively from his own wallet: framed modern paintings of chaotic shapes hovering in nondescript spaces and photos of metropolitan staples like park benches and garbage cans. There are now two IKEA chairs in the far corner, crookedly facing one another with a folding table between them as if they are ashamed of their new home and whispering back and forth, trying to figure out some way to escape. There's even a gurgling Zen garden and waterfall that sits babbling in the center of the room on Stanford's desk.

Marty smiles wide in an attempt to not give away what both Stanford and I can read in his face: shock, and perhaps second-guessing if he'd even want to be represented by us in the first place. The satellite office is not a space that would put confidence in anyone — and if Stanford and I couldn't stand it, of course someone who wasn't paid to be there would think even less of the place.

"Tragic, right?" Stanford asks, shrugging at the shabby surroundings. "I know. I'm working on it. Bit by bit. Can I get you a bottle of water?"

"Actually," Marty is nervously ruffling his hand through his hair, which makes it poof out and renders him all the more cute, "I'd rather do my song first."

"Have at it!" Stanford claps his hands, jumps out of his chair, and bounds across the room to a keyboard. Marty walks quickly yet cautiously over to him and hands him the sheet music to his chart-topping "Lost in the Wilderness."

"Oh, Stephen Schwartz," Stanford laughs. "Critically panned, loved by audiences everywhere. What's your rhythm?"

Marty snaps his fingers to illustrate the beat and Stanford picks it up immediately, digging into the notes like a wild animal. I'm staring at Marty's face, solid yet tepid. He's petrified, and so am I. I imagine his voice cracking. As though what I saw last week was just a dream, because no one could ever possess a talent like his. Maybe memory would prove better than reality? My fingers are crossed instinctively. I am voicelessly cheering him on and praying for him.

Wasted worry. I am immediately transported by Marty's first note, and it only gets worse from there. He's a siren, except he's not beckoning my ship closer to his island so he can devour me and my crewmates and spit our bones upon the shore. I find myself mouthing the lyrics I remember from the day he performed it at the showcase. The song that rendered each of his fellow students pointless and talentless. I am falling for his voice, and that love is mixing with a sense of achievement at having stolen Marty right out from under those other agents. I may not know talent like Stanford does, but I know Marty has plenty. I've brought home a golden goose.

Stanford stops playing the song but gestures for Marty to continue singing, and Marty doesn't miss a beat. My boss and I sit silently as he takes us through the chorus a cappella, then the second verse and the chorus again. And then that final high note. Those glorious, over-confident, hopeful final words of Cain:

"Lost in the wilderness, finally we'll be found!"

And then: clapping. Stanford's face is stone but his hands are on autopilot just as mine were and are. I'm not even thinking. Just clapping, because it feels not just like the right thing to do but the only thing that can be done. Words won't do justice, but in the thunderous applause of our four hands, maybe we're communicating how we feel about what he's done for us.

When the clapping stops, we fall into a silence that hums so loudly it's practically crying out for Marty to fill it again with those delicious notes. Marty doesn't speak, just smiles. Stanford is smiling too. I'm smiling the most.

"Can I get that drink now?" he asks.

"Absolutely," Stanford says. "Gully? Please get Marty a bottle of water and a contract."

Now it's Marty's turn to be speechless. "Just like that?"

"If you've sung it like that twice now, it proves it's no fluke. Hell, even if it was, I'd sign you just to wait around for another fluke!"

Marty glances at me, beaming and blushing. I want to go over there and give him a big squeeze, plant one right on his lips. Instead I am standing stiffly trying to force my grinning mouth closed lest I give too much away in my pride.

"I don't want to know what Gulliver had to do to get you to come meet with us before any other agency..."

Marty's face flashes with panic, which luckily Stanford misreads.

"Bribes? Blackmail? Death threats on a beloved pet? Oh, Marty, I kid. Gulliver may be green, but he knows what he's doing. This proves it. He reminds me of myself at that tender young age, always with my eye on the prize."

I smile at the compliment to avoid wincing at the accompanying lurch of guilt. Of course I must hide the details of my "acquisition." Marty and I talked it over last night, deciding it was probably best for both of us to keep business and pleasure separate as far as Stanford's knowledge is concerned. Naturally Marty didn't want to say anything that might jeopardize his chances of getting representation, though he did wonder whether or not my boss would be able to smell it all over us. So did I. I took a gamble on Stanford being so focused on the glory of Marty's singing that everything else would fall away, and it appears I was right. Stanford grabs Marty by the shoulder and shakes him half-violently in excitement. I opt for only a polite handshake and say, "Welcome aboard."

My ecstatic boss runs his hand through my hair playfully, gracing me with a look he's never given me before. But I know what it means exactly. I have just brought Stanford his first official New York City star. Me. Gulliver Leverenz. For the first time since starting this job, I finally feel like I belong here.

CHAPTER 11

It's Wednesday night and I am lying comatose on the couch, one hand down my sweatpants, the other clicking through the DVR while Señor lies passed out and snoring on my stomach. The week has been nuts and I'd like nothing better than to stay right here, sinking into the generous cushions and finally succumbing to my heavy eyelids for the night. Soon Todd will be home, attempting to drag me out for another night of the same clubs and bars. I plan on telling him I'll be staying in and catching up on the sleep I've missed during a week of long hours with Stanford and additional long hours at the clubs with Todd. The thought of rolling off this couch and jamming myself into a pair of jeans to take to the sweltering streets is about as attractive as a frontal lobotomy without anesthesia. Actually, I'd opt for two lobotomies so long as I could stay right here while they're performed.

I'm also texting Marty for the fifth time. He's in the bittersweet midst of his graduation month and strangely hasn't responded in over 24 hours. I wonder, is it unrealistic of me to expect daily communication from him? Things had been going so well up until now. On the night before he headed out of town again, I came clean about Brayden. He was appropriately shocked that I was friends with his ex, even more stunned that I witnessed the impromptu title fight at Barrage. He wished I had told him right away; I said I thought it'd be unprofessional, given that my initial advances in inviting him to drinks were solely on Stanford's behalf. "When would have been a good moment to let you know? While we were blowing each other in the bathroom? Or rolling around on the floor of your hotel room making out?" Marty conceded that any way you cut it, it would've been awkward. In the end, he was just glad I told him at all. And so was I — keeping Marty a secret from Stanford, Brayden, and the crew was bad enough. Keeping that secret twofold would likely have driven me into an asylum.

So what happened? Until today, Marty and I didn't let a day go by without at least four exchanges, even if the content was sappy and unnecessary. Just yesterday we were sending smiley faces back and forth (along with a few naked photos to keep things interesting), trying to figure out the first possible chance we could see each other when he moves back to the city (or, well, to Astoria). Last night he went out with his theater friends to some local gay dive bar and I assumed he would text me upon waking. By four in the afternoon, I was imagining all sorts of terrible things: him cheating on me with a townie or falling for some classmate and deciding to just never call me again. And after all that, him being gay bashed and killed. Days like today remind me that I'm my mother's son, having inherited her propensity for over-exaggerated fear in situations that don't warrant it. I have since promised myself to always call her in the morning so she doesn't go through what I've been going through today. On some of those calls, I'll probably yell at her for cursing me with this worthless worry gene.

I throw my phone to the other side of the couch in frustration, which startles Señor awake for a second at most.

The door opens and Todd enters. His phone is clutched between his shoulder and ear and a voice is screaming out of the speaker. "I get it. No, no, it's cool. Hey, listen. Shit like this happens. No, don't worry about it. What? He said what? Well you tell him Todd says he can't dance on the pole tonight. I don't CARE what the manager said. The manager doesn't have a say in where the go-gos go. I do. If he gives you shit about it, let me know. I don't want to come down tonight. But I will. And if I do, you let him know he will be out of a job."

Todd holds the phone away from his ear, rolls his eyes dramatically, and blows me a kiss as he makes a beeline for his bedroom.

I don't understand how Todd is alive. He's up every morning at 6 AM. I hear him walking around the apartment, going through his morning ablutions. There's the smell of coffee seeping under the crack of my door by 6:30 and he's already on his Blackberry, talking the language of financial analysts, using words like "amortization" which I'm too lazy to Google. He leaves me two cups in the brewer and is out the door by 7 AM. He doesn't come home until after 7 PM.

I'm guessing a lot of his energy comes from caffeine. The strip on his auto-refill Starbucks card is worn more ragged than even his American Express. When we're on our way out at night, the first stop is the bodega on the corner where he buys the largest can of sugar-free Red Bull and two small bottles of energy juice. He pounds the Bull so fast he can throw it away in the trash can right outside of said bodega. He chases it with one of the small energy juices, saving the other for a few hours later. While many might go psychotic with such caffeine intake, Todd just continues with a baseline of somewhat-enthused confidence and sexiness. The fucker has enough energy to hit the gym five times a week, where he spends an hour to an hour and a half working out various muscle groups to the point of perfection. Meanwhile, I am still riding on the perhaps undeserved luck of a naturally toned and skinny body that comes as a result of a hyper metabolism.

Todd returns from his room, now changed into a pair of long gray sweat shorts with UCLA inscribed on the right thigh and a tight baby blue tank top.

"Hey, Gullzo — sorry about that. If anyone ever tells you that go-go boys are easy to work with, just punch them for me."

"Everything defused?"

"For now. We'll see what happens when I get back from the gym. You wanna come? I get guest passes because I promote them in my weekly emails."

"No thanks. I'm getting plenty of cardio right here petting Señor."

The dog shakes awake at the sound of his name and stares me in the face. I pout back at him. Back to sleep he goes.

"Come on, bro, beauty is fleeting. Get your shit together before you end up fat, bald, and saggy."

"I doubt your gym will help me keep my luscious locks," I say dismissively from the couch, now nervously picking at a strand of hair.

"Alright bro, when you end up on *The Biggest Loser* at age thirty, don't come crying to me."

"You know I will."

"Yeah, and I'm going to remind you of this day."

"So long as you help me wash the parts I can no longer reach in my weekly sponge bath..."

"Gross, bro. I'm gonna vomit and go work out my pecs." And with that, Todd is out the door and I am left with the snoring Señor and the fine hosts of *Access Hollywood.*

It was this way in college, too. Todd was a superman. He possessed a bottomless reservoir of energy that rocketed him to the top of the Dean's List, the top of our fraternity, and the top of anything else that happened to find its way into his sights. He was the president of our fraternity. He ran the college's activities council, bringing bands and artists to UCLA. He had a radio show. He was the treasurer for the gay-straight alliance. And me? I was more than happy to tag along and catch some of the stardust blowing off him.

In college, it was a sweet benefit. But now it's harder. A daily reminder that I might never actually make something of myself. Todd was a race car that turned into a jet upon graduation, like something out of *Transformers*. I was a tire that hit a speed bump and deflated, like something out of a Laurel and Hardy movie. As if this isn't enough, there's another part of me still that beats myself up about hating Todd for his success while so happily suckling at his teat for my steady stream of New York City debauchery.

For the next hour and a half I will lie here, pet the dog, and enjoy the embarrassing downfall of celebrities I used to see in LA. Here in New York, celebrity sightings are rarer. They're also handled differently. On the West Coast, paparazzi are everywhere so stars tend to look their finest. They will be recognized. They have no hope. Here, they tend to hide themselves away. Look as shabby as possible. On the streets of New York, you're just another pair of elbows, another body blocking the entrance to the 1 train. Nobody's that special.

And as he works out, Todd will be sending invites to the parties he promotes. He sends thousands of invites to five different events a week. Saying, "Todd sent me" earns you free or reduced admission all around the city — even to parties he doesn't promote. Standing next to him at a bar ensures a handful of drink tickets and a pocketful of numbers supplied by the endless parade of boys he will introduce you to before the night is out. He's also sending day job-related emails intermittently, all while his body treads closer and closer to a physical perfection I could never achieve, even with the help of cosmetic surgery.

With this much nightlife celebrity, you'd think Todd would never have an empty space in his bed. Yet to date, I have never seen him take advantage of his position with a single star-struck boy. Sure, they flock to him like pigeons to a pizza crust in Times Square, and he'll let his hand rub their back or make a quick grab of their butt, but never any more than that. "Never mix business and pleasure, Gully," he counseled me one night when I asked why he so happily passes these tight, toned, dumb-looking kids on to anyone else in his vicinity (including me). "I get my guys elsewhere. There is no shortage of places to go when you want to get laid. Don't want to become the creepy promoter who dips into his audience."

"I guess that makes sense."

"Plus, you'd never get laid if it was me versus you," he laughed, messing up my hair. He's probably right, and that makes me even more jealous — even as he's handing me my fourth free top shelf drink of the night.

For years and now more than ever, Todd has made me feel like a fat lazy ass, a failure with no successes in sight, an advantageous nobody, a useless human being not worth knowing. And he's the closest thing to a best friend I've ever had. Perfect, right? Of course I never gave a second thought to his advice — never thought I needed to. It's only now that Marty's not returning my texts that it's sinking in: Marty's not just the current leading man in my love life, he's also my lifeline at work. Losing him would be bad for business in addition to the suck it would bring to my personal happiness. Maybe I should have taken Todd's words to heart before piling so many eggs in this Marty-shaped basket?

But to give myself a bit of credit, I feel less like a failure recently. I could do worse than working for Stanford. No, I don't have to be up at 6 AM like Todd — thank God, because if I did, I may not have made it to my fifth day of work. But the hours run long and hard, and I like that. It's fun to whip out my iPhone and take a work-related call on a Friday night, holding up a finger for Todd and the crew, covering my phone to mouth the words, "I need to take this," and fleeing to the street to handle some Very Important Business. Granted, that Very Important Business usually has something to do with being sure to order more copy paper on Monday morning. But it's still business and still looks professional.

Tonight I have also been exchanging emails with Stanford, who has been up the past few hours in search of new furniture for us to celebrate the acquisition and future fortune collected thanks to our golden goose. Turns out he's not too talented when it comes to picking out matching colors and wood types for tables and chairs. I guess everyone has one flaw, at least.

My phone vibrates. I pick it up, expecting Stanford again while hoping for Marty. Instead, an unrecognized number pops up above a text message.

Well, my phone doesn't recognize the number — but I do.

"Hey, how are you?"

Anger. Señor hops off of my stomach as though he can feel what's bubbling up inside me. I remember hearing once that animals can detect spirits in haunted houses. Maybe he senses the ghost of Graham haunting me now.

Before I can even decide whether or not to respond, the phone vibrates again.

"Gully. Please. Talk to me. I'm sorry about our fight."

Fight? It wasn't a fight, asshole. A fight has two sides. What happened between us was the equivalent of a drunk yelling at a stop sign.

Again, vibration. *"Your parents said you told them you missed me."*

That's a lie. It's bait. I am deleting these messages. One by one I throw them into the ether of nothingness that is my delete folder.

"Gully ANSWER ME."

Delete.

"Please please please?"

Delete. Delete. Delete.

I knew this would happen. He's panicking. He doesn't know what to do. He's been staring at his phone all day. Checking to make sure there was a signal. Powering on and off in case the phone "forgot" that I called. He's kept the volume on and waited. Now he's cracking. He's thrashing. He's begging me to respond.

Too fucking bad.

The phone vibrates again. This time for longer. Because Graham has abandoned texting and begun calling me. I won't answer, but I won't send it to voicemail either. That's a form of response. That's me moving a digit, expending energy to shut him up. It'll give him comfort in his ability to inspire some sort of action from me.

Graham's call goes to voicemail naturally. The phone rings again. He may keep this up all night.

Fine by me.

I turn off the ringer, plug it into the wall, and leave the apartment. Clearly Marty won't be texting me — and if he does, my non-response might be a bit of silent revenge for putting me through all this stress today. I'm not wasting another second staring at my phone.

I'll get some ice cream. I'll sit in the meat market of the courtyard where Stanford hired me. I'll make eyes at the early evening foot traffic. Then Todd will come back from the gym and we'll go out and drink. Because I suddenly don't want to stay in and sleep any longer. I want to be out and wild with my best friend and the boys, while three thousand miles away, Graham grows more and more desperate, realizing there's nothing he can do, no way to reach me short of hopping a plane and scouring these streets until he finds me.

And he'd never do that.

CHAPTER 12

Someone must be dead.

Maybe Mom crashed into a traffic light on the corner of La Brea. Maybe Dad had a heart attack. I STILL haven't heard from Marty. Maybe he's been gay bashed after all?

Surely something terrible must have happened to warrant the urgent, brief text that Todd sent, causing me to apologetically tell Stanford I have to take a half-day and get back to my apartment. (Stanford's face crumbled with worry as he told me to take as long as I needed and that he hoped everything would turn out okay.)

Now I am pacing around Todd's apartment, Señor following me and bouncing back and forth, his throwing toy (a knotted rope) dangling from his maw. I grab it once and throw it as far as I can, behind a couch, leaving the dog to strategize a way to get to it and me to worry and wonder what the fuck is going on.

Finally the door flies open and Todd enters. His phone, as always, is attached to his ear.

"Pack a bag. We're going on a trip," he says to me.

"Huh?"

"Two days' worth. Hello? Yeah, hey boss — listen, I'm not going to make it out there tonight. Can you cover?"

"Two days of what?"

"You can? Great! Thanks, babe, I owe you one…" And then, to me: "A cute pair of underwear or two. I got us a house on Fire Island as part of my payment for promoting their big July beach party."

Todd sprints into his room and I hear drawers flying open and clothing being sorted through. I don't have my answers, but now that a tragedy is clearly not what caused Todd's urgency, I am able to breathe and start packing. I run into my room and grab whatever looks good, jamming it into a duffel bag.

Todd pokes his head into the room to utter: "Hurry. We have to catch a 7:30 train at Penn Station and a 9:45 ferry to Fire Island." And then he is gone, stomping back across the apartment causing a fit of yelps and barks from the now super-charged Señor.

"What's Fire Island?" I call out.

The blur of Todd returns to my room. His eyes are slits of suspicion. "What'd you say, bro?"

"What's. Fire. Island."

"You're kidding, right?"

I shrug.

"Un-fucken-believable. Pack your bags. You'll find out en route." Then Todd's back on the phone, asking one of the thousands who owe him a favor if they can puppysit for a couple days. I do as I'm told.

I've already seen Penn Station, I realize. On my first night when my cab brought me into this city from JFK. At that time all I saw was a large subterranean staircase between entrances to the mammoth Madison Square Garden, a gaping maw that ceaselessly spits commuters out to the street.

Now Todd is yanking me into this maw and down into the depths of an entirely new world. Penn Station is a labyrinth and Todd is my sherpa. First we run through a line of homeless men and women who each take a shot at getting a donation. Todd scoops a handful of change out of his pocket and hands it to a bald man closest to the door, who also happens to be holding it open for us. We take the left side of a long escalator, allowing us to run past the exhausted commuters leaning and sighing on the right. We are running to the Long Island Rail Road (LIRR) via a public concourse — an expansive, arched corridor filled with pizzerias and a smattering of magazine and cigarette stands. We hustle between clusters of tourists, shoulder bags bouncing on the smalls of our backs. Down another escalator, around a corner, down a set of stairs, past a corridor that features two Starbucks within two hundred feet of each other (and a Jamba Juice coming soon!). Luckily, Todd towers above most of the commuters — keeping him in view even when he breaks ahead. I am running as fast as I can while trying to evade people running in the opposite direction. Because if I lose Todd, I'll never find my way out of this maze.

He's on his phone again, screaming into the receiver: "What track, bitch? What track? Are you sure? How long? One minute! Fuck!" Todd's hand shoots out and grabs mine, dragging me to a stop and down a set of stairs under a sign that announces Track 19.

We barely make it through the closing doors of the train. I can barely breathe. The air conditioning is strong and my sweating body feels like it's been submerged in an ice bath. My hands pat down my midsection in a panic to make sure I haven't lost my wallet, iPhone, apartment keys. All is accounted for, and my breath settles, slowly. Maybe I should start going to the gym after all.

"All aboard!" screams Servando, raising a brown paper bag that poorly conceals a tallboy of Bud Light Lime. The whole crew is sitting in two rows of seats that are facing each other at the center of the train car. Unlike the commotion we just found our way through, just about every single person on this train is both male and gay. And they are angry. Because we are crammed in like peasants in the *Titanic*'s steerage. All look as though they've been chewing on lemons; it's hard to believe they are excited for the journey we are about to take. A chihuahua sits yipping in a bag somewhere. Cell phones ring, ping, and vibrate all around us. No one's too happy that the two latest arrivals have seats saved. We sit, trying not to meet the razor gazes leveled at our heads.

"Fire Island here we come!" shouts Brayden, cheersing Servando and offering me a sip of his beer. Todd (composed and seemingly unfazed) and I (heaving and gasping) drink hard. The crew is all decked out in spaghetti strapped tank tops or dark colored polos. Servando has brought a pair of ridiculously oversized baby blue sunglasses that makes him look like the long lost brother of Mary-Kate and Ashley.

The train is so packed that conductors give up trying to navigate through the aisles to collect tickets. Conversation surges all around us: accounts of wild sex from previous Fire Island excursions, hazy memories of drunken nights over the past week, griping over politics, the latest fashion lines from design- ers I've never heard of. When the train finally begins moving, the mood in our car seems to pick up along with it. Suddenly all is dark and my ears pop as the train passes through a tunnel that is apparently taking us underwater and then out the other side to Long Island. There is a *whooooosh* as the dark- ness of the tunnel falls away and purple twilight and Queens apartment buildings paint the canvas of the train's many windows.

The train crawls slowly along a track raised at least fifty feet in the air above the gridlocked lanes of some major highway. It takes me a minute to realize this is the very highway I careened along two months ago on my way from JFK to Hell's Kitchen. My magical trip is now playing out in reverse, as if I'm heading back home again (made all the more believable since I'm headed to the beach). The train winds its way past apartment complexes made of brick and stucco, surrounding backyards filled with out-of-commission playground equipment, pools clogged with floaty toys, and eviscerated car bodies.

"Oh girl, please, he wants me to bottom for him? Tough shit. My hole is closed for maintenance!" someone shouts from the other side of the train.

"You tell him!" someone not directly involved in the source conversation shouts back. The entire train laughs. It's as if the pressure inside the tunnel has sucked out all the bad juju that was festering in the angry eyes of the commuters. The common mood now seems to teeter between giddy, drunk, and horny. Which, from what little I've heard, seems perfectly in line with what I should expect on Fire Island.

"We didn't think you were going to make it," Brayden confides to Todd, drinking from a bottle of Vitamin Water that probably has close to no actu- al Vitamin Water in it.

"Yeah, I got held up with some party business. And then when we hit Penn,

I was afraid Gully wasn't going to be able to keep up with me."

"Yeah, yeah," I wheeze. "I kept up, jackass."

"Bee tee dubs," Todd continues, "turns out that he has no idea what Fire Island is."

The crew's reaction, I imagine, is similar to how a gay man might react if you asked him who sang "Toxic" at a club. In my mind I'm seeing an island engulfed by nonstop flames, gay men running wild like savages, stripping off their clothes and tossing them brazenly into the inferno. But surely that can't be right. "I'm guessing it's hot?"

It takes five minutes to convince them that I am not kidding, nor have I been living under a rock. Then, with that sorted out, the boys take turns telling me exactly what Fire Island is. Choice words of note include "Gay Mecca," "Never-Neverland," "Boy Heaven on Earth," and "Drama City, USA."

"Isn't that just Hell's Kitchen?"

The boys gawk at me silently. "You'll get it when we get there, Gully," Todd says, patting me on the head delicately.

We then descend into beer and jokes and catch-up. Todd bitches about his stressful day. Shane talks about the party he danced at on Thursday (which Todd hosts). Servando and Rowan are equally concerned about the fate of their jobs at Kenneth Cole and Express, respectively. Brayden is seeing a guy who may end up being The One. (Fast? Sure. But that's fine.) I am nodding and avoiding Brayden's gaze as he talks, so heavy is the guilt. It doesn't help that I want to share my frustration at Marty's textual disappearance but must keep the whole ordeal hidden away. I check my phone for a call, an email, anything from him, but all remains silent on the digital front.

An hour into our journey we have to change trains. Todd lines us up at the door so we can elbow our way through the throng. Across the platform is a double-decker train that reminds me of the Pacific Coastliner I once took to San Diego on my way to a graphic design conference. There the sky was purple with a sweet breeze that filled me with excitement. I watched the ocean flow by as I exchanged texts with Graham, back in happier times (though, in hindsight, I now know he spent that entire weekend with his secret second boyfriend Kevin).

As soon as the train wheezes and whines to a bouncing stop, Todd jumps into the position of linebacker, clearing our way with his wide shoulders and forearms and earning our fair share of derogatory commentary from the poor souls cast aside. They'll probably have to stand in the aisle now — but we won't.

The sky grows darker still. The houses and businesses we pass light up the darkness with a warm glow. The tall buildings of Queens have become blocks and blocks of single-family suburban homes, all huddled around a small village with the proverbial single main street. When the train stops again thirty minutes later, we are off and running to a parking lot that is home to at least a baker's dozen idling vans and minibuses. A pockmarked driver in a Yankees cap takes five dollars from each of us and grunts and hoists our bags into the back as we take our seats. We are then, finally, slowly rolling down side streets and past vacated schools to what I am told is the final leg of our trip.

Sixty bumps later we are dropped off at a dusty gravel parking lot that leads to a dock where we will wait for a ferry. I feel completely disoriented. In the span of three hours I have run through the streets of Manhattan, sprinted through the bowels of Penn Station, ridden in two trains, sat in a van, and now am hopping on a ferry. I couldn't show you where I am on a map unless there were pink triangles pointing out the destination. Not knowing my whereabouts is both horrifying and exhilarating. I am also exhausted, pondering injecting myself with Red Bull. If this is a party island, I am anything but prepared.

We step to the end of three lines of two hundred boys. At the front of these lines is a ticket booth and a full service "restaurant" peddling alcoholic drinks. (Very smart, ferry owner. Very smart.) The bar is run by a woman and her kids who pour vodka sodas despite the inherent illegality of minors serving liquor. I guess when you get this far out on Long Island, the police turn the other way. The tickets aren't cheap, but Todd insists on paying my way and won't hear otherwise. To my credit I fight with him for five minutes until I discover that he slipped the cash behind my back to Servando, who bought a round-trip for each of us already. With our tickets purchased from the flustered, stone-faced woman in the air-conditioned booth, we find our way through the men and suitcases and dogs-in-bags and come to a rest at the edge of the dock.

There are actually two docks that protrude from the gay traveler holding pen where we are standing. Over one is a sign that says "Pines" (where we are going) and over the other, "Cherry Grove." This was a subject of much discussion on our long train ride from Penn Station. Servando spoke for ten minutes explaining that there was a hard divide between the types of gay men that went to one or the other. Then Rowan summed it all up in four words: "Youngins: Pines, Fogeys: Grove."

"So Fire Island is out there?" I ask no one in particular, staring out across the first true expanse of water I've seen since I left California. The reflection of the fat setting sun rides across the slow-dancing waves like a flattened orange balloon.

"Thirty minutes by boat and we'll be homo sweet homo," says Rowan, slipping his hand into the back of my shorts for emphasis.

Servando squeals with excitement, skipping where he stands. "Gully, you're going to LOVE it! It's a magical, wonderful place, like nothing you've ever seen."

"And maybe nothing you'll ever want to see again," Shane grins.

"Just you wait," Brayden smiles. "You'll be floating the idea of a half-share before we're back on that boat."

Conversation gradually dies as the crew becomes more content to measure up the long line of guys. No longer contestants in the reality show *"Who Will Get One of the Limited Seats on the Train Ride Here?"* we are all friends now — and potential lovers. Servando has already picked out his "weekend husband" and Rowan has already threatened to steal him. Their peace treaty involves sharing the unknowing guy — a fate I am all too familiar with.

I step away from the group to lean against a railing, looking out across the water. It is now that it dawns on me: I am feeling more at peace than I have in months. Even scarier, I discover this is because I haven't left what is essentially a ten-mile-long island in four months. New York, with its many floors both above- and below-ground, its many diverse interiors and occasional leafy exteriors, fooled me into believing otherwise. Right now, staring at the waves, I feel like a rat that has escaped its cage, striving to regain some feeling in its atrophied legs.

My hypnotic lull is broken by a loud crack of thunder as complimentary lightning shoots across the sky, five separate lines of charged white descending in a cone from one single point originating in a sloppy pile of clouds. There are moans of displeasure from the crowd around us but Todd is all smiles. "They're queens. Rain stops nothing on Fire Island, you'll see. Plus, I forgot to shower today. Staaaank!"

It occurs to me that I should contact Mom to let her know where I'm going. In the insanity of the day I completely forgot to text or call her. But my phone shows no signal. I hold it up to the sky, waving it around like I'm an air traffic controller, but to no avail. Shane smiles. "Good luck getting any signal out here."

"There's no signal on the island at all?"

"There's some. But it's spotty as hell. Think *Survivor*. But gay. And the challenges all involve sucking dick."

A cheer erupts from the crowd as the ferry appears over the horizon, taking its sweet time to reach the shore. When the two-story boat docks, Todd has positioned us perfectly so we can get to the ramp first and board while the other gays fight to fit on the narrow walkway. We bound up a narrow metal staircase to the top of the ferry and secure seats toward the front.

The boat rumbles to life, draining my ass of all feeling as the engine kicks into full gear. And then we are off across the water, at first slow as we pass restaurants, houses, and houseboats. Then, once we hit the open water of the Long Island Sound, we ramp up to full speed. The wind whips past. The threat of rain manifests itself as a far less horrifying steady mist that moistens the front of our shirts. To our right we hear a scream followed by a groan as another traveler's hat is swept off his head, up in the air, and then off the back of the boat.

When we dock again thirty minutes later, all is rush and chaos and racing again. Todd pulls me by the hand like a misguided toddler and yanks me past this wall of boys, who I apologize to as we leave them in our trail of dust. It is only after we are spat out of the boat that I can take in Fire Island for the first time. No skyscrapers. No lines of cars, buses, cabs, and pedicabs. It's all wooden boardwalk and throbbing party music.

Along the right side of the dock is a row of two-floor wooden buildings —

a real estate agent, two restaurants, the entrance to a pool, a grocery store, a place called the Hotel Ciel. Bass is throbbing and colored light sneaks out of a row of windows, bathing the wooden dock in reds and blues and pure whites. Directly in front of the boat is a barricade of trees and a parking area where people can leave their wagons (what they use a wagon for, I have no idea). My face must spell amazement because Servando says, "Aww, look at our baby Gulliver. He's never been anywhere quite like it!"

It's true. I haven't.

There is a welcoming committee for some of the travelers we hip-checked to get here. I hear the distinct smacking of cheek-kisses and hollered hey-girl's in the darkness. Todd slings his bag over his shoulder, pulls a piece of note paper out of his pocket, reads the address, and leads us past the buildings. We pass a small folding card table underneath a large banner that features a tan, muscled, brunette naked man (his privates discreetly cut off by the edge of the printed area). This man is pointing and smiling at the word "BayDance," written in the same infamous font as *Baywatch*. Beneath the title, in a wide bold sans-serif font and italics is: *"Hosted by Todd DiTempto."* About fifteen other names I may or may not recognize fall in line beneath his, all so tiny that they can comfortably fit between the first and last letter of his name.

I am turning toward the source of the bass and light when Todd grabs me and says, "First things first. Gotta get to the house and make sure no one looted it and last week's guests aren't still fucking in the pool."

Leading us to the left, Todd continues with the schedule for the night: "Drinks, wardrobe change, suitcase drop — then Sip n' Twirl!" I assume the establishment with the thudding bass is the one he just referred to. And so we fall in line behind the gays from the ferry. There are no lights overhead. We walk in pairs along an uneven narrow boardwalk with loose, weather-worn planks. We tightrope-walk precariously six feet above a gravel service road. I almost plummet twice and I'm not even drunk. Bad sign.

"At least five Fire Islanders fall off this thing on a given night," Shane informs me. "We'll make sure you don't become one of the statistic."

"I'm trying!"

Without service, cell phones apparently serve a separate purpose on Fire Island — they are internet-era lanterns. Everyone holds them out front, waving this way and that to cast a dim light on where the boardwalk ends, where it goes up, where it dips, where a board is missing. We follow the sounds of wheeled suitcases dragging on wood, of catch-up conversations between strangers about who already slept with who and who helped cement Sip 'N Twirl's unofficial other name: Drink N' Hurl.

We only have to walk for two minutes before Todd directs us up a connecting boardwalk via a sharp left turn. According to Shane, many of the gays in our parade have a lot longer to walk, some as much as twenty minutes to get to their houses. Of course we are the lucky ones. And of course it's thanks to Todd. I can imagine the jealous looks and seething rage, but can't see them in the dark.

The fact that I have no idea where I am despite my sobriety fuels the decision to keep a bit of my wits about me tonight. Because if I lose my way, I'll probably end up sitting on the boardwalk crying until a nice gentleman comes and takes me home. His or mine? Doesn't matter, so long as I'm safe.

My phone buzzes in my pocket and dumps a handful of notifications that must have queued up while I was out of service. Emails from Stanford hoping everything's okay, texts from Mom letting me know Todd took the liberty of telling her where we were headed and not to worry about getting back to her. Still nothing from Marty. I have reached full-on stress mode but can't show it. Double torture. I don't want to go out tonight. I want to spend hours on whatever bed I'm allotted and call Marty's phone over and over until the fucker picks up. At this point I'm convinced he's in someone else's bed, cackling about his loser quasi-boyfriend back in New York.

"You okay man?" Todd asks, as though he can feel the stress seeping through my pores.

"Yeah," I shake my head. "Just thinking about work."

"Fuck work, man. This weekend, we party."

Our house is a four-story mansion. From the outside it looks like four square boxes stacked on top of each other to resemble a rudimentary staircase built by a five-year-old. Once inside, I feel as though I have been transported back to the 80's. Every surface is glass. Three bathrooms, all with Jacuzzis. A pool, barbecue, accompanying pool house in baby blue shingles, and gurgling hot tub in the spacious backyard. There are framed paintings of Venetian landscapes on the walls in the Tropicana orange living room. My room sports a

101 / JUSTIN LUKE ZIRILLI

queen-sized bed and writing desk as well as a flat-screen television mounted on the wall across from the bed.

I decide then that if Marty is over me, I will be over him. It takes a shitty sort of person to drop you without the courtesy of a call, text, or email. To lose to him would be to sulk and let my first weekend on Fire Island plunge into murky depression. Fuck him. Like Todd so sagely said, this weekend we party.

And so I change into my outfit — a pair of checked shorts from Express and a tight graphic T-shirt from Lucky Brand Jeans. I throw on a puka shell neck-lace, determined to bring it back into style if it kills me. Elsewhere in the house the boys are screaming and laughing. I hear the clinking of glasses as Servando makes his famous Get Fucked Cider Punch, which probably contains no juice whatsoever. Shakira sings her way into my room via a speaker mounted inconspicuously in the corner like a hidden security camera.

"Sing it, girl!" Rowan screams from downstairs.

When I finally make it down, Beyonce is singing her anthem to all the single ladies and Shane and Rowan go through the perfectly executed moves in the middle of the living room. Todd tries to join in but he only knows the part where you march forward, punching the air while knocking your head back. I don't even know that part, so I help myself to the cider punch which, as I suspected, is pure vodka. I add Red Bull to bring the drink down to 98% alcohol content.

My first Fire Island night quickly transforms into the familiar fucked-up blur in a different locale, which makes it seem shiny and new. The boys and I make a major entrance (also known as any entrance where we don't trip all over each other stumbling through the door) at a party known as "High Tea." Apparently Fire Island hosts three "Teas" a day — low, mid, and high. No actual tea is served, except of course the Long Island variety. And nothing specific, I am told, separates any of these from the other except a change in location. Low Tea takes place at an outdoor bar; Mid Tea kicks off an hour into Low Tea at a club called Pavilion directly next door, and then High Tea kicks off as Low Tea wraps up and Mid Tea rages on one story below. Someone might question the logic behind this if they were sober enough. But who'll complain when there's always a drink special somewhere? The gays, much like herds in the savannah, simply migrate to the next vodka-filled watering hole to quench their thirst for sex and SoCo.

The Red Bull mixed with punch didn't do its trick. I feel my eyes grow heavy, so I quickly gargle down four vodka-spiked cups of the energy stuff. Then the hours pass and begin to spin together as they tend to do. And while a good number of the people drinking and dancing around me are familiar faces from Hell's Kitchen, I find a few that stick out as strangers I've never met before.

Then I'm making out with one. I don't remember approaching him, dancing up on him, or anything. It's like one second I was alone, the next our tongues are sumo wrestling. I erroneously call him Casey until he corrects me (between all the spit-swapping) and slowly re-pronounces: "Chase."

Chase is no more or less special than anyone else here. He possesses the perfect abs, the Ken Doll chest, the toned biceps, the killer tan, the bedroom eyes, the swoopy/choppy blonde hair, the sexy grin, the half-filled drink swishing around in his hands, the single meaningful piercing (above his right eye), the maybe-sensuous voice that strains to be understood over the blasting tunes, the growing bulge in his pants he tries to hide as he bats my inquisitive hands away, the alcohol-flavored breath that mixes with mine when I back him into the wall to kiss him more.

"Wait," he says, weakly pushing me away from him. "I have a boyfriend."

"And?" I ask.

And nothing. We're kissing again, I am letting my mouth lick and tug away at Marty. With each peck and suck of the lip it's like I'm pushing the asshole farther and farther into darkness. His features fade away, his voice grows tinny. Because this weekend, I party.

On Fire Island, nobody locks their doors. Every house is most likely vacant during party hours. An intrepid gay could easily slink into any house, sleep with whoever may be there, and then have his run of the rooms, taking all the dollars his pockets can carry (including the ones hid in every freezer for the housekeepers). I learn this fact from Chase, who is calming me down as we reach Todd's house and I realize I don't have a key.

"Look!" he says, opening the door and pushing it wide. "That easy. You done freaking out?"

"Maybe," I say with a lick up his mouth.

We are kissing against the open front door, then against the wall by the kitchen, knocking red plastic cups to the floor. We are kissing on the couch in the living room with the double-wide and double-tall glass windows looking out to the pool. Then we are laughing and stumbling down the needlessly spiral staircase that leads us down to that very pool.

We are stripping down and having at each other along the side of the lapping, chlorinated, green-lit water. Britney Spears' "3" mixes with the breeze blowing by us and the ocean roaring a few hundred feet from the house. Our only audience is the tall black shapes of the other ridiculous Fire Island houses that make no sense standing next to each other — each a vision of its creator who could care less about how the structure looked amongst the other houses.

Then Chase and I are fucking. Flip-flopping, because it's only fair. My head falls so far back that it dunks into the pool and I whip it back up, my hair dousing Chase's abs and chest, leaving them glistening in the moonlight.

When we are done and drenched in each other, it only makes sense to roll over and fall into the pool. We swim naked and kiss, splash and dunk each other's heads under the water. Now that we know the sex is good, we are free to actually find out about each other — take the time to figure out where we are from, what we do, and how we plan to take over the world someday. I am too drunk to retain anything Chase says. And I'm starting to think about Marty, which makes me feel guilty. Are we boyfriends? No, we're not. I did tell him I loved him — but only because he said it first, and how could I not say it back? Plus, I STILL haven't heard a fucking word from the bastard.

And then I think about Graham, and force myself to think of nothing. Nothing at all.

"Holy shit! You have a tattoo!"

Chase looks down at the permanent illustration on his skin, laughing. "I didn't realize it was such a radical concept in this day and age."

"No, no. I just didn't notice it until just now."

It's an ornate one, too. No Far East symbols or astrological signs. This one is an antique-looking golden pocket watch on a likewise-golden chain. The chain loops and curves, pointing to his belly button. The hand on the clock's face is spinning so fast that it blurs, yet it is also frozen in the middle of the blur, pointing just past the 12.

"Pretty observant, Gulliver. You like it? Cost a ton to get." He stands there, looking down at his tattoo, his ab muscles flexing, his sizable (even when limp) dick wagging between his legs.

"What does it mean?" I ask.

"None of your business what it means to me. What does it mean to you?"

I am struck by the forcefulness of his reply. I fumble for words. "Um. That it's TIME to change the subject, I guess."

"Cute," he laughs, walking past me to get his underwear from the side of the pool. "You want to do something tomorrow? They have a great brunch across the Meat Rack over at Cherry Grove."

I don't know what the Meat Rack is, but I figure it's some sort of steak joint. And I know the Grove means otters and bears and older guys. And I know that a meal the day after a night of drunken sex is the point where shit gets complicated.

This is Fire Island. No commitments, the boys assured me. What happens on Fire Island stays on Fire Island. Or at least that's how it should be.

"Sounds good. Assuming I'm not too hungover or asleep until the next party." I squeeze his ass for emphasis.

I give Chase my phone number but for the last digit, which I change, and then kiss him goodbye. Fortune has it that the crew is walking up the board-walk as he is walking away, guaranteeing that he won't come back for more action, and also earning him a full-on stare from each of the crew before they make it up to the porch where I am standing in just a towel.

"Good work." Todd claps me on the back.

"Seriously, shit," Brayden adds.

"Whooore!" Shane bellows too emphatically to be taken seriously.

"We're going to get drunker and go swimming. You in?" Servando asks, finishing an unidentified substance from a plastic cup he's brought back from the party. My answer, of course, is in the affirmative.

"Excellent!" claps Servando. "Who wants some more of my famous punch?!"

And though earlier I thought I couldn't possibly stomach another ounce of the stuff, now I realize: I do. I want plenty more. I raise my hand accordingly.

CHAPTER 13

There's not much to do on Fire Island besides drink, visit the houses of strangers you meet during the day, have sex, and lay out. Or so it seems, judging from the behavior of my friends.

This isn't necessarily a bad thing.

Servando, Shane, Rowan, Brayden, and I are in our tiny bathing suits laying out on the beach — which is blissfully right beyond our backyard fence. Todd was up earlier than the rest of us, of course, cursing the lack of cell phone signal and slowness of internet, brewing enough coffee to fill a bath tub (it was needed) and then gone to set up his big party. The price one pays for celebrity, I mused, before crashing back into my pillow for four more hours of sleep.

The rest of us woke up after noon, still groggy and hungover. One by one we shambled to the kitchen, downed the coffee left behind for us, and stumbled our way to the beach. Servando mentioned mixing up a large thermos of his famous punch but abandoned the idea when stabbed by four sets of icy stares.

And so now we lie here, telling each other where last night's antics led us, since a second round of Servando's punch was only the beginning of five separate adventures that ended with the sun up, taunting us from the sky. No one ended up alone in their bed (and Rowan ended up in someone else's bed, in a house that he claims almost rivaled the one we're staying in). Our mouths hurt too much to go into further detail, and I tell no one that I went to sleep when everyone else departed with the group of strangers who stumbled into our backyard unannounced. And so we watch gaggles of Fire Island weekenders pass us on the beach, whether running with their dogs along the ocean's edge or putting up a volleyball net or setting up camp close enough to shoot us flirtatious glances (but far enough to pretend they were doing no such thing in case we aren't interested).

"So, Gully, what do you think of Fire Island?" Brayden asks, turning over to give his back the sun's glowing attention.

"It's a bit much to take in. Like, in a good way. I can't think of anything like it on the West Coast. Maybe Will Rogers Beach. But not even that is a secluded island."

"Yeah, that's why New York rocks," Shane laughs, catching the eye of a Justin Bieber-haired Latino walking by.

My phone explodes again as the signal fairy alights briefly for the second time since my arrival. Texts from Mom, emails from work, Facebook stuff from Cali people asking how I am. Nothing from Marty. I send a quick text to Mom saying I love her and queue up a painful one to Marty that simply says:
"Are we over?"

The signal fairy leaves before my question to Marty can escape the phone, so I erase it to make sure there's no trace of us in case Brayden gets a peek.

After lying out for another hour, we slip into our flip flops and gather our things to head back to the house. Next up is lunch at a place called the Blue Whale where the hamburger is the cheapest meal, clocking in at just over nineteen dollars. Expensive, sure, but since everything else this weekend has been free, it's a fair and enjoyable expenditure.

With the crew complaining that now they are going to look bloated from all the french fries, we are back at the house lying around, nursing the remaining dribs of our hangovers with large, sweating glasses of Gatorade or Vitamin Water. Servando and Shane are playing a Wii that came with the house while Brayden reads and Rowan wanders the house with his Blackberry to try and fire up Grindr, hoping to find the guy he blew the night before.

When my head ceases its internal drumming I excuse myself to explore the island. I walk the boardwalk, occasionally checking my phone to see if my signal has returned, and every once in a while it does, springing to life with missed calls, emails, and text messages. I try sending the text to Marty again, and this time it makes it. I put my phone back in my pocket, basically resigned to the fact that he won't be responding. Guys wander the narrow boardwalk with big red plastic cups, nodding and smiling at me as I pass or ignoring me altogether. I say hi and grin at the ones who ignore me, enjoying the shocked reactions this gesture solicits. The sun has flash-fried the boardwalk to what feels like a hundred degrees and I am thankful for the pair of Camo flip flops I threw into my suitcase at the last minute.

I could probably live here. The absence of car horns and screeching subway cars, replaced by invisible bird chattering and lapping ocean waves, has me feeling like I've found my way into some alternative universe. This feeling is magnified by the fact that I've seen so many faces here around the gayborhood — it's as though all of Hell's Kitchen was mystically transported to this island. And now they're just going to drink, dance, and have sex with each other. No need for a job. No running to catch the subway. A lazy porn paradise.

When I get back to the house, all the boys are either done with their hangovers or determined to power through them. Music is blasting through the speakers (Katy Perry this time). And everyone is dressing, showering, drinking, singing, and dancing. Low Tea is almost upon us, they tell me, and God forbid we miss a single chance to party.

By the time Low Tea is over my hangover has either disappeared or been pushed down a flight of stairs by my hastily returned drunkenness. We skip Mid Tea to head back to the house because a bigger party is on the horizon. At the house we are drinking more, dancing more, singing more. Prettying up, redoing our hair, checking our eyebrows and tan lines, applying concealer to our dark circles. I check my phone one more time to see if Marty has texted and come up with a blank screen — my phone is dead, and I've left my charger back in the city. I shrug and throw the phone on the bed. Marty won't be writing, and Mom already got her text of the day. Time to party all over again.

We are in the dining room just off of the main entryway, dancing to "California Gurls" when Todd descends the staircase.

"Okay, boys, let's get a move-on!" he announces. And, one by one, shirts and pants drop to the floor. I am left standing by the punch in my clothes.

"Um. Did I miss something?"

Todd slaps himself on the head. "Shit, Gullzo. Did I forget to say we're going to an underwear party?"

"I was wondering why you told me to bring a few good pairs. I've never been to one — what do I have to do?"

The boys laugh. Todd says, "Just go put on underwear, bro. The rest will come in time."

The pair I am wearing is not fit for primetime — far too loose — so I sprint double time up the stairs to my room, tripping on my way up. I rip into my duffel bag to find the best pair I brought — a pair of deep blue Andrew Christians that improperly identify me as a member of a police force on the butt. The shorts and shirt can impress another day. I throw my clothing on the bed, leaving just my underwear, sneakers, and white ankle socks.

When I get back downstairs, my first visual is an inspired one. As if by divine intervention (or more likely, a specific plan I didn't hear about), the boys are each wearing a solid-colored pair of underwear — the sum total of their G-strings, boxer briefs, and bikini bottoms is a gloriously gay undergarment rainbow.

"Sure, there's a clothes check," Todd tells me. "But why bother? Shit gets stolen ALL the time from there. Those check boys are fucking thieves."

Todd shows me how to embrace creativity in how I store my belongings when there are no pockets to be used. You fold up your money and put it in your sock or between your sock and shoe. Cigarettes can be tucked into the side of your waistband. Your lighter goes in the ankle of your sock. You hold your phone if you aren't stupid enough to have forgotten the charger, in which case you leave it at home charging, using Servando's graciously-provided plug.

After a few too many more drinks, we are bar-bound. The crew's cell phones are out, their glowing displays lighting our way back to the main drag. The lights spin and whirl from bush to tree to boardwalk to guys passing us, like Tinkerbell on a bender. The bass has gotten louder, hitting us almost imme-diately. Even the underlit trees on the main drag shake and dance along to the music. An empty ferry pulls away from the dock, Long Island-bound. It seems to float on nothing due to the dark water buoying it. At the last moment before we go into the party, while waiting to have our IDs scanned, I notice a single passenger on the second level of the ferry, his or her head hung low — a featureless blob. And then we are inside and climbing the stairs.

I have never been to an underwear party. The very concept seems odd to me. In LA, you just take a trip to the beach to see all you need to see. Plus, I am a slave to my pockets. I feel unnerved without my wallet, phone, cigarettes, lighter, keys, and gum on my being. And Graham was never a fan of such publicly slutty events — at least not to my face. I later learned that when he was out with Kevin, they went to all sorts of wild parties he always told me he didn't care for.

But no. Enough Graham. Tonight I party.

The room is a surging tide of abs and chests. The music is so loud my ears ring on contact. Packages and butts bob before me. It feels almost creepy to let my eyes wander down to take in what everyone has put in full view, and I blush when someone catches my eyes after I've done just that. We are all so vulnerable. Nothing is hidden. Everything on display. Every mole. Every hair follicle. The fact that this many drunk near-naked guys can be stuck shoulder to shoulder in such a suffocating hot space without an accidental orgy start-ing is astounding. It's just like any other night at any other bar, except we all forgot to bring our clothes with us.

A screaming fight breaks out at the clothes check we bypass because some-one's Diesels got lost. Todd punches my shoulder with a quick "told you so."

It becomes immediately apparent that Todd is even more of a celebrity here than in Hell's Kitchen. Drinks are free. Introductions are constant and, despite my best intentions, instantly forgotten. I am greeted by four or five Davids. Three Chris-Christian-Christophers. Two Tylers. Seven Ryans (though they each apparently spell their name differently). My head is spin-ning, my ears throbbing, my dick unsure what's going on. And so I steal away from the crowd.

Windows line the space opposite the bar. Because there are no lights, the only glow is what comes from the stars and moon above. I walk to the side and take in the calm waters, the bobbing boats, putting the party to my back for just a few seconds. Another ferry is approaching — this one brimming with gays. Another hundred or so guys descend, hug, whoop, cheek-kiss, and wheel their suitcases toward their rentals, all trying to see what's going on inside the windows I am peering out from. The captain steps out of his little wheel room and lights a cigarette, shaking his cell phone to try for a signal.

"See any drag queens?"

It's Rowan, screaming into my ear while wrapping his arms around me and grabbing a strong hold of my dick.

"Should I?" I ask, incredulous, grabbing his hand back and kneading it deeper in.

"Well, drag queens invade the Pines once a summer," he tells me, his hand now down my underwear and stroking. "This weekend, actually."

I laugh and grow hard, his strokes picking up in speed. "Ridiculous."

"No, I'm serious. Ask anyone. It's a huge event. Once a summer a ferry docks and seventy or so drag queens invade the Pines."

On the verge of climax, I bite Rowan's ear and whisper, "I'm picturing it like *Braveheart* — blood-curdling screams, bleach-blonde twinks running in all directions, blood-soaked stilettos wielded like battle-axes."

"The reality is far more fabulous. There's a runway show, drag queens showing off summer fashions while the Pines guys cheer them on."

My dick is out of my briefs. I gasp and shoot directly onto the floor, my head up and eyes closed. "I still think my version is more interesting."

"You would, bitch." Rowan bites my lower lip and disappears into the crowd, leaving me to tuck myself back in, stop my head from spinning, and contemplate that this marks the closest I've ever come to public sex. Thrilling. Scary. I'm shocked no one kicked us out for the carnal act. Then again, maybe such behavior is encouraged here.

Seconds, minutes, or hours later, Todd appears, parting the sea of underwear-clad boys with a trail of strangers behind him. "Come on, Gullzo. Let's go do some shots, shots, shots, shots, shots!"

One of the five bartenders is an ex of Todd's — a guy named Kenton. Kenton is the good kind of ex. He and Todd still brunch on occasion, and when a new potential boyfriend crawls up out of Hell's Kitchen's primordial ooze, Kenton or Todd has veto power. He also pours shots in full-sized glasses, so he's alright by me.

Shots are poured. And shot. And poured. And shot. The flavor burns with sweetness. Oh God, I'm getting drunker still. With the inebriation comes enhanced bravery or less shame. Either way, I am now surveying the party-goers beneath the waist. Everyone is wearing their sexy Sunday best. Stitching is impeccable. Colors are vibrant. Patterns emphasize package girth and space-age fabrics add definition to ass dimples. Logos abound. For some, being in underwear isn't revealing enough, so they've shredded the butt fabric to give no-hassle access to their crack. Others still have rolled down the elastic waistbands to give just a glimpse of what is hardly hidden below, including impeccably trimmed pubes. Some of the guys are so cut it looks like their legs can be plucked from their torsos like Ken dolls.

I meet the many strangers following Todd around like he is Fire Island's own pied piper. Names rise up like fireworks and disappear like smoke moments later. Everyone is a honey, sweetie, or sexy. If we ever meet again, maybe I'll try to remember what to call them. Not now. The crew splits after the shots dry up, with Servando disappearing first, then Rowan. Todd is making out with Kenton, which mystifies me — the only part of me I'd ever let near Graham's face is my fist. I do a walk around the bar so I'm not the only one left standing there. All is elbows and dancing sweaty bodies. Booties are popping, bulges are bouncing, hot breath with a twist of booze is the air we all inhale.

I haven't even made one full revolution when I crash into the guy from last night.

"Oh! Hey!" I say.

He looks up and measures my assets from feet to face. "Cute underwear, Gully."

I am grinning. I have forgotten his name. While we scream inaudible words at each other, I get a load of his own wardrobe: a pair of bright white briefs with a vintage cowboy illustration on the right thigh. His package is so massive I have a hard time believing it was in me last night, and I wonder if that's the true size or if the underwear is built to allow some extra depth and dimension. His long hair is spiked tonight with a product that leaves no trace of moisture, a chunk of it brushed across his face and between his eyes. I respect him for this. I don't think I could ever go through an entire night with my vision obscured. Then again, considering how much I've been drinking, my vision is plenty obscured presently.

Just above his underwear line is that tattoo of the gold pocket watch with the blurred minute hand, and I think: time's always blazing by. What a terrible thing to be conscious of while you're fellating someone.

We grind up on each other. I'm disappointed that he doesn't mention trying to call me. When I admit that I might have drunkenly given him the wrong number by mistake, he laughs and says, "Oh, I see how it is. Good thing I didn't try to call you."

Well, that settles it. What a cocky dick. But before I can turn and walk away, he is kissing me. This I don't mind.

Now doubled in size, our crew continues to drink and dance. We trade, we create a daisy chain, we become a circle again. And sure, Chase and I are kissing. But I'm also kissing Rowan. And Shane. And Brayden — only briefly, though, as his phone buzzes and lights up and he walks to the windows to check the incoming message.

After a few minutes, I am no longer aware whose mouth I am kissing. I can only tell that I've moved on because of the change in technique. Some mouths are aggressive and frantic, delivering rapid-fire pecks to my upper and lower lip. Others are slower and deeper, plunging the depths of my mouth with brave tongues. Some are nibblers, pulling at my lip while licking the underside. And we're all hard — it's not a chore to discover this at a party of this nature.

More drinks! Todd is yelling, dragging us to the bar. Kenton lines up the shot glasses, does some magic with his cocktail shaker, and strains a long line of shots, precious alcohol missing some shot glasses altogether and soaking the wooden bar underneath.

The party is getting more crowded by the minute. I wonder if we'll reach a super-saturation point that will eventually end up pushing people out the windows, down to the dock two stories below. Every time someone passes, I end up with their dick in the crevasse of my ass or their hard nipples brushing my back. This is not a problem. Every once in a while, just for shits and giggles, I snake my hand behind my back and give the passerby a quick, playful tug. Sometimes they grab me back and push me in deeper. Sometimes they start licking the back of my neck. Sometimes they start grinding into my ass.

And sometimes they spin me around and slap me across the face.

Wait.

That's not right.

I'm on the floor, my face on fire. The heads and bodies above me spin. I'm stuck in the middle of a human carousel. Then a face emerges from within the spiraling black. It's Brayden, and he's screaming at the top of his lungs.

"WHAT THE FUCK IS THIS?"

He's waving his cell phone in my face. I can't read it. It's all glow and blur. But then, much like his face, everything becomes clear. I am staring at a text message from Marty to Brayden. I can't read what he's said because the Blackberry is banging against my head over and over. I'm throwing my hands up in the air to stop the blows raining down on me, but I'm too drunk and all I'm actually doing is flailing helplessly. Only a few scattered words make it all the way to my ears: "trusted" "traitor" "slut" "fucking fake-ass bitch."

I am trying to will someone from security to come and save me — as if we both have the power of ESP at our disposal. But I don't remember seeing any bouncers here. Just guys. Bulges. Underwear. Everything is growing darker with brilliant flowers of red and orange whenever the phone collides with my face.

My drunk brain is trying to figure this out. Brayden's fury and the text on the phone being slammed into my face over and over again just do not connect.

What did Marty say?

Smack.

Why did he say it?

Crack.

Why is Brayden killing me?

Splat.

And then Brayden's weight is lifted off me as though he's just taken flight, disappearing back into the darkness. A strobe kicks into gear and I see Todd holding Brayden in the air from behind, rendering him a fly stuck in a spider-web in slow motion, Todd's thick arms wrapped around his midsection. My face is throbbing. There is wet. I taste metal. I'm going to throw up. I do. I am facedown in my own vodka vomit. Brayden must have somehow broken free of Todd's grasp because he is now kicking me in the side. My ribs get their fair share of pain, enough to make my face jealous of the extra attention.

Over the roar I hear: "YOU FUCKING BACKSTABBING SLUT! YOU WHORE! I'LL FUCKING KILL YOU!"

I try to talk, or scream, or cry, but it only serves to push my vomit back into my own mouth. Maybe I'll be lucky enough to die right now. They'll carry my body out and drop me into the Long Island Sound. The next day, drag queens will invade and everyone will forget my blood- and vomit-soaked Fire Island Pines premiere.

But no, I'm not that lucky. I'm plenty alive and now suddenly sober as well, which lets my body go on full pain overload. It decides everything that went in tonight must now come out. Todd restrains Brayden again and Servando and Rowan wrap him tightly in their grip. He is still kicking and screeching. Now freed from Brayden-handling, Todd is helping me up.

"Fuck, Gully! Get up."

Todd is carrying me across the dance floor, through the crowd that parts to let us pass. He is telling some older guy that yes, he'll get me taken care of, and no, he doesn't bring drama, and yes, he'll be sure this doesn't happen again while he's here.

All eyes on Gulliver. They've turned on the lights. The music has stopped. Everyone is left as they forgot they were — near-naked, and in complete silence. The only sounds are the ringing in my ears and whisperings between the boys Todd carries me past. A short Mexican man runs past me with a mop and bucket.

Todd carries me back to the house, stopping four times for me to throw up over the dock and into the water, into a garbage can, off the boardwalk, and onto the service road. My head hangs and I'm catching blood in my vomit-smeared hand.

"I can't go back to the house," I slur to him through my bloated lips. "Brayden will be waiting. He'll unleash the wrath of his Blackberry on me again. I'll die of massive digital head wounds."

"Servando and Rowan got Brayden. They took him down to the other side of the docks to calm him down."

"What did I do?"

"It's fine, bro. It's fine."

But Todd's face isn't reassuring. He's thinking. He's concerned. And why wouldn't he be? His best friend from college just drove a wedge into the heart of his New York crew.

"No, it isn't."

"Not now. You need some bandages. Ice. A lot of water. But…"

"But what?" I mumble through my busted lips.

"Maybe you should go home first thing in the morning. Just… until Brayden cools down."

I nod, fully aware that life in New York as I know it is now officially over.

CHAPTER 14

I am too busy throwing up to sleep. At one point during the night, Todd comes in and takes the garbage pail he left on the side of my bed to empty it out. He makes it back just in time for me to fill it up again.

Todd leaves a glass of water on the side table, says something that sounds like echoes in a dripping cave, and rubs my head delicately before leaving and shutting the door, unleashing darkness on the room again. My head, ribs, and mouth all throb in tandem — a percussive pain that I start blinking in time with.

If I sleep, I don't remember it. The morning's hangover, however, is respite from the spins and tilts of the night before. Sunlight comes in through my window and I crawl out of bed to the bathroom, strategically avoiding the mirror; I am not ready to face what's left of me. I pee and flush and throw cold water on my face before returning to the bedroom. I scrape my clothing off the bed and into the suitcase. I shove my iPhone in my pocket and wince. The iPhone makes me think of Brayden's Blackberry. Last night is seared on the frontal lobe of my fucking brain.

I descend the stairs without saying anything to the other boys, who are all gathered around the dining room table. Last night I was one of them. Now, like a foreign antibody or a recently transplanted organ, I am being rejected. Pushed out. The empty punch bowl is still there, stained red along the rim. Obvious lines have been drawn, and they look up silently from the table in the dining room as I walk by. No doubt Brayden (who is not here) showed them the text message. Someone whispers something but I don't even want to think about what they're saying. Even Todd doesn't say a word as I pass. Doesn't even meet my eyes.

"That's fucking shitty," Servando says as I open the door. "Who dates someone's ex-boyfriend and hides it like that?"

We all know the answer, so I leave.

The boardwalk to the main drag is barren. All the Pines boys are still in bed, sleeping soundly or not so soundly. I wonder: what happened after Todd escorted me out? Did the DJ start spinning again? Did the bacchanalian revelry continue where it left off? Did people grind and kiss on the spot where my blood mixed with my vomit as I curled into the fetal position?

One thing is certain: the name Gulliver Leverenz (or, more likely, "that blonde twink") was on the tongue of everyone at that underwear party. I will go down in Pines history as the subject of one of the most brutal beatings anyone has ever witnessed. This morning's brunches will be anchored around solving the mystery of what caused it.

Every step I take feels like there's a nail in the sole of my foot, stabbing a nerve that leads straight up to the center of my head. My eyes dart this way or that every time a bird chirps or a wave laps or a window opens. My brain panics, thinking: is that Brayden? Is that? I imagine it like it's a movie, the camera behind me, Brayden suddenly entering the frame — sprinting toward me, his Blackberry held above his head, far deadlier than any chainsaw, axe, or butcher knife.

A ferry pulls up and gleeful weekenders descend. Their smiles fade as I pass and they take in the reality of my face, which even I'm not ready to confront. I am the only passenger on the return trip to Long Island. The train to Manhattan, however, is packed with families. I stand in the back of the car, my head buried in an unfurled, outdated train schedule.

Manhattan welcomes me back with a rainstorm. I hail a cab outside Penn Station and traffic gifts me with a twenty-dollar fare to travel ten blocks and one avenue. I don't tip the driver. What's one more enemy?

I plug in and turn on my cell phone when I get back to the apartment and the text message assault begins. Marty sent ten of them. They get more and more desperate and apologetic.

First: *"Gulliver, I can't do this anymore. I'm sorry. It's not right. I have to tell Brayden. It's not you. It's me. I know that's a tired saying."*

Second: *"Gulliver, are you with Brayden? He just called me flipping his shit. Get away from him! I'm so sorry!"*

Third: *"FUCK! GULLIVER! I HEARD WHAT HAPPENED. ARE YOU OKAY??"*

Fourth: *"He's fucking insane! I'm so sorry! Oh my God! Why aren't you answering your phone?? I didn't want any of this to happen! Please call."*

And then there are assorted, all-capitalized texts from Brayden. I'm every kind of slut and tramp. I am a piece of shit and if he ever sees me again I'll reminisce about last night's beating with fondness. (This, of course, is not put so eloquently in the text message.) To top it all off, there's Mom, wondering how my weekend getaway is going. I send her a text message to let her know everything's just dandy, because if I call her, I will break down into hysterics and she will fly here just to drag me back to California.

There are no texts from Todd. This hurts more than anything that's happened all weekend.

It takes twenty minutes to compose a text message to Marty. When all the deletions and rewrites are done, it ends up saying: *"I'm fine."*

"Can I call you please? I'm so sorry baby."

Now I'm "baby" again. I don't get it. I'm digging through Todd's medicine cabinet for Extra Strength Tylenol.

"Make up your mind. Is being with me wrong or not?"

There are minutes of silence, then his responses pour back in staccato bursts:

"It was. Then."

"Not anymore. Not after that."

"He's the same psycho he always was. I thought he had changed. I was wrong."

"Please Gulliver. Please let me call you."

"Don't let me lose you."

I'm crying from a text message. Tears are splashing my phone screen and I try to wipe them away, leaving smeared fingerprints. There's still blood caked under my fingernails. Someone in this city doesn't hate me. At least one person hasn't kicked me aside. But if he felt so wrong about us, why didn't he just talk to me about it? Was Brayden on his mind the whole time we were together, like he was deep in the back of mine? Did Marty do this to get back at him — or back WITH him? The confusion is too much for me right now.

"Not now. I have to do something," I type back, my fingers skidding on my tears.

"What do you have to do?"

"Move," I write back, heading for the closet where my suitcases reside.

CHAPTER 15

I am all packed with nowhere to go. I can't be here when Todd gets back, just to have him sit me down and tell me this isn't going to work anymore. I have two days to get the fuck out of here. But where to?

When I hit the Craigslist ads, it becomes obvious that Todd has been all-too-generous with my rent. To continue living in this city I will need to live in the upper reaches of Harlem with at least one roommate, if not more. Or I will need to abandon the magical island altogether with sights set on Queens or Brooklyn instead.

A panic sets in as I read listing after listing. Every price too high. Every apartment too inconveniently located. Even in Queens and Brooklyn. Every one will involve drastic life changes. My commute is going to suck now. Going out will no longer be a convenience. I will need to use subways. Busses. Are there even gay bars in Queens? God, I'm crying, viewing apartment listings through my swollen, tear-shedding eye.

It is then that I realize my life has already changed drastically. Which is less a comfort than it is another heaping pile of anxiety. Suddenly my salary from Stanford looks like pennies. How can anyone afford to live in this fucking place? I have no connections. The ones I did have chose sides; they won't help me find a place, and they won't be living with me. I'll be lucky if they even look at me after this. I am still nauseous and the blazing white background of Craigslist is only making it worse.

I make a few calls and schedule some immediate viewings. It is while I'm making these calls that I catch a glimpse of myself in Todd's hallway mirror. The sight is so horrifying that I drop my phone, disconnecting from a potential new roommate in a Bed-Stuy, Brooklyn two-bedroom apartment, 5th floor walkup. I look worse than I imagined. I am purple all over. My right eye looks like a grape marred with a jagged slit through the center. My lips so swollen they look six times their normal size. There is reptile skin on my cheek — a scab that is still black with my insides and not quite fully reformed. Who would lease a room to someone who looks like this? Who'd even let me past the front door?

I'll need a story. If asked, I will say I was gay bashed. I put my alibi together as I make a few more calls and jot down addresses on the back of a receipt. The story begins with three guys outside of Barrage (of course) the other night. A night spent in the ER. Fractured ribs (this part might not be a lie). The tale has a happy ending: the three guys were incapacitated by security until the police showed up. Part pity, with a shot of triumph. The perfect ingredients for defusing any averse reactions and maybe even earning me a few points toward getting a place.

I'm woozy and weak when I emerge from Todd's apartment. I haven't eaten since that nineteen-dollar burger. Despite the heat, I am wearing a hoodie that hangs down over my face. My shoulders slouched and head low, I take the subway to Roosevelt Island — a tiny island across the river from Stanford's office that is marked with one main road, its own non-MTA bus system, and no cars. I walk down the one main road bordered by skyscrapers that seem completely out of place. The potential roommates here are nice and the room is spacious, but I can't imagine being trapped on an island with only a single subway or a ski lift-like tram to get me back to Manhattan. I also don't have enough money to both eat and live there — I'd have to pick one.

So instead I walk around the entire island in thirty minutes. Across the East River, Manhattan looks like it has been sliced into a cross-section — skyscrapers with a double-decker highway in the foreground. I imagine swimming back but think again when I see rough waves lapping at the shore. Before abandoning the island, I stop at the northernmost tip and lie beneath a lighthouse. It's quiet but for the inner throbbing of my damn destroyed head.

From Roosevelt Island, I'm off to Brooklyn (via Sky Tram and then two subways). This borough is a new land filled with high-priced strollers, squat brick apartment buildings with rooftop gardens, independent coffee shops, torn jeans, torn jean jackets, beards and mustaches and all lengths of creative facial stubble, organic soul food restaurants, fried chicken joints with bullet-proof glass protecting the cashiers from the customers, farmer's markets with pickled green beans, a park with a zoo buried somewhere deep inside, gay bars with back porches and barbecue grills, a museum, a botanical garden, and real estate offices hawking apartments that cost as much as my parents' house back in LA.

After visiting five apartments, I still have nowhere to live. The subway is too far away. Or the neighborhood is colored by too many police sirens for my comfort. Two of them weren't even available any longer. And so I am back on the train, back into Manhattan. At this point, my body is starting to feel better. I stop at Grand Central Station to pass beneath a grand arched and painted ceiling in its main corridor, walk between rushing commuters and screaming children, and grab a bite to eat. Right now Todd's crazy party is just wrapping up. I probably would have had the time of my life.

The last stop is Astoria, or as Servando used to call it: ASS-toria. Here there are many diners, tons of feta cheese omelets, strange produce in stands outside of groceries, a lot of cute gay actors. I cannot afford even the small apartments on what is considered "the right side of the tracks." I must cross under the raised tracks of the N and Q and R and whatever other trains to find lodgings in my price range.

Here the businesses are shuttered and vacated. Here the streets are pock-marked with potholes. Here even the pigeons look a little mangier as they fight each other for scraps of bread in the clogged gutters. The sky is visible, unlike in Manhattan, but it is gray and heavy and overcast, and who wants to see more of that? It is here on the wrong side of the tracks that I find my future home sweet home.

It is a two-bedroom apartment with two roommates who have already been living together for over a year. My room is actually half of their living room; one of the walls erected for the express purpose of shoehorning in one additional renter to make things more affordable. I'm paying two hundred dollars more here than I was to live with Todd.

My new roommates are Kieran and Rosa. Kieran is a straight, beefy ex-football player who works as a bartender at a lounge three subway stops from the apartment. Rosa is a spindly, frizzy-haired graduate student at Hunter majoring in education. She hopes to take advantage of the influx of Obama money into education to land an English-teaching position. They both seem nice enough. I sign a check for my first month's rent after they agree to wait until Stanford pays me again to deposit it. I just don't have the money right now.

While on the platform waiting for a train back, I text Todd the news. He and I are no longer roommates. I've found a place and will be out of his hair before he gets back to Manhattan. One less thing for him to worry about when he gets back.

Todd texts me furiously: *"fuck you bro, dont give me this drama shit now. its been a hell of a weekend."*

"No drama. I'm serious. Don't worry about me."

"gully youre pissing me off. this isnt funny."

"Agreed. Thanks for helping me out when I moved here. Sorry I fucked it up."

There's no response. Maybe the signal fairy flew off again, or maybe it's Todd's sympathy that departed.

It'd be so easy to stay put. Simply call my future roommates to let them know I made a mistake and they should reactivate the Craigslist posting because I won't be banished from Manhattan after all. I know Todd would never put me out on the street without warning, no matter what happened between us. He'd give me the time I needed, no matter how awkward that time might be.

But then I see Brayden. I see the rapidly attacking Blackberry. I see Todd sitting with HIS friends around the table yesterday morning as I left, not speaking a word to me. I can't bear the thought of coming home to that every night. Watching Todd get ready to go out on the town with my former crew, hiding in my room pretending I'm not home if any of them come by to pregame. It was bad enough taking advantage of Todd before I'd completely betrayed his trust — we all did. Todd's good fortune was ours, too. We were spoiled.

But I don't deserve that anymore. He knows it, I know it — they all do. Sooner or later this wedge will drive us apart, and when that happens, this apartment will be gone, and who knows where I'll have to move? I can't take that chance.

So I power down my phone, grab my suitcases, drop my keys into a dish by the front door, and take one last look at what was once my Hell's Kitchen palace.

Then I slam the door, and I'm gone.

ROUND II

CHAPTER 16

It's been a week, and I haven't told Mom and Dad that I moved. Maybe I won't bother — they're better off not knowing. Not worrying. If I ever decide to come clean, I better have a great story to accompany what will seem like a hasty decision. Because why would anyone leave what I had for what I have now?

When I get to the apartment after work every day, Kieran is working and Rosa is taking an evening course in comparative literature (so says the white board hanging lopsided on the freezer). The apartment is cramped but clean. In my room is a single free-standing closet missing one of its doors. There's enough space in my room to stand in the center and spin 360 degrees, but walking in any direction would cause me to collide with my bed or closet, or place me out in the hallway.

My bed here is a twin. What was once an elevator is now five flights of stairs. Todd's doorman has been replaced by a buzzer that produces static and only sometimes lets you in. I venture to the street daily to find a place to buy bread and sandwich ingredients, unable to afford finer cuisine (and even more unable to eat out, since what used to be my food and beverage budget now goes almost entirely toward my rent).

There is a supermarket around the corner. The racks display products I've never seen — sodas flavored with fruits I didn't know existed, tall glass candle holders painted with the likenesses of various saints and prayers written in Spanish. The sidewalks aren't half as crowded here and the people on them are a lot older. The sky is still as gray as it was the day I looked at the apartment, but the threat of rain doesn't make good on its promise. The meat in the deli section looks questionable so I end up stocking up on Lean Cuisine, being sure to check the expiration dates before settling on my selection.

When I get back to the apartment I come face-to-antennae with a roach that courageously catwalks across the counter. I watch him crawl up a half-eaten banana, march around it a few times, his antennae flailing in a circular fashion; then I knock him off his perch with my sneaker and squash him flat as he tries to figure out what happened.

Todd calls me three times a day. I let each one go directly to voicemail. I text him responses immediately afterward to keep him calm: that I really can't talk right now, but I'm safe and okay; that I'll talk to him as soon as I've thought things through. He calls again every time I send that message. I know texts will follow soon, so I shut my phone down and plug it in (there are no working outlets in my room, so I charge it in the kitchen near the roach's final resting place).

The commute is an unpredictable pain, and I loathe not being able to depend solely on my feet to get from home to work and back again. I have to get up earlier than ever every morning until I get a sense of how and when the N and Q trains run. So I go to bed early — or at least get into it. My bed has a support bar that juts out through the thin cushion of the mattress, right where my spine belongs. Sleeping can only be accomplished on my side, with my arm and leg dangling off the edge. Lying there, I ponder if I would rather sleep like this or chance waking up with a sore back and neck. I also realize there will be no more sex at my apartment — I am embarrassed to claim this squashed hovel as my home. The mantra that only sometimes lulls me to sleep has become, "This is only temporary, this is just for now." But until what? I become a millionaire? Todd comes and rescues me from my fate? The thought of this living situation as anything but temporary is a crushing one, yet it's just as hard to imagine a plausible alternative.

Tonight I can't sleep, which comes as no surprise. At some point, Kieran enters the apartment. Light leaks over my fake wall and I hear him stomp around, clearing his throat. He turns on the TV in the half of the living room I don't live in. Its flickering glow creeps over the wall and seeps into my eyelids. I'll need to buy an eye mask. I'll need to buy earplugs.

I am still in shock. To think it's been a week since I was on Fire Island. Since I lived in a luxury two-bedroom apartment in an elevator building in Hell's Kitchen. Since I had friends. Since I was blissfully unaware of just how good I had it. Now I have nothing. My life was an inflatable raft I punctured with my dick not seven days ago. I shouldn't have gone to Fire Island. No — I shouldn't have fucked Marty. Nor kept it a secret from my friends. The "I shouldn't"'s start piling on top of each other. I arrange the events of the past couple months and it's crazy how one thing led to another. I'd call myself a victim of chaotic fate if my predicament wasn't obviously a result of my drunken, boundaryless libido. And my tendency to eschew the truth rather than face the consequences of said drunken libido. Feeling sorry for myself might work had I not so easily ducked all the obstacles most transplants to this city face upon arrival — stuff I took so easily for granted. Now I'm finally getting to see what my move to New York would have been like without Todd's deity-like assistance, and I wonder: how are the streets not filled with hopeful newcomers fleeing the scene, running and screaming from the reality of this place like it's a CGI Godzilla?

I get back up, since sleep is impossible. I get dressed and slink out past Kieran, who has fallen asleep on a futon with an infomercial blaring the benefits of some new food processor. I grab my phone, fire it up, and walk down the five flights of stairs out to the street. At least now it's cool. The streets are quiet instead of alive. I can hear the chime of a subway at least four blocks away. My phone says it's 2:30 AM and my stomach churns to think of how I will feel tomorrow morning at work.

As I'm rounding my corner for the fourth time, smoking my third cigarette and wondering if there is somewhere I can buy another pack (and if they are maybe cheaper here in Astoria), my phone chimes. It's Marty. For the first time in seven days, I answer.

"Gully? Did you actually pick up?"

"Guess so."

I don't know what to say to him. Whether I should yell or cry. He sits on the other end of the line, breathing, maybe thinking the same thing.

"Baby, how are you?" His voice is shaky — it breaks my heart the instant I hear it. I imagine him holding back tears.

"Well, the bruises are fading. I look less and less like a rape victim every day." I manage a grim snort at that one, but Marty doesn't join me.

"Gully, I'm so—"

"—No. No more 'I'm sorry's, please. I have enough of those from the texts. I could print them up and make a very apologetic lampshade out of them."

"Okay. I'm sorry. Shit. Sorry, didn't mean to — ah. How many times did I just apologize trying not to apologize for apologizing?"

I laugh. I can't help it. "Do you know ANY other words besides 'I'm sorry'?"

"If so, I think I forgot them. Did you go to the hospital?"

"No. It's all superficial damage. If I had a concussion I'd know by being dead already. But to look at my face, maybe I'd be better off that way? At least then an undertaker could finally give me those cheek bones I always wanted."

Marty's laugh makes me smile. It lifts so much of this heavy Astoria air off of my chest.

"I'm sure you look rugged. That's sexy. I wish I was there with you."

"Do you?"

"Yeah. But do you want me to be?"

I think about it. "I don't know. One moment we're great, then all of a sudden you disappear on me. And next thing I know, I'm having my ass handed to me in a fight sponsored by Blackberry. Their logo is now permanently implanted on my face, thanks to you."

"I won't apologize, only because you said I can't. But — I had doubts. I started feeling really guilty. Didn't you ever feel that way?"

I can't lie. "Yeah, I felt pretty fucking guilty. It was tough to keep a secret. It's just — we were having so much fun..."

"And we still can. Guilt-free this time. After I heard what he did I called him. Not texted. I called Brayden a fucking psychopath and said I had no idea what I ever saw in him. He called me a lying, cheating bitch. And that was it."

I exhale, watching the smoke from my final drag of this cigarette curl into the air and then disappear. "You make it sound so simple. Like we easily could have avoided all this. Hindsight's 20/20, right?"

"All week I've been thinking about you. Us. The only bad part was the guilt, you know? And now that's gone. If you can trust me again."

I don't respond. I'm not ready yet.

"Please, Gulliver. I want to be with you. I miss you so fucking much."

I'm seeing Brayden's face. I'm feeling his Blackberry. I should cut Marty off, shouldn't I?

But then again, with Brayden and the whole crew no longer talking to me — what more damage can be done?

Without them and without Marty, I'm alone. So fuck Brayden. I won't live in fear of him. I don't owe him anything. If we're no longer friends, what the hell do I care how he feels?

"Okay, Marty. When are you back in my life?"

There's more silence. "Wait, are you serious? Like for real serious?"

I laugh again. I want to keep laughing. "Yes, fool. I'm serious. When are you back?"

"Oh my God! Thank you! Ten more days! Ceremony is tomorrow. I can't wait to see you!"

"Me too. But I should probably go. Have to get up early to get to work."

"Okay. Goodnight, baby."

He delivers that final word with exquisite care, like he's slowly advancing on a cornered snake that might strike at any moment. And that word hangs between us in a pensive silence that is broken by a horn a block away.

"Goodnight."

With my phone tucked back in my pocket, I head back to the apartment, stomp up the stairs, jiggle my key in the lock until the door decides to allow me back inside. I take a hot shower and breathe the steam in, feeling my lungs open. I feel relaxed. I feel tired. And most importantly, I don't feel the least bit guilty, which is probably the greatest sensation I've had in awhile.

CHAPTER 17

I feel like a wanted criminal, one who would love more than anything to flee the country but cannot because he'll be caught at the nearest airport and brought in for a sit in the electric chair or a cocktail of lethal injections. Or maybe I'm more like a drug addict going through withdrawal, constantly sweaty and forever on edge.

Stanford's moved us to a new office in the heart of Hell's Kitchen. It should have been a blessing — allowing me to jump out of bed post-partying, right into my chair. Even hungover I would be the model of a perfect employee — at my desk clicking intently at the computer, even if I was dying like an exorcised demon on the inside. But since moving to Astoria, I haven't been to a single party. I don't jump out of my bed so much as crawl out of it, often with shooting pains in my back. The irony is that I think I felt better after a night of nonstop partying than I do after a night of jerking off and struggling to sleep in my half-room, listening to my roommates stomp around.

Even worse, Rosa has a set time she takes her shower in the morning, so I have to go in either before her or after her — and if I went after, I would be late to work. I am consistently underslept, which feels worse than any tequila hangover. My eyes burn until noon; my stomach is a roiling container of acid until three. By nine at night I am too exhausted to move, even though it takes my brain another four hours to shut up and get ready for bed.

Marty is the only good thing going for me right now — and he's not even back yet. The good news is I'm no longer on the prowl for supplementary sexytime. I have officially devoted myself entirely to Marty, who I now have epic hours-long conversations with every night. Sure, maybe half the reason I'm willing to give the long distance thing a try is that I can't have anyone over to my place, anyway. But I give myself credit knowing this is the 21st century in New York City and if I really want to get laid, it's as easy as hopping online or firing up Grindr — or just making eyes at the right cutie in the right neighborhood. Why bother, though? Marty and I have had enough drama, enough opportunity for the powers that be to rip us apart. And yet we managed to come back together. Why tempt the fates?

So I walk the streets of Hell's Kitchen trying not to make eyes at anyone. I never know if one of them will be Servando, Shane, Rowan, or — God save me — Brayden. When I hear someone yell, my instincts are to cover my face and back against a wall, my body already reverberating from phantom punches. To date, these have only been false alarms. But, as the New York Lottery ad taunts me from every phone booth: *"Hey, You Never Know."*

At times I think I am overreacting, but then I flash back and see a Blackberry coming at my face and think: no, this isn't overreacting, this is survival. I remember the rage and hurt in Brayden's eyes — the look of someone who would run in front of speeding traffic to have another shot at me. I'm not saying he doesn't deserve to be angry — I would be, too. But I'm past guilt. I've received my punishment. Now I'm on the defense. I already have my plan should we come face to face: I will go for his throat like my mother learned in that self-defense class she took after seeing a news report on the rising rate of crime in Los Angeles. I will turn my hand palm-up, stiffen my fingers, and scoop upward quickly, right under Brayden's prominent Adam's apple. As he stumbles backward grabbing at his throat, his eyes wide in shock, wondering if he's about to choke on his own tongue, I will take off like a shot, abandoning my shoulder bag and laptop on the street. I may not have the strength to take him on, but I know I have the speed to escape him.

Luckily, since my exile from the Garden of Manhattan, I haven't seen a single one of my former crew. According to some number Todd once told me, during a normal work day there are over eight million people surging through this city, standing back-to-front on more than fifteen subway lines, waiting in line for coffee from street-meat vendors, walking the streets above and navigating the tunnels below the island. I only need to stay clear of five of them. So far, so good.

Today's lunch break is like every other I've had over the past few weeks: the last thing I feel like doing is putting food in my body. I order a salad from some place that sells only salads and makes a huge show of chopping the contents of your healthy lunch into unrecognizable bits. But every *chop-chop-chop* has me flinching, thinking back to the night on Fire Island. I end up sitting in a dark corner by overflowing garbage cans where no one bothers to sit. It is sunny and wonderful outside and here I am hiding away and praying over and over again that I don't see a single familiar face.

Will I have a heart attack every time I hear someone yell? Every time someone bangs a door shut or crashes into a garbage can? Every time I see a guy that even vaguely resembles Brayden? It's becoming unbearable. I almost wish I would run into him. He'd attack me, I'd chop his throat, and we'd get this whole thing over with.

My walk back to the office, half-eaten salad swinging in a plastic bag at my side, is a choreographed dance of quickly looking around for predators, and just as quickly dropping my head so no one recognizes me. For the fourteenth time this week, I wonder if things would be better in Los Angeles. If I moved home.

But then I think of Graham. He'd be there waiting. And I'd be going through this same routine trying to avoid him instead. That, still, would be worse than this.

So eyes downcast, I power through my walk of shame, just waiting for my boyfriend to come home.

CHAPTER 18

It is yet another summer Friday in Hell's Kitchen and Stanford is long gone. He is on his way to Boston for a monthly checkup with the superiors. And he's excited. The state of Diedrick, Kemnitz & Hobbs Casting International's New York satellite office is the complete opposite of my own — immensely successful. We are representing five actors, two of which are already packing their bags for non-equity national tours. Then, of course, there is Marty, who will be in this city soon (and, turns out, just around the corner from my new apartment). From there we will hustle him from audition to audition.

Stanford is a golden-tongued god of representation. Hearing him pitch Marty to the casting directors of various shows so far has been inspirational. He seems to know each one so well, and they seem to trust him. Even though it's not like Marty is a tough sell in the first place.

"No, Jane, you have to hear him. And get this, already halfway to his equity card! Yeah, *Jersey Boys*, tore the house down. No, I know he's not a star yet. But don't you want to be the one to say you set him up? Because, listen, I'm not kidding when I say this guy has jet-packs tied to his shoes and Tony noms a few years out. Whoever's hanging onto his shirt when they take off is… yeah? I thought so. I'll email over his resume and headshot. Love you too babe. Sure. Drinks next week. Kisses."

Every time I hear that pitch, my heart soars. For Stanford. For Marty. And, I guess, for me. Because I'm holding on to Marty's coattails, too.

Okay. So perhaps I'm being over-dramatic (go figure). Not all is going wrong in my life — work is fine, clearly. And I have to remember, as Mom always counseled when I would tell her about everything going to hell in LA, to keep my eyes on what IS working. And work, at least, is working. Stanford gave me a raise at the beginning of the week. "Early, I know, but Gulliver, you're making my life and job so much easier. Keep it up, and we'll take each other to the top!" I am saving as much of my take-home as possible so I can move out of Astoria and back into Manhattan, even if Hell's Kitchen is no longer on the table.

So here I am in the office answering phone calls, adjusting PowerPoint files, and checking and double-checking Word documents Stanford will be passing around to the agency partners. Every time I tell him what he's called to ask me for is already in his inbox, he confirms that I'm a saint of the highest order and says that I can go home early... until he remembers this one other thing he really needs my help with.

"You okay to stay a little later?"

"Of course it's okay, you're the boss."

"Ooooh, don't like that B-word. It's icky."

"Captain?"

"Hmmm... no."

"What about Admiral?"

"Only if you buy me a hat."

Laughs commence, and Stanford's brand new iPhone cuts him off mid-laugh, causing my phone to beep a robotic apology. Oh well. This happens all the time since he treated himself to the Apple must-have — the signal loss and call dropping. It's like he's forever ringing me up from inside Hitler's bunker.

We're hoping the bosses up in Boston are going to be as excited as we are at our progress. With that we may end up getting more money, which Stanford has already committed to buying us a couch, a flat-screen television, desk chairs without missing wheels, and another round of raises. Frankly, if his bosses know what's good for them, they'll give him more than he's expect-ing. Because if they don't, he could go anywhere and name a price. The guy is a superstar the likes of which I have never seen, except maybe Todd.

The phone rings again and I scoop it up saying, "You want that document spell-checked again, huh?"

"Bro, I'm going to fucking kill you."

I almost drop the phone. It's like I fucking used The Secret to get him on the other end of the receiver.

"What? How did you get this number?"

"That's not the point. You're meeting me for coffee. Now."

It's a lot easier to ignore Todd's pleas in text format. I agree to coffee, but tell him to bring it by the office. I don't feel safe coming outside.

I buzz Todd in five minutes later and he enters, coffee-less, and stands hulk-ing in the doorway. He is still dressed from work, his pale green and bright white striped shirt tightly clinging to his muscular frame, his biceps bulging at the rolled up sleeves. His tie is undone and hanging (flopping, really) at either side of his thick neck. If you were to search Google Images with the query "Important guy after work," this is what would come up. Especially if you added "pissed off."

Todd's voice is monotone. "Bro."

I rise out of my chair and back up, wondering if he'll jump over the desk to get to me. "I'm sorry..."

"Shut the FUCK up and listen to me."

I shut the fuck up and then some.

"What you did was stupid, yeah? We all know that. Everyone does. We got it." He isn't even looking at me. His eyes are trained on a far corner of the room, where the paint starved wall reaches to meet the ceiling unevenly. He brushes his matted hair out of his face, the product all but obliterated. "But because of that you fucking disappear without a trace? You barely answer my calls or texts? Dude, we're fucking BROTHERS. What would you do if I did that to you?"

And I thought I felt like a criminal before.

"Well?" His eyes descend and stare me down. The effect is chilling. He is heaving, like maybe he ran here the second I told him he could come.

I mumble, "I'd lose it."

"Yeah, exactly," he pounds a fist into an open hand. "What do you think I've been doing? I mean, first I thought maybe you were being dramatic. That I'd come home and you'd be locked in your room and I'd have to coax you out. But no, I get back and you're gone. I almost contacted your parents to find out where you were."

Oh God. I imagine Mom. She'd drop dead right there, every fear she ever had of Manhattan coming true — the big, bad Apple swallowing her precious Gully whole, bones ground to dust by the E train. She'd send the police. She'd hop on a plane and comb the city streets and avenues, one by one, until she found me.

"Oh no..."

"Chill. I didn't. Because as I was tearing apart your room, I found your business card behind the bed. PS: I thought you were working on the East Side." He flings it on the floor — almost comical considering all the force he puts into the lob and how it swirls delicately in the air like a falling leaf.

"We just moved here this week. Once upon a time, that would have been a convenient bonus."

He swallows hard and walks toward me, his fierce green eyes narrow. "I didn't know what I was going to do when I found you." He steps back, crosses his arms, shakes his head violently. "First I was scared. Then sad. Then pissed. You DON'T do that, man. You don't disappear when I'm the only fucking person accountable for you. I told you we could've made it work. Brayden's chilled out. Well, he's getting there. We all do stupid things with our dicks. We get that. All of us."

I've never seen Todd like this. Sure, I've seen him fuming, but it was over a bad grade in class, or a guy he was seeing who had Manhunt open when he came by for a surprise romantic night in the senior dorms. But never at me. And now I'm crying. Not just silent tears; I'm choking and wheezing, my nose is leaking. Todd pauses to see that I've fallen back into my chair, my elbows on the desk, my face stuffed in my soaking hands.

"I'm so sorry! I didn't know what to do! I didn't want Brayden to kill me. I just ran." The office phone is ringing, but I'm in no condition to answer it. "Your life is SO fucking perfect. You did everything for me. And then I... just..." I melt into more tears and words I can't even understand.

Todd's hard, angry face softens. His shoulders slump and he releases a giant, built-up sigh. "Bro, come over here."

I shake my head. "I don't deserve you — I said that when I first got here. Then I proved it. I should just go back to LA."

"JESUS!" he bellows, his arms in the air. "Haven't I had enough drama these past few weeks? Can you spare me, please? Can you do me this one little favor and make this easy on me? Just get your twink ass over here."

I suppose, given everything I've done wrong, I can do this for him. His arms are open and then I'm up in them. He's holding me over his head like a barbell. I am a human feather. I am flying.

"Do you UNDERSTAND ME, you MOTHERFUCKER? You will NOT do that again. You dig?"

He shifts me so he has his hands in my armpits, holding me clear above him with my feet dangling. I look down on his smile, stretching from jawline to jawline.

"Consider it dug."

And he drops me. My legs give out and I'm on the floor. Oh Stanford would love this. He'd be laughing his ass off, clapping wildly, asking for a repeat. I stand up and Todd punches me full-force in the arm. Numb. Tingling. But I'm laughing, and so is he.

"I guess, yeah, maybe I overreacted a bit..."

"Jesus. I love you, Gully. You could have an orgy with every ex I've ever had, then come to my house and knock my mother out cold. And yeah, I might beat the shit out of you, but I'd still love you. Dig?"

"Dug. Dug. Dug." I can't stop laughing. God it feels good to laugh — to use my lungs for something besides crying. To feel a pain in my gut that's from peals of laughter, not Brayden's sneakers.

"Good, now let's go get a drink. You're moving back in with me this week-end."

I stop laughing.

"No, I can't. Not yet, at least."

Todd looks up at me, sucking air through his teeth. "Gully…"

"I'm serious." I hold my hands up. "I got spoiled. I got careless. And all because everything just came so easily to me. Friends. That apartment. Even this job." Todd's about to protest, but it's his turn to hear me out. "And yes, Astoria sucks. Specifically my current apartment. Yes, Kieran comes home smelling like Coronas and sawdust and yes, Rosa leaves her clothing all over the place like we live in a washing machine. But it's real. I'm paying real rent for a real apartment, not a Disney ride in Fantasyland."

"You sound like a nut, Gully."

"I feel like one, too. But I need to earn it. At least until Kieran and Rosa and the roaches and the busted N and Q trains drive me out of my mind."

"So I'll be seeing you back in my place in about a week and a half," he says.

"Yeah, probably."

"Okay. What about a drink? You can at least give your old buddy one of those, right?"

It's past seven. I assume Stanford has safely arrived at the office and is in the midst of delivering the presentation that will hopefully allow our new digs to meet all of New York's current building codes. So I tell Todd to wait while I finish up a couple things, then power down the computer and lock up.

We leave the office ten minutes later and head to Vintage, a not-necessarily-straight bar where Todd promises none of the boys will be in attendance. They are all at a party where artists sit around a stage, sipping wine and sketching nude models while a DJ spins palatable trance tunes. Shane is one of the models, and as I would expect of them, the other boys are being supportive (and taking advantage of the free Riesling). For a moment my mood sours, imagining myself with them. Drinking the wine. Joking around about Shane's dick (which I never had the opportunity to see). Not only am I excluded, but they are also probably having a fine time without me.

But then I look at Todd and think about him tracking me down like a private eye, and the feeling is gone. At least I'm still worthwhile to him.

Vintage is the spitting image of all the gay bars in Hell's Kitchen — dimly lit, loud music, hanging fabrics serving as dividers, scantily clad bartenders and waitstaff. The only difference is the larger percentage of heterosexuals. It's a nice change. I'm still edgy, but a few drinks from their encyclopedic menu of martinis unknots my brain and gives me a welcome buzz.

I don't want to talk about the crew, and Todd is more than happy to oblige. Instead we go full-on into nostalgia mode. We revisit our adventures from UCLA — the late night trips to TigerHeat with our fake IDs, sitting around the fountain in the quad during our shared lunch time, the student films we starred in because we looked convincing enough during fake sex scenes. It's hard to believe this all happened over three years ago. As we share stories, shooting back martinis, it feels as if we're talking about memories that happened just yesterday. The martinis hit me and I excuse myself to find the bathroom.

My phone goes off on my way back: Stanford telling me that the presentation was an astounding success. We're performing above and beyond every expectation and they're extremely excited about Marty. Stanford ends the text with the announcement that there will be yet another raise in my upcoming paycheck. (*"Nothing big. Maybe a few more drinkies on a Friday night tho."*) He also invites me out to a night of drinking and dancing with his talent friends, too. I happily share the Marty-free part of the message with Todd.

"Who the fuck gets two raises in a week?" Todd howls. "You're buying this round, moneybags."

And so I buy that round, and then the next one too. It isn't until the third that I realize this is the first thing I've bought for Todd in New York. Until today I have accepted whatever he paid for, mooching on the many hookups he got for free. Maybe Astoria living is doing me some good after all. I can't give him lodging or VIP status anywhere, but I can at least get him drunk. It's my thank you for the apartment. For dragging me out to New York, out of my going-nowhere stasis in Los Angeles. For hunting me down and still being there for me.

Of course, if I told him this, he'd punch me. So I just toast him and gesture to the waitress for another round.

As we drink, Todd tries to convince me that the other guys aren't as harsh on me as I think they are. I roll my eyes and try to change the subject to a couple across from us, too busy making out to realize their waitress is standing there waiting for them to finish paying out their tab.

"But, seriously." He takes my chin in his hand and spins me to face him. "The boys aren't as pissed at you as you think."

"Whether I agree or not with how Brayden reacted, they're all his friends, not mine. And there's no way to tell this story without me coming across like a heartless piece of shit."

"True, they were pissed at first. But don't forget your bro is a genius. I had more than enough history to remind them of."

"Like what?"

"You think we've all been on our best behavior since the dawn of time? What did I tell you? We all make mistakes. Everyone has slept with everyone — sometimes drunk, sometimes really, really drunk. Exes find their way in and out. Did you know that Servando and Rowan used to be boyfriends?"

I did not. Now their present sexual activities confuse me even more.

"Yeah. And that was BEFORE the crew came together. Actually, their breakup might have been the beginning of us. They HATED each other for the longest time."

"Even so—"

"And finally, don't think you're the only person Brayden has laid a smack-down on. Actually, I'm probably the only person who hasn't faced his wrath, most likely because I'd school the shit out of him. So I cherry-picked a few stories over drinks this week. That cooled most of them down real fast. Plus, it helps that you were an awesome lay for Servando and Rowan."

I blush and give my best Goofy "gawrsh" as the waitress arrives with our next round of martinis. Brayden, he says, really is chilling out a bit — to the point where he won't try to sever my spinal cord when he sees me, at least. Perhaps just a stiff bitch slap is in order. The cocktail of Todd's words mixed with the martinis opens a hole in the top of my head, through which every ounce of saturated stress and fear is now mercifully flowing out.

But there's a part of me that remains cautious. Brayden seems like the sort who might say one thing and mean another, especially when it involves something as explosive as what I did — and with whom I did it.

"Whatever, man. It's Marty. He's a fucking slutty twink and a liar. Not worth all this drama."

At these words, my stomach lurches and the instinct to defend my man's honor kicks in before I squash it immediately back down. I want to explain his side of things. Dealing with a hot temper like Brayden's couldn't have been easy. Hearing him referred to this way puts red flags up. How could Marty be the awful person Todd and the crew think he is? Could it be he's just playing me? Of course, he wouldn't be the first of my boyfriends to do so. What do I do? Break up with him — just because of hearsay from the crew about what a shitty guy he is? The thought of losing him again makes me queasy. I can't do that. I won't do that. No matter what.

"Brayden said you and he had a major heart to heart that day at Central Park."

I had forgotten about that. "Yeah, we did."

"I think that's what really did it. He spilled his shit to you and then you turned around and slept with the kid. Which, by the way, is over?"

Fuck.

Fuck. Fuck.

Todd's eyes measure me. My mouth hangs open, some martini still sloshing around my tongue. My answer is taking far too long.

Must. Say. Something.

"Yes. Absolutely, one hundred percent dunzo."

"See? That's what I told Brayden! You're not one for repeats, bro. I know my Gully." This statement is followed by a round of hair ruffling, and me physically reminding myself to take in and expel oxygen so I don't pass out.

We finish drinking sometime after 2 AM, and Todd persuades me to crash at his place. He promises no one is expected to show up and besides, the N and Q will be running so infrequently I'll end up waiting in the station forever. The thought of swaying back and forth drunk and alone on a dripping subway platform that smells like puke and spoiled milk turns my stomach enough to seal the deal.

I've only been gone for a few weeks and yet the homesick pang hits me hard when Todd unlocks the door to my former residence. Señor comes running up to me barking like a lunatic and commences humping my leg as soon as he reaches it.

"He misses his walkin' buddy, Gull. I make him pee in the courtyard."

My room is empty: "Because I'm banking on you giving up this bullshit and coming back." Our framed pictures remain on the wall. "One of the best pics of us ever, bro. I used that on Manhunt for EVER."

We stay up late, drinking from a bottle of Stoli sitting in his freezer, watching YouTube clips of old Saturday Night Live skits. When that's done, we put *Aladdin* in the DVD player and sing along with each of the songs (I do Jasmine's part in "A Whole New World" — don't judge). It's like old times — not a week ago, YEARS ago. We're back in the fraternity house, drinking PBR and doing shots of Popov vodka (or as we called it, "Burn"). Todd isn't making a six-figure salary. I'm not working for an agent I met walking Todd's dog. We may or may not have an exam we should be studying for. Everything was easier. Graham and I were still enviable college sweethearts. Drama was getting soaked on one of the infrequent days it rained because no one in LA owns an umbrella, or a tiff with a guy we were casually dating. The only thing that hasn't changed since that time is Todd and me.

Tears return to my ravaged eyes and I have to thank him again — for everything. I am babbling. Blathering. Blubbering. He gives me thirty seconds to get it out before he shakes his head and punches my arm again

"Enough emo, bro. Don't make me give you something to cry about."

"You already have. A whole lot of stuff."

"Uh-huh. Right. Pizza?"

We order Domino's — a large pie and a carton of over-buttered cheesy bread. The pizza delivery boy is way too cute and definitely digging either or both of us. We send him away with a generous tip and flip a coin to decide who gets to have sex with him in the story we'll fabricate later. The grease is so terribly delicious we polish off every last crumb, picking at the remaining bits stowed away at the bottom of the box.

"You've had quite the time here, bro," he says through his last bite of pepperoni, chewing with his mouth open dramatically. "Seriously. Aren't you glad you came out?"

"You're funny, Todd. Really. Hysterical."

"I'm serious. Put the Brayden shit aside. You got into some drama back in LA, too. I was there, remember?"

I want to say: tell me one situation that was in any way similar to the Fire Island beatdown.

"There's a difference between flung drinks and screaming battles and what went down three weeks ago."

Todd burps and doesn't excuse himself. "Okay, okay, I get it. Brayden's crazy and he took it out on you. Now put that aside and tell me: are you happy you came out here?"

"I'm still deciding," I say.

"Oh, come on. What's on the other side? What are you missing out on?"

The answer: not much.

"I have the money I'd need to go back. And I haven't yet, right? Mom would throw a parade if I told her I were coming home."

"And yet," Todd gestures at me, at us, at his apartment, and burps again. "Here you stay. Woof! Jesus. Sorry bro, that one's foul."

Why haven't I gone back to LA? After what happened on Fire Island, why didn't I pack my things and take a cab to JFK and call Mom to surprise her from LAX? It wasn't even something I considered. I went looking for other places to live. Like New York has some sort of hook in me, like it is my new center of gravity.

And it's not like California has anything better to offer. Living at home? No can do. Without a job in an economy that's worse on that side than where I'm standing right now? No. And Graham. God knows what he'd do when he got wind of the fact that I was physically reachable again.

Graham. Career. Life in general. Enough failure — New York won't be added to that list any time soon.

"You've got your thinkin' face on. Not a good idea when it's this late and you're drunk and full of shitty pizza," Todd says, shaking me by the shoulders. "Can it for now. You're here. You're queer. Let's get some beer?"

If we had some sort of lame fraternity brother handshake, we'd probably do it now. Because we're drunk and covered in grease, it'd probably be a hilarious sight to behold. But we don't have a handshake. So we just break down in laughter, fall back on the couch and I let my hand drape over Todd's broad shoulders as we watch Prince Ali defeat the evil Jafar once and for all, condemning him to a life enslaved inside an antique lamp.

"Shit. Imagine being trapped in a lamp forever. That's gotta be worse than living in Astoria," Todd says.

"That's spacious compared to my place. And no roommates to share the shower with. And hey — that reminds me, we never went antiquing!"

Todd considers me for a full minute, picking at a piece of pizza lodged in his tooth. "God." Another belch. "Gully, you are one gay motherfucker."

CHAPTER 19

"To fame, fortune, and the gorgeous boyfriends we'll get as a result!" Stanford raises his drink above our matching aged strip steaks. Our glasses clink together.

We are at some pricey steakhouse in Midtown where ornamental cow carcasses hang from the ceilings and walls. In front of us is a spread from an issue of *Carnivore Monthly* magazine. The steaks themselves cost half my weekly take-home and, according to the waiter who took us through the menu like he was selling a diamond, they are aged for days until a rot forms around the meat, whereupon the rot is cut away and tender meat revealed to the world like a protein-rich butterfly. Despite the horror of the genesis story, I figure if the steak is that expensive, it must be safe to eat. Update: not only is the steak safe — it's the meatiest, fattiest, butteriest thing I've ever allowed myself to consume. The side dishes — carby, veggie, creamed, and fried — are in bowls bigger than my head. We don't have napkins, we have tablecloths on our laps. And we need more of them to mop up all the stray steak juice.

"I don't normally eat this way, Gully," Stanford says between chews. He looks me in the face — a rarity granted only because he pledged to keep his iPhone in his pocket for the entire meal. "But I determined that a proper celebration has not been had if we don't achieve heartburn and bust through our pants."

Stanford has been back in town for three days and already things are picking up. The Boston office is handing us some of their mid-tier clients. Before

Stanford returned, men arrived at the new office with deliveries — the couch he promised, a black leather number from West Elm. Along with that came an oak coffee table, a metal magazine rack, and a 52-inch flat panel television which the deliverymen mounted on the wall. In less than eight hours I was working in a brand new space.

All this excitement is nothing compared to one bit of news: tonight Marty returns. He texted me earlier letting me know his bus was pulling out of the Charcoal Drive-In — a greasy spoon with a framed coffee cup apparently used by Bill Clinton when he passed through for a stump speech. We have plans to meet later tonight at his place.

I should be savoring this meal more, but all I think of is Marty. It's not that I'm not enjoying dinner, it's just that I wish the food were already in my stomach, me already on the train to Marty's, and Marty's bus actually a tele-portation device that would transport him immediately back to New York.

Stanford recounts for me the entire meeting with the Bostonian Big Wigs in detail. Next time he goes up he has been ordered to bring along his golden boy (that's me, apparently). I am all blush and modesty but Stanford won't allow it. Our meeting wasn't chance, he informs me. It was blessed fate. Without me none of this would be possible. I don't believe him, and am in fact rather confident that he could take over New York, and then the world, all by himself — maybe with his arms tied together and a blindfold over his eyes. But it feels good to hear him credit me with even a portion of his suc-cess.

I take another bite of the steak, as soft as an overstuffed pillow. I wipe my mouth and dig in to the creamed spinach. After this evening I will make good use of yet another benefit Stanford secured for us while in Boston — gym memberships. Todd's going to be very excited that he's got a workout part-ner after all these years of peer pressure. (Well, that's assuming I can com-plete a single chin up while he bench presses the weight of three horses.)

We don't even come close to finishing our meals. Stanford has the remains wrapped up in foil and deposited in a brown paper shopping bag. It weighs at least five pounds. "How exciting that we now have a working refrigerator in which to store our spoils of war!" he cheers.

The office is only a few blocks away from this kingdom of steak, so we swing by to deposit what's left. Then it's on to the bars. Stanford has no regular spots and happily surrenders the selection to me. I figure maybe it's time to give the east side a shot, so exclusively west as I've been since my arrival. We pick up the latest copy of *NEXT* magazine — the gay nightlife bible in New York. I expertly flip past drag queen interviews, promoter highlights (this week it's Todd, go figure), and porno reviews to the back pages that list every gay bar and event in New York City.

"It'll be like a safari!" he says when I admit I have no idea what any of these bars are like.

Between the map in *NEXT* and Google I am able to get Stanford and I to the East Village, by way of Union Square. First I take him to a bar that has apparently been closed no less than three times for an "active" back room. The dangling black ropes along one wall, hardcore gay porn on a projection screen, and handlebar mustaches on the bartenders' and patrons' faces are too much for Stanford, so I move us on to another bar defined by deep red lights and Russian-themed wall decorations; then yet another with a pool table and distinct dive vibe; then another whose reputation is apparently even more scandalous than the first; then two other bars directly across the street. The summer evening is cool and gays are out in full force. We stand in the crowds, yelling for the attention of rushing bartenders. We drink crammed up against walls. Stanford talks about his life before becoming an agent.

"I was a theater major myself, believe it or not. Not a very good one. And one day, while sitting in rehearsal trying to find the character and purpose of a walk-on role with two spoken lines, I realized I didn't want to be an actor. Well, I realized I'd never be an actor, and therefore shouldn't waste any more time wanting to be. I made a last-minute shift and sacrificed my last two college summers to internships — the second of which was Diedrick."

"Wow, that worked out pretty nicely," I laugh, amazed at how it all seemed to come together for him.

"Speaking of stardom, Gully. I want to talk to you about your title."

Over the blasting music, Stanford tells me he believes in sink or swim. And am I interested in representing Marty?

"Boss, I think you drank too much!"

"One, enough with that B-word. Two, I may have drank too much but I made up my mind before imbibing. Now take your promotion before I beat you with it!"

He goes on to say he'll be watching over my every move, of course. But he wants to see how I handle all of the responsibilities I've seen him performing so many times since I began working under him.

"I just don't get it! How could I be ready? I don't know anything!"

"We've yet to follow any sort of traditional ladder of progress, partner. Why start now?"

I think this is a huge mistake. I wonder what the hell I've done to convince Stanford that putting me in charge of Marty is a smart business move. Even if I'm not entirely in charge, I feel like any ounce of responsibility placed on me is moronic. Plus, if he knew I was dating Marty, he'd think twice about this conflict of interests. But as his boyfriend, won't I be working even harder to make sure Marty becomes a star?

"Well?" Stanford asks, finishing his drink. "What do you say?"

My phone buzzes and I pull it out. My "client" has arrived safely in Astoria. I put a finger up to Stanford and text: *You can call me boss now, boyo. See you in 30.*"

"I accept," I say, stuffing my phone back into my pocket and shaking Stanford's hand firmly.

Stanford and I part ways only after I perform an "acceptance speech" for my new position. I thank the Academy and Lea Michele for being the next coming of Barbra Streisand. And then, after hugs and goodbyes, I am sprinting through the East Village to find the first train that will take me to Marty. There may be a closer one than where I end up, but I might as well be wandering the streets of some foreign alien city for all I know about this side of town. The N train is pulling into the station, an increasingly rare event that hits me like a divine favor.

I am Marty-bound in record time.

I check the address on my cell phone for a third time before I press the buzzer outside of a four-story brick building five subway stops from my apartment. It is past four in the morning but Marty assured me he'd be awake and waiting.

There's a squeak from beyond the front door, quick steps that increase in volume, and the door flies open. He's wearing a loose sleeveless T-shirt that hangs off his frame, exposing a pierced nipple, and a pair of tight running shorts. A chilly, refreshing shiver climbs up from my groin and fills my head. I'm surrounded by freezing air. My eyes are hot-wired to my mouth, providing a direct feed of his face and body that powers a smile so wide it hurts. It's like I haven't seen him in months. My memory of how beautiful he is wilts before the real deal standing in front of me. He looks so much like Brayden it's eerie. But he's far hotter than Brayden. No contest.

"Hey there, boss."

"Good boy." I stick my tongue out at him.

His hand snakes out and grabs hold of mine. We're kissing and undressing before we have a chance to close the door.

The apartment is dark and Marty puts his finger over my mouth, tiptoeing backward as he leads me through what I assume is the living room. In the dark I can make out the silhouettes of couches, chairs, and a coffee table. Somehow, despite the alcohol imbibed during what turned out to be my promotion dinner, I avoid tripping over anything.

And then we are in his room. It is smaller than even my room, all the more choked from stacks of bags and boxes he has yet to unpack.

There is so much to talk about, yet nothing so pressing that it needs to be said at this moment. We fall onto his bed and are naked in an instant. He is kissing my neck, my chest, my stomach. I am kissing his back. I am licking between his pecs, along the lines of his stomach, the backs of his knees, the hollow sides of his ankles, the inside of his elbows. I will leave no place unkissed, even the most trivial.

He holds me down and ties his discarded sleeveless tee around my eyes. I am cast into a world of darkness. I do not resist much, just enough to keep him excited. Hypersensitive, my body quivers every time I feel the wetness of his mouth. Now on my nipple. Now on the inside of my bicep. Somehow, almost too quickly to make physical sense, the same wet warmth between my legs. Echoes of pleasure bounce around inside me. He is a floating warm entity. A ghost of warmth and wetness. He runs his fingers up and down my chest, my stomach. He gently kisses my almost-back-in-action face.

Now a condom is on me. And then he is on me. I am slowly, forcefully thrusting myself into him. He is on me and off of me, on me and off of me. I am moaning and he is putting his finger on my mouth, breathing heavy while trying to shush me lest his roommates awaken. I am biting his finger and grinning. I beg him to remove the blindfold so I can see him. He tells me to use my imagination.

"I'm home, baby. I'm home."

He feels so good. He feels so right. He smells like fabric softener and body wash. We are panting and moaning. Tumbling and wrestling. He is hanging off the bed, then I am. Hushing each other and laughing. I can't see his face, but I feel it on me. I feel him around me. And then I feel him tightening and quaking. I hear him scream silently through sealed lips — a vicious whisper. My name, over and over and over again. I feel new, warm wet on my stomach and chest, jet after jet. I feel my own release and the relief that follows.

He removes the blindfold and I can fly into his eyes again.

Breath and energy leave us. All is right with the world again. My loneliness is caught, spinning, in the ceiling fan above us, flung out his open window and down to the street below. We don't get up to wash. He has strategically placed a roll of paper towels beside his bed. His eyes can't stay open.

"I can get used to this — living so close to each other," he says, kissing my right ear.

"Anything's closer than Allentown." I kiss him back. Our hands are intertwined, our opposite legs delicately crossed over one another. "Astoria just got so, so much better."

And then I am asleep. Tonight my dreams are forgettable and unexciting, which is such a welcome change.

CHAPTER 20

I am wrenched out of dreamworld by my cell phone, which vibrates itself off of Marty's bed and onto the hardwood floor. I pick it up, staring hard to read the name on the screen, take the call, and mumble through my sticky, no doubt stinky, hungover mouth: "Mom, you're up early. Everything okay?"

"My sweetie! Happy Saturday!" Each syllable is a cymbal around my ears, slamming my head. I hold the phone back like a shrieking mandrake root as Marty opens one eye and looks at me, then at the phone, then at me, and then at the ceiling.

"Heyyy, same to you. Why are you so cheery?"

In the background I hear a crackly voice over a loudspeaker: *"Bienvenidos a JFK Airport. Rosa Vazquez, your family is waiting for you in baggage claim C."*

Like coffee injected straight into my brain. Now I'm awake. I am in full panic mode and jumping out of bed. Marty is sitting up and looking at me in alarm, both eyes open wide. "What happened? What's wrong?" I am jamming my legs into my pants, holding my phone out as I slip on my shirt (backwards).

"Mom, you didn't..."

"Surprise, Gully! We'll be at your apartment in an hour!"

In other words, she'll be at Todd's apartment. Where the drawers are empty.

Where I am currently not. Where my mom will be having a complete nervous breakdown in one hour's time. My mind is desperately trying to work, come up with an excuse, something to delay them, a plan of any kind. But it's like trying to start Rufus back in California after a long week of driving — buzzing from the motor, but no actual ignition.

"Okay, Ma! Can't wait to see you!" What else can I say? *"Funny story, Ma... I don't live there anymore! You see, I went ahead and slept with this guy..."*

Don't think so.

"See you soon, sweetie! Love you!" And she is gone. I am left staring at my phone dumbly. I have just enough time to kiss Marty and explain that my family has decided to show up completely unannounced and uninvited as I tie my shoes.

"I swear, Gully. Your life is ridiculous."

"You want to trade?" I ask, spinning my shirt around the right way and checking my hair. The bruises and gashes are all but gone, which is a relief. "Oh God. What am I going to do?"

Mom, Dad, and Leo are probably already in a cab and Manhattan-bound. I am praying for baggage mixups. Hoping beyond hope that there is a never-ending line of obnoxious tourists clogging the taxi line. Even a flat tire! Construction on the highway! Anything.

"First things first: eat." Marty jams a breakfast bar in my mouth. I chew obligingly. "Now call Todd. So at least if they get there before you do, he'll be prepared."

Marty's right. Marty's a genius. Actually, Marty's just used common sense, which is more than I'm capable of right now. I frantically try to locate his name in my contacts, and then, thankfully, do. Now all I can hope is he'll answer his phone and be conscious enough to lend assistance. I turn around and kiss Marty hard.

"It's not always this way. I swear. Just. Thanks for coming along for the ride. Assuming you still want to."

He kisses me back. God, his smile is amazing. I haven't seen my family in months, yet all I want to do is go back to bed with Marty. Kiss him between dreams.

"Whatever. It's exciting. And I have a lot of unpacking and re-acclimating to take care of. Have a nice impromptu weekend. Don't be a stranger, okay?"

As I run down Marty's block toward the subway, I am calling Todd over and over again. I reach voicemail five times before he finally picks up, his voice worn with his own Saturday morning regrets.

"Bro, you better have been raped or robbed or arrested or something."

"Even worse — my family is at JFK!"

Suddenly Todd's hangover voice is gone. "No shit! Sharon and William are in my city!"

"This is bad!"

"What do you mean? You haven't seen them forever!"

"They think I'm living with you!"

"Oh, fuck bro. You're right. Whatever! They're here! I haven't seen them in YEARS!"

"Todd, this is not a time to celebrate, it's a time to panic. It is a time for blood to rain from the sky and drown us all."

"Glad to see your hangover doesn't fuck with your ability to overdramatize. Get your ass over here. I'll make your room look like you still live in it. Hopefully your rents won't check the size of the T-shirts in the drawers. Plus, I've got a bag of shit you left here. I'll just throw it all around to make you look like a slob."

"You'll do that for me?"

"Of course. But you owe me big time. Like, permanent wingman wherever we go. Just bring coffee with you — I'll tell them you ducked out, it'll make a fan-fucking-tastic surprise."

It all makes so much sense. Of course Todd rocks at emergencies — he may have missed his calling in the ER (the real one, or the TV show). I jump up the stairs to the subway just as a train is approaching — once again, at the exact moment I need it to be.

"I love you, Todd," I say, swiping my Metrocard, spinning through the turnstile, and jogging up the second flight of stairs to the open-air platform where the subway is now pulling up, its doors opening.

"Permanent. Wingman. I'm not kidding, bro. I think there's puke lodged in my nose. See you soon." And then he is gone. Off to save my life once more.

CHAPTER 21

"My sweetie!" Mom is up, across the room, and assaulting me with perfumed kisses. She's short enough that her head can rest in the crook of my neck. Her many-dangly necklaces and earrings clinking and clacking all over my chest. The Starbucks I picked up teeters precariously in my hands.

"Hi, Ma!"

"So sweet getting up early to welcome us with coffee."

"You raised him well, Mrs. Leverenz," Todd quips, winking at me.

"I'm surprised you were awake when I called," she continues, taking the cup holder and dispensing of the caffeine I picked up. "Leo said you'd probably be hungover and we'd be in trouble!" I shoot a glance at Leo, who smiles at me knowingly.

There are many hugs. Leo's brutish and obligatory. Dad's warm and supportive. Mom's desperate and tugging. I guzzle my entire coffee before we've even had a chance to sit down. And then we talk.

Dad, a tall man with a full head of slicked-back gray hair and a forehead that wrinkles like a crinkle-cut french fry when he thinks, takes occasional calls from colleagues back in LA, who are up and worried about financial things way too early for their own good. Leo, on the other hand, is content to chase Señor around the apartment, making cooing noises at the overstimulated pup.

"Be sure to wash your hands when you're done touching him, Leo!" Mom calls after him, her command cut short by the slamming of Todd's bedroom door.

"You're trapped, you cute bastard!" my brother screams from beyond it.

"I'm so sorry, Toddy. You'd think he never saw a dog before."

"It's fine. Señor loves that sorta sh... err, stuff."

Mom demands a tour of the apartment. I fight off the headache monsters to make it so. Walking her through the rooms, I again wonder why I left this place when Todd told me I didn't have to. I am also impressed by his "Gullifying" my old room — which is peppered with wrinkled shirts and pants (no underwear in sight, God bless him).

"What a palace!" Mom says, opening the two oven doors. "This kitchen is better than mine!"

"Yeah, I'm really lucky, Mrs. Leverenz."

"Be careful, Toddy. We might just move in here with you, too! It certainly seems like you have enough room to accommodate us."

"You know, no one else calls me Toddy, Mrs. Leverenz," he says, hugging her.

"Good! I've always wanted to be seen as an independent woman," Mom says, planting kisses on Todd like he's one of her own kids.

When we return to the living room, Mom wants to know about everything and I just don't have the energy to tell her yet. It's okay though, because she's more than content to speak a mile a minute and let me know how great their flight was. How nice the cab driver was for helping them with their bags. How she prefers to travel early because she can avoid the traffic. How the plane had a quiz game that Leo played and won since she wouldn't let him turn his phone on during the flight.

Since we speak twice every day, Mom only has so much news to report, so she speaks in exquisite detail about everything from the snack menu on the plane to the commercials that were on the television screen in their cab. Leo, at this point, has passed out on the couch with Señor snoring next to him. Todd clearly would like to follow suit. After another few minutes, my father returns from the bathroom, re-holstering his Blackberry.

By the time Mom's monologue ends, my hangover seems to be receding and I can consider standing up and walking. But where to? What the hell does someone do in New York City that is both family-friendly and doesn't involve drinking?

"Toddy, do you have any suggestions on what we can do today?"

"Give me five minutes, Mrs. Leverenz," Todd says, running off to his room with his phone.

Mom and I sip our coffee, her scratching the back of my head, while Todd makes the calls. It is hilarious hearing him try his best not to drop a single F-bomb while talking to his people. When all is said and done, Todd has much to report: "Okay, so I got you guys a bunch of stuff. First there's VIP tickets to see a show called *Fuerza Bruta* tonight. Tomorrow night, you'll be seeing *Wicked*. Then I've got us some lunch and dinner reservations all around the city. Couple of museum passes. And some new tour bus with stadium seating and hired actors that perform for you on the street. Hope you brought your walking shoes, Mrs. L."

"They're in my suitcase!" she cheers, producing them from a Louis Vuitton wheelie. "Are you going to shower, Gully? Before we go out?"

I wasn't planning on it, but if I don't, she'll be upset about it all day. So I excuse myself to quickly attend to my unwashed body. When I come out, Leo, Dad, and Mom are all ready to take on the city. After another round of hugs and kisses to Todd, we are on our way to take Manhattan.

Mom is on happiness overdrive. We walk the streets with her arm hooked in mine, my dad on the other side, Leo behind us, continuously on the phone with his girlfriend back home. With Mom here, I am quickly becoming the kind of tourist I often want to hip-check into the street. The kind that stops to listen to every nonprofit worker's pitch about why we absolutely MUST contribute to their cause. Every poster must be read to completion. Every looping video of a Broadway show outside its theater must be watched in its entirety. Postcards are bought. *I Love New York* T-shirts are purchased (ironically, or at least I hope so).

"Suckers!" she hisses as we pass the lines of tourists waiting to purchase tickets from the discount TKTS booth in Times Square, before lapsing into a round of schoolgirlish giggles. "We're rolling VIP this weekend!"

She learned that from Todd, like, an hour ago. It's cute hearing her say it, like she's trying to pronounce the Swedish name of a sofa at IKEA. It's not like we come from the boondocks. Yet here Mom is, squealing with disbelief at the fact that the streets I walk to work are visited by tour buses on a daily basis.

"Do you wave to them when they pass by?" she asks.

"Of course, all the time," I say.

I haven't seen my family in a little over two months. They look fantastic — Dad has cultivated a healthy tan despite the fact that I know he's in his office more than anywhere else. ("Tanning beds. He wants to get cancer and leave me a widow, Gully.") And Leo — I swear the kid is five times more muscular than last time I saw him. He towers above me, looking more like an older brother than a younger one. ("Too long at the gym, Gully. Tell him he needs to study more!") And Mom, who was never heavy but always thought she was, looks positively radiant — tan, skinny, less harried. ("Who, me? Please, Gully. I'm an old goat. Put me out to pasture!")

The weather is on our side — although at times maybe a bit too hot. Mom has insisted I pay for absolutely nothing this weekend, and I pretend to challenge this offer. But free Frappuccinos and hot dogs are eventually accepted gladly.

Our full first day in the city consists of The MoMa and The Museum of Natural History. Mom purchases postcards and books at every gift shop, takes a picture in front of every iconic structure. In between she is hugging onto me for dear life and asking when I'm going to return the favor and come back to see her in Los Angeles. She is kissing my cheeks and telling me that even though he doesn't show it, my big buff brother misses me and also wants me to come back.

"It's not true, I like you being gone. She pays more attention to me without you there," he says before going back to his phone conversation.

"Oh, shush! I love you both the same! Plus I think he's dating an alcoholic," Mom whispers to me a bit too loudly.

Leo places his hand over his phone and says: "She's a college kid, Mom. She drinks. I drink."

"You're NOT legal!" Mom yells.

Leo rolls his eyes and returns to his phone. Knowing Mom, this is a conversation that has been hashed and rehashed to the point of dust. Of course, if Leo were to turn around and say, "You're right, maybe I shouldn't date her," Mom would quickly come around to the other side and say something to dissuade him from cutting her off. Because that's what Mom does.

Despite constant hydration and ample stops to rest under any sort of shade, we are all exhausted by the time dinner rolls around. Heretofore absent all day doing his nightlife thing, Todd is able to join us for dinner at a place that sells empanadas and nothing but empanadas. Mom loves this. I astound her by speaking of restaurants that sell only grilled cheese, macaroni and cheese, and so on.

"Only in New York!" she laughs.

"You can be honest with me, Todd," Mom giggles over her second white wine sangria. "Is Gully a slob? He was always a messy kid. Especially back before he had a computer and had to do all of his designing with crayons and colored pencils. Thank God for Photoshop! But you should have seen his Mac desktop. Horrifying."

"No, Mrs. Leverenz. It's like he doesn't live with me at all!" Thankfully Mom's too tipsy to pick up on the sarcastic tone in Todd's voice, or the soccer kick I administer to him beneath the table. He smiles back at me and shoves a cheeseburger-filled empanada into his mouth.

"I hope you're not giving Gully a free ride either," my father pipes in. "I want him to have the REAL New York experience."

"Come on, guys, this is supposed to be happy hour," I say. "Not Debbie Downer hour."

"I just want to be sure you're really living out here Gulliver, and not on a vacation," Dad says. He's not trying to offend me, but is doing so all the same.

I'm pissed. Not just at Dad. Also at the fact that telling the truth about where I'm living and what I'm really doing with my time is not an option. As much as my parents claim they want to be sure I'm living a "real New York life," if they found out I was doing just that, Mom would be panicking and Dad would be dealing with her panicking.

"No worries, Mr. Leverenz," Todd says through chews of his fifth empanada. "He's living a real New York life."

After dinner, we go to *Fuerza Bruta* with Todd in tow. The show is a psychotic gymnastic orgy that doesn't bother with technicalities like gravity or the safety of its performers. Watching near-naked men run around all four walls of the space — or flying above us in a hovering, plastic-bottomed pool — to the blasting beats of a live DJ with a hose he uses to soak us has all of us over-energized, drenched in water, and physically shaking by the time we exit the theater.

Todd has to separate at this point, his attendance expected at his Saturday night party. Mom gives him a huge hug and kiss and thanks him profusely. I do the same. A cab pulls up and swallows Todd whole, leaving us to walk back to Times Square so that the evening breeze dries our hair and clothing.

My family is staying at the Marriott Marquis right in Times Square. I walk them back to the hotel — a towering building that looks out on the crossroads of the world with a circular bank of bullet-shaped all-glass elevators on the ground floor. I've already texted Marty to let him know I'll be spending the weekend at Todd's, sparing him the technicalities as to why I'm doing this. Despite the fact that I am balancing three levels of lies — to my family, to Todd, and even to Marty, I find myself remarkably calm.

"Wait here for a minute," Mom says when we reach their room on the fifteenth floor. "I'll drop off my things and we can get a drink together?"

"Honey? I thought you were tired," my father says.

"Oh, one more drink won't put me in any deeper," Mom laughs, trying to jam Dad into the room like an article of clothing that won't fit in her suitcase.

Leo gives me a hard hug, smacking my back. Dad slips me a fifty and says, "You treat your mom, okay, Gully?" (And I wonder: why bother asking me if I'm living a REAL life if every time we interact, you slip me money?)

"Okay, Dad. Thanks."

He stops at the open door and adds, "And remember, she loves you more than anything."

I have just enough time to text a digital kiss to Marty before Mom emerges from the room, changed into a pair of jeans and a hoodie. "It's so chilly in this hotel!" she says. "Take me to the bar, Gully."

Marty's response text is almost instantaneous: *I miss you! When is your STU-PID FAMILY LEAVING? :-)*

Mom doesn't wait for the elevator doors to close before she corners me.

"So, Gully... enough pretending. How are you really doing?"

"I already told you, Ma! I'm great."

Thank God the elevator is empty. I'm pretty sure Mom would have laid into me regardless of the audience.

"Gully, you need to give your old mother a little more credit than that."

I am suddenly hyper-aware of my face and how I am standing. I am also confused. Today was an absolutely amazing day. Mom herself was on an endless 'roid rage of enthusiasm from the first minute in Todd's apartment all the way up until now.

"I don't know what you're talking about. I'm having so much fun." Suddenly the words sound so hollow and unconvincing, I wouldn't even believe me.

Mom nods, her lips pursed. She knows. She's letting it lie. Her strategy is being revisited and augmented. Meanwhile, my guard is up. She turns around to observe her reflection in the elevator's great glass wall and rubs a speck of lipstick off of her tooth. "I see. Who were you texting when I came out of the room?"

We end up on the top of the Marriott, in a rotating restaurant where the host begrudgingly allows us to sit at a table meant for six even though we tell him we won't be eating. There, over two Grey Goose extra dry martinis, I tell her about Marty — well, selectively at least. The audition becomes our first meeting. Our dating from there on in becomes pretty standard. Without the Brayden coincidence and the altercation on Fire Island, it all suddenly seems so boring.

"Is he what's keeping you here?" she asks, considering an olive before dropping it back into her glass.

"What? No. New York is what's keeping me here."

"Gully." She's so serious all of a sudden, her giggles and wide-eyed grins on a shelf somewhere deep inside. "You think I don't hear you while we're on the phone?"

"I don't know what you're talking about…"

"We didn't just come here for a surprise. I wanted to see you for myself. Your father thinks I'm paranoid. Your brother is distracted. But I'm not a fool. Never was. Not starting now. And now that I've seen you, I know for sure. You're not telling me something."

The truth is bile rising up in my stomach. Is my mouth quivering? It feels like it. Are my eyes saying something my lips aren't? I wish I could have rehearsed my face prior to this loving shakedown with Manhattan and its many skyscrapers ever-so-slowly rotating behind me.

"I understand that maybe you can't tell me. That hurts, but I'll leave it be. I didn't come here to be the motherly inquisition. I came here to bring you home with us."

"Mom…"

She reaches her hand across the table, takes mine in it. It is smooth and warm and rubbing my palm. Her eyes lock with mine and I feel like a guilty murderer when I break the glance to watch the spires of the city slip out of my range of vision. But if I look back at her I WILL cry.

Because my head is filling with images of my house. My home. My old room, which I'm sure they haven't touched besides dusting the belongings I left behind. And with these images comes a relaxed sensation that rolls over me like a wave of the Pacific Ocean. I can taste the clean air of our living room. I can smell the meals she'd be cooking for me. And I realize, with all the many secrets I've been keeping from everyone in my life, how good it would be to finally unload on someone. But I can't — because then my decision would be made for me.

"Before you fire back, Gully, think about it. Something here isn't right."

"I'm not giving up, Ma."

"Who said it's giving up?" she shoots back at me, like a rubber band suddenly stretched to its breaking point.

"I do!"

"What if it's home that you gave up on? Us? Did you ever consider that?"

No. I guess I didn't. But now I am, and the first thing I think about is Graham. The entire state of California seems inextricably latched to him. My car — in which he rode shotgun (or drove, while I was drunk). My apartment — which he more often than not spent the night in. Our house — which he often visited for Sunday night dinners and watching football with my Dad. But even this, suddenly, seems manageable. Could I coexist with Graham in California?

Probably.

Most likely.

No.

"I didn't give up on home. I'm making something of myself here. It's not perfect, but LA never was either, okay?"

"You can be so damn stubborn, Gulliver." She finally pops the olive in her mouth and munches down on it discontentedly. "What if we bought you a newer car and funded your apartment for a year?"

"It's not about MONEY, Mom."

"Oh please!" she hisses at me. "If you were living anywhere other than Todd's apartment, you'd be singing a different tune. How much is your salary? Do you think you could live in this city without the immense amount of luxury you've been afforded?"

I cannot fight this fight because I cannot tell the truth. If I told her where I'm actually living, and took her on a twenty-second tour of the room that is actually mine, she'd spin around on her argument and suddenly it'd be all about how I'm living in squalor and she won't leave New York until I'm sitting next to her in business class.

"Don't yell, Mom. Please."

Her face crumbles. Her tears follow. My heart breaks on cue. "Gully, I'm just worried about you. All the way out here. By yourself. What if something happened to you? It was so much easier when you were nearby, and with Graham."

"Graham destroyed me."

"You know what I mean. Your entire family is in California. Your friends are in California."

"I have friends here now." Okay, not exactly true. I have one friend, who I met in California. "And I have a life here now." For better or worse, that's the truth. "And I'm doing pretty well, despite what you think you have figured out." Also, strangely, true.

"I hope you're right, Gulliver. It's going to kill me to get back on that plane tomorrow night without you on it."

"You're going to have to trust me, I guess. And know that, if anything ever got too hard, I'd come back home." Though even now, with things as they are, I wouldn't. And I think she can read that in my face, too.

Mom finishes her martini and drops the remaining olive into mine. "Take me back to my room, honey. Your mother is a tired old goat."

CHAPTER 22

Sunday morning arrives pleasantly now that Friday night's alcohol is long gone from my system. Being sober and regret-free is like a new lease on life and I skip from Todd's place to meet Mom, Leo, and Dad in the sky lobby of the hotel. Dad has been up early on calls and, while walking the streets screaming numbers and stuff I don't understand, found a place where he could secure real New York bagels. Leo is munching on his second one — all the while saying there's no difference between these and the ones he can buy in California, the stubborn motherfucker. Mom is back to her cheery routine, giggling uncontrollably at something in a copy of *New York* magazine Dad picked up for her. I'm waiting to see if she'll bring up our conversation or try again to persuade me to come back with them, but that doesn't happen.

We have matinee tickets to see *Wicked*, leaving us a few hours of free time beforehand. Walking through Times Square, my mother wants to take a picture of every street performer — the guy who acts like a robot, wheezing through a whistle he conceals in his mouth; the naked cowboy (who's not really naked, and apparently has his own website); the women on stilts made up to look like the Statue of Liberty.

I take them shopping on 5th avenue and Leo buys a new wallet at the H&M. Dad wants to stop at St. Patrick's Cathedral so we stand in the corridor while he walks up the aisle between the pews to stare up at the world-renowned ceiling. Leo has heard about Madame Tussaud's wax museum and it's all he cares to see. Mom protests, but not too hard, so we walk amongst petrified imitations of celebrities they could see in the flesh on the streets back home. One by one, Leo has Mom capture photos of he and Leonardo DiCaprio, Johnny Depp, and Michael Jackson. I send a picture of myself and Beyonce to Marty, who promises it will be on Facebook in seconds.

From there it's lunch, then to the theater. Our seats are the premium kind that sell for $250 a pop, all of five rows from the stage. Mom says she might move to New York if this is the treatment Todd can provide on a regular basis. I tell her he went out of his way to make this weekend for us, and she swears she'll be sending him a thank you card as soon as they get home.

When we leave the theater, humming some song from Act II, Mom glances at her watch and begins panicking. Their flight departs in three and a half hours and she won't be comfortable unless they get to the airport with two hours to spare, in order to wait in a long line at security that will not actually be there.

"Take us back, Gully? We need to get our things. Don't want to miss our flight! Your dad has work tomorrow."

And so we all walk the five blocks back to Todd's apartment. He is out, so Mom leaves a note on the refrigerator ("Just to hold him over until I can send that card"). Her high spirits are gone and she is silent, her face drawn and emotionless. I've seen this face before: the morning she dropped me off at LAX for my flight to New York. She stood at the gate and wouldn't leave until I made it around the bend and onto the plane (I came back to check, only to find her there, smiling weakly as she waved).

It takes five minutes to grab their bags and make last minute bathroom stops. We take the elevator down to the street. Outside, New York is full of honks and chatter, sun and wind. But we four are silent. I reach out my hand and a cab pulls up alongside us, its trunk popping open before it comes to a full stop.

Hugs commence. First Dad, who pats my back and slips a few hundred dollars into my pocket, whispering, "Get yourself some fall clothes, okay?"

Then Leo, who pulls me far enough into his wall of breathing muscle to suffocate me. "Be good, Gull. I miss you."

They each get into the cab — Leo in front ("Because his legs are longer, honey") and Dad in back. Mom has left the trunk open. She gives me the Look.

"Are you sure, honey?"

"I'm sure."

She sighs again. She's been sighing every minute and a half since the show ended. "Please be careful. Please be safe."

"C'mon, Ma. You'll see me again before you know it. Maybe I'll come home for Thanksgiving."

"You WILL be home for Thanksgiving." Her face challenges me, her eyes squinting.

I laugh. It breaks the awkwardness between us. At least for me. "Yes, Thanksgiving then. And you know I'll call you two times a damn day."

She is hugging me. Her arms pull me in tight. I smell her perfume and sun-tan lotion. "Any time you change your mind, honey." She is crying but hiding it. I am fighting back tears as well.

"You'll be the first person I call."

Her shaking stops and she backs away from me, sniffling and wiping her eyes. "My sweetie!" she performs for Dad and Leo and the pedestrians passing us by. "Now go take a nap, you look like someone dragged you through the streets."

I kiss her and say, "Yeah, that someone was you. Have a safe trip."

The cab slowly drives down 9th avenue, forced to stop before they can clear the red light. Dad is probably cursing the traffic. Leo is most likely on the phone with his maybe-alcoholic girlfriend. Mom is hanging out the window and waving like some 1950's movie star who has just boarded a train and is about to speed beyond the horizon.

I am not yet back at Todd's when my phone comes to life with a text: *"You look too skinny sweetie, eat something! I left you a check on your bed. Use it. xoxo Mami."*

Todd is back in the apartment when I return. He expresses his dismay that he missed out on saying goodbye to my family. I promise he hasn't seen the last of them. On the bed that once was mine is a check for $550, which is about the price of a one-way ticket home when last I checked. My Mom's illegible signature is scrawled across the bottom. Affixed to it is a piece of paper that says, *"Just in case. XO."*

I fold it up, shove it into my wallet, and return to the living room. It feels good to crash onto Todd's couch. And I am now torn: do I stay here and spend the night? It's air conditioned. Free food could be involved.

Or do I get on a train and drag my ass all the way out to Astoria? Marty awaits...

"Wanna stick around tonight?" he asks, his eyes heavy.

"Maybe," I say.

"Well, at least stick around and let's watch *Beauty and the Beast* and order pizza?"

"That I can do."

I text Marty to let him know I won't be over tonight, that the family is staying one more night. I would love to see him, but I'm just so drained.

I fall asleep as the Beast first lets Belle into his expansive library. Well, half-asleep, really. I can still hear the movie and feel Todd readjusting himself on the couch, getting up to answer his phone, letting the pizza guy in. And as I'm nodding off, I feel more relaxed than I have in ages. I had a lovely weekend with my family, Todd and I are chilling like old times, Marty's waiting for me back in Astoria. With my brain just barely aware of a jaunty Disney tune playing in the background, I feel fortunate. I feel blessed.

And then I feel like I have to pee. The urge jolts me out of my sleep.

When I get into the bathroom and let loose, something isn't right. In fact, something is horrifyingly wrong. It burns — like acid tearing through my piss slit. It's unlike anything I've ever felt before. I wince and grit my teeth. I try to stop the flow but then it hurts at the base of my dick. I have to let it out, all the razor blades and flame.

I rush out of the bathroom, grab Todd by the shoulders, and tell him what happened. Like I don't know what this means. Like I'm twelve and haven't sat through high school health courses. I'm praying he'll say it's something I ate, or something else. ANYTHING else.

He looks down at my jeans as if my dick is hanging out and rotting. "Oh. That's not good, bro. That's definitely not good."

Shit.

CHAPTER 23

Embarrassing. Mortifying. I'm an unwilling contestant on the most private quiz show ever created. The whole situation would make a reality show that only Fox could love.

How many partners have I had in the past month? Have I had unprotected sex? Oral? Anal? Do I use recreational drugs? Do I drink to the point of blacking out? I am sitting with a disinterested nurse who has done this one too many times for one too many dumb pretty boys. She is checking off my answers, one by one, on a clipboard. She doesn't even look me in the eye.

All night I kept going back to the bathroom to pee, even when I didn't have to. Hoping the burning was a fluke, that all would be clear. It wasn't the case. Before the fourth time I switched my strategy, trying not to pee at all. That didn't work either. I couldn't decide which was worse: frequent yet brief periods of searing pain, or far fewer but far longer stretches of penile agony. Of course I didn't sleep. Not that I expected to be able to.

I told Stanford I'd be coming in late. He asked if anything was wrong, and I tried my best to convince him that, no, I just had some run-of-the-mill business to attend to. The Chelsea clinic is a brick building in the midst of a garden right by Penn Station. Anyone passing by might think it was actually an old mansion. If only they knew. I arrived so early I had plenty of time to stand outside of the locked doors, smoking cigarettes despite a sign informing me that I wasn't allowed to. Arriving late would mean a long wait or, worse, a chance that they wouldn't be able to fit me in at all. Another 24 hours of urinary torment.

Inside the clinic are echoing empty corridors of outdated tile, rattling dusty fans, and uncomfortable wooden chairs. Yellowing posters on the walls feature photographs of genitals in horrible states of disrepair. Red and seeping growths. Rotting skin. Oozing orifices. I have never been so focused on my dick. I have never wanted to not see another dick ever again so much in my life.

The waiting room quickly filled with other dreary-looking guys, a few of whom I recognize from bars in the neighborhood. None of us met eyes; this is not the place to smile, flirt, and start a conversation. I sat silently in the awkward company of both single patients and couples — where one half had apparently come to lend support regardless of the outcome. Good for them.

Todd, ever the comforting friend, offered to take a half day in order to accompany me, but I told him no. "Relax," he said. "It's either gonorrhea or chlamydia, both get taken care of with a single pill. Happens to the best of us. The worst of us too, you little whore. Think of it like it's a cold... except your dick has it. And the sneezing kills." I know he meant to help, but it didn't work.

After an endless stream of embarrassing questions and equally embarrassing answers, the nurse wordlessly excuses herself to get my test results, slamming the door behind her like I just told her we're getting divorced. I have been poked and prodded, grabbed and massaged. I don't need her shit. I feel disgusting enough without her making me feel like some idiot whore to boot. And all the while, I'm wondering — how the hell did this happen? Why now? Why me?

The only guy I've been with in weeks is Marty, who I haven't told yet — but will as soon as I get my results from the bitch nurse. I'm furious. No, worse — there are no words for the bubbling in my stomach and my sweaty, clenched fists. We'll call it strikes two and three. Maybe he WAS sleeping with someone those days he didn't call me before the Fire Island explosion. Maybe whatever was going on with that guy didn't work out, so he came crawling back — and infected me.

Marty. Every time I think of his face or even his name I want to cry. I want to slap him. The night we spent together has transformed from sexy to sinister in the blink of an eye.

And I couldn't even tell Todd when he asked, "Who do you think gave it to you?" The answer, of course, would ruin everything he and I have rebuilt. In hindsight, I wish I hadn't freaked out like I did — because then I wouldn't have had to tell him about my symptoms. Then he wouldn't be wondering who infected me, as he is most likely doing now. But then again, I wouldn't have known where to go to get treated, either...

The nurse waddles back in. I try to read her face. What will she say? Do I have gonorrhea? Chlamydia? Am I HIV-positive? I think of the guys in the waiting room. Did this happen to them out of nowhere, too? Did a condom break? Did someone cheat on them? Did they end up in a backroom orgy and wake up with the same burning sensation I did? I've slept with a total of four people since coming to New York, and I'm sick already? It's not fair. The boys from the crew make sex a hobby. I never heard of them coming down with something.

Or did they? If my rendezvous with Servando and Rowan had been more recent, I could include them on my list of (four) suspects. But given that my fiery little friend popped up just last night, only a few days after reuniting with Marty, it seems safe to assume that he's my culprit — and that he got it somewhere between when he went back to Allentown and our recent reunion. Mystery solved. Case closed. Fucking bastard.

Finally, after sighing and sitting in the chair across from me with a thud, the nurse speaks: "For HIV, you have tested..."

That last word hangs in the air. Again, I'm in a game show and the prize is that my life DOESN'T irreversibly alter after she spits out the rest of this sentence. Why is she holding out? It's minutes that are going by. Hours. I wonder if she's enjoying this. Can I phone a friend?

"...Negative."

I am relieved only slightly.

The nurse then passionlessly reads through the rest of my results with the same pause right before the punchline. In the end, Todd was right. It's chlamydia. Or it might be. She isn't sure, but the discharge she squeezed out of me like toothpaste from a tube points to the probability. She'll know for

177 / JUSTIN LUKE ZIRILLI

sure in two days, and I can call her for the results.

The unibrowed judgmental cunt finally looks at me for the first time. Her gaze is like that of a disapproving mother. She shakes her head and says, "Please try to be more careful next time." Like I haven't been. Like I've been running around town dipping my bare dick in every orifice presented to me. I nod, fuming.

She gets up and shuffles across the room to a cabinet, throws it open, roots around with a soundtrack of clanging and rattling, and comes back with a bottle. She shakes out two off-white pills into a paper cup and hands them to me. "Take these as a preventative measure. And please do not drink or have sex for at least twenty-four hours."

I swallow like a good boy.

It's sunny and warm when I emerge from the clinic, the polar opposite of my current mood. I want to go back to my apartment and bury my face in my pillow and scream. I feel disgusting. Filthy. Ashamed.

I'm thinking of Marty, at the top of a large chart. Stemming from him are lines to men I don't know (and maybe some I do). The mouth he kissed me with has kissed so many other men, who have kissed so many other men. For all I know, there are six degrees of separation between Marty's ass and Germany's skeeziest bathhouse. I could have been sampling the saliva of meth addicts, HIV-infected porn stars, drag queens, and rent boys. I duck down a side street, look both ways to make sure I'm alone, and vomit in a garbage can. I vomit again.

I have to run to the bathroom when I finally get back to Astoria, after a subway ride that crawled along the tracks, making me dizzier with each stop and start. I shit my brains out. Streams of liquid flying out of me. My stomach is spinning and forcing everything that isn't anchored inside back out again. I crawl from the bathroom to my phone to call Todd. Is this another STD? Do I need to go back and get tested again? No, he tells me, it's because I didn't eat before I took the pills.

How was I supposed to know? That whore nurse didn't tell me anything. I imagine her on her lunch break, perpetually shaking her head about the slutty California transplant with sex disease coursing through his veins. I am toxic.

I thank Todd for his help and hang up the phone.

My next call is to Marty. I scream from the second he picks up. He is prompt-ly crying. He's so sorry. He is sobbing and heaving. He didn't know.

His voice is a whisper: "Are you sure you didn't sleep with anyone else?"

I respond with a scream: "No, I haven't slept with anyone else! Not since we started seeing each other!"

He's whimpering, but I feel no pity for him. Because my shame and self-dis-gust are so much stronger.

"I didn't even know! I'll go get tested, treated. I don't have any symptoms! If I knew I never would have put you in danger. Oh my God, Gulliver. I love you. I love you so much. Please. I would never do that to you on purpose!"

Lies. In my head I don't see just Marty. I see Marty getting fucked by every guy that has ever fucked him. He is on his back, legs spread and in the air with a line of guys stretching beyond the horizon. Each one walks up, whips out his dick, and goes to town. He is a dripping bag full of disease. He put me at risk. I was safe with him and he STILL infected me. I tell him not to talk to me anymore. That I will not see him or say anything to him ever again. That he should be more careful where he puts his dick next time; that he should take a closer look at the cocks he sits on; that I wish I never met him.

It's because of him, I shout, that I lost my friends. My apartment. My dream-come-true life. He came in and like a sexy pack of dynamite, obliterated everything while distracting me with his beautiful eyes. His chiseled face. His gorgeous legs. Pretty poison, sexy cyanide. His inverse Midas touch has turned everything I had to shit. I will not believe a word he says to me now — I heard this all before, with Graham. Denials. Apologies. Proclamations of love. Bullshit. All of it, in the end, bullshit.

Then Marty starts screaming. "Fuck YOU, Gulliver! I will not take responsi-bility for your actions. It takes two to make this shit happen. I didn't even KNOW you were friends with Brayden when you picked me up outside the showcase! And stop being a fucking BABY! People get STDs. It happens. You don't want one? Then start a life of fucking celibacy! Find one man, get tested together, and never sleep with another fucking person for the rest of your life. *Voila!* Problem solved! No more scary clinic visits! You are so fuck- ing immature!"

I am speechless. My breathing is slowing. But Marty keeps on going.

"But something tells me you don't want to do that, do you? Let's not forget that it was YOU who came back to my hotel the FIRST NIGHT WE MET. That was YOUR choice. Your suggestion! You knew I was Brayden's ex! You didn't say anything until AFTER we fucked! After you told me you LOVED me!"

I'm not apologizing. I'm not speaking.

"You're an asshole, Gulliver. You didn't even give me the benefit of the doubt? Fuck off. Now you'll really wish you never met me."

And then he disconnects. Marty is gone. And I am on my bed, starving but too afraid to put any food in my system for fear it'll find its way to the speed tube right back out. I am blinking and staring at the wall. Minutes pass. The anger drains out of me, the fury evaporating. And I realize: I've become Brayden. Or, at least, I'm acting like him. Flying into a frenzy of jumped-to conclusions instead of talking it out? Attacking Marty when I'm just as cul- pable myself? I feel estranged from the words that just flew out of my mouth.

My phone rings. It's Stanford.

I wheeze: "Hey boss, sorry I couldn't come in today. I'll be back in tomor- row for sure, though."

"No you won't."

Stanford's voice is slow, disappointed. I have never heard him use this tone before.

"What?"

"Don't come in tomorrow, Gulliver. I just got a call from Marty."

There goes my stomach. In a blink, chlamydia is the least of my problems. Of course Marty called Stanford. Of course he threatened to seek representation elsewhere if I wasn't immediately fired. Now it's not just the nurse that's ashamed of me, I've earned the disappointment of my now-former boss as well.

"Why would you sleep with him? I said you could have your pick of the hungry actors that came your way. But never. NEVER. The ones we represent. You don't shit where you eat. It's stupid and unprofessional."

"I know." I'm trying not to sound like I'm crying as, once again, my world falls apart. Dollar signs are disintegrating in front of me. My raises, past, present, and future. The months of hard work. The potential. All of it dies right there while I sit on my bed, phone clutched to my ear.

"Maybe if you'd come and told me, said you made a mistake, it was a one-time thing? Or at least given me some kind of heads up that you guys had feelings for each other, so I could have figured out what could be done..." And as he rattles off these possibilities, they seem so obviously like the right thing to do it's a wonder I did otherwise. "But how can I trust you after hiding this from me for so long?"

"You can't," I mutter. It's the only possible response.

Because of my hard work, Stanford will give me one week's severance at my current salary. Nothing of mine is in the office and he would prefer that I not come back. He also asks, from human being to human being, that I not speak to Marty anymore. We can be men about this, he says. He doesn't want to have to threaten me with legal action. I don't want him to, either.

"Stanford, thank you for seeing something in me."

"Good luck, Gulliver."

And then Stanford is gone, along with my job. I'm alone in my room, alone in the apartment. My cell phone, now a portal to ruin, sits by my side. I am blinking quicker, staring at the wall.

Everything happens so fucking quick in this city. One second you've got a sweet job and you're living in a luxury apartment in Hell's Kitchen, and the next...

I pick up my phone and call Todd. I won't be able to afford the Astoria apartment when my salary dries up. And I'm ready to throw in the towel on this whole "making it on my own" experiment. At least I still have him to fall back on.

"Bro."

"Hey." I'm still crying. "I need to talk to you."

"Yeah, I know you do. Brayden just called me flipping his shit. He got a text from Marty."

Oh God. Oh no. Marty is on hyperdrive, a cyclone determined to tear its way through my life until there's nothing left standing.

"Todd, I'm sorry..."

"So it's true. You were STILL sleeping with him. You lied to me — AGAIN. After everything that went down?"

I'm back in Marty's room the night he first got back. We are laughing, tickling each other. He is riding me, telling he loves me. Except now he is reaching behind his back, almost as if to slip me inside of him, but instead his hand reappears, clutching a gun. He's crying. Tears all over his beautiful face. His eyes are drowning in the blue. He's shutting those eyes and slowly pulling the trigger, the gun shivering just in front of my forehead.

Bang.

"I don't think I want to talk to you right now." Todd's voice is a wall of monotone. He could be reading instructions from a VCR manual. "I've got a group of friends who think I've been helping my slutty, backstabbing college buddy maintain a relationship behind their backs. They think I'm in on your stupid shit."

Crying. I'm never, ever going to stop crying. "Todd! No! I need your help..."

There is a prolonged silence and I think that maybe he's already hung up on me. Or maybe he's considering what happened. Digging deep down into that vast store of love he has for me.

He knows he can fix this. He can fix anything. He's King Todd — the undisputed master of the universe.

"Dude. Go help yourself."

And everything shatters.

"Please...?"

My voice is tiny. My head is spinning. My life is ending.

"Oh, and FUCK YOU for bringing me into this. Fuck you, bro."

He hangs up.

Nothing. I am left with nothing. I am in an empty, shitty apartment in the middle of Astoria. An apartment that, in a month, I will no longer be able to afford. My one friend in this city is done with me. The boy I was falling for just systematically destroyed my life with two phone calls. So fast. So ridiculously fast.

I look at my phone. Despite its recent double-delivery of bad news, it can also become a portal that will transport me out of here so quickly and effortlessly; I need only push one button and then it is done. My finger finds the entry in my contacts labeled "Home," hovers over it...

But that is as far as my finger is willing to go right now.

I set my phone aside and feel nothing. I become nothing. I am completely free.

I jump out of bed and take a shower. The water is scalding and I stand under it, my skin turning red from the heat. It stings but I stand defiantly under the jets.

I step on a roach with my bare foot when I get out, dripping.

I dress, do my hair, and steal a few spritzes of Kieran's cologne from his room. My phone, left to wait on my bed, has new text messages. One from a number not in my phone book; the area code is Brayden's. Another from my mom. I text her to let her know I had a great day at work and I miss her already.

I delete Brayden's text without reading it.

I go to the kitchen and open the freezer. Cold smoke belches into my face. One benefit of Kieran's job is that he can easily sneak bottles of the mid-tier booze out of the bar and nobody seems to mind. I crack open a frosted bottle of Svedka and pour it into a glass. It goes down like sour bubbles. But the glass doesn't deliver drunk enough quick enough, so I slap my fist around the neck and start drinking directly from the bottle. I am pacing the apartment, swigging, wincing, breathing, blinking, swigging, pacing, drinking.

When I'm halfway through with the bottle, my cell phone goes off. The message is from Marty.

"Fuck you, you piece of shit. Now I have to go get tested to see if I got whatever YOU picked up somewhere. Go give your guilt trip to whatever slut you ACTUALLY got it from. Brayden told me about the guy on Fire Island."

Oh, right. Him.

I delete the text message and polish off the bottle in three quick swallows. My lips are now numb. I go to the bathroom to pee and it doesn't burn — but I have peed all over the seat and floor. I don't clean it up.

Now nothing matters. My head, my fingers, my throat. All is tingling and bubbling. I'm smiling. I'm laughing! Because this is all so ridiculous.

I'm giddy and drunk and my life can't get any worse than this. I'm alone on a coast hated by everyone who knows me and I can't stand up straight and I'm rolling along the wall on my way to my room. I grab a handful of condoms, they crinkle in my hand. I stuff them into my pocket because if I have no job, no friends, no boyfriend, and no place to live, then I'm fucked. So why not GET fucked and make it literal? New York has ruined me and I'll be heading back to LA before the month is out. Might as well go out with a handful of bangs. And if I give someone chlamydia, well then tough shit for them. They should know better. Like I should know better. I will be karma: give the gift that keeps on giving.

It is black, black dark when I stumble out of the apartment. I crash into a man carrying a pizza box and it lands *smack!* on the sidewalk. I giggle and sprint off. He curses but is too busy checking the status of his dinner to come after me. A driver of some gypsy cab sits on his horn when I dash in front of him and across the street, tripping up the steps to the train platform as I go. The train is once again waiting for me when I make it to the platform after wrestling with an uncooperative turnstile. New York is making it as easy as possible for me to annihilate myself.

I've got the condoms and a blood alcohol level that would break a breathalyzer. I'm Manhattan-bound. And in this state all I want to do is everything I shouldn't because when has "shouldn't" stopped me before? Never. Look where it got me! I'm free for the first time since I flew into this hyperactive, hateful city. New York beat me and I don't care. I don't care about a fucking goddamned thing, myself especially, and this city has made it clear that it feels the exact same way.

On the subway I sit alone. Everyone else has come in groups of friends. They are laughing, sharing silly stories with punchlines I am too drunk to appreciate. I think I see Marty, but it's actually an old woman wearing a hairnet and a pair of glasses that belong on a diner waitress you'd find in a 1950's drive-in. I stare ahead through the windows as Queens zips by, Manhattan in the background. I want to spit and piss all over it. I want to scream: "You win! Are you happy now?"

Once on the island, I fling my way through oncoming clusters of commuters on their way to a madcap night of blackouts and drama. I transfer trains and find my way somehow to the East Village. I come back up above ground to the chilling kiss of misting rain. The streets change from packed and bustling to quiet death as I stumble further east still.

The unshaven man at the door doesn't bother looking at my ID, far more interested in the fact that I am cute enough to be a boon to the establishment. After getting past him I navigate those dirty, steep stairs I once traveled with Stanford the night we were celebrating my promotion. Now they are far harder to traverse. I trip, tearing a hole in the right leg of my jeans. I don't care.

Inside, the bar is empty except for a dash of guys in a far corner and two bartenders who are busy pouring shots for each other. Hard house music is blasting from a vacant DJ booth that looks over the empty dance floor. The walls are lit with red. I feel like I've stumbled into a David Lynch movie.

"Fuckin' dead tonight?" I slur at a burly man with a buzzed head who is leaning against the bar, admiring me. On his arm is a tattoo of a skull on a toothpick resting in a martini glass full of what looks like blood. He smiles at me for a second and I can't tell if he's swaying back and forth, or if I am.

"Back there, cutie." He puts one hand on my shoulder and spins me around slowly, extending his other hand to point.

My eyes slowly follow and see a part of the bar I hadn't noticed. There is a curtain of long black ropes hanging from an archway that spans from one wall to the other. The ropes are writhing, cascading ripples like you might see on a windy day on the Hudson River.

"I'm Sebastian." The man shakes my hand, my whole arm jelly. He holds on a bit too long for my comfort. "Want me to take you back there?"

I spin around and collapse into his chest, turning my head up so I can rest my chin on his sternum. "I'm Gulliver!"

"Like *Gulliver's Travels*?" He thinks he's so fucking smooth. Asshole. I roll my eyes so hard I almost fall over, but he catches me and rights me up. "You're not here alone, are you?"

I shrug.

"You didn't want to bring any friends with you?"

"I don't have any friends," I slur again. I'm not even sure what I've said counts as English, but Sebastian nods, and I can tell he understands.

"Let me guess. You don't have any money, either."

This time I don't answer. That's enough questions for today, nurse. "Take me back there, please."

His sweaty hand engulfs mine and he leads me across the room. I am stumbling and he stops to help me up a few times, laughing and saying, "Don't give up, Gulliver! Almost there!"

The few guys at the bar stand sentinel as I walk closer to those wiggling ropes, which grow larger and fatter in my blurred vision. They are coiling and uncoiling, lifting and falling. They are sponges at a car wash and I am the dirty Toyota on its way to be scrubbed. As I get closer I begin to hear it: moaning. Someone shouts "YES!" Another roars, "Take it, you fucking whore!" Grunts and groans and hums and whines smash into whinnies and growls and screams. The black ropes are alive. How many people are back there? I imagine thousands. On the other side there isn't a room, but an entire new world. Some place where New York can't get me, where I can get lost in the dark forever. I am getting closer and closer.

But I stop. A tiny voice is screaming inside of me. I shouldn't. There's self-destructive and then there's this.

But that tiny voice didn't stop me before and it's not stopping me now. Because I'm too drunk, I'm too horny, and I really don't care what happens tonight or ever.

Sebastian's hand cups my ass. "What do you say, sexy? You wanna show me what you can do?"

Yes. With Sebastian as my guide, I walk through the screaming wall and into the welcoming darkness. The ropes are the first caresses I receive. Cold and sticky, they skim across my goosebumped skin. They're in my face. And then I am beyond them and there is nothing but heat. Movement. The bodies around me are rutting shadows. Ink blots in motion. Monstrous silhouettes. I am being pulled into a world of shadows and those shadows want a piece of me. Here I am.

Hands are on me, snaking out to take hold of my knees, my thighs, my chest. They are hands of all sizes, all colors. Large and sweaty. Skinny and feminine. Wet and dry and hard with calluses. Some scratch at my back, leaving marks that make trails down the sides of my spine. Others gently crawl up my stomach, to my nipples, pinching them like zits. Others go right for the kill and free my cock from my jeans. I am hard and dripping. The hands are hungry and immediately attentive.

The next hour is a blur of arms attached to bodies and faces I can barely make out in the dim red lighting. I am grabbed and fondled, I am poked and prodded. It is my STD appointment from this morning except I get my rocks off at the end. Again and again and again. And no fucking nurse will ever hear about it, shaking her head in prudish disapproval like she never wanted to be used.

Through all of this fucking and sucking and cumming and moaning, Sebastian watches. I can make out his hulking form across the space, leaning against the wall as I'm bent over, sucking off another faceless stranger. But Sebastian doesn't touch. I'm hurt, wondering why I'm not good enough for him. Why he won't take me like all the other sexy shadows? At one point, I wonder if I'm only imagining him there. And then I forget about him completely.

Four times. Four times I cum and I wonder where my seed ended up. On a face? In a mouth? On a leg? Maybe one of the couches against the wall.

Then I wake up. My eyes open and I find I am back outside of the black rope curtain. My drunkenness has been fucked clean out of me. I am not sober, but at least the room isn't tilting back and forth, threatening to knock me off my feet and down the stairs, back down to the street. The bartenders have abandoned their posts and patrons are helping themselves to drinks. The action from the back room has also trickled out onto the floor, the couches, the tables, the bar itself. Two go-go boys are fucking each other with neon footlong tubes.

"Have a good time in there, Gulliver?"

It's Sebastian, in the same place I found him when I first arrived. Same position, too. He is nursing a Heineken and looking me up and down from head to toe. Taking stock.

"I think so, yeah. Fuck yeah." I zip up my fly and notice there's cum on my forearm. I wipe it on my shirt, already wet with sweat, spit, and God knows what else.

"You're pretty hot, have to say." He smiles and offers me his beer, which I shake my head at.

"Thanks."

"I'm not coming on to you, by the way," he chuckles — a "ho-ho-ho" that comforts me somehow, like a pervy Santa Claus. Can I sit on his lap and whisper what I want this year? "But I do have a proposition for you."

Because apparently when God closes a door, he opens a glory hole.

"I'm listening," I say. Or I try to say. I can't tell if those words have left my mouth, or if my mouth is even moving. Because I'm suddenly drunk again. Drunker than before. I am running down a hallway in my own head, a flood of vodka gaining on me as my feet catch in the carpet. I can smell it getting closer, hear it colliding with chairs and tables, upending them. And then it overtakes me. Sebastian is floating away from me — like he is on a conveyer belt pulling him in the opposite direction. His voice is echoing, distant. I cannot even read his lips. And then Sebastian is spinning. He is on his side.

No, wait — I'm on my side. He's standing over me, screaming wordlessly in my face. I wait for a Blackberry to come out of nowhere and end my life.

Finally the ringing subsides and I hear Sebastian shouting my name, asking if I'm okay, but I can no longer see him...

CHAPTER 24

I wake up not knowing where I am. The room is not my own. Not Todd's. It's not Marty's either.

It is larger, for one. Clean, too. Outside the window behind my head, a bird chirps. Further away, kids are laughing. I am in a bed that is as wide as it is tall, and I am alone. From the looks of the sheets tucked tightly around me, I've been alone since I got here. Wherever here is.

Last night slowly comes back to me in still images, like I am flipping through a photo album I'll never show anyone. I think maybe I've been raped — then I recall my activities and realize the soreness I'm experiencing has been asked for and duly earned. Why would someone bother to rape me after I presented myself to anyone and everyone who could get close enough to have a piece?

I cannot remember leaving the bar. Whether by cab or train to wherever this is, that bit of my evening is lost. Maybe that's good.

Strangely, this looks like my college dorm back at UCLA on the day I moved in. There is a wooden desk, a chair underneath. There is a chest of drawers and a wardrobe that, upon careful and quiet inspection, I discover are empty. I pull out the chair from the desk to find my clothing, neatly folded and clean. My wallet is there. My keys are there. My iPhone is there, fully charged.

Okay. This is getting creepy.

I dress and then sit for minutes, afraid to open the door. I'm trying to figure out where in God's name I am. My best bet is to quietly sneak out — unless whoever brought me here is waiting outside. I imagine an old hermit sitting in a rocking chair, a shotgun cradled in his hands...

I send a good morning text to Mom because the last thing I need to deal with right now is her hysterics. I've got more than enough hysterics of my own.

Then I gently open the door.

The fresh, chemical smell of air conditioning assaults my face. In front of me is a spacious, well-appointed, sun-drenched kitchen. Stainless steel appliances that make Todd's place look like a shithole. A table divides the kitchen space from a living room area that boasts a leather sectional, love seat, recliner, and glass coffee table. Generous sunlight pours in from a skylight above and floor-to-ceiling windows throughout the wide open area. My sneakers squeak on the waxed hardwood floors.

I am in the middle of a long hallway. There are three closed doors to either side of the one from which I emerged. A piece of note paper sits on the kitchen table.

"Hey, Gully. Cereals are in the cabinet. Juice is in the fridge. One of the other residents may show up with bagels and muffins if you're lucky. If this morning is particularly harsh, I've left some Advil. Seb."

And now I remember Sebastian. I deduce he must have recovered me after I went down for the count. Is this his place? What did he mean by other residents? This isn't an apartment building, I don't think; chances are it's more of a brownstone, as evidenced by the large staircase at the end of this hallway of doors. I really have to pee, but have no idea which of these portals is the bathroom — and I'm not about to disturb any of the other "residents," whoever they are. If this were any ordinary one-night stand I'd be out the door by now trying to locate the nearest subway. But I'm not sure this was a one-night stand, and I've never been in a place this posh before.

My hunger for cereal is stronger than my thirst for clarity and understanding, so I sit and pour myself a bowl, housing it in record time. I pour a second bowl and notice: it's so quiet here. Am I even in Manhattan? Frankly, I'm not sure I haven't died and gone to some kind of weird heaven. Which, given my devilish behavior lately, I suppose is not the worst possible result.

Pat-pat-pat.

Someone is briskly padding their way from down the hall behind me. A second footfall joins it and suddenly there's a *pat-pat-pat, pat-pat-pat.*

"I'm surprised you're up this morning, girl," comes a young, boyish voice.

A second, queeny voice responds: "Oh, don't EVEN. You won the Hot Mess of the Year award last night, slut."

"Oh no you didn't!" hoots the first voice.

The source of this chatter is two boys about my age in superb physical condition. They are tan and totally hairless, chiseled with long, toned limbs. Their faces have that squinty I-just-woke-up-and-need-coffee look to them. One is a brunette with a tattoo of the astrological Scorpio symbol to the right of his belly button, the other is bright yellow-blonde with a silver crucifix necklace.

Oh, and they're both completely naked.

"Hey, look! A guest!" says the tattooed brunette.

"Did you come home with us?" asks the blonde.

"I'm not sure who I came back with," I say, forgetting about my cereal and trying my best not to stare. "Maybe Sebastian?"

"Look, everyone!" the blonde screams to the empty apartment. "We have a guest!"

My eyes dart around the room to confirm what I already know. Yep... nobody else here. This is getting more and more bizarre.

"I'm Gulliver," I say, for that's the one thing I'm still fairly certain about.

The brunette says, "Gulliver. You're cute. You into morning sex?"

I don't know how to respond to such a forward question. Of course the answer is yes, but I don't even know this guy's name. Granted, I didn't know the name of any of the guys I got it on with last night, either. But for some reason, I am now shy.

"Never mind," says blondie. "It's no big deal. We just have to take care of something."

"Well, don't let me stop you..."

They don't. The blonde falls to his knees with the speed of a dropping sand-bag and takes the brunette's dick into his mouth. "Nothing like a big fat cock to wake you up after a rough night!" he mumbles through his full mouth.

And there I sit, my half-glass of juice losing its chill, my cereal getting soggy, and my dick doing just the opposite as these gorgeous guys go to town on each other five feet in front of me like I'm not even there. They take turns fellating each other, then fall together onto the couch. The blonde reaches between the couch cushions and produces a condom, suits up, and dives in.

I am frozen and completely aroused. What if I joined in? They did invite me. But I'm stuck to this chair. I can't get up to partake, can't get up and leave, either. What is going on? At one point the blonde quickly gestures for me to move a bit to my left. I don't ask questions, just shift my chair and continue staring, my mouth agape.

I am tempted to at least whip it out and address the throbbing going on between my legs. But my hands remain nailed to the table, my eyes stuck on the porno unfolding in front of me. Does Sebastian know this is happening? Before I can pointlessly ponder this tableau the boys erupt into simultaneous orgasm, their moans hitting a fevered pitch and their stuff shooting all over each other and the floor.

"Hope you boys enjoyed that!" the blonde says, blowing a kiss above my head. I spin and see for the first time a camera rigged up to the corner of the kitchen, just above the refrigerator, its red lamplight blazing.

I fumble for my spoon and take a bite, mostly so my mouth can do some-thing besides hang open.

"So," I say through my mouthful of mush. "I think I have a lot of questions."

The boys are very friendly. They tell me all I need to know as they towel off. It turns out I am indeed in a brownstone, but not just any standard brownstone — it is the top secret studio of NewYorkScrewniversity.com. A gay pay-porn website. It has won countless awards since its founding four years ago. It's basically considered a stepping stone for the major gay porn studios out west. There are HD video cameras in every room, including the one I slept in. That one, however, was shut off for the night, says the blonde (whose name, I learn, is Joey Gambit). Eight boys are currently living in the house.

The boys report all of this with no small amount of pride in their twinkling eyes. As I try to grasp the information being thrown at me, the other boys are gradually emerging from their own rooms, each one also as bare as the day they were born. Joey introduces me to all of them. Their names are lost before I can even try to come up with mnemonic devices.

"So Sebastian offered you a gig?" asks Joey. "Gulliver. That's your porn name?"

"No, I think he just let me crash here. I passed out last night after meeting him at a bar."

"Well, he's not one for charity cases. Especially when it comes to boys who black out at gay bars. Plus, you're hot."

Hot is the last thing I'd consider myself amongst this group of naked super-models. In fact, my self-esteem has never been so low in my life. Each of them is a different definition of gorgeous. And they're all nodding that I'M hot? Maybe I'm dreaming after all. I'm probably still passed out on the floor of the bar, the janitor vacuuming around my head. I'll wake up, hung over and groggy; this magical house of lithe, hairless, impeccably tanned naked guys who are a hundred times hotter than me will fade away into the dreamy distance.

Or this is actually happening, and they are joking. I can't compare to these guys. Not by a long shot.

"I don't think so," I say.

"Why not? You're so cute!"

"Not as cute as you guys," I say. I'm blushing in front of a ragtag bunch of buck-naked porn stars, like wearing clothes is abnormal, and I'M the one who has something to be embarrassed about.

"Sure you are," Joey says. "I'd fuck you right now! But you might as well be getting paid for it."

I shrug. How else could I respond?

Before I leave the house, I scribble my number on a piece of paper and hand it to Joey, telling him to give it to Sebastian if and only if he asks for it. Outside it is sunny and warm. Google Maps informs me that I am all the way downtown in the Financial District. The "dorm," from the outside, looks like any other brownstone, nestled cozy-like in a row of similar structures. It takes me fifteen minutes to navigate the criss-crossing named streets and find a subway back to Astoria. In the meantime, I completely lose track of where the dorm is.

When I get above ground and back to Astoria, I have a voicemail.

"Gully! Sebastian. So sorry I missed you. Wish you stuck around. Anyway, Joey said he spoke to you and I want to echo what he said. I'd like you to come work for us. The guys said they really like you, they all want to fuck you. That's the most important part of our audition process, of course — chemistry with the other boys. The rest I think was taken care of last night, so call me. Let's talk pay. Let's talk move-in dates. We think you'd be a valuable addition to the team."

I sit dead still for minutes. Possibly hours. I'm flattered. I'm intrigued. Of course I can't actually do it.

Can I?

What's my alternative? I am in my shitty half-room in Astoria with Kieran and Rosa. No part-time job will pay me enough to stay here, and finding a new full-time job will take weeks I can't afford. The economy has only soured all the more since the last time I looked for work.

But then I'm thinking of Mom, Dad, and Leo. What if they found out? I can imagine Mom kicking me out of the house. Dad forever ashamed of me. Leo shutting me out. Then again, I moved to another borough and they were none the wiser. This doesn't have to be a permanent solution, just a temporary remedy. I can search for jobs and do porn on the side without telling anyone. Then who gets hurt? Even if I found another place, it would never compare to the dorm.

I call Sebastian from the bathroom with the shower running so Rosa and Kieran can't hear the conversation.

"Gulliver! I didn't think you'd be calling me back."

"Well, I am. I'm just not so sure what to say. I never really considered, um, acting before."

"Acting? Nah. My site's not looking for actors — God knows they aren't hard to come by in this town. We just want good-looking boys who do what comes NATURALLY to them around other good-looking boys. I've seen you in action, mister, and you weren't ACTING like you enjoyed that. You were a a star back there. And if you're gonna get off, why not do it with everyone watching, make a buck or two while you're at it?"

"It's just…"

"What? Not enough money?"

"Well, no, you didn't even tell me what you're offering…"

So he tells me, and I'm seeing double. I'd be living rent free and earning three times the salary I made working for Stanford after two raises. My meals will be covered. My wardrobe will be funded by a weekly stipend. I'll be having sex with those visions of perfection I met this morning, massive dicks and swinging balls lined in front of my face.

"Come on, Gully. Give it a chance. If you don't like it, you don't have to stay. All my boys are in open-ended contracts. All I ask for is two-week's notice so I can go scouting again."

Yesterday this all would have sounded ludicrous. I wouldn't have given it a moment's thought. But they say things change in a New York minute here, and an awful lot of minutes have passed since I was in that clinic yesterday at this time. I have nowhere else to go — besides back to California. And come what may, I've already established that as Plan Z. This has all come together too perfectly for me to just dismiss it flat-out.

"Okay," is all I say. It's all I need to say, and probably all I'm capable of saying. More words would find me actually thinking this through and immediately changing my mind. I can hear Sebastian grinning on the other end of the line.

"Okay! Swing by later?" He blows me air kisses and disconnects, leaving me sitting on the toilet in the foggy bathroom, pondering what I've just agreed to do with my life. Gulliver Leverenz, porn star? That doesn't sound right.

I should probably start thinking about changing my name... because why not? I've just gone and changed everything else, haven't I?

ROUND III

CHAPTER 25

If you want to see me naked, you're more than welcome to. But it'll cost you.

My new home, the web-famous NewYorkScrewniversity.com, charges its members a sensible thirty bucks a month (or sixty bucks for a three-month package — what a deal!). For that reasonable fee you can get a glimpse at the lifestyles of the rich and gaymous — the sexiest "college" guys on the east coast.

Of course, anyone who pops my name into a Google search would be shit out of luck. Because on the site, my *nomme de porn* is Marty Brayden — my own little shout-out to the boys who paved my way here in the first place.

And before you judge me for this current line of employment, think it over. If someone told you they'd pay you the equivalent of an investment banker's salary in exchange to live in relative luxury, masturbate frequently, and sleep with some of the hottest men you've ever seen… how easily would YOU say no?

The Dude Dorm is made up of three floors that consist of a sauna, ten bedrooms, five showers, three hot tubs, two living rooms, a kitchen, a dining room, a wrap-around balcony, a private backyard and garden, and a game room. In these rooms, the other dudes and I live our daily lives and fuck each other's brains out under the watchful eyes of men we will never meet.

In exchange for two sex shows and five jack-off sessions a week, I get to live here free of charge. Plus the pay is fantastic — Sebastian's project has earned him a fair amount of cash, since sin industries always thrive during a recession. People are so depressed about their sky-high home loans and the escalating price of everything from tomatoes to Winnebagos that the only way to ease their minds is to get drunk and have a lot of sex. And for those who can't necessarily get horizontal with some hottie whenever they want... well, that group of people matriculates at New York Screwniversity.

I already have a fan club — a collection of faceless screen names, that is. Anonymous monikers like BigDaddyBoyLover and CharlieCumsTwice and BarebackBoyo who click on the weekly schedule to find out when Marty Brayden will perform. I am consistently at the top of the "Most Viewed" section of the site, voted three times into tawdry sexual situations with two of the site's other stars (who also happen to be the first boys I met here). They would be Ryan Roberts, a skinny, tanned boy with spiked brown hair and thick legs, the reigning king of the dorm; and Joey Gambit, a muscle-bound Jersey boy to the umpteenth degree with cornstalk yellow-blonde hair.

I sleep in a king size bed (which allows for more movement when I'm performing) decked out in deep blue sheets and comforters with half a dozen pillows. I shop weekly with a stipend provided by Seb to buy scandalous underwear and skimpy, tight outerwear that now fills my armoire and dressers. I hesitate to call this a dream job, but I have no other words with which to describe it. The pay is absurd. The time I'm actually required to "work" is minimal, and that "work" is the very definition of pleasure. It consists of walking around the house naked, doing whatever I want to do — eat, shower, swim, work out, play video games, talk on the phone, tend to the outside garden, whatever. Sebastian prefers that we are physically aroused as often as possible, which isn't much of a task considering the eye candy wandering the dorm's many rooms and corridors.

Some might worry about the threat of STDs, and for many companies, that might be a legitimate concern. But Sebastian doesn't run all of the world's porn studios, he is solely in charge of NYScrewniversity. And as far as STDs go, I couldn't find a safer place to be. Here we are rapid-tested once a week before we begin our sets. Getting the blood drawn sucks, but knowing we're all healthy makes up for it. To date, there have been no positive STD results at the Screwniversity. I was more at risk having sex with regular New Yorkers than bedding down with my housemates. Despite this, we all have mandated protected sex — because Sebastian values our health above all other things. We are his prized stallions, and he's not about to sacrifice the stable because of a few audience members who'd rather see us go at it raw.

So there it is. Life in the dorms is easy as soon as you learn to forget (or grow to accept and enjoy) the fact that there are cameras everywhere, and behind those cameras are the eyes of thousands of horny men who are more likely than not pleasuring themselves to whatever you're doing — be it showering, sleeping, or making a peanut butter and jelly sandwich. For the first two weeks I couldn't take a shit in the house because I was too busy thinking: I'm being watched. Sick fucks are jerking off while watching me defecate. I would instead take care of my business at a Starbucks a few blocks away. But three weeks ago, it was pouring and I just didn't have it in me to make my fecal trek. So I dropped trou and shat for a fawning audience — some of whom actually emailed me to ask what had taken so long. Since that day, everything has been that much easier.

And despite the illusion of spontaneity members expect from a "dorm," Sebastian runs a tight ship. He circulates a weekly schedule to let us know what we're doing with whom when and in what room. We're always on time. Wouldn't you be, if this was your job? I'm only expected to be in the house for five conscious hours a day when not performing, but there is incentive to stick around longer — Sebastian pays overtime. Also, if I decide to do a pick-up (which entails having extra, unscheduled sex), there is a bonus there, too. By being so generous in free time and rewarding of extra effort, Sebastian has created a place that is always teeming with man-meat, shaking with sex. No wonder he's making money hand over fist.

He's a total professional, too. Sebastian pays each of us on the books. We have W-9s signed and filed (under our real names, of course). We are taxed weekly and receive full health and dental benefits. We have bank accounts and direct deposits. He's even working on getting us 401(k)s. The operation is more airtight than even my last job for Stanford's agency. Nuts, right? If someone had approached me months ago and told me that web porn was as legitimate a business as any corporate 9-to-5, I would have checked their forehead for a fever.

I was driven here by desperation, sure, and planned to leave almost immediately. But as I first worried, there simply were no design jobs to be had. I sent the cover letters, I attached the resumes. No one got back to me, and Sebastian kept finding more excuses to pay me more money. And when you don't have to pay for room, board, food, utilities, or even clothing, that money stacks up faster than a snowdrift in Tahoe. So it looks like I'm staying, for the time being. I'm not at all troubled by this.

Besides our weekly government-sanctioned paychecks (with a legitimate if somewhat obvious business name: College Buddies, LLC), we also receive PayPal checks funded by voluntary online donations from our visitors — the digital equivalent of a businessman stuffing singles into the jockstrap of a go-go boy. Except our donations are usually a lot more than a buck or two. In any given week, I can make up to nine hundred dollars from kind strangers who love the size of my cock and hope I'll respond to their email requests to let Ryan Roberts and Joey Gambit double-dick me. I don't think I'll go that far — then again, I never thought I'd go this far, either.

When I'm not on the clock I wander the streets of the Financial District, trying to get a feel for my new neighborhood. The gay nightlife scene is only just discovering this no-man's land, still haunted by the falling of the Twin Towers. A new club just moved in a few blocks away — its management now in their fourth home. Just like me. So once again, it seems I have been saved from losing my battle against New York City. I'd say there's a horseshoe shoved up my ass, but honestly, that's probably the only thing that hasn't been up there lately.

And I don't have to worry about calls or texts from Todd or Brayden or Marty or any of the crew anymore. The moment my funds allowed (it took all of five days, really), I cancelled my phone contract, moved to Verizon, and bought myself a fancy Droid X. When asked if I wanted to transfer my number, I kindly told the woman behind the counter no and watched as a new telephonic identity was borne out of thin air. I promptly texted Mom and Dad and Leo, letting them know I had lost my phone and this was how they could now reach me. Then, hedging my bets, I dropped a postcard addressed to Todd in a mailbox. On the cheap, shiny stock featuring a glamour shot of the Statue of Liberty and the capitalized, italic words: "*I LOVE NEW YORK*," I wrote the following:

"*Todd,*
If you wonder where I am, don't wonder. If you don't care, don't care and throw this away.
See you when I see you, assuming you ever want to see me again. Please don't call my fam.
G."

I left no return address.

I figured the name change would deter my family from ever finding me online (Mom loves Google and knows how to use it). But just in case, I also underwent a small visual transformation. First, I dyed my hair — bright blue ("Neon Blueberry," to be exact). Joey Gambit helped me pick the color and administer the follicle treatment. We turned the bathroom into a wall-to-wall Smurf stomach, but Sebastian didn't mind because viewer numbers were huge. We were innocent and cute, he said, showcasing a very Bel Ami-esque quality that his members adored. Sebastian even suggested I get an eyebrow or tongue ring to complete my evolving ensemble. I got both.

On Tuesday morning of my fourth week I went into a small sterile shop in Chelsea and let the bear-hairy, oddly soft-spoken man there punch a hole above my right eye and in the center of my tongue. The pain was extreme, but it didn't hold a candle to a Blackberry attack — or the acrid sear of chlamydia. While waiting for the deed to be done, I had the sudden thought that maybe a tattoo would be nice also. Someday.

I completed my new look with what is still the scribbly, faint beginnings of a chinstrap — a thin path of very light brown hair that parades from one ear to the other, along the narrow line of my chin. This part was not easy, because my body and face never really expressed the desire to grow hair and, until now, I never asked this favor of them. The other boys in the house laugh at me, since most of them have to shave and wax and Nair to keep their bodies so sinfully smooth. For me, this state comes naturally. And so they are glad I am frustrated daily, peering into the mirror and all but taking a ruler to my face to determine if there's been any progress.

Add to the piercings, dye job, and chinstrap a pair of bright blue contacts and you have the full transformation of Gulliver Lerverenz, Los Angelino, to Marty Brayden, up-and-cumming New York City gay porn star.

This metamorphosis is probably what made me so popular in the eyes of the website's many visitors — I am a punky-looking twink who loves to get fucked by the biggest dicks swinging around the dorms. I regularly receive emails from my fans offering me large sums of money to meet them for weekends in exotic locales. Sebastian is not opposed to this, as long as I give him a cut for the lost screen time. I haven't done this yet, but anything is possible.

As days pass, I look in the mirror (with hundreds of fans looking at me look at me) and hardly recognize myself. I think about Todd and the crew. Stanford and (the real) Marty. My family. Even, every few days, that asshole

Graham. Would they recognize me? Would they want to recognize me? I imagine not. Not unless I sat right in front of them and let them stare awhile, pick apart my features. But on a subway or jam-packed avenue, I'd just register as some cute, freaky-haired punk kid in the crowd. I like this idea — flying beneath New York's radar. As long as I stay unnoticeable, even the city won't recognize me. So it can't take another shot at sending me home.

I've earned myself another fresh start. Third time is a charm, right? God bless this chaotic, crazy, sinful city. You can reinvent yourself every damn day if need be, and make a hell of a living doing it.

CHAPTER 26

It is a run-of-the-mill Wednesday afternoon and I am chilling with a handful of the other dorm dudes, eating lunch. Sebastian sent the pizza delivery boy unannounced. I've just about gotten used to the many pleasant surprises he throws in our general direction, but even this was unexpected.

(Contrary to what you'd expect to happen in this scenario, we did not all fuck the pizza guy.)

I sit next to Rowell Adrian, one of the good ol' boys of the dorm. He is the shortest of us, a buzzed-headed, tight-and-toned package that makes up for his height with the length and girth of what lies dormant beneath his Diesel briefs. He is in the process of showing me a new phone widget that Sebastian uploaded to our phones earlier this week.

"Technology, shit," Joey says through a bite of white pizza. "I don't get it. I think I was born in the wrong century."

"It's not that hard," Rowell says. "Look. You just press 'sign on.' After you put in your password, it'll remember it."

I do as I'm told and the screen comes to life with a control panel of candy blue buttons. Each one has a label that corresponds with one of the rooms in the dorm.

"Good, now just press any of the buttons." He is gently running his fingernails along my naked back. It feels like heaven, like Jesus himself is massaging me. If I could somehow have someone feed me pizza simultaneously, this might qualify as one of the best moments of my life. I press "Living Room."

A live video stream fed by the camera focused on us appears on my screen. So this is what all of those thousands of members are seeing right now. Looks pretty boring if you ask me. Next to the video is a column that says "Viewers" and beneath it, a slowly rising number, which is now at 453.

"Seriously?" I ask through a bite of salad. "Four hundred and fifty people are watching us eat lunch?"

"It would be more," Joey says. "But I think Coti and Matt are showering together."

"How boring are their lives if this is what they're doing for entertainment?" I ask.

"Be nice," Rowell says, scratching the back of my head. "Not everyone gets to spend their days in a Dude Dorm."

"Whatever. They can't hear me," I mumble. "Until someone turns the volume on, I can say whatever I want!"

"Plus," Joey says, "it would be a lot more if one of us did something sexy."

"Hey, guys, how do you like this?" yells Chris Van Cleave, the newest addition to our gang — having recently moved in three weeks ago. The tall, wire-thin, red-haired boy stands up on his chair and drops his pants, exposing his goods for the four cameras stationed at different corners of the kitchen and living room. Moments later, on the widget, the number under "Viewers" begins to slowly climb.

"How do they know?" I ask, amazed.

"Chat rooms. Message boards. Word spreads fast. Come on, Chris, tease 'em a little more, you slut," Joey says, jumping on my other side to watch my phone screen. Now both Joey and Rowell are stroking the nape of my neck. My eyes are getting heavy.

"You guys keep that up and WE'LL be the show that gets the viewers pouring in," I murmur.

Chris hops over to the coffee table and begins to sway his hips to a synth horn solo he makes up himself. He swings his limp, hefty dick around counter-clockwise in a speedy circle, pumping his fist. All I can think is: if he smashes his balls into his leg, it's gonna be a shit show. But this doesn't happen. Chris' faux-innocent all-American freckled face is precious, a mix of seduction and sweetness — good girl gone bad. He pinches his nipples and licks his teeth and starts beat-boxing as his dick gets hard.

The numbers are skyrocketing.

"What's everyone laughing about?" asks Matt Mager, entering the living room with a monogrammed towel wrapped around his head (and none around his waist). Coti Tyler comes up right behind him, equally disrobed.

"Testing out the new widget," Joey says. "And seeing how much of a crowd Chris can drum up."

"What the hell?" Chris says. "I'm past due for my show any way." He slows his spinning and instead works himself to the point of full-on erection — an astounding sight, of course (no boy in the house is allowed to be under seven inches, and Sebastian prefers eight and up). The number of onlookers triples.

"Wow, look at them go!"

"Whatever," Coti rolls his eyes. "It's just because our shower scene is done."

"You wish, bitch," Chris gasps through clasped teeth.

"Credit where it's due," Joey says, popping Chris' dick in his mouth for all of five seconds. Chris' eyes close and his body quivers in response. Then, after removing it, Joey orders, "Now sit down and finish your lunch."

"One sec, I can't stop now," Chris says. "Anyone want it?" He spins 360 degrees on the coffee table, aiming his dick at each of us. We all recoil, pulling away, yelling.

"Not me!"

"Chris, no!"

"This shirt is new!"

"I just showered!"

"Don't get any on the pizza!"

"Hit me," Rowell says, walking up to Chris. "I have to shower anyway."

So Chris gasps, stops breathing for a few seconds, and pumps out all over Rowell's face. Rowell's eyes are closed, his cherubic face doused in pearly white Chris juice. It looks like a mix of boogers, glue, and spider webs. I am laughing and completely turned on, which is a great descriptor of every day here.

"Thanks," Rowell says. "Gully, teach the boys the widget while I wash this shit off my face. God, Chris, did you eat asparagus last night?"

"Funny," Chris pouts, pulling up his underwear and returning to his half-eaten lunch.

The number on the widget slowly trickles lower as the viewers wait to see if any of us will decide to hop up and improvise another scene, while others flee for the bathroom feed in hopes that Rowell starts a vignette of his own. I click the "Bathroom" button and see that Rowell has done just this. He is flexing in the mirror, admiring his muscles while using Chris' stuff as lube for his own jack-off session. Sure enough, the viewer numbers are speeding to the top.

Today we boys are on the clock for another two hours, at the end of which the visitors have decided that Joey Gambit and I will reprise our sex scene from my first day in the house. "God, I'm going to get tired of you, Marty," Joey said upon seeing our weekly schedule.

Even though I chose the name for myself, it still stings when I hear it. While sticking my tongue out at Joey, I think of Marty. I imagine he spent the week auditioning. Hell, for all I know, he's already cast in something and I'll see his fifty-foot face grinning at me from a Broadway billboard within the month. Because that sort of shit happens to me. Because I would be that lucky.

But, on the other hand, who cares? It's not like I'm unhappy where I am, right here in this gay Garden of Eden.

When our lunch is cleaned up, I bring my laptop out to the living room to see what's going on online. I have hidden my Facebook profile from basically everyone. On there, I'm still Gulliver Leverenz. In my photo my hair is still blonde, my face unpierced. There are a few comments on my wall from various frenemies on the West Coast. Where have I been? Why am I not updating? It's been weeks since I've said anything. I update my status with: "*Another gorgeous day in NYC… love it!*" Then I sign off.

After that I fire up Photoshop, where I am working on an idea I had for the NYScrewniversity logo. The current one is a hideous and boring beast — a Helvetica font in rainbow colors in front of a plain black rectangle. My versions play with some more collegiate fonts, some lighter, less offensive colors.

Sebastian texts me to meet him in his office — the only room without a camera because, as he puts it, "People aren't paying hard-earned money to see a daddy like me hulking around. It would ruin the mood." In fact, there are no cameras on the path Sebastian takes from outside the house all the way to his office. I've told him he has nothing to be modest about, but this is always followed immediately by his trademark "ho-ho-ho" and an immediate dropping of the subject at hand. Rumor has it that Sebastian himself used to be in porn until he discovered he could make a ton more money behind the cameras.

Sebastian lets me into his office on the first knock. It's a large carpeted room with floor-to-ceiling windows that look out on our backyard. The walls are lined with bookcases filled with tomes I've never looked at, along with framed photos of Sebastian and his husband Bud and their two dogs on what appears to be a ton of very exciting vacations. Sebastian's desk — a large restored oak panel — is flanked by exotic plants and flowers he lavishes with love and water every hour or so. Between two bookcases across from his desk is a large panel of screens — the variety of which you'd see in your typical villain's evil lair. Each screen corresponds with one of the house's cameras.

"Gully, I couldn't help but see you were playing in Photoshop?" he asks, not looking up from his computer screen.

"Yeah?" My guard is up. Was there something in my contract that forbade the use of Adobe products?

His eyes meet mine, his chin dropping into his hands as it often does when he's escorting a thought from his brain to his mouth. "How good are you?"

"I mean, I'm pretty good. Here, check out my portfolio. Most of the stuff is old, but I've added some new work recently, since I started having all this free time," I say, as I lean over him and fire up his computer.

"No shit," Sebastian says, his eyes burning holes through the monitor as he scrolls and enlarges, taps and clicks. "You did all of this?"

"I was a graphic design major in college?" I ask, rather than say, as if Sebastian will be the sole decider of whether or not this is true.

"This is great! You should have told me you had this talent sooner!"

I smile, watching as my promos, logos, web mockups, brochures, posters, and stickers zip by on the screen. It's like a visual buffet and Sebastian is gorging himself.

"I may have yet another gig for you. Paid, of course."

"Well, since you brought it up, I've actually been working on some revisions to your logo." I proudly hoist my laptop up so he can see the work. "They're just drafts right now, but…"

"Are you kidding me? These are awesome!" Sebastian jumps up from his desk to grab the laptop and scroll through my logos. "I don't know which one to pick!"

I am speechless, all smiles, and blushing I am sure. I realize it's been a long time since I got a compliment that wasn't related to the way I look or fuck, but rather, an actual skill.

"Tell you what. Finish doing whatever you were going to do to these, then tell me which you like best. We'll get it up all over the place right away. Okay?"

"Yeah, sure! Thanks, Sebastian."

"Thank me nothing. This is gorgeous. Great work."

"Marty! Get your tight ass over here!" Joey shouts from up the stairs and down the hall.

I sigh dramatically and say, "A blue-haired bottom's job is never done."

"Knock 'em dead," Sebastian says, patting my butt and pushing me out the door. "And get me that logo ASAP, Vincent Van Go-Go!"

CHAPTER 27

Some companies have dress-down Fridays, encouraging employees to wear jeans and comfortable shirts and take the day just a little easier. Since dress-down at the dorm would involve us peeling off our skin and walking around as skeletons, Sebastian instead gives us the entire evening off and encourages us to go out and get plastered, often leaving money on the table to fund our exploits. It's not entirely charitable — his hope is that we come home with a date, get him to sign a release form, then fuck him senseless when the cameras go back on at 3 AM. According to Joey, these guest stars appear more often than one might suspect — because it's a compliment to sleep with a porn star, and an even better compliment to actually be one for the night.

To date I haven't brought anyone home. I've been teased endlessly about this, but I fend it off saying no one at the club is hot enough to compare to what I get day in and day out at the house. The truth is far more emo — I simply just can't have non-porn sex yet. Even making out with someone at a club immediately brings visions of Marty to mind, and any chance I have of sustaining an erection is obliterated in seconds. Why this doesn't happen with my dorm boys is beyond the limits of my own internal psychologist. It's just a fact I've learned to deal with.

At 8 PM sharp the house's cameras switch off and, on the site, all screens transition to a message that says we are off to have "college dude fun in NYC," but we'll be back after 3 AM. There is a link next to this that sends our visitors to the donations page and video and photo archives to keep them orgasming in our absence. A stack of hundred dollar bills — one for each of us — waits on the table by the front door with a handwritten note on scented stationary telling us to have fun and not to come back too late, unless it's with someone else.

The evening is warm but breezy, a salty-smelling wind coming in from the South Street Seaport. It is the middle of August and the streets are clogged with twenty- and thirty-somethings en route to their evening's entertainment. From open windows and doors we hear live bands playing their opening chords, drunken karaoke participants warbling hits from the 80's, the clink and scrape of forks and knives in countless cafes and restaurants. We boys walk the streets, earning the wanton gazes of total strangers. To them we are your run-of-the-mill clan of sexy guys on their way out to get crunk. We hop into three cabs and are West Village-bound — to a one-time party that has advertised that thousands of dollars will be dropped from the ceiling at 1 AM. Not that we need the money. We're actually going to this party by special request from Sebastian — his best friend and sometime business partner is helming it, and he wants us to meet him and get a feel for the space.

"Big things are on the way," Sebastian cautioned us with a bit too much intentional foreshadowing.

Joey, Chris, and I are in the back of one cab, windows down, air blowing in. The television is broken and the driver is screaming into a Bluetooth headset. Chris floats the idea of us having a three-way next week, but only after heavily promoting it. The scene proposed isn't an innovative one, but the aggressive advertising is. Joey and I think this is a great idea. We know Sebastian will love it too.

Our three cabs wind through the confusing named (versus numbered) streets, running red lights sometimes, almost taking out pedestrians at others. Back when I lived in Hell's Kitchen, the crew made sure to never venture this far "off the gay grid," despite the fact that some of the hottest parties made their home down here. Without my phone, I could quickly get lost here for hours. This labyrinthine setup makes me feel safe, ensuring that I'll never be spotted amidst the beautiful buildings and cobblestone streets.

And yes, that is still a fear of mine. While I have come to love my new calling, I am still constantly afraid I'll bump into one of the old crew. That they'd recognize me through all of this blue and all of these piercings. And then what? What would they do if they found out about my new line of work? Call my parents? Roll their eyes and lose whatever remaining shred of respect they had for me? Too many questions — none of which I'm interested in answering any time soon.

Sebastian's friend's party is raging in some huge space I've never been to but probably passed a number of times since I came to New York. I also have no idea how we got here, despite being completely sober. The street is empty — lined mostly by what appear to be vacant warehouses. The club itself is one of said warehouses, identical to the others except the brick exterior has been painted tar black and above the entrance hangs a giant billowing flag emblazoned with a rainbow-colored skull on both sides. Bass shakes the sidewalk all the way to the adjoining avenue. A line of gay men wraps around the block. As with most clubs we visit on our nights off, we walk right past this mass to the front and are escorted inside by the doorman.

"Why do they get to cut in front of us?" demands a curvy-hipped boy in a shirt that stops above his belly button.

"You want to get in tonight?" the drag queen guarding the door barks.

"Yes."

"Then shut the fuck up, bitch!"

She turns to us. "Go right in, boys. Michael is upstairs." I realize that I have never had to wait outside of a club at the mercy of a disinterested doorman, praying for entry before my fingers fall off from the chill. It's a privilege I am sure very few newcomers to this city enjoy immediately.

Inside the party is packed. The drinks are overpriced and strong enough to burn your lips off — our hundred extra dollars won't go far. I reach for my wallet before Joey stops me. "Don't even think about it, Marty."

Joey leads us through the three floors of impeccably dressed and insanely drunk crowds. I notice so many people I remember from what probably qualifies as my past life. Actors from the slush pile. Party people from Todd's events. Our eyes meet briefly, but the combination of my recent physical transformation and the potency of the booze makes it so that the fleeting moment of potential recognition fizzles immediately.

After much walking, we land in the VIP room at the top of the club, hidden on the far side of the dance floor. The room must have once been the office of the owner of the building, since converted in the fast-fabulous style of so many parties that take over a space temporarily. The cinderblock walls are masked with curtains, decorative rugs are strewn about the floor, and couches are randomly placed throughout, as if deposited this afternoon by distracted deliverymen. The host of the party, Michael Porcelain, makes himself known the second he sees us. He is a big fan of our site and best friends with Sebastian, and he welcomes us in with an immediate flurry of activity and issued orders, seeing to it that we are treated like royalty.

"Get these boys drinks!" he howls. "I don't want to see a single empty glass tonight. Whatever they need, get it for them! I don't care if they ask for fried chicken or a blow job, *capice?*"

The VIP lounge is just as packed as the rest of the club, but here the drinks are free, sponsored by a new brand of caffeine-infused gin served by cocktail waiters wearing nothing but cutoff jeans and skinny black ties. The crowd is made up of the who's who of the gay elite. I recognize two guys from TV; Joey nods and puts a finger to his mouth before telling me he's slept with both of them. He then puts his mouth to my ear and points out the other celebs I haven't noticed — a host of some reality show on ABC, a director of action movies, three anchormen from Fox News, and two congressmen from districts in the Midwest.

Michael Porcelain is one of those Chelsea-Boys-turned-Chelsea-Men. He wears a pair of pink sunglasses indoors, his ears amply studded, his hair proudly gray, and he is double-fisting sponsored caffeinated gin drinks. "Fucked up AND awake, this shit is brilliant!" He offers each of us a bottle, which we happily take.

Drunk comes quick and Rowell says it's time to explore. Joey, happily relinquishing his power, tells him to lead the way. Michael has his shirtless waitstaff give each of us a bracelet for easy reentry to the VIP lounge, telling us to come and find him if we require anything — more booze, drugs, a boy or two. None of us bother to tell him about Sebastian's strict anti-drug policy (we're tested weekly for that, too).

Back downstairs, the main dance floor is surging with activity under a blanket of ear-bleeding bass. It is roughly half the size of a football field, its ceiling as high as Madison Square Garden's. On the stage is a live sex-ish show with two go-go boys stripping to nothing and fondling each other. To the boys and men on the dance floor, it is something to behold — they desperately scramble to capture the scene on camera phones, elbowing each other to get as close to the stage as possible. To us, it's just another couple of boys making a living.

"Just wait until we do our show here next month," Joey laughs. "They better have paramedics on staff for all the heart attacks."

"So that's what Sebastian was being all vague about," I say.

"Yep. Big blow-out event. He and Michael have been working on it since before you got here. It's going to be a sexy shit show. *NEXT Magazine* cover story material."

Above our heads, aerialists swing back and forth on heavy-duty fabrics fastened to the ceiling. They are pure muscle, making even my hunkiest dorm mates look anorexic. Too much muscle, I think. If they didn't break my bed when they sat on it, they'd break me in half by the time I got ahold of their suit-of-armor appendages. Drag queens promenade around us, all under Michael's employ, paid merely to look overdressed and insult the clientele. Some new pop diva is performing with naked backup dancers at 2 AM. I have no idea how our event can outdo tonight's, but I'm sure if anyone can make it happen, it's Sebastian.

"I can do that," Chris says, pointing at one of the aerialists back-flipping over our heads. "I just don't want to."

Looking past Chris' smile, I catch the eyes of a boy with shoulder-length blonde hair. He is twenty feet away but I can see his face clearly between the shoulders of two other guys between us. My breath is gone.

His shirt is off, and with good reason — he has a tight, toned swimmer's body that should never, ever be hidden under clothing. He smiles and winks at me and I feel like I might shoot a load directly into my pants. He's fucking me with his eyes and I'm letting him. He dances with a short, stocky girl who might as well not exist. Her hair is half-black, half-pink. I imagine her working at an indie record store, snorting when people ask her who Arcade Fire is. But the guy. I want him.
And I'm shocked that I want him — it's been months since I've wanted anyone.

I smile at him. He looks around to make sure that no one else is making eyes at me. I shake my head and point at him — YOU, gorgeous. I'm talking to you. He coolly throws his head back and to the right, beckoning me over. I walk as though I'm in a trance, narrowing myself to get through the crowd, leaving my boys behind me.

His name is Tracy, I think. It's hard to make out what he's saying over the music. We spend some time pretending we can hear each other before we settle for dancing up on one another. His girlfriend all but disappears in the crowd — no doubt heading home pissed that she got ditched. (I'm sure this isn't the first time it's happened.) I was worried she would prove to be an adversary in my quest to get him; clearly I gave her far too much credit.

Tracy and I are rubbing together, sweat waterfalling from our bodies, mixing molecules. My shirt is off. And then we are kissing, my tongue ring clacking against his teeth in a way I learned from a history of making out with Rowan. It shocks Tracy at first but he adapts quickly, figures out how to give the metal the right of way, learns how to appreciate the tiny shiver it creates when it clangs the back of his teeth. He is driving me crazy. I want to take him to a corner and have my way with him, let him have his way with me.

An hour later, Joey emerges from the crowd, pointing at an invisible watch. He makes eyes at Tracy. I nod, and whisper to my first guy in so many fucking nights: "You wanna get out of here?"

His response is a deep kiss and a firm grasp of my hand as I lead him out of the throng.

CHAPTER 28

We take four cabs home to account for our extra guests. Each of the dorm boys made a big, dramatic show of the fact that Marty is actually coming home with someone tonight. Punches and pushes were doled out accordingly. Tracy seemed pleased that this wasn't a common occurrence, making an assumption about my relative chastity that will be cleanly annihilated before the night is through.

It is late enough that the streets in the Financial District are dead silent, ensuring us a speedy trip home. Tracy is clearly confused — well, drunk and confused — by the fact that these other stunning men are all walking back into this one brownstone with us. Maybe he thinks we are part of some sexy cult that's going to sacrifice him to our god of gay beauty. I wonder how I'd react if I were in his situation. Would I walk into the brownstone?

Who am I kidding.

Tracy is speechless and wide-eyed when he first sees the dorm's interior. I take him on a mini-tour through the space, showing him the rooms, grabbing a bottle of water from the fridge for each of us. As we go from room to room we pass my other housemates, giving similar tours to their impressed one-night stands. Until tonight, I never took part in this ritual. I would walk back to my room, jerk off if it was on the schedule (and sometimes still when it wasn't), and go to bed to the stereo sounds of sex all around me. Not tonight. It's exciting to finally be a part of this hallowed tradition. We bring our guests to the living room where there's a beep and the lamplights on the cameras spring to life.

"Smile!" Joey says. "You're on candid camera!"

The other boys are confused, their heads spinning this way and that. Except for one — Ryan's take-home — who must have been briefed earlier in the cab, or has been to the dorm before. He's just grinning goofily in anticipation.

"What's going on?" asks the guy Rowell brought back. He is a dark-skinned Latino with perfectly-shaped eyebrows and a head that is completely buzzed to the skull minus sweeping bangs spiked out from his forehead.

"Ever heard of NewYorkScrewniversity?" Rowell asks.

The other boys have, and can't believe that they are here.

"No," says Rowell's guy. "What is it?"

"Are you too drunk to take a guess?" Joey asks, his hand absently stroking the chest of the guy he brought home — one of the buff bartenders from the VIP lounge.

Rowell's guy blinks and stares ahead. I wonder if maybe he's on something besides too many drinks and far too much dancing.

"Porn," I speak up. "It's a gay porn website."

All eyes on me.

"What? Someone was going to have to say it."

Everyone breaks into uncontrolled drunken laughter. Someone spills a drink that nobody moves to clean up.

"Seriously?" Rowell's date breaks in.

"No, we just have these cameras all over the place because we're extremely protective of the coffee table," Chris says with a condescending smile.

"You're for real right now?" He's blinking quicker, looking at the cameras like they're part of some elaborate hoax that he hasn't quite figured out yet.

"Yes. New York Screwniversity. Google it when you get home. Or check XTube. We've got trailers on there," says Joey.

"I don't know..." Chris' date wavers, clearly tempted. "I have a future modeling career to consider."

Chris just looks at him for a long moment, one eyebrow raised. "Really?"

His date thinks it over, looking at the floor. "Hey, it could still happen."

"You're fucking prostitutes!" Rowell's guy jumps up from the couch, backs his way to the kitchen, measuring us up.

Rowell's head hangs down. "Jesus, sorry guys. I thought I told him in the fucking club."

"No you didn't!" Rowell's will-be zero-night stand shouts. "I wouldn't go home with a slut like you if I knew that shit!" He backs himself up into the kitchen counter, knocking over a full bottle of caffeinated gin that shatters on the floor.

"Party foul." Joey speaks through rolling eyes. "Feel free to leave, the door locks automatically."

"Excuse me for having some fucking self-respect!" the guy yells, flinging his finger into the air like a desperate disciplinarian. "All of you are disgusting."

"Whoa, chill out there, Captain Drama," Joey says, his guard coming up. "If you're not interested, you can just go. No harm done, okay?"

"No, there IS harm done!" the guy says. "You're the reason we can't get married! You and your slutty site, and the other thousand just like yours. YOU'RE THE REASON people think we're nothing but sex-starved, amoral monsters!"

"So you were coming back with me to play chess?" Rowell asks, his eyes lost in the back of his head.

The rest of us are silent. Some quietly snickering. Tracy squeezes my hand hard, reminding me that he's been there the whole time. Rowell's freak is frothing at the mouth, his voice straining to break out of his face.

"Disgusting. All of you! And you perverts, too!" he screams at one of the motion-sensitive cameras that has located him. In a blur of activity he jumps up and yanks down the camera, its wire guts shooting all over the place, slamming the high-tech toy to the floor. Heaving, he pulls his leg back and punts the camera straight down the stairs. I wonder if Sebastian can see this. I wonder if he's in the building. Is shit about to go down?

The guy gives us a good, hard middle finger and stumbles down the stairs, slamming the front door behind him. Rowell fires up his iPhone and checks the front door camera, catching the fuming Latino for a split second before he disappears. "Well, I'm sorry about that, boys. Talk about a boner-wilter. Guess I'll be going solo tonight. Assuming I can even get it up."

"Ridiculous," Joey says, turning to his date. "In the mood for a third?"

The bartender shrugs, checking Rowell out for a hot second and clearly approving of the prospect. "Sounds good to me." They help Rejected Rowell up and lead him out of the living room. With the drama behind us, we go our separate ways.

I lead Tracy by the hand to my room. I close the door and rub his shoulders. "Sorry about that."

"Whatever," he laughs. "Clearly you have better taste than your dorm buddy."

He kisses me, and my insides explode. I don't want to stop, but my professional side pops up, refusing to let me go ahead without doing what must be done. I stop temporarily so I can pull out the contract Sebastian keeps in piles in each of our drawers. On it, in actually readable type, is a lot of legalese that says Tracy will let me have sex with him on camera, that he is eighteen years or older, that he surrenders any and all rights to his appearance in the video. I'm explaining it to him, blushing like I'm admitting that I have erectile dysfunction or a gastric problem.

He is surprisingly okay with the whole setup. In fact, he seems impressed by it all. He is no stranger to performing for the eyes of hundreds, he tells me — he's a recent dance school grad, and to help pay off his college loans, he dances on the weekends at a host of clubs. Well, that explains his body.

"Let me see your ID, and sign this please," I say, my face burning up.

He signs the contract: Chase Bliss. So, not actually Tracy. Stupid loud music.

"Really?" I ask.

"No, but hell, if I'm gonna be in a porn movie, then I might as well pick a good name, right?"

I check the ID for his real name: Chase Winterman. Just as sexy, if you ask me.

With the documentation made official (which involves, I kid you not, tearing off a yellow carbon-copy sheet and handing it to Chase — who can't stop laughing about how not-hot and professional the porn business actually is), I launch into prep mode. I fire up my computer, log into the video program, and put myself back "on the clock" in Sebastian's time-tracking software. I switch on the many lights around the room, all set to make my skin look its best, positioned to hit my bed and the space immediately surrounding it for the optimal dramatic effect. When I'm done, Chase has already stripped out of his clothing down to a pair of tight and tiny green briefs that probably cost as much as ten pairs that would cover 300% more of his skin.

"You like?" he squints through the lights, adjusting to the glare.

I gasp and, just as quickly, cover it up, saying, "Yeah, definitely." All the while I am forcing myself not to stare at the tattoo just above his underwear line: a gold pocket watch on a likewise-gold chain that loops and points to his belly button. How did I not see that before?

Chase. Fucking Chase. Fire fucking Island fucking Chase. Who I fucked on fucking Fire Island! This world is too small, and it's shrinking, shrinking, shrinking all around me. The posh lifestyle of Marty Brayden fades away and I am back at the underwear party on Fire Island, drowning in my own blood and vomit as Brayden wails away at me with his Blackberry.

And then I realize Chase has no idea who I am. We were trashed those two nights, as we are now. My hair was a different shade. My body a lot paler. My face a hell of a lot less pierced. He looks different, somehow, too — maybe a different haircut. Or maybe my transformation into Marty Brayden is more complete than I anticipated. Now I'm thinking like a new man as well, forgetting all the experiences I had as plain old Gulliver.

(All except the most scarring, that is.)

"I'm ready for my spotlight, Marty," Chase grins. God that smile and those perfect teeth are so fucking sexy. I force myself not to picture the actual Marty, not to remember the last time I had sex with someone I was actually into. And, thanks to my inebriation, it is a resounding success.

As if on cue, my computer explodes into bleeps, boops, and bings with instant messages from those who have been watching this whole silent moment take place.

"Let's do it, then," I say. "Take a seat, Mr. Bliss."

I motion him over to my desk. He sits in a chair beside mine. For the next ten minutes, I let him interact with the viewers while my heart calms down from cardiac arrest to a mere steady thump.

"Oh hai! Who'd you bring home with you, Marty?" messages one of the multitude.

"His name is Chase," I say aloud. "You think he's cute, guys?"

"OMG SO FKIN QT!"

"Yes yes yes!"

"Top or Bottom?"

I look over to Chase.

"Um… verse, I guess?" He's giggling. And I think: I can vouch for that.

"Take it off Chase!"

"Yeah! Let's see what you got!"

Despite his confident smile and flirty persona, Chase is actually shy. He agrees only to stand up and show his underwear, covering what's gone back into limp hiding underneath.

"Relax," I whisper to him, licking his ear. "You'll never meet them. They don't matter. Plus, think of all the guys that are about to get off to you."

"That is kind of hot," he whispers back, smiling and growing back to full attention. The bulge is even more impressive through a camera lens and my fans quickly vocalize this observation.

"So who tops and who bottoms?" I ask them, then say to Chase: "Check this out."

I click some buttons and a box pops up on the screen. It says: *"Pick the top and bottom!"* with our names next to two colored bars, both at 0%. Together we watch as the votes tally in.

"Holy shit, there's so many of them!" Chase says, watching "Chase Tops" and "Marty Tops" fight each other for dominance, their numbers quickly rocketing into the mid-hundreds.

It's a close call, but "Marty Tops" wins by forty-four when time is up. Chase howls, demanding a recount, earning a stack of LOLs from the guys in the chat room. But in the end Chase concedes, shrugs, and says: "The audience has spoken. To the bed!" He telegraphs his final statement by spinning his chair around and leaping across the room to the California king, landing on his stomach with his perfectly curved ass in the air.

The sex begins with tickle play. I want to get right into it, but I'm being paid to put on a show — the first of this type I've done on the site. Sebastian will review it tomorrow if he isn't one of the two thousand watching now. We are wrestling on the bed, holding each other down, kissing and pushing and pulling and kicking. When we're finally naked and rubbing up against each other, our breathing getting harder and faster, I pull out my phone and fire up the dorm widget, now a master at its workings thanks to Rowell's tutelage.

"Thirty-nine hundred people are about to watch me fuck you."

Chase laughs. "Hopefully none of my family members."

"If your family has a membership to New York Screwniversity, you've got a lot more problems than that."

Tonight I top Chase in every way my drunken mind can conjure. He is on his back, on his stomach. We are against the wall. He lies back with his shoulders on the floor, his legs up on the bed, while I jackhammer him from above. We are side-saddle. He is sitting on me, bracing himself only on the balls of his feet — such fantastic balance despite his inebriation. He is moaning Marty's name over and over again, and I am staring at the golden pocket watch, its hands spinning frantically, never stopping. I wonder why he chose the hand to be frozen in time just past the 12. I wonder if he even has a reason. And then I think, does this count as a third date? Even if he has no idea there were two run-ins preceding it?

With each thrust I get harder and happier, because I am imagining four thousand strangers sitting at desks and lying in beds, jerking off while watching me fuck a near-stranger. I am in a competition with all the other sex going on right now: Joey and Rowell and Joey's bartender friend. The wannabe model Chris brought home. The sexy black guy that shared the cab back with me and Ryan. What are their numbers? Who's winning tonight? I'm having too much fun to bother checking the other cameras on my phone, which fell off the bed long ago and will require an expedition in the wee morning hours to relocate.

When we are done, we bid the audience goodnight and let them know, hey, if they want to stick around, we might go at it again in the middle of the night. But we don't. I don't have a show again until tomorrow evening, and I plan to sleep straight through my hangover.

Chase finds his way comfortably into my arms, our bodies connecting perfectly. "Are they still watching us?"

"Some are."

"Don't you think it's weird, having a bunch of strangers watch us sleep?"

"They just watched us act out the gay Kama Sutra from A to Z, and that's what you think is weird?"

Chase yawns. "Well, when you put it like that..." His breath is sweet, not a hint of liquor on the warm air that hits my face. Hearing him hum in his sleep is the perfect white noise that finally escorts me into a similar state of unconsciousness.

That night I dream of Chase and me. We are in complementary bathrobes

— his green, mine blue. We're eating breakfast on the veranda of my parents' house in LA. But instead of our spacious backyard, we are looking out at the Long Island Sound, which laps at the shore. He takes my hand across the table, knocking that day's *LA Times* to the floor (the headline reads: *"Rufus Wainwright sings that Life Is Beautiful on the New York Times"*). His mouth is moving, but all I can hear is the water, some seagulls, and further away still, Madonna's "Like a Prayer."

When I wake up in the morning, Chase is gone. He's left his number on a slip of paper on my desk:

Hey Marty,

Thanks for last night — had to meet some friends for brunch. I'm more than up for a reprise performance if you are. Hope to talk soon.

Xoxo "Mr. Bliss."

I tear the note, crumple its many parts, and let them gently glide into my garbage can. Because there's fate, and then there's coincidence. And I'm not about to tell him who I am. Or who I used to be. Not now, at least. In the unlikely event that we ever cross paths again in this over-populated city, maybe then.

Maybe.

CHAPTER 29

His name is MartyMan22.

He surfaced a week ago in my daily chats. Since then, he's never missed a single session. From the minute I sign on to when I bid adieu, MartyMan22 is there, chatting me up. He has a habit of cutting through the chat clutter because he uses full sentences, knows how to spell, and LAYS OFF THE CAPS LOCK. It helps that he's always there with a witty comment that makes me snort-laugh and break my sexy persona. It didn't take him long to win the favor of most of my chat room regulars, too, with his quick jokes and cutting pop culture knowledge.

At first he caught my attention with his praise, not to mention the dedication of his screen name — something you're not allowed to change once you register. He's always telling me how attractive I am, again in full, properly-spelled sentences. Like a modern day Romeo standing outside of my window, comparing my ass to a rose. At first I was suspicious, thinking maybe this name wasn't truly dedicated to me. But the boys in the dorm confirmed that I was the first ever Marty to walk through their hallowed and horny halls.

So then, this was officially the biggest and most devoted of my admirers. The president of my fan club. And he was intelligent and funny! This was cause for jealousy amongst the other boys. Joey, who had a ton of users with his name as part of their online identities, lamented that, alas, none of them could put words together into something novel or meaningful. Rowell, meanwhile, had yet to earn his own dedicated fan and pretended to weep when I told him about MartyMan22.

Now I often find myself awake at night pondering the screen name. Does that mean my fan is only twenty-two years old? I spent so long assuming the men watching me do my thing were in their thirties or forties. I imagined most of them as unattractive — unable to land someone who looked like me in real life, and therefore resorting to life as an anonymous onlooker of my nightly hijinks. But maybe that stereotype was silly. Prior to my enrollment at the Screwniversity, I watched porn, didn't I? Didn't everyone? Maybe MartyMan is caught in some hateful town in Middle America where he has to keep his identity secret. Maybe I'm his window to the gay world he longs to be part of someday, once he's saved up enough money from his day job as the associate manager of a Pig 'n' Poke. Or, far less romanticized, maybe he's just some gay living in Chelsea or Harlem or Long Island with enough spare cash to afford our monthly membership fees.

On Tuesday morning, I catch myself jerking off to my imaginary version of MartyMan22 while doing a shower show. Behind my eyelids he is a brunette with a runner's body and a farmer's tan. He works a respectable job in an advertising firm where he makes good enough money. He spends his free time doing charity work. MartyMan is close with his family and friends, friendly to everyone he meets. He's everything I wanted Graham to be, the real Marty to be, and dreamed Chase might be the other night (for whatever odd reason — let's blame it on the drink). He's also a monster in the sack. What? Sex is important, too!

Later that day, I get a call from Sebastian.

"Marty, you're fired."

I'm going to faint. My mind is scrambling through the past day, wondering what I could have possibly done. (Certainly sleeping with the talent is not the cause this time around.) Did I not look like I was into sex with Chris Van Cleave this afternoon? I was still hungover, but I tried my best! I am counting through the money I've saved and calculating what the fuck I am going to do next. And I am still wondering: where did I go wrong?

"But... why?"

New York City found me again. I'm finished.

Sebastian's laugh explodes through the earpiece. "Of course not! Shit, Marty! You're amongst the three top-earning boys on this site. Don't tell the others, though. Not interested in fueling jealousy among the ranks."

My heart is still racing. The state of California, which seemed to be ever-so-slowly creeping closer while New York geared up to kick me cross-country, recedes again. I laugh with relief.

"Did I scare you there?"

"No. No! I guess I'm just wondering why you called me?"

"Actually, I come bearing glad tidings," he says, clearing his throat. "You have an admirer."

"Huh?"

"Yeah, a serious one with a checkbook to match. That MartyMan22 guy just offered us five hundred bucks in exchange for a private chat and cam session with you."

No 22-year-old would have access to that much cash. My imagined version of MartyMan is going down in flames.

Still, that's a lot of money.

"That's three hundred extra for you, babe. But I'll leave it up to you. Wouldn't mind the extra cash, myself. I'm saving up to buy a guitar."

"Of course I'll take it. Get a nice guitar, I expect you to write a song about me."

Wednesday night hits and I'm on cam as scheduled. I've been teasing my dick, but not getting off for 55 minutes. The chat room users are going out of their minds. I'm a huge tease, they scream (always with the DAMN CAPS). They threaten to leave me for Joey's room — he's actually jerking off, they tell me. I shrug and dare them to, knowing full well that Joey is off for the night. Of course my viewer numbers continue to climb as I do this. Then, the cherry on the sundae, I tell the boys I have to go because I have a private chat with one of the members.

Oh, they're pissed now. Cock-blocked by one of their own. It's unacceptable! Digital mutiny is growing amongst the ranks. I shrug and tell them I am more than happy to have a private session with any of them, but that sort of treatment doesn't come free. With that, I tap a few keys and enter a private chat room, turning my camera off to all but MartyMan22.

I click a button that invites him to turn on his webcam so we can see each other. This opens a second screen on my monitor. The box showing the pending invite disappears and a new box pops up: *"MARTYMAN22 HAS REJECTED THE CAMERA CONNECTION."* I am left to stare at my own dumbfounded face next to a blank box displaying a generic silhouetted man's head, a question mark floating over his face. I can think of no more fitting image.

I lean back in my chair, pulling the wireless keyboard with me so I can rest my bare feet on the desk. My legs are open, my hole on stunning display.

MartyMan22: *I was beginning to think you wouldn't show!*

MartyBrayden: *Well here I am. Thanks for the donation :-)*

MartyMan22: *It's my pleasure… anything to get you alone.*

MartyBrayden: *Heh. You're making me blush. Turn on your cam? I wanna see my generous donor. No one's ever done this for me before.*

MartyMan22: *Haha. Right. Well my cam is broken, sadly :-(And I'm not that special, I'm sure you've had tons fawn over you before.*

MartyBrayden: *Maybe I haven't.*

MartyMan22: *:-) So how long have you been doing this?*

MartyBrayden: *Not too long, a couple months.*

MartyMan22: *All the boys say that.*

MartyBrayden: *Maybe, but I'm telling the truth.*

MartyMan22: *Well, that's good. I've been watching you. Listening to you. You're too good for this. So I'm glad to see you haven't been wasting your talents for too long.*

MartyBrayden: *I'm sorry?*

MartyMan22: *This is beneath you, Marty.*

MartyBrayden: *Wow, this just got so serious. Haha. You do what you gotta do, ya know?*

MartyMan22: *I'm sure there's something else you could do for work. Isn't there anything else you're good at? You seem like a pretty smart guy.*

I have been typing so quickly that my knuckles are sore. My dick is limp, lying dead and deflated on my desk chair. In my head I am thinking: who the fuck is this? Why is he lecturing me? For a second I wonder if Todd or one of the other guys has found me here, is fucking around with me. But they wouldn't pay five hundred bucks upfront for that pleasure.

Would they?

MartyBrayden: *Why aren't you on cam?*

MartyMan22: *Do you want me to be?*

MartyBrayden: *Well it's up to you, baby. Whatever you're comfortable doing.*

MartyMan22: *I think this is fine. This is about you.*

I audibly sigh and then panic, realizing my microphone is on.

MartyMan22: *Stop typing, Marty. I'd rather hear your voice.*

"Okay," I say too quietly. It's already an odd experience speaking out loud to my own face and silent text. "Can I hear yours?"

MartyMan22: *Sorry, don't have a mic.*

I do a sad puppy-dog face.

MartyMan22: *Aw, don't be too disappointed. You don't need to see me, do you? You chat with plenty of guys who you've never seen before, right?*

"Well, yeah. But maybe you're different."

MartyMan22: *No. I'm not different at all. Is this a problem?*

"No. It's fine, baby. We can still have a good time." It's weird saying these things that are so easy to type. I reach for the keyboard, but MartyMan's IM box pings.

MartyMan22: *Huh uh, baby. I wanna hear your voice :-)*

"Okay. So what do you want me to do? Jerk off? Fuck myself? I just bought a new dildo."

MartyMan22: *No, thanks.*

"Um. Do you want me to get someone else in here? I mean, you did pay all that money."

MartyMan22: *I just wanted to be able to speak to you without all those other perverts in the chat room. Can I have your phone number?*

So that's what this is. I've heard of guys like this from the other dorm boys. One in every hundred or so users thinks they're special. Thinks they see something in us our other thousand admirers can't. Thinks they can break through the digital divide, rescue us from this horny squalor, and start dating a porn star. And we'll gladly give it all up for them, because now we know true love. It's the same sort of clueless guy who slips his number to a go-go boy instead of a tip (which I once learned from Todd, they HATE).

"Sorry, babe, against house rules."

MartyMan22: *Where IS the house, anyway?*

I am trying to keep my voice sultry. Trying not to ruin the playful persona I've been putting up. If I ruin this, MartyMan22 could submit a complaint to the website. Demand his money back. Then Sebastian really would fire me.

"New York."

MartyMan22: *But where in NY?*

"I can't tell you that either, babe."

MartyMan22: *For someone who was willing to do anything, there sure is a lot you're NOT willing to do.*

I give a big overdramatic shrug. "These are the rules."

MartyMan22: *Are you getting pissed at me?*

"No. You're really generous and smart, but I can't treat you differently than everyone else. I could lose my job."

MartyMan22: *That would be a pity. What if I wanted to meet up with you?*

The truth is that MartyMan22 could meet me if he wanted to. For the right amount of money, with the honest agreement and interest of the boys, Sebastian is willing to let pretty much anything happen so long as we aren't in any sort of danger. But I'm feeling increasingly uncomfortable speaking to MartyMan in this one-sided conversation. I don't want to meet him. I'm afraid of ending up facedown on a garbage barge in the Hudson River.

"No can do. I can't even see what you look like!"

MartyMan22: *Does that matter?*

"I'd say so! And I'm guessing you didn't devote your screen name to me solely based on my personality, either."

MartyMan22: *Well, what if I told you I'm a 22-year-old stud with an 8-pack and more muscles than you could ever imagine?*

I'm instantly aroused by the thought. "It sounds hot, but I'd need proof to back that statement up. Don't you have a picture to send me?"

MartyMan22: *What if I said I was a 500-lb. 70-year-old with millions of dollars and a terminal illness and that I'll write you into my will, no questions asked, in exchange for one final night of passion that will probably kill me with a heart attack, turning you into an immediate billionaire?*

A sexy smirk: "You're funny."

MartyMan22: *I want to meet you, Marty.*

"Oh yeah? What would you do to me when you do?"

MartyMan22: *Talk to you.*

"Yeah, and what else?"

MartyMan22: *That's it. But it'd be worth your while. BTW. What's your real name?*

Sneaky. Part of me fears the worst: he's some psycho who has enough information about me already to hunt me down and kill me in my sleep. The other part is super curious and still hoping he's a hottie. Am I hopeless or what?

"It's Marty!"

MartyMan22: *But how'd you choose the name "Marty?"*

I'm starting to get flustered. "I didn't! My parents did!"

MartyMan22: *Everyone says their porn name is their real name.*

"Yeah, but I'm telling the truth! I'm new to this, you know?"

MartyMan22: *I see. So, "MARTY," you're telling me there's NO WAY I can ever meet you?*

"Well. We do these events. We'll be doing one Saturday, actually, at this club called eWrecksion. Are you in New York?"

MartyMan22: *Maybe.*

"Now who's not answering the questions? What's YOUR name, by the way?"

MartyMan22: *MartyMan22.*

"Your real name?"

MartyMan22: *Marty Mann.*

"Fucking smart ass."

MartyMan22: *Haha. Okay. Yes, I live in NYC. You guys are going to be at eWrecksion?*

I comfortably snap into my promotional voice. "Yup! It's gonna be a blast! Drink specials, me and all the other boys will be in attendance. May do some sexy shows after they lock the doors at 3 AM. You gonna come see us?"

MartyMan22: *Without a doubt.*

"Great! So how will I know how to find you?"

MartyMan22: *I wouldn't worry about that. I'll find you.*

"Hot. Then I guess we'll meet there."

MartyMan22: *K, I'm going to sign off now.*

His rejection hits me like a punch in the face. He did pay five hundred dollars for this, right?

"You don't want me to jerk off? I've been teasing for an hour and a half. I'm going to shoot at least ten gallons. Might hit myself in the face."

MartyMan22: *I already told you, I just want to talk. Stay safe, okay?*

"You know, it hasn't even been a full hour..."

Too late. *MartyMan22 has signed out of the room.*

I stare at the screen, my lone cursor blinking weakly. I rush back to my public chat room, where the guys are waiting.

"How was it, Marty?"

"Was it hotttttt?"

"How much do I have to pay for a show??"

"Who were you chatting with? Which one of these bitches do I gotta cut??"

MartyMan22 is not on the chat room attendee list. He has signed off for the night.

I feel like I've been fucked. Directly through my ear to my brain. Hard. And then, when all was said and done, left on my bed to wonder what the hell just happened. But I'm still on the clock for ten minutes.

"Leave me a donation of more than five hundred dollars and send a request," I say with a wink. "And yeah. It was super hot."

Digital groans, a ton of WTFs, and a few yellow frowns scroll past the screen.

I try to jerk off for my fans, but it's like my dick is stopped up. It stays hard but nothing comes out. I pull and tug until the skin is raw and dry. In the end, I pretend to shoot into my hand, my head tilting back in faux-ecstasy.

"yeaahhhhh!"

"So fucking hawt!!!!!"

"Nice big load Marty?"

I feel nothing, but it works for my adoring fans. Which I guess is all that matters.

CHAPTER 30

The next day in the living room, the boys and I are gathered around the TV watching a DVRed episode of some VH1 comedy clip show — one of our favorite genres. Four hundred people are watching us watch the show. I wonder if the rants of lunatic talk show hosts are half as entertaining with no volume.

During the commercials (which we forget to fast-forward through) I catch the boys up on the recent MartyMan22 episode and our absurd digital date. He has been a topic of conversation for weeks now and I owe them the latest developments. As I regale them with the story's details, it pains me to own up to the fact that my admirer turned out to be a creeper with a fat wallet after all.

"Wait," says Rowell. "After dropping all that cash, he didn't even have you jack off?"

"No," I confess. "He signed off. It's not like I didn't offer. I've never felt like such a whore in my life, listing everything I would do like I was a Chinese take-out menu."

"That's shady," says Chris, pounding a fistful of popcorn into his mouth.

"You didn't tell him where we live, did you?" Ryan asks, an eyebrow raised.

"Yeah, and I gave him all your real names and phone numbers, too." I expect laughter and am met instead with blank stares, panic-stricken mouths hanging wide open. I roll my eyes. "Of course I didn't! He did ask, though."

"It's not really THAT creepy," says Joey, wearing just a green G-string and a tiny yellow tank top (his justification: if all these people are going to watch us watch TV, we might as well give them something to look at). "I've had my fair share of creeps, at least he's the boring kind — not asking you to wear a diaper for him or whatever. And he MAY actually be twenty-two. And hot. And rich. You'd be surprised by who our members are — a lot of them are our age. Plus, when we go to events, Seb springs for a limo and tells the driver to take side streets and highways to sneak back to the building, so it's not like he can hop in a cab and stalk us all the way back."

"Yeah, Marty, I'm sure he's a 22-year-old gorgeous millionaire," Chris laughs. "If he is, I'll give you a hundred bucks."

"Fine. And if I lose, I'll let you top me on camera," Joey says, grabbing Chris' dick through his sweat pants and shaking it firmly.

"Deal!"

The rest of the week goes by so, so slowly. Every time I sign on to do my nightly chat, MartyMan22 is nowhere to be found. I ask the other guys in the room if they've seen him and suddenly they are all jealous. I have a crush on one of my fans, they say. They want to find him and kill him. He must be gorgeous if he's gotten the attention of the one and only Marty Brayden.

I assure them this is not the case and jerk off for them twice, three fingers up my ass and my legs in the air, proving my loyalty to each and every one of them. A handful swear they are pooling their resources together so they can get me in a private chat. I wish them luck.

Thursday night is my three-way with Chris Van Cleave and Joey Gambit. It's become a big deal and Sebastian has been extra-enthused by our genuine excitement. We all promoted it in our separate chats. I fired up Photoshop and created a promo graphic featuring the three of us naked and huddled together. Joey is center, of course, his massive chest and shoulders facing front. Chris and I are in profile clinging to him on either side. A heading in a font aptly named "Fucker" obscures our precious bits and proclaims:

For the first time ever, newbies Chris Van Cleave and Marty Brayden get it at the same

time from Dorm RA Joey Gambit.
The three-way of the century!

Sebastian then took my promo and, after many effusive comments and an offer to pay me extra every week to create similar ads, popped it into his weekly email to the site's members. The "open rates" were apparently 400% higher than ever before, which, judging from Sebastian's dancing when he found out, was a very good thing. In a final feat of genius, Sebastian decided to charge an extra four bucks per user who wanted to watch, an idea generated by a recent article on the success of something called "micro-purchasing" — a model that has been perfected by none other than Apple and Farmville, amongst others. The cost was low enough that it was impossible not to justify the price of a cup of coffee to see us three go at it, even though members were already paying by the month and could see not-dissimilar events regularly without the surcharge. Sebastian was worried there might be an uproar, but he went with his gut. The micro-purchases came flying in. This was shaping up to be an Event with a capital E.

We decided to stage the scene in an extra room Sebastian then redecorated and relit, dragging in a giant bed as well as a pool table. It took him a whole day to get it just right, giving us all the props we could ever need. When all was said and done, the room we had until then referred to as "the appendix" due to its apparent uselessness became the ultimate porn set — with more surfaces and toys than you could shake a dildo at. A veritable Willy Wonka Factory of sex instead of candy.

There are actual butterflies in my stomach the night of the shoot. Sebastian huddles us together like a Junior Varsity football team (in a corner with the camera shut down, of course). I'm nervous! It's like I'm backstage during one of my high school plays, getting ready to hit center stage and sing the solo.

"All right, boys, this is the biggest official event we've ever done here. How tonight goes determines everything. If you kick ass and make people feel like they got their extra money's worth, you've just helped me discover an all-new revenue stream. And if that happens, you'll get a cut."

We're smiling — Chris most of all, since this all came from a drunken musing he voiced that night we headed to Michael Porcelain's party.

"Joey, you're topping. Marty, if you wanna top Chris, go on ahead. Chris, we'll save your topping for a completely separate event. Gotta leave them wanting more, right? Use everything in there. Get creative. Stay hard! I know it's tough. Pretend it's just the three of you. Picture the audience naked — ha, ha. But seriously, just try to get back in touch with the days you had sex because you were drunk or horny or bored. Not being paid to do it. So have fun! Go Bel Ami and smile and laugh and wrestle. The users love that shit. And when you can't go any longer, try your best to have a triple climax. Whisper to each other when you're getting close. Okay, guys? Now forget everything I just said and get in there and fuck the crap out of each other. The cameras are already rolling!"

The show goes like this: Chris and I both bottom for Joey and then we're in a chain, me in the middle, Chris in front, his red hair minty and fluffy when it mashes against my face. We're on the pool table, on the bed, on the floor. Legs are up, legs are spread. We arch our backs. We flex every muscle we have (and strain for others to materialize just for tonight). We are all a bit louder than usual so we can then whisper instructions for transitions. Every blow job is wetter. I even take a ride on a huge dildo that Joey seems to pull out of nowhere. I will be sore for days (thank God Seb said we can have the next two days off to recuperate). The chemistry is unbelievable — you can just feel it. We're going all out. We're holding nothing back. We fuck and fuck and fuck.

Sebastian, meanwhile, is running a camera control room he stationed just outside the appendix, switching on the fly from shot to shot.

And then the grand finale: we each shoot three times, leaving us a cum-covered, heaving pile on the floor, legs intertwined. Red lamplights on the six cameras in the room go dark. I am half-expecting a burst of applause, instead met with dead silence.

I am sore. I am exhausted, heaving, coughing. I may have lost my voice. Chris has to pee and Joey actually farts, sending us all into hysterics. Our widgets tell us that we've been watched by seven thousand users — both in the United States as well as abroad.

At the exact same time, from beyond the door I hear Sebastian scream: "Seven thousand fucking viewers! Boys, we're fucking RICH!"

Joey excuses himself to shower our collective seed off. Chris spanks me and says he's topping next time. And then I am alone in the room, listening to Sebastian banging pans in the kitchen, shouting "Seven thousand!" over and over again.

As I towel off, my thoughts go back to MartyMan22. Was he watching? Is there a way to find out if he was one of the users who paid to witness Screwniversity history in the making? I know it's crazy to have such an intense reaction to someone I've never met, never even seen a picture of. Yet despite the possible creep factor, I can't deny the unmistakable chemistry we had even just typing to one another. He sees something in me, something no one else does currently; for now, I'll give him the benefit of my doubt.

And then I wonder, will he show up on Saturday? Did our conversation mean anything to him? Or was I not good enough for him one-on-one?

And if he does show up — well, what the fuck happens then?

CHAPTER 31

Since moving into the dorms, I've taken to calling Mom and Dad less. They think it's because things have gotten so busy at work. On our now once-weekly calls, I share the names of actors I make up on the spot and lament the late nights I've been facing since Stanford began picking up more clients for us to place in shows that I'm not even sure have tours or productions currently running.

As I fabricate a rosy life for myself, I occasionally catch myself thinking about my old boss. Is he taking over the world as I initially forecasted? What if something went sour and the big wigs called him back to Boston? What if the whole firm went under? Times are tough for everyone right now. Well, everyone except me and my dorm buddies, plus anyone else in the "adult arts." I assume that, no, Stanford's doing just fine, if not spectacularly. He wouldn't have it any other way.

And of course, where there's Stanford, there's Marty. When I think of him, I am filled with a palpable regret that proceeds to plague me for at least a day. I hear my own voice tearing that boy down, hear his voice coming back at me and setting in motion my employment's end. There's anger there, but I'm not sure if it's with Marty or myself. In the end, I hope he's doing well. On tour somewhere. One of the good ones with generous per diems and posh travel arrangements and long stays in each city. He deserves it — probably more than I deserve all this.

For porn star Marty Brayden, life's a peach. It's when I have to talk and think like Gulliver that things get complicated. I don't call my parents for a hand-ful of reasons: one being that it's hard to tap my creativity on a daily basis to make up a 9-to-9 corporate day that didn't actually happen. If I could lie in my bed and recount the pounding I gave Rowell on the kitchen counter or the five-person oral daisy chain I played a part in one night after clubbing, that would be one thing. I also can't call from the dorm because of unpre-dictable ambient noise. A single strange male voice shouting something com-pletely inappropriate would be hard to explain away, and here, such sound bites are far from a rare occurrence. Thudding on the wall accompanied by Chris Van Cleave's high-pitched moans as one of the dorm boys has his way with him can't be confused with a construction crew working on a scaffold outside of Todd's apartment, as much as I wish it were that easy.

As far as Mom and Dad know, I am living the life I left behind months ago. Talking to them is one of few reminders that I ever had another life here. My parents keep offering to send me money if I need it, when in reality, that's the last thing I need. If they only knew how much I was making on a week-ly basis — and thank God they don't.

On Friday, I get a call from home. I am in the middle of jerking off for roughly fifteen hundred guys, taking requests on which sleeve of my Fleshjack butt toy to use. When my scene is done I hop in the shower, then take to the street. There is a small cafe around the corner that serves really salty edamame and a latte with peanut butter on the rim of the cup. This is where I call them back.

"Gulliver, Todd called us last night."

Stunned silence. I am the deer. I have just spotted the headlights. We all know how this scenario ends, right?

"Do you have anything you'd like to tell us?"

Smack.

My edamame will not be consumed any time soon. My heart is racing, as it likes to do when my life is on the verge of collapse. Which, since I moved here, has been all too often.

So this is fear. This is embarrassment.

This is the end.

"He's so sweet! He just called to say he hoped we're doing well, and that you two are going upstate for the weekend. Why didn't you tell us that, Gully? Honestly, I don't know what I'd do if that boy wasn't looking out for you..."

Seems I'm not the only one making up an imaginary life for myself.

My pulse is still on overdrive despite the fact that it was only a false alarm. Too many of these little evaporating shocks to my system. Sebastian and the boys will find me dead in bed one morning soon.

"Well, uh, we weren't sure if it was going to work out or not, you know, with my job being fucking insane and all."

"Gully, you've become so filthy-mouthed in that city. Watch it! You might say it sometime when you don't mean to."

Oops. It's funny — when you shout four-letter words over and over again, covered in sweat and lube and cum, you forget that the rest of the world doesn't necessarily toss around such language so liberally.

"I hope that place isn't corrupting my sweet boy."

"Sorry, Ma. But yeah, that's why. Turns out I will be able to head up with him. I'll probably pay for it next week with even later hours and all, but it'll be worth it."

"Of course it will, honey. You deserve to lie back and relax. You've been working so hard. We're so proud of you, sweetie!"

I wince. That doesn't feel anywhere near as good as it should.

"No, Ma. It's not really that big of a deal..."

"No, no, no. Stop it, sweetie. You know I wouldn't say it if I didn't mean it. Your father and I were just talking about you this morning on our walk."

"I was telling her to admit she was wrong about you," Dad pipes in, confirming that I am indeed on speakerphone.

I shove a piece of edamame in my mouth. It's too salty. I'm not hungry anymore. "Wrong?"

"Yes, sweetie. Record this for the archives. The moment you told us you were moving, I told your father it wouldn't happen. That you wouldn't do it."

"And then, when you DID do it..." Dad adds.

"Yes, yes. When you DID move, I told him you wouldn't be staying. That you wouldn't be able to apply yourself, just like how you didn't apply yourself while you were here."

Tears. My cheeks are wet. My latte is cold and I just want to hang up and go for a walk to the water's edge. Maybe there I'll scream at the dinner cruises slowly motoring by. Or maybe I'll just dive in and go for a swim with the garbage and bobbing Mafia victims. That's where I belong right now.

"But you proved me wrong, honey. And your father right. You've made something of yourself. And you're making something of New York."

"Mom, I have to go."

"Are you okay, my honey?" Now she's all worry. Of course.

The truth, meanwhile, is pushing at my teeth. It would be so easy to just tell her. Just a few words: "Mom, I've actually been making a killing doing gay porn. My costars are the best friends I've made here, my boss adores me, and thousands of kind strangers spend hours a day getting off to my likeness."

But the reaction to these words? That wouldn't be easy at all. I find myself mouthing the truth, wondering if I'd be able to speak it, wondering if she could possibly understand — and maybe feel just a sliver of the sense of accomplishment I possess despite the nature of my newfound glory. But that's hopeless.

"Yeah, Mom, I'm fine! It's just that Todd's wildly signaling at me. Gotta catch the bus. We're going to be late."

"We'll wait a day before I beat you up about your drinking, Gully. I'll let you sit with my motherly pride and wallow in a sense of being right for once."

I laugh, air-kiss my parents goodbye, and kill the call.

I don't leave right away. With a plate of food and a quickly cooling beverage in front of me, no one pressures me to vacate. At one point, my waitress stops and drops the check next to me, whispering that I can stay as long as I need to.

Oh, Mom. Fuck you for being proud of me now. Of course the son who finally earned this much-sought-after and rarely-achieved pride is one who disappeared over the summer. Her real son and his actual success would fill her with shame until the day she died. I don't know if she'd ever speak to me again.

I smoke six cigarettes outside the cafe until I am nauseous and dizzy. I consider drowning out the feeling with the dregs of my latte, only to find that my table has been cleared and a happy couple has taken up residence, staring longingly into each other's eyes and sharing a wire basket teeming with french fries.

Back at the dorm, I take another postcard out of my desk and write:

"Todd,

Miss you a lot. Hope you're having fun in Hell's Kitchen. Maybe someday we'll be neighbors? I'm doing fine. Well, sorta.

Either way, I love you. And thanks for playing along while I stumble around this city and try to make it work for me.

- Gully."

I add my contact info, including the dorm's PO Box number, to the bottom corner. I jam it into the dorm's mail chute before I can change my mind.

CHAPTER 32

And then it is Saturday. Sebastian shuts the cameras down early, putting up another ad he paid me to design (an extra hundred bucks!). It reads:

Come meet the boys of NewYorkScrewniversity.com!
Join Joey Gambit, Ryan Roberts, Marty Brayden, Rowell Adrian, Chris Van Cleave and all of your favorite college studs in a one-time only event!

Hosted by NYCs' hottest promoters, including the famous Michael "Porcelain" Peterson. Held at New York City's exclusive club eWrecksion.

Extra special surprise at 3 AM.
Get there early!
Doors CLOSE at 2!

Behind the headline I've placed a group shot of the twelve of us, Joey Gambit at the front and the other eleven of us behind him, to both sides, fading into the black background. Joey's holding his arms open wide and I've put the NewYorkScrewniversity.com logo I designed in such a way that it looks like he's actually holding it.

Meanwhile, Sebastian has been a blaze of activity all week, running to the print shop where he ordered a run of three thousand of my glossy promo cards. He gave me time off from my regular scenes so I could create twelve versions of the ad, each with a photo of just one of us. On the back of these shiny heavy-stock promos is a code that allows the bearer to get a free three-day membership to the site — the gateway drug to a prospective lifetime of paid addiction, we hope.

Sebastian also ordered three large banners, the logo and our likenesses popping out of a background of the New York City skyline. There are tons of other promotional materials too — coasters, cigarette lighters, condoms, little lube packets, tank tops, baseball caps, helium-packed balloons that will float to the ceiling, weighted to hover in such a way that hundreds of our logos will be looking down on the party.

MartyMan22 has not reappeared. I assume he won't be coming to meet me because he doesn't actually live in the city, and that's probably for the best. The unknown reasons for which he paid all that money to be cautionary and shady leaves me uneasy, but I have too much else to think about — namely, tonight's public performance. Engaging in a three-way with Chris and Joey in the appendix is one thing; executing a twelve-person orgy live on stage in a club, on the other hand, is a completely different world altogether.

Sebastian gave us the big day off and hooked us up with his friend Jayare, a gorgeous glam gay who owns a spa and salon. There we underwent a fierce makeover the likes of which you'd see on some model-competition reality show: booth tanning (with sessions longer than the cancer warning on the rocket-shaped tube allowed), haircuts, dye jobs, waxing, trimming, manicures and pedicures and copious amounts of primping.

We are all slightly nervous, even Joey. The fact that none of us can look to him as a support beam and voice of experience and reason doesn't help. Plus, we're already exhausted after spending three hours today running through the choreography. It's difficult. It'll be even harder when we're naked and having sex in the midst of it.

Then, before we know it, it's time to go. We pile into a party bus featuring a stick-on sign advertising the site. (Why not promote on our way there, too?) Sebastian is waiting with a bottle of champagne. He pops the cork and pours generously. His energy, thank God, is contagious. We lift our glasses, toasting a performance that will take New York City by storm.

After the first glass our moods are already lightening. We blast Lady Gaga as our driver winds up and down the side streets of the Financial District. Joey and Chris poke their heads out the windows, out the moonroof, catcalling the cute boys we speed past, telling them to come by eWrecksion for the show of the century. Mother Nature has blessed the performance with a beautiful, starry Indian summer night. No rain to keep the gays away for fear of melting into the gutters.

When we pull up to the club, Michael Porcelain explodes out of the front door, reducing Sebastian's energy and enthusiasm to molecules.

"The boys are here! Look at you! Oh my God! I think I got hard and fucking shot at least four times in the past minute! Get your sexy asses in here!"

He drags us, one by one, out of the party bus, escorting us past a line that is wrapped around the block. There are some cheers from the crowd and tons of camera flashes. We blow kisses, kiss and grab each other, as per Sebastian's coaching on the ride here.

"Who's ready to fucking party?" howls Joey, flexing and then turning on his toes to march into the club.

Above the entrance is the first of three banners Sebastian had printed. There I am, right next to Joey, smiling, hands on my hips, my pointer fingers drawing attention to the bulge I only Photoshopped a tiny bit (a camera puts on ten pounds, but I'm convinced it takes off an inch and a half). The other boys look up too. Seeing your photo on a web browser is cool. Seeing your near-naked self on a banner four times larger than you, blowing in the warm wind? Well, that's a total trip.

The black drag queen at the door demands a photo. Michael herds us around her and the flash goes off. Afterward, she gives us each a wet cheek-kiss and goes back to hassling the long line of boys and hags, scanning their IDs and giving out free entry tickets to those lucky enough to know someone who knows someone. The rest will be paying anywhere from forty to sixty dollars at her discretion.

Though I've been here before, the club looks all new to me. I walk through the many rooms and dance floors. I don't remember it being this huge. I also don't remember being sober, so that explains a lot. The NewYorkScrewniversity balloons are already on the ceiling, behaving exactly as Sebastian predicted: hundreds of copies of our logo hang like gay stalactites. Everywhere we walk, there are television screens displaying a hyperactive, speeding feed of words and numbers. It takes me a minute to realize these are text messages from the people drinking and dancing around us.

Sexual propositions. Shout outs. DJ requests. A seemingly endless torrent of communication.

The corridors connecting the rooms and stairwells are completely dark, but the dance floors and lounges are bright blasts of color and brightness — thousands and thousands of dollars of moving and stationary lights. We'll perform on a theatrical-style stage on the main floor, Michael shouts over his shoulder as he leads us toward the VIP lounge.

Michael gathers us at a door behind one of the four bars on the main floor. Above it are the specials for the night: one named after each of the twelve dorm boys. The Marty Brayden is Blueberry Stoli, blue curacao, and 7 Up, garnished with a blueberry.

Past the bar and through the door is an unlit staircase that takes us to a smaller VIP area we apparently weren't exclusive enough to get into last time we visited. The room is a shotgun, warmly yellow-lit corridor with a dark area rug and plush couches and chairs lining all four walls. Despite its small size, there are at least a hundred people milling around. Tonight's major sponsor, according to Michael, is a caffeinated vodka. There are large bottles of the stuff in ice-filled carafes all over the place.

"I love this shit! They need to infuse EVERYTHING with caffeine!" Michael yells, swigging straight from a bottle and then violently shaking his head like he just hopped out of a swimming pool. "You boys want some?"

We all nod and are promptly attended to by a cocktail waiter who's dressed like an old-fashioned fraternity brother in an unbuttoned wool sweater that exposes the requisite hairlessness and musculature Michael seems to prefer from anyone on his staff, be they waiter, bartender, coat check, or bathroom attendant.

"Sebastian!" Michael yells, running away from us as our boss appears in the doorway. "I don't think you have a fucking CLUE how big tonight is going to be."

"Michael, dear, I saw the line outside. I think it stretches all the way to Jersey!"

"Every promoter who's ANYBODY is working this fucking thing," Michael cackles. "The invite has gone out on Facebook, Twitter, Manhunt,

Adam4Adam, BarebackRT, DList, MySpace, Friendster, through texts and emails, word of mouth like you wouldn't believe. I had my go-go boys papering every gayborhood from here to Albany all fucking week! RSVPs are through the roof! We're going to break the fire code! The cops will come! Even Jesus is going to offer to blow the bouncer to get in here!"

"You think our Lord and Savior would be any good at fellatio?" Rowell whispers to me, earning a hard elbow in his side and a quick kiss on his cheek.

Todd.

Whoosh. It's like all the color drains out of the room, all the chatter reduced to a tinny hum. I see my former roommate before he sees me, beyond Rowell's shoulder, past the fraternity boy waiters and ultra-VIPs who must be the top tier promoters Michael just mentioned. Todd's leaning against the back wall, drinking one of the caffeinated concoctions and laughing that dumb, straight jockish laugh of his. It penetrates me to my core, like someone just stabbed me in my stomach, spilling my guts all over the bar.

"Marty, you okay?" It's Joey, putting both hands on my shoulders and stepping between me and my former roommate and guardian.

"Yeah, just nervous, you know? I've never done anything like this before!"

"You'll be fine!" Joey proclaims, clapping me on both shoulders. "Trust me. I've had plenty of tastes of that Marty Magic!"

I smile sheepishly and then slowly turn to face Ryan, who is behind me, thereby putting Todd behind me as well. I try to enter a conversation about which waiter is the cutest but the whole time it's like the back of my head is burning. I can feel Todd staring at me. What is he going to say? What will he do? Maybe I'll get out of here before he notices me...

"Fucking Todd!" Michael screams. "Fucking Todd Fucking DiTempto! Don't think I don't know that ninety-five percent of this crowd is on your list! Get your ass over here and meet tonight's entertainment."

So there is no avoiding it. I feel the heat of approaching bodies and Todd is standing right next to me, facing the cabal that is me and my dorm mates. And now that we're this close, I can see that something is terribly wrong.

Todd is trashed. He never drinks at his own parties — ever. But tonight his face is beet red and his eyes blink hysterically, eyelashes like dragonfly wings.

"You're too sweet, bitch," Todd slurs.

I don't think I've ever seen him this drunk — I distinctly recall him once telling me that a good promoter never gets trashed at his own parties. He also looks about 25% less muscular. His face is drawn, walked all over. Those dark circles that have always resided around his eyes are now black holes that all but swallow them. To anyone who didn't know Todd, he'd still be one hell of a sexy specimen of humanity. But for someone who's known him for years, Todd looks like total shit. Sick. Beaten. Is this my fault? I imagine him up all night, scouring the city for me all these weeks. Waiting for the day my parents or the cops call him with my whereabouts — stuffed in a dumpster somewhere.

But why would he bother, after everything that happened between us?

"Have you met the boys of NewYorkScrewniversity?" Michael gestures at us with a hand like we're the new Ferrari in a showroom on Lexington Avenue.

"No. I haven't." He smiles, leaning forward and almost falling over. "How's it going, guys? I'm Todd."

He's offering his hand to me. I reach out and shake it. "Marty Brayden," I say quietly, doing my best to disguise my voice without calling attention to the fact that I am doing so. My fingers are warm, clammy, vomiting sweat as his big hand envelops mine. And he doesn't let go. He's just shaking and shaking my hand for what could be hours. His eyes don't leave mine. Those dark circles get bigger and bigger, threatening to consume both of us and the entire party.

Then he bites his lip, swallows hard, and breaks his gaze. "You're cute, bro," he winks, then continues around the semicircle, meeting the rest of the boys.

Now he's rubbing abs and pinching nipples and flexing his still-formidable biceps for Joey and Chris and Rowell and Ryan and everyone else. They are falling all over him. This, of course, is nothing new; it's especially bothersome now, however, because these are professional porn stars who have driven thousands to show up tonight. Even sex-celebrity means nothing in the presence of my old buddy Todd. His aura is that of a dominant top who will have you on your back, legs in the air before he even opens his mouth. I am tempted to tell the drooling crew that I used to see him naked. Daily. But of course I keep my mouth shut.

With his greeting and posing done, Todd gives me one last glance and smile, then returns to the other side of the room, where he begins putting the moves on a punky-looking kid with a neon green mohawk that sticks at least six inches straight up. Since when did he start breaking his "don't get caught hooking up with people at your own events" rule? What the fuck is happening to the man I still can't help but consider my closest friend in the world?

I feel tears coming. I excuse myself and run down the stairs, almost falling as I go.

The dance floor is packed. People are too busy dancing to notice me. I go to the bar and order a Marty Brayden. The bartender asks for twelve dollars, not realizing I'm its namesake. I pay with a twenty and don't wait for the change.

My breathing slows. Did Todd recognize me? Were the hair and piercings enough? Was our elongated moment merely a drunken stutter — or a moment of realization? Did he get that postcard yet? Is that, in part, why he's here? These questions go unanswered and will stay that way, because either Todd couldn't see me through the hair and tan and metal — or he did, and has decided to pretend otherwise.

"Marty!"

It's Sebastian, calling me over to the VIP door.

"Yeah, boss?"

"Your number one fan is here."

I'm too dazed to respond. I just stare at him blankly.

"MartyMan22? Ring a bell?"

I'd forgotten. Completely fucking forgotten. My eyes dart in all directions. "Where is he?"

"Oh, somewhere around here. He got access to the VIP room, came up to me just as you ran down the stairs. Are you okay?"

When it fucking rains, it fucking pours.

"Yeah, it just got too hot in there. What did he say?"

I'm cycling through what few faces I can remember from inside that room not five minutes ago. It's useless. All I remember are Todd and that guy with the mohawk.

"He didn't have a mohawk, did he?" I ask.

"No," Sebastian laughs. "But he did ask if he could meet you after the show. I figured you'd be up for that."

"Well, what does he look like?" My voice is high. So much is happening. In my mind drunk and destroyed Todd circles around the question marked silhouette from my private chat with MartyMan22, circles around the fact that I am about to go on stage and have sex in front of a crowd the size of fucking Woodstock.

"Oh, he's CUTE, Marty. Very cute. I would offer him a job if we had an extra room in the dorm. You'll love him. I guarantee it."

I dig for more description, but Sebastian has to talk to the DJ and give him the memory stick he prepared with music for our choreographed show. So I'm stuck with merely knowing my number one fan is, in fact, cute. At least by Sebastian's standards. Then again, those standards are high. Under any other circumstances, this news would have me stoked — but that wave of panic in the pit of my stomach is still going strong and I am riding it, knees slightly bent, arms spread wide to anticipate my inevitable plunge into the dark ocean below.

I can't even make it back up the stairs before my boys rush past me.

"It's showtime!" Joey yells, grabbing my arm and yanking me back down the stairs, my Marty Braden hitting the wall and shattering in the darkness. "Oops! Someone get the clean-up crew!"

I fall in line with my boys and we run along the perimeter of the main dance floor. The lights zap this way and that, alternating between pure darkness and blinding brightness. I want to break away, to find my mystery man and figure out what the hell happened that night. But getting away is hopeless. I am completely surrounded, being dragged to the stage. My eyes have but a second to adjust and register a sea of heads and shoulders — some kissing, others drinking, still others smoking (illegally). We find our way to the far end of the main stage and enter a door by yet another bar. Inside is chaos. Go-go boys are coming in from their shift, flirting with each other, doing shots, asking for our autographs. We are their inspiration, some say. Others say we're the reason they have such formidable forearms.

"Stick around," Joey says. "We'll sign after the show. Especially you, you're ridiculously cute."

Rowell breaks into the circle we've formed with a tray of caffeinated vodka shots courtesy of Michael Porcelain, who's probably screaming and swearing somewhere nearby.

Over the million dollar speaker system, I hear my former roommate's voice: "Boys, are you having a good time?"

Deep breaths. No time to wonder. MartyMan22 is here and I will meet him in a matter of minutes. I'm scared. I'm psyched. I can't tell what's more nerve-wracking — the performance I'm about to stage or meeting my secret admirer immediately afterward.

"One, two, three... NewYorkScrewniversity!" Joey yells, holding out his hand, which is immediately covered by the rest of ours.

"Get it!" we yell back.

"Make me proud, boys," Sebastian says as he hands Joey a microphone and pushes us out to the stage one by one.

"Put your fuckin' hands together for the boys of NewYorkScrewniversity.com!" Todd fist pumps, stepping downstage as we come running out, taking our positions as best we can remember them. The DJ gives us a thumbs up and familiar music pumps in, blanketing the club in bass.

The first song is Ke$ha's "Cannibal." So many lights, once all over the place, come together and land on our little slutty chorus line. We are dancing.

Gyrating. Our hands are over our heads, rubbing down our sweaty faces, down our chests.

Then we pair off. Joey, Chris, and I are at the front, an homage for anyone in the crowd who saw our scene two weeks ago — and chances are a lot of them did.

Nerves are gone. I am adrenaline. I've always known I was attractive, but right now I feel sexy. Super sexy. Godlike. My brain isn't thinking. I am all sensation and motion. I am impervious. Wanted, coveted. I am known and recognized. We all are. It's the most energizing feeling I've ever known. (Or is that just a side effect of all that caffeinated alcohol?)

"Hellooo, New York City!" Joey yells, with Chris and I dropping to our knees, our legs each wrapped around one of his. We each throw a hand up to his chest, ripping the easy breakaway shirt to reveal his hairless chest. The crowd is all flashes and iPhones urgently recording video. "I'm Joey Gambit, the head RA of NewYorkScrewniversity.com!"

The audience knows who we are. Sebastian assured us of this. A lot of them may not be paying members, but our videos are being stolen on illegal porn sites all over the net. People in the crowd have apparently made mashup videos and porny homages to us, hosting them on every site from XTube to PornoTube to RocketTube to God-knows-what-else-Tube.

I look out into a dark sea of heads and hands. I can't make out a single face, but I'm looking for MartyMan22 regardless. Is he in the front row? The spotlights on us have rendered me blind — casting the entire audience in a throbbing black blur that certainly isn't helped by the alcohol I guzzled upon arriving.

"We want to thank you for coming out tonight. We love having a chance to meet new friends, and maybe take some back to the dorm with us."

Screams and cheers that border on the manic wash over us like a wave that comes from the back of the main dance floor. We're the fucking Beatles. This is nuts! Seeing "7,000" as a number on the dorm widget is exciting, but seeing seven thousand actual people in front of you...

Wow.

"Now let's turn the heat up. We want to see you sweat!"

And off we go. Britney Spears' "Hold It Against Me" is pumped into the room like sleeping gas and we resume our choreographed dance. First we remove our shirts, throwing them into the audience (each has the web address prominently displayed on the back, as well as a secret code that provides the user with a free month-long membership). We are all six-packs and chests. We are sparkling nipple and belly button rings.

Next come the pants, which are track-style, lined along each leg with snaps. One hard pull and we're down to jockstraps, briefs, boxer briefs, or bikini briefs (with my NewYorkScrewniversity.com logo emblazoned on the ass, if room on the fabric allows). The boys are reaching from the dance floor up to the stage. Sebastian encouraged interaction and we obey. I run to the edge of the stage and sit, my legs hanging over the side. Like piranhas on a cow, hands are all over me. I guide some up to my abs, between my legs. I get hard immediately. I am sweat-slick and the hands sip up every droplet of perspiration. A hand finds its way up my underwear and I spin around to my knees, humping the hands that are able to reach me. Down the line, all the boys are doing the same. Joey and Ryan are all over each other, licking nipples, rubbing hands up and down, down and up.

Britney begets Robyn begets Gaga begets Black Eyed Peas begets Britney again. We are all rock hard. We flash peeks of our web-famous goods. And as I do this, I wonder, is MartyMan22 one of these hands? I look down into dark, indecipherable faces for a clue but all I see is desire. He could be any of them or none of them. I look to the wings to see Sebastian and Michael enraptured by our performance.

Todd, however, has disappeared.

We are sex on stage. Ryan plucks Joey out of his underwear and the crowd is insane. They are demanding, begging, pleading, *please please please put it in your mouth*. Ryan shrugs and goes to town. If there's a plainclothes cop in here, this club will be shut down for good. Of course, Michael Porcelain could care less. The street cred that comes with shutting down a club will have them rich for decades. They can throw a party on a garbage barge with a transsexual puppeteer performing the songs of Tiny Tim after tonight and still sell out in advance.

The mix ends abruptly and we run offstage, waving and blowing kisses, with

Joey promising we'll be back for an extra special scene in two hours, and that if anyone has a friend who hasn't made it yet, they better hurry, because the doors WILL close at 2 AM.

"The shit show's just getting started," he teases. "We'll see you boys REAL soon."

CHAPTER 33

Back in the VIP room, Michael Porcelain is waving, screaming, drinking, and sweating. "Fucking amazing! You boys are insane! I told you, Seb! Did I tell you?"

Sebastian nods and gives us a few notes on our performances. We should strike harder angles and always look up into the light, even if it's raping our retinas.

Michael tears his ever-present sunglasses off his face, eyes wild with success and filled with dollar signs. "They fucking LOVED you guys! We're running out of promo cards and coasters!"

This isn't a problem, because Sebastian ordered a second round of promo materials in case this happened. He sprints out of the room to help the promoters restock all the bars. Michael, ablaze and manic, rushes back out of the room to his party of the century, leaving us and the other VIPs to relax between sets.

Todd never returns, and if MartyMan22 is here, he's hiding from me. I meet actors, dancers, Broadway guys who are expecting Tony nominations this year. They tell me they've never seen my work, but now they intend to. I blush and nod and thank them for the compliments, all the while wondering — is he one of them? Is he playing with me?

"Marty!" Joey whisper-screams at me, pulling me away from my new fans and friends. "It's MartyMan22! He's here!"

"Where?" I ask, my head darting in all directions, trying to see through my drunken fog to make out the face.

"Right there!" I follow Joey's finger to the corner of the room where Todd sat before. MartyMan is facing away from me, talking to one of the potential Tony triple-threat hopefuls I met a moment ago. Thanks to the hundred or so people between he and I, all I can see is the top of his shoulders and his hair, and only when the sea of humans between us ebbs in such a way that I am gifted with a clear sightline.

"He's HOT, Marty!" Joey says. "Crazy or not, if you don't take him home with us, I will. Fuck! Van Cleave owes me a Benjamin!"

Joey laughs and fades into the background. I am sucking in my stomach and squeezing past this person and that. I am knocking over drinks despite being careful and ducking between go-go boys stripping out of their first pair of underwear and into their second pair of the night. MartyMan is getting closer and closer.

I am right behind him. My heart is racing. I wonder if maybe this is all some joke my dorm buddies are playing on me. Maybe MartyMan22 will turn around to reveal that he's actually Rowell in a wig.

"So you're my number one fan..." I say, arranging a sexy grin in preparation for his eyes and what could very well be love at first sight.

He spins around.

I am staring my ex-boyfriend in the face.

"Marty," Graham smiles. "So nice to finally meet you!"

Not love. HATE. And not first sight, either — but rather, someone I never wanted to see again. My smile is a frown is a grimace is a frozen flat line of fury. Seething. Heat surges inside me. My fist clenches and collides with his nose. It is the first punch I've thrown in my entire life.

Graham's arms shoot up to deflect the full force of my knuckle. I make direct contact and feel his nose crunch under my fist. I spin on my heels —

almost falling, thanks to a puddle of caffeinated vodka — and rush across the room, straight for the exit.

"Marty!" one of the boys screams.

"Gulliver!" Graham is coming after me, trying but failing to hold the blood in his nose.

My knuckle is throbbing. My brain slams against the inside of my head. My throat has closed. I shove my way out the door and down the stairs, the voices of Joey, Ryan, Chris, and crew asking where am I going? They are trying to stop Graham from chasing me but he wriggles through them, keeping up with me.

I don't make it to the street because Graham catches my arm. "If you don't talk to me, I'll call your parents and tell them EVERYTHING."

I stop. My fury is sky-high. My eyes are made of tears. My ears are ringing and my stomach hurts so much I want to throw up. Maybe I will — all over him.

I turn to look my ex-boyfriend in his gorgeous (and blood-gushing) face for the first time since April, when I told him I never wanted to see said face again.

"I hate you," I spit.

"That's fine!" he yells, trying to get a word in over Kelis blasting from the bass speakers right next to us. "We still need to talk."

"No, we don't. Get the fuck out of here before I call security."

"Go ahead. I've got your Mom on speed dial." He holds up his phone to prove it.

I have no choice. This is a fucking hostage situation — he's got a gun to my future's head — and as long as that's his threat, I'll do anything he wants. Anything.

"Be outside in five minutes," I say. "Around the corner."

"If you disappear on me like you did a few months ago, I've got a pic of the promo for that little three-way you did just waiting to be sent to your mom. Leo. And all our friends back home. I'm sure they'd find it just as stunning as I did."

"Fuck you! I heard your pathetic little threat the first three thousand times!" I throw over my shoulder as I walk back upstairs to tell my boys I'm fine.

Back at the party, I laugh. I have a drink. I tell the boys that MartyMan22 turned out to be some kid with a grudge against me for sleeping with his ex-boyfriend, a nice spin on the real events that led to the recent birth of Marty Brayden.

Then I tell them I need to hit the bathroom and slip outside, unnoticed by all.

Outside eWrecksion, around the corner from the line of gays who have fingers crossed that they make it in before the doors close and they miss the show of the century, I slap my ex-boyfriend across the face. The slap echoes on the empty West Village street — a loud, resonating sound that bounces back to my ears.

It isn't enough.

I slap him again.

Graham rubs his reddening face. His nose is no longer bleeding, but it has dried blood rings around the nostrils. There are tears in his eyes. "You get one more of those, Gull. Better make it count."

I pull back and put every last bit of me in the sweeping arc, my hand cutting through space and displacing matter, bringing kinetic energy to a forceful smash on the side of Graham's stubbly cheek. I am slapping Marty. I am slapping Brayden. I am slapping Marty Brayden. I am slapping myself. This slap goes out to all of New York City, and the direct recipient is the one who sent me here in the first place.

Graham falls backwards. And despite this, I am the one crying.

"You asshole. You fucking psychotic asshole!" I rub my face like I actually have been slapping myself. "You had to come here?! You had to come and fuck EVERYTHING up?!"

Graham rises slowly. Cautiously. "Everything looks pretty fucked up already from where I'm standing."

"You're wrong," I wheeze. "For the first time, I am making it. By myself. I am MAKING something of myself."

"Yeah, making an ass of yourself. You call this making it? You're DESTROYING yourself. Jesus. Get a clue, Gulliver."

I am wearing underwear, socks, sneakers, and an unzipped hoodie — the outfit of choice for go-go boys and scantily-clad bartenders on their smoke breaks all around New York City. Graham is dressed the same as when I last saw him — the sleeveless tee, the tight distressed jeans, the flip flops and socks.

"Destroying myself? I think you're being a touch dramatic. In case you didn't notice, every single person in there LOVES me."

Graham laughs a little, shaking his head. "Everyone fucks, Gulliver. Just because you let the world watch doesn't make you special."

"Well, there are a lot of people in there who disagree with you."

Graham pauses. He looks at me like there's a roach crawling on my face. "Um. Is that a tongue ring?"

"Yeah," I sniff. "So what."

"Nothing. It looks good. Not sure about the blue hair. And that chinstrap makes you look like such a douche bag."

"Did you fly all the way out here to let me know I look like shit?"

"You don't look like shit. You look good. You just look… different. Not the Gull I remember."

No one since I moved here has called me Gull. No one before or after Graham ever happened upon that nickname. Every time he says it, it's like he's smacking me with the past. Every date. Every time we had sex. Every fight, including the last one. All of it loaded into a sack, tied at the top, then swung backward and hurled forward directly at me. That name is latched to everything. I fucking hate it.

"I am different."

"No, you're not."

"I'm NOT the 'Gull' you remember."

"Sure you are."

"You don't know shit about the last few months of my life and you DON'T know me anymore!"

"Okay, okay." His hands are up, his voice getting lower. "You're right. I'm sorry."

"Great. Now why are you here? WHY THE FUCK ARE YOU HERE?"

A bouncer comes around the corner, shining his little handheld flashlight in our faces and mumbling something about not disturbing the neighbors. We nod in understanding, which seems to appease him as he shuffles off.

"How could I not be here?" Graham asks, his voice lower.

"How long have you been here?"

"Two days. I'm staying with Kevin."

Kevin. Graham's ex-roommate and fucking ex-secret-boyfriend. I had thought Kevin was just one of the guys Graham and I slept with toward the end of our relationship, back when monogamy was the least of our problems and random special guests seemed to work as far as keeping things interesting in the bedroom.

As I later found out, the first time I slept with Kevin was not the first time Graham slept with Kevin. Not by a long shot. When Kevin came out to me, I assumed it was news to Graham, too. Turns out I was the only one who'd been kept in the dark. It had seemed hot at the time — seducing Graham's newly gay former roommate, who still had that slightly awkward "straight guy" vibe radiating off him. Now it sickens me to know I was every bit as much a guest star in their frequent fuck-a-thons as Kevin was in Graham's and mine.

"I didn't know that asshole lived here now."

"Yeah. He got a great job out here. He's dating someone who's not me. He's the one who told me he thought he saw you on XTube. I told him he was full of it, of course. That you would never, ever do porn. Or dye your hair blue."

"Enough about the hair, Graham."

"One more. BLUE? Really?"

I'm laughing. And then I'm angry because my asshole ex is making me laugh.

I pull back to slap him and he puts his hands up, catching my wrist.

"What the fuck happened out here? I thought you were living with Todd. I thought you were working as a talent agent."

"Someone's been doing their fair share of Facebook stalking."

"Always a talent of mine. So?"

A cab rushes around the corner and speeds past us. I jump at the sudden sound.

"Shit," I say then. "Shit happened. Point is, I landed on my feet."

"You landed on your back. Legs in the air."

"Still so fucking poetic." I'm zipping up the hoodie even though I'll be shucking it once I get back into the club, which stands to be any moment now. "We done?"

"I. Will. Call. Your. Mom."

"You wouldn't dare."

"YOU wouldn't dare walk off knowing that I might."

I stop mid-zip. Hostage.

"As my biggest fan I'm sure you're aware I've got a show starting soon. They'll be closing those doors any minute now. So I really should be on my way, and so should you. If you don't want to miss out on the New York City gay nightlife event of the century."

He just dangles his cell phone in front of me, Mom's cell phone number already loaded onto the screen, his finger covering the "Send" button. He's calling my bluff — which is still considerably better than calling my mother.

God. What would she do? What would Dad do? Would they disown me forever? Tell me I'm never again welcome in their house? Leave me to rot here? Tell everyone I'm dead? Maybe they'd even hold a funeral. Bury an empty casket to make it all the more official. I can imagine their tearful faces at the services, still better than the look I picture on Mom's face when she Googles "Marty Brayden," hoping and praying that this just an evil scheme of my vengeful ex-boyfriend. That it couldn't possibly be true of their darling Gulliver.

And then the confirmation as my bright, smiling face popped up on the NewYorkScrewniversity homepage atop my bare torso (one of the site's top three earners!). Of course, they'd need to pay a pretty penny to get any further, but there'd be no need. All twenty-some years of love and parental pride would be flushed right down the toilet in the blink of an eye. To avoid this, I will beg and plead and strangle a defenseless child with my bare hands to get Graham to put that phone away.

"Fine. I'm here. What do you want?"

"I want you to go back on stage and do whatever the fuck you've planned to do with your fellow screw-dents."

I'm measuring his face for sarcasm.

"Okay…"

"And make sure you do it well. Because tonight you're retiring."

"What? You can't make me do that."

"Well. I am."

I'm crying. Because this is it. Despite all the money I have, it'll dry up real fast when I have to start paying for food and rent and utilities and clothing back in some shithole. Six months if I'm lucky. Maybe less.

"I can't make you forgive me. I can't get you back. But I can't let you do this to yourself. It isn't you."

"It IS me! This is who I am now! Marty fucking Brayden!"

Graham's palm connects with my face. The back of my head hits the brick wall, knocking me to the ground. Graham stares at his hand like it's an unwelcome guest. He shakes it out and shoves it into his pocket.

"Fuck, Gull. Fuck!" And now he's joined the crying party.

I stay on the floor, the city lights twirling above me. Inside, the boys of NewYorkScrewniversity.com are getting ready for our live sex show. Michael Porcelain is instructing his doormen not to open the doors under any circumstances (and if a plainclothes cop shows up, the correct code to whisper into their walkie-talkies). I should be in there. I should be joking, primping, positioning my dick just so. I should be prepping to fuck and get fucked in front of the better part of gay New York. So why aren't I? Why, instead, am I here?

The reason, of course, is Graham. He's the reason I'm here outside, and the reason I'm here in New York. Throughout everything, he's had that power over me. The power to chase me out of LA, the power to keep me struggling to stay afloat in New York just to keep away from him. Now he has more power than ever, and I have no choice but to let him have it, or any hope of returning to my old life gets dashed to pieces irreversibly.

"You did this," I sneer. "NONE of this would've happened if you didn't lie to me. We were SO happy, Graham! Our friends were jealous of us! My parents were ready to make fucking marriage arrangements! And then you go off and fuck another guy for MONTHS without telling me!"

Graham's hand comes back out, but it is in the air, hovering there, silencing me. I back up instinctively.

"I've beaten myself up enough about it, Gull. I apologized to you for months. I stopped talking to him. I stopped going out. That day I asked you to meet me Starbucks? I was going to tell you that. I wasn't going to ask you for another chance. I just wanted to look you in the face and genuinely say how sorry I was."

I tell myself it doesn't matter, my jaw tight. There's no amount of sorry that's sorry enough.

"But now? I am done feeling bad about what I did. I'm sure it sucks to be cheated on. But let me tell you, it's a whole different type of torture when you're the cheater. Because then you're not just afraid of trusting other people, you're petrified of trusting yourself. And worst of all, you only have yourself to blame for losing the one person who could make you feel better. It fucking sucks."

"Good," I sniff.

"Okay, so now that we've both blamed me for everything, why don't YOU try taking some fucking responsibility for your actions?" Graham yells. "People break up all the time. Do you think you're that special? Or WE were that special? Come off of it! Not every heartbroken fag ends up in porn. That's all you, Gull."

That F-word hangs in the air between us. I invoke another.

"Fuck you."

It's the summation of everything else I'd like to say, that I just can't anymore.

Graham sighs and rolls his eyes. But he's quiet for a long moment.

"I guess I've said what I wanted to say. Thanks for listening."

"Like I had a choice?" I stand up and zip my hoodie again. "So was it worth it? Five hundred bucks, and a plane ticket, and the time off work?"

"If it means I never run across another video of you getting a facial on XTube, knowing I'm a large part of the reason why you're doing so in the first place, then yeah, it was. You're still new. But a lot of bad things can happen to you in your line of work. You think I want that hanging over my head?"

"I think you just want to surf porn and jerk off in peace, without the boner-killer reminder that you lost me," I smirk. "Now if you'll excuse me, I have a show to do. And apparently, an early retirement to announce."

Sebastian is going to be so pissed. I need to check my savings. I've made enough to find a place, I'm sure. But again, I'm back at square one — homeless, jobless, friendless. Can I do this all over again?

Yes. Why not? I'm an expert by now.

"Okay. Enjoy your swan song. I'll tell LA you said 'fuck you.'"

"Right." I'm turning around now. "Be sure to save most of that message for yourself."

Now I'm walking back to the club. Now I'm trying to figure out where the hell my life is going. God. When will it just get easy?

"Gulliver!" he calls out to me.

I turn and look at Graham. He's standing under a streetlight that casts a pale beam of light over him, making him look like a ghost with long shadows under his eyes, nose, and chin. I wonder if this is really it. If this is the last time I'll see my fucking asshole ex-boyfriend. Now that he has successfully ruined my life not once but twice, maybe he'll finally give up.

"I'll always love you. You know that, right?"

I stand still for a moment. And then I shrug. "Maybe."

Graham wipes tears off his face and blows a kiss across the empty space between us. "Good. And good luck."

I leave his kiss floating in the air behind me and walk away. He makes no attempt to follow me back inside.

When I reach the front, I nod at the bouncer who pats my chest and lets me

269 / JUSTIN LUKE ZIRILLI

in past the line. Some recognize me, compliment me on the scene from the other day. I blow them kisses and tell them I'll see them inside.

What I don't tell them is that they will now be present for a historical moment in the East Coast amateur gay porn scene — the first and final live performance of that smutty spitfire, Marty Brayden.

CHAPTER 34

Here's how it all went down:

Sometime after 2 AM, Sebastian and a hired crew brought in two beds from the dorm and, behind the cover of a large velvet curtain, worked with ten members of Michael Porcelain's staff to construct a sexual wonderland on the stage. The beds were surrounded by every apparatus a porn connoisseur should recognize: couches, chairs, a pool table (always a pool table). Even a sling.

At 3 AM, as advertised, the boys of NewYorkScrewniversity.com took the stage for a live sex show gay men would talk about for years to come. Those who saw it swear it was the hottest, most spectacular event they had ever witnessed (and would ever witness) in their lifetime. Those who missed it — and bemoan that New York's gay nightlife scene was scraped and scrubbed clean by responsible senators and mayors — consider this story to be preposterous, collectively fabricated by those who claimed to have been there.

But we know better.

We saw the one and only Marty Brayden on a bed getting plowed, tag-team style, by Joey Gambit, Ryan Roberts, and Chris Van Cleave, each taking turns on his notoriously tight butt. We remember the money shots, each well worth the price of admission. We recall all the hot, carnal chaos surrounding this centerpiece — Rowell had a good thing going with David Michael and AJ Zirpoli, two relative newcomers to the dorm. They began with a daisy-chain arrangement, their bodies folding over one another, sweat glistening under the burning stage lights.

Some of us remember that Todd DiTempto disappeared that night, right after announcing the first performance (the tamer of the two shows). This is something no one understood, because the boys of NewYorkScrewniversity.com were right up his alley. Why leave right before a momentous nightlife occasion that, like an eclipse or a double rainbow, might never, ever happen again? A few overheard Todd tell someone he felt a little nauseous, blaming Marty Brayden — not the twink, but the drink. Seems he ordered one too many of the blue-hued cocktails and returned home to ward off the quickly-approaching hangover. Of course, some of us wonder at the absence of DiTempto's crew, too — Shane and Rowan and what's-his-name, at his side anywhere and everywhere — but not that night. Those who inquired later didn't get much of a response. They just weren't really in the mood to go out that night, they said.

We remember Michael Porcelain manning the microphone and calling the action like a play-by-play announcer with such a frenzy that paramedics on hand took bets on whether he'd drop dead of a heart attack right there. We remember him howling and running across the stage, continuously shouting out the address for the website, holding his microphone in the center of the copulating couplings and triplings so that their moans might be amplified for the rest of us in attendance to hear.

We recall the lights and the music, a bass that rocked every last person in the three-floor club to our very core. The actual songs didn't matter, because the sound guy turned up that bass so dangerously high. Ears present that night rang for days after, like a teakettle whistling from three rooms away.

We remember the bartenders stepping away from their posts to admire something that, to date, was reserved for fictional TV programs like *Queer as Folk* (British or American, take your pick). Joining them were security who, true to their promise, had bolted the doors shut and killed all exterior lights, blanketing the street (and anyone who didn't make the cutoff) in darkness. Even the VIP room cleared out.

No one spoke. Not a person in the entire club could think of anything worth saying that compared to what was unfolding before their very eyes.

And of all of those gay men who remember this gay night of nights — this porn come to glorious life on a stage surrounded by more than seven thousand frothing fans — almost all will remember it as the last public appearance of porn star Marty Brayden.

Marty went out with a bang, of course. He took it up the ass from no less than five of his dorm mates, eyes rolling back in his head, face always positioned at the most perfect of angles, abs and chest swelling to the point that they appeared as if they might pop and deflate. And then, when all was said and done, Marty hopped up from the bed as though he had been napping rather than getting furiously fucked by piles of muscles and tattoos. He blew kisses to the cheering crowd. A few of us swore we saw tears in his eyes as he took his bow; those of us with more common sense assumed it was merely a glean of sweat or perhaps stray droplets of a dorm mate's seed.

The boys didn't stick around after the show because Sebastian decreed that the crowd must be left wanting more. We remember Marty cramming himself back into the NewYorkScrewniversity.com party bus, back to wherever this magical dorm existed, waving at the fans who had followed them out to bid a fond farewell — for the night, they thought. Not for good. But then Marty disappeared from the porn scene forever without another word.

In following weeks, as autumn began to sneak up on the city, porn blogs published reports, rumors, and blind items. Fleshbot and QueerClick were on the case like it was the second coming of the Jon Benet murder. Interviews with anonymous sources exploded across the web, half fictional, the other half dubious. People swore they had seen Mr. Marty Brayden on and around the gay New York nightlife scene. Some saw him at Pacha. Others claimed he was drinking at Campus Thursdays, even hopping up on the bar with some of the go-go boys to dance the night away. Still others would snap photos of attractive gay boys roaming the streets of New York, sending them in as proof that Marty was indeed still in the Big Apple. But nothing was ever confirmed.

Then the rumors increased in implausibility. Marty had taken the small fortune he amassed and moved on to Paris or Tokyo or Rome. He was starting his own porn company there, amassing a studio of studs to take down NewYorkScrewniversity (which, in such tales, had made him an enemy by screwing him out of money, or not featuring him enough, or maybe he secretly dated one of the other boys until things went sour). Others claimed he died of an overdose (despite Sebastian publicly repeating, ad nauseum, his strict no-drugs policy). Still more said Marty took up an escort job with

RentBoy.com, using his "assets" to make well-dressed visiting businessmen and entrepreneurs look all the more influential at their sexy parties before blowing their minds in their boutique hotel rooms later.

Again, all rumors. Because nobody had a shred of proof to support a single claim.

After six weeks, memorials to the blue-haired ingenue of NewYorkScrewniversity sprang up online. The famous three-way rose to the top of the most viewed videos in the archive. Sebastian created a special section to house back-footage of all Marty's performances for those who were only just hearing of him thanks to these flying rumors. All in all, the publicity became quite profitable for the site.

Emails came in by the boatload asking if Marty was working for other companies or behind the cameras in a more strategic position for the Screwniversity. They begged to donate any untold sum to get him back, if even for one single scene. Sebastian responded to all of these messages with a form email:

Dear Subscriber,

We at NewYorkScrewniversity.com are sorry to report that Marty Brayden has permanently retired from adult film work.

We will miss his presence at the dorms and wish him all the best in his future pursuits.

Please keep coming back — we promise his replacement will blow your mind, amongst other things!

The replacement foreshadowed in that email was called Billy Rage. He appeared in the dorm on September 1st — a smooth, tanned, tattooed boy with dirty brown hair and only one dimple. Billy kicked off his enrollment with a four-way featuring Chris, Joey, and Ryan. He knew he had a lot to live up to, but he was a go-getter and determined as all hell. Rumor has it he studied Marty's videos to learn from the master.

By October, Marty Brayden was forgotten, and Billy Rage was — well, all the rage.

Meanwhile, a day after Marty's vanishing, a boy with an eyebrow ring and a shaved head moved into a small studio up in Harlem — far beyond the sexy bars of the Village, Chelsea, and Hell's Kitchen, near 145th street. It was owned by a lesbian makeup artist on tour with *Jersey Boys*. She knew very little about her new tenant, except for the fact that her cousin Sebastian said he was a reliable fellow. She was more than happy to accept his first month, last month, and security, which was paid for in cold hard cash.

The boy's name was Gulliver, inspiring her to say, "Well, Gulliver, I'm sure your travels in Harlem will be plenty adventurous. And quite different from those you had in LA."

"I'm sure you're right," Gulliver laughed over the phone. "I've always been down for an adventure. And PS: I love your apartment, it's gorgeous."

"Thanks. You'd be surprised the deals you can find uptown when downtown you'd be living in a shoebox for this price. So. Welcome to New York."

"Thank you," he told her, and hung up.

The studio was fully furnished and cozy from the second he arrived. Hardwood floors and red-painted walls created a homey feeling he had missed. The walls were covered in relics from the owner's theatrical career — masks, sets from previous productions, signed Playbills and group photos. It took Gulliver less than two hours to unpack his things.

But it took a week before he was ready to pick up the phone and place a call to a contact he hadn't contacted in quite some time. It was answered before the end of the first ring.

"Hey, bro."

"Gully?"

"You remember my voice."

"Yeah, no shit. Where the hell have you been?"

"Harlem, of all places."

"Does this mean you're officially back from the dead?"

"Guess so. A zombie, anyway. Better keep a close eye on your brain. Which reminds me, have you eaten dinner?"

"If I had, I'd stick my fingers down my throat right now if it meant getting to see you again. Mind if I bring the boys?"

"Um. Does that include Brayden?"

"Time heals wounds, bro. And having a friend disappear from the world for a couple months puts shit in perspective. We were fucking worried about you — yes, even Brayden."

And, in the background, a shriek: "Tell that fucking cunt I have an iPhone now. It's way too expensive to break over a bitch's fugly face!" The accompanying howl is joined by a chorus of other recognizable laughs.

"Noted. And tell THAT fucking cunt I now own a hockey mask and will be wearing it upon his arrival."

"Put it on, bro. Text me the new addy and we'll be up in an hour with Chinese food, and housewarming gifts like candles that smell like sweet shit and new, fugly towels for your bathroom. You dig?"

"Yeah, bro. Consider it dug."

"Awesome. Señor is coming, too."

ROUND IV

CHAPTER 35

The Musical Mondays party is a show queen's dream held at Splash every week down in Chelsea. It's the same bar that hosts so many other parties I frequented more than I'd like to (or can) remember, but you wouldn't know from stepping inside on a Monday that it is even the same location. The go-go boy dancing blocks are removed, the floor filled instead by metal tables and stools. Leather daddies and twinks in G-strings are replaced by wannabe actors and theater addicts. On the large projection screens surrounding the dance floor, instead of Ke$ha and Kylie and assorted other pop goddesses, you get Chita Rivera, Angela Lansbury, Patti LuPone, and Bernadette Peters. I love Splash because, daily, it is always changing — its crowds, its music, its skin — and yet if you come the same day every week, it's the same as the week before. A constant chameleon returning to its roots every seven days.

The boys who come to Musical Mondays are there to sing at the top of their lungs. To show off how they memorized the entire opening number from *A Chorus Line* (well, the entire show, probably). To stand on one of those metal stools, an invisible (or sometimes actual) broomstick in one outstretched hand as they belt the dramatic end to "Defying Gravity." The bar fills up at 7 and empties by 12:30 when all the actors go home for beauty rest before the next day's auditions and cattle calls (or to another bar, if they are not so lucky). You can get trashed on the "Buy one, get one" special by 10 and still end up in bed before midnight, getting more sleep Monday than you will for the rest of the week.

This is where I work now. As a bartender.

The manager started me out last month down on the basement level — the same space where Todd auditions go-go boys every Thursday. The job came from Todd, of course, and for the first time, I accepted it gladly and guilt-lessly. I proved my worth quickly, always pouring perfect shots and earning my own little fan club — people who came to the near-empty basement to drink with Gulliver.

Todd and I have been working out since I moved to Harlem, so I'm starting to bulk up — which is important since the bartender dress code consists of small underwear, sneakers, and socks (which, ironically enough, would be overdressed in my previous line of employment). All the hard work with Todd and his trainer has paid off with a six-pack and a healthy set of "man lines." Between my following and the way I'm looking in my briefs, it didn't take long before I graduated to the main floor, right by the entrance — high traffic, high octane, and even higher stress.

It's funny how different a club feels when you work there. You gain access to the offices hidden in the back, the familiar fluorescent lights and slow-mov-ing PCs you'd find in any other business. Here you can't really hear the music. This is where paychecks are cut and notes line the walls, warning go-go boys not to "tie off" to make their dicks look bigger and bartenders not to give free drinks to their friends. The mystique is gone. The sexy, sinful darkness is a bit lighter when you walk a path you've walked so many Mondays before. The club also loses its glitz when you're sober and physically exhausted and have ten people shouting detailed drink orders at you.

Not that I'm complaining. I love it here.

I owe thanks, again, to Todd. After I "returned" to New York, Todd became a speeding tank for my cause — committed to getting me a job that could help me stay in my Harlem rental with ease. He took me to parties where I met every bartender, every promoter — and instead of getting trashed and making out with someone, I watched and learned. Todd threw me behind the bar on quiet nights at events he ran, where I learned the trade. I was a natu-ral, thanks to my history of working at Starbucks. I quickly learned to make all the drinks I've been imbibing since arriving in New York. From there, it was a few phone calls and Todd had me working the basement on Musical Mondays. From the basement to the top floor, and from Musical Mondays to four parties a week. In record time.

The old crew drops by to say hi (and get free booze) weekly; my apology to them comes in liquid form, a never-ending tidal wave of Long Island Iced Teas. No one has mentioned their conspicuous absence that night at eWrecksion, which is reason enough to believe they're keeping quiet for a reason. Maybe they know everything. Maybe Todd just asked them to trust him and please not show up that night. Whatever it is, I don't need to know. By now I know there's no such thing as a totally clean slate. The past comes back, often when you'd least prefer it to. I'll never totally abandon the fear that Mom, Dad, or Leo will somehow stumble across an image of Marty Brayden someday; never be fully satisfied that Graham won't pull another stunt and tell someone who tells someone, and so forth. If there was ever any danger of me running for political office, well, that won't be happening now. But that's life. We all have a little something we hope will stay buried until long after we are. If my dirty laundry ever comes up for air, I'll deal with it then. For now, I just live my life.

Brayden and I are speaking too. It's still awkward. I'm not sure if it's me, him, or the both of us. But we're trying. And while the conversations may be labored, they're getting better. He's seeing someone — someone I haven't met yet, and if he had his way, maybe never would. But I will. Eventually.

Oh, and I served a certain globetrotting talent agent a martini two weeks ago. He almost didn't recognize me. Stanford's doing fantastically, of course. He now has an office with three employees, freeing him up enough to permit an occasional night at Musical Mondays. He wants to meet for lunch in a few weeks when he's back from another trip to Boston. I accepted the invitation.

And Marty? He's on the road like I expected: one of two *Wicked* tours currently crossing the United States in a never-ending figure-eight. I'm not ready to speak to him yet, but have been working on getting up the nerve to at least send a text to say I'm sorry. I have no interest in getting back together — I don't want to be his Graham. And two strikes with the crew is already two too many. I just want to make amends, and move on.

Mom and Dad are fine. Leo still has that girlfriend Mom thinks is an alcoholic. Now she thinks I'm one, too. Mom wasn't too hot on me working as a bartender until the wee hours of the morning, but it's better that she complain about this job than the one that preceded it, so I patiently cope with her endless chiding. It's good to call home once a day again. I never realized until now how much hearing their voices for even a few minutes every day can cheer me up and give me what it takes to keep on keepin' on.

I see Joey and Ryan and the other dorm boys sometimes, too. They followed a trail of "sightings" of me online, cornered me one night when I was still working in the basement (at that point, my head was still buzzed down to stubble). Joey and Ryan leaned against the bar, winked, and asked if I knew how to make a Marty Brayden. I actually did. (It's delicious!) They are now regulars. Ryan is thinking of retiring, trying to get into bartending as well. Joey, on the other hand, is going to be working in the dorms until he is too old to be on camera. Then he will no doubt step behind the lens and work alongside Sebastian as they turn the site into a force that tramples all the best-known adult studios in the world.

So maybe New York City isn't as cruel as I thought.

After three hours of running, pouring, shaking, icing, bottle opening, money taking, pretzel bowl refilling, shouting "what!?", squatting, ice well restocking, tip collecting, and bottle flipping (a little trick one of the other bartenders taught me, both fun and attention-grabbing), I am able to sneak out to the street. The autumn air is cold and the street is gleaming with a recent sheet of fallen rain. This will mark my first fall in New York; Todd has warned me that my first winter might also be my last, depending on how I deal with the frigid temperatures. I told him I'm not going anywhere.

I light a cigarette and check my texts. Between drags I read and erase, read and erase.

Mostly the messages come from guys who asked for my number while I was working. I've gone out with a few but slept with none. I've had my fill of sex for a while. (Or, as Shane puts it, I've declared a moratorium on my ass.) The other text messages are from Todd and the crew, who will be down as soon as Rowan decides what fucking pair of jeans to wear. (*"Like it fucking matters? These Broadway bitches will ignore his ass the second he admits he has no idea who Judy Garland is!"*) And one is from Todd's nightlife boss. He wants me to help him promote a party this weekend. I tell him sure, why not. I'm not working that night, and Todd has been helping me create a list of emails and phone numbers in case I want to dip my toe in promoting. Maybe that's my next step here in New York — I'd love to see my name alongside Todd's on glossy promos handed out by stunning boys on every corner of every gayborhood.

"Todd DiTempto and Gulliver Leverenz present:
something something something."

The creative part will have to come later. Right now, I just bask in my future fame. With that plus bartending plus the slew of small freelance design projects I've been picking up on Craigslist, I may be able to start a savings account — one with an actual savings in it, that is.

"Hey, got a light?"

I turn and come face-to-face with Chase. My one-night fling from Fire Island; my one-night "special guest star" at NYScrewniversity. My two-night stand.

He's cut his hair since I last saw him. Now it's messy, flying out in all directions. He leans against the wall and measures me up and down. And from the look on his face, I don't think he has the slightest clue who I am.

I light his menthol and he leans up next to me.

"Thanks."

"No problem."

And then we're both silent, our backs against the cold, slightly wet bricks on the exterior of Splash. Cabs are speeding down the block, the bouncer (Louey) is telling people they can't smoke in front of the entrance, and could they please move somewhere else, like perhaps the designated smoking area?

"You having a good time tonight?" I ask him finally.

"Thanks to those drinks you're pouring, for sure."

I'm laughing. "Oh, wow. I've been serving you? I'm so sorry, I didn't even notice…"

"You're a fucking speed freak back there, it's totally understandable. Anyway, I'm Chase."

"Gulliver." I shake his hand.

"Gulliver?" He studies my face. "Okay, if you would've said Joe, or Daniel, or like, any other name, I probably never would have remembered. But unless there are two guys out there whose parents hated him as much as yours did

— did we meet on Fire Island?"

"Hmm," I say coyly, tapping my chin as if trying to recall. "Yes. And I remember the time after that, too. About two months ago. You were going by the name Chase Bliss?"

Chase turns to face me, looks me up and down from sneakers to package to face. "You're kidding."

Cat's out of the bag. I don't know why I told him — it's the first time I've come clean about my pornographic misadventures since quitting the dorm. But meetings like this don't happen three times. They just don't.

"I am not, actually."

Now Chase is laughing. Hard. He's having difficulty breathing, his face crinkling up in the cutest way I've ever seen. "How the hell did I not recognize you?"

"I'm a bit of a chameleon. Or used to be, anyway."

"No shit? Well, I like you better like this. That chinstrap made you look like a douche bag."

"Yeah, I've heard that before."

"A sexy douche bag, though. Obviously."

Our faces are getting closer as we flirt. Our breath, visible in the chill, grazes each other's faces.

"I gave you my number," he says. "At the dorm."

"I gave you MY number on Fire Island."

"Yeah, that was a shitty weekend. My phone was broken and then I found out I had chlamydia. Right after we hooked up, actually."

"Thanks for the gift," I laugh.

"Oh no!" His cigarette drops to the floor. "Did I give it to you?"

"You sure did. Hurt like hell."

"I am so sorry! I got it from this guy I was dating. Fucker was cheating on me, I found out, like, two days before Fire Island. I was sort of in a crazy place that weekend, trying to forget him. But if I had known, I never would have…"

I kiss him, leaving his face permanently etched with shock. He shakes his head. "Gulliver. How can you still be talking to me?"

I put my hands on his shoulders, push him back against the wall. "It's fine. As much my fault as it was yours."

"But then I went home with you and had sex on camera! Oh my god, you must think I'm such a…"

I put a finger up to Chase's mouth and shush him dramatically. "Enough. It was my camera, my audience. And that's all in the past now."

He nods slowly, and then I'm kissing him. Hard. In between laughing and shushing him. I must look like a crazy person. And a slut. A crazy slut. When's the last time you told someone you gave them chlamydia and received laughter and kisses as a response?

But he's playing along. His hand is rubbing my naked back. I put my hand up his shirt to rub his torso, lifting the shirt higher to see the chain of the old-fashioned gold pocket watch.

"After that night at the dorm, I stared at my phone for days," he says. "I know that makes me seem pitiful and lame. But I did."

"All I can say is I'm in a different place now. A place you might actually want to get to know me."

"You mean I don't know you yet? What about all the quality time we shared in front of thousands of anonymous online viewers?"

"And the pool on Fire Island. Don't forget the pool."

"Oh, I haven't." Chase finishes his cigarette and stomps it out. Patti LuPone is belting "Everything's Coming Up Roses." Her voice — which to me sounds like a flat vacuum cleaner switched on reverse — blows out the open window next to us.

"I should get inside before they come looking for me," I say.

"I'm afraid to give you my number. What if you never call me?"

"Here," I pull out my cell phone from my sock. "Put your number in. I'll call it right now."

"So that's where you guys keep your phones." He types it in, fingers flying on the keypad. "Third time's a charm?"

I dial the number and his phone rings from inside his pocket. "I'm here until 3:30. Not sure what your schedule is like, but if you want to do breakfast at four, I know a diner nearby."

"You talk like I don't dance in this neighborhood on a weekly basis," he laughs. "Sure, I only have a midterm study session tomorrow. Fuck my perfect attendance."

"And who is this?!" Servando screams in his trademark sky-high register. He and the crew are quickly approaching on the sidewalk, arms crossed to fend off the cold since their fashionable thin jackets won't get the job done. Chase looks up, confused, and backs into my arms, which wrap around his torso almost instinctively.

"He's cute, for starters," Brayden says, sounding as close to genuine as he can. "And familiar?"

"His name is Chase. You may have briefly and drunkenly met at Fire Island."

Brayden's eyes are anywhere but on me when I mention the cursed island where our epic battle began. (Well, my epic ass-kicking.) Everyone nods in recollection and it's hard to determine which of us is most eager to change the subject.

"So you guys finally made it out? I see Rowan found the right pair of jeans. Well worth the six hours everyone waited on you."

"Whatever, bitch," he whines. "They're not the ones I wanted. But Todd said he'd kick my ass if he had to wait one more minute."

"I would've, too, bro," Todd says, clenching a fist and faking a shot at Rowan.

I lead the boys back toward the wall of show tunes blasting out the front doors. Bruce, a bald muscle-bound man with a scar above his stomach, is drenched in sweat, working double-time so I could smoke. I tap him on the shoulder. He takes a deep breath and runs from the bar to suck down his own cigarette. And I get back to work.

Refreshed by the nicotine and cold air, I am a blaze of energy. I'm pouring Long Island Iced Teas. Screwdrivers. Vodka cranberries. Madrases with Stoli Vanil. Someone orders a 007 and is shocked that I know how to make it. Plus there are plenty of beers (domestic and imported) I yank out of the cooler and crack open. I am pouring and pouring to show tunes. My boys are stationed near my corner of the bar (Chase included). They dangle tips in front of my face, sometimes snatching them back when I reach with a peal of laughter. They flirt with men who stop by to order drinks — the ones who look rich, anyway.

As the booze continues flowing, Rowan and Servando are at it. (Oh, they're dating again, who saw that coming?) Todd makes eyes with one of my regular fans — a boy clearly using a fake ID that is good enough to get him past the bouncer and his high-tech scanner. I nod and call Todd over, whispering that the kid, Joel, is an out of work actor — but if Todd doesn't mind that, he's completely and totally available.

Todd, of course, doesn't mind. They disappear within the hour.

The night is on fast-forward. One by one, my crew departs. When I finally have a chance to survey the crowd, I realize Chase is gone, too. I search the near-empty bar. In the pit of my stomach: jealousy. Did he go home with someone else? That fast?

Then again, given our past, what the hell else did I expect?

I hurriedly count my tips and cash out my drawer in the basement, saying goodnight to my fellow bartenders. I am equal parts despair and fury — as if my heart had been holding back all these times we've met and re-met, and finally let loose tonight, puking emotions all over him.

And just like that, he's gone? Story of my life.

I run outside, almost tripping over Chase's leg as he leans against the wall where we were kissing earlier.

"Jesus. I didn't think you were ever coming out." He spins his cigarette, pointing the filter at my mouth.

And so the anger-sadness-fear-jealousy melts and I am left staring at him, and he at me. I pull a hard drag from his cigarette and gag on the minty taste.

"I don't understand how anyone smokes these. I heard there are bits of glass in it."

"Cigarettes? Bad for my health? Man, I wish I'd known sooner."

"Smart ass," I laugh, and kiss him against the wall. "Come on, I'm starving."

"Lead the way, sexy," Chase says, offering his hand.

The diner is empty — we're between the 2 AM drunken gay boy rush and the 7 AM senior citizen attack. Because of this, Jenny (our waitress and usually my sole breakfast companion) has no problem with Chase and I taking up one of her largest booths. Over challah bread french toast (me) and an egg whites omelet with turkey and broccoli (Chase) I am racing through the story of me. Gulliver's travels. Because he made the mistake of asking what brought me to this point in my life.

His eyes don't blink once. It amazes me that what I thought was a Cliff's Notes version of my past six months takes over an hour to tell. In my defense, we did stop every now and again so he could ask the requisite, "Are you serious?" and so Jenny, making sure our coffee cups were never empty, could assure him: "Trust me, honey. It's all true."

"Wow. That's certainly not how I remember the story of *Gulliver's Travels*. When I read it as a kid, there were fewer three-ways."

"You only get one of those," I say. "And yours is gone now."

He points a bite of omelet at me accusingly. "I've been meaning to ask about that."

"It was all my mother's idea. She was reading it when she was pregnant with me. She said Gulliver carried her through to the moment of delivery. She also said my head was the size of a bowling ball."

Chase grimaces. "Well, in a world of Apples and Pumpkins and DiShontelles and all that, at least this one has some real meaning behind it."

I point my fork at him. "Easy for you to say. You don't have to fucking live with it."

"So change it." He puts his lip around my fork. "Pick something else. You've changed everything else forty or so times, right?"

"I've thought about it. Growing up Gulliver wasn't easy. It's an easy target: Seagull. Gilligan. Liverwurst. Plus that stupid travel joke everyone makes. EVERYONE makes. Even though none of them ever read the book. I mean, not even I have. Nor did I see the movie."

"It was a shitty movie." Chase takes a breath and gulp of decaf, wipes his eyes and stifles a yawn. I gaze beyond him to the street outside. Cabs fly by, "Off Duty" signs blazing bright white. Other than that, everything is as silent as New York can possibly be. "And now that your adventures are behind you, what's next?"

"Next, I get you on a train headed home. Which is where again?"

He grabs both of my hands over the crumb-covered table. "Oh, I think at this point, we both know where I'm sleeping tonight."

Actually, I hadn't thought about that. But between his smile and the fact that he didn't run screaming from the diner at any point during my tale, I am more than happy to take him back with me — and to pay for his omelet, too.

It takes five minutes to find a cab willing to make the long trek uptown. As we wait, we huddle together, our arms wrapped around each other to stay warm against New York's killer winds. Maybe this is New York's next move: literally freezing me out, sending me screaming back to my warmer homeland.

On the ride up, Chase naps, his head on my shoulder. I look out the window, watching the neighborhoods change. We pass so many of my personal landmarks, historic locations of pleasure and pain. The bars from my first night here, the courtyard where Stanford hired me, the theaters and stores I brought my parents to when they surprised me with a visit. All of these places are closed now, of course; cleaning crews inside work to get everything set for tomorrow. New York doesn't sleep — but if you're out at the right time of morning, you might catch it blinking.

I look up at darkened apartment windows, thinking about the people within. Todd once told me that few are from New York City. We come from other places and stay as long as we can. We allow ourselves to be stacked on top of each other in places we can't afford that are not worth what we can't pay for them. We cram into subways infested with germs and listen to crazy people tell us the wrath of God will soon be upon us. We travel from bar to bar to listen to the same music and drink the same drinks and see the same people every Thursday, Friday, and Saturday. Lunch is never cheaper than ten dollars. Dinner is never south of twenty. And yet, we fight tooth and nail to stay here. We'll do anything and everything to avoid packing up and heading back where we came from, those boring, uninspired places filled with people who still can't believe we're actually "making it" here.

Because once you've been to New York, you can't leave. You cannot fail. You cannot let this city win. All these daily sufferings are medals — shiny decorations we buff up and show off to those who were too afraid to come or unable to stay. New York is a bucking bronco and we are all riders doubling as rodeo clowns, trying desperately not to be thrown off. Why? Who the fuck knows.

As Chase and I climb up the three flights to my apartment in Harlem, I think: I did it. I've beaten New York.

And a split second later I wonder, have I? Or is this metropolis just taking a breather, stepping to the sidelines to strategize and come up with a new plan of attack? Biding time until I get comfortable, and then *BANG!* Something else comes out of nowhere?

I am wary, New York. But I am ready for you. The events of the past six months are so far away, and yet so close. Two months ago I was getting fucked in front of thousands. Three months ago I had just moved into the dorm. Four months back I was scaling the ladder of talent representation. Five months ago I was living in a luxury apartment in Hell's Kitchen. And six months ago I was hastily packing my bags and fleeing the City of Angels.

Nobody knows how it all happened. Maybe Graham. Maybe Todd. And now Chase, who is so adorable lying on my bed, wrestling to keep his eyes open. But not my old friends from Los Angeles. Definitely not my parents. And really, not even me. It's like I've been spinning in circles and only now have I stopped, with the world around me still rotating and blurred.

Before bed I hop in the shower. Chase mumbles that he'll be awake when I get back. I know he won't be. Under the warm water I scrub myself with something featuring sweet hints of vanilla and honey from the corner bodega. Todd called it girly, but it relaxes me and does a great job of cleansing the secondhand booze out of my system.

When I get out, it's 7 AM. My phone is ringing.

"Ma, why are you awake right now?" I ask quietly as I slip into a pair of flannel pajama pants.

"My sweetie! Your old goat mom has insomnia. I was just going to leave you a message."

"Don't you have to be up for work in a few hours?"

"Yes, my honey. Yet here I am, suffering hot flashes."

Money's tough back home, so Mom is working again. She's teaching English, which she did until Leo was born and often pined for quite verbally in the years following her hasty retirement. She's trying to convince her principal to put *Gulliver's Travels* back on the syllabus.

"And here I am getting back from work."

"How does it feel, being a vampire?"

"Like you should talk, Ma."

"I'm kidding, baby. You work hard. I'm proud of you. Make good money tonight?"

And that's something else I'm loving: silently accepting pride from Mom that I actually deserve this time.

"Yes." I am actually flipping though my take-home right now — just under four hundred bucks. "And now I'm going to bed."

"Sleep tight, my baby. You're sure everything's okay over there?"

I look at my bed, with Chase on it, snoring softly. He is shirtless and I stare at that gold pocket watch tattoo in the early morning sun's glow, its arm a blur yet frozen just past the 12. As if time is always flying by, but also always bringing a new day, a new beginning. I'll have to ask him if that's what it means to him. Someday.

"Yeah, Mom. Better than okay. Everything's great."

"Good. Love you, baby. Sleep tight."

I lay down slowly, gently. Chase greets me with a sleepy hum. His left leg kicks like a puppy dreaming of running. I sidle up next to him, wrap an arm around him, and pull myself closer. We are interlocking, my legs with his legs, my midsection with his midsection, my face with the back of his neck.

"You smell clean," he mumbles.

"Shhhhh," I say, kissing his neck.

"You wanna have sex?" he whispers, already halfway back to sleep but grinding his butt against my groin feebly.

"Maybe tomorrow."

"Okay…"

And then he is snoring again. My arm rises and falls with his chest. My breathing matches his. I smile and don't know why. We are going deeper and deeper into sleep together.

New York City is so funny sometimes. You get up, shower, and get on the subway. From there, you have no idea what will happen. Planes may crash into landmarks and kill thousands, or maybe you'll crash into Sarah Jessica Parker on the sidewalk and she'll sign an autograph. Maybe you'll get mugged on the street three times on three consecutive nights. Maybe you end up in a drug-fueled backroom orgy, or maybe you end up grabbing a slice of pizza after a few drinks at the bar and then just call it a night. Or maybe, just maybe, you'll share a cigarette with a guy you've fucked two times — one of which was in front of an audience of thousands, while the other gave you an STD — and he still doesn't recognize you. Then maybe you'll go home together, to your new apartment, where there are no cameras or hot tubs, and you'll not have sex. Just spoon and fall asleep.

Basically, absolutely anything can happen or not happen at any second.

I should be terrified.

I am so fucking excited.

ABOUT THE AUTHOR

Justin Luke is a gay nightlife promoter and the co-director of BoiParty.com, an events and production company based in New York City. He's also a blogger (www.JustinPlusOne.com), a podcast co-host (www.InTheKitchenNYC.com), an indie filmmaker, a new media consultant, and a huge video game nerd. Justin graduated from Muhlenberg College with far too many majors and minors, and grew up on Long Island before fleeing for Manhattan as every Long Islander is raised to do.

He has written many novels, but never felt that one should be published until he met Gulliver. He is already working on the sequel to this novel, *Gulliver Travels North: Pride and Provincetown*.

Like him and drop him a line on Facebook right now:
www.Facebook.com/JustinLukeNYC

To find out more about Gully and his upcoming adventures, visit www.GrabGully.com.

ACKNOWLEDGEMENTS

First for my Grandmother, Edith Zirilli, may she rest in peace, who used to write at home in Queens and dream of someday being published, having a job, and being more than a housewife. She was my first best friend, and she taught me a lot considering the short period of time we had together.

And then to my Grandfather, Frank G. Zirilli — a retired knife salesman who's still alive and kicking today, and counseling me every week to do more than what is expected of me, and to bring to everything I ever do nothing but Enthusiasm (with a capital E).

And then my Mother, Dian Zirilli-Mares, an independent and inspirational woman who has celebrated the most important moments in my life with poetry that I still have with me today, to remind me that I must have some talent in these veins, even if only a tiny bit was passed on from her to me.

And to my Stepfather, Ray, who gave my mom happiness that is too surreal even for a novel, and gave me someone to look up to when I needed it most.

And to my Father, Jay Buchbinder, for loving me and supporting me despite his own challenges and troubles. And for never, ever, ever giving up, no matter what is flung his way.

And then my brother, Jared Zirilli — the straight muscle wall of a man with triple threat talent and Broadway in his sights. Thank you for always being my best cheerleader — both in my presence, and to everyone else when I'm not around. Thanks, also, for giving my character Todd a voice I could work with.

Next, to my partner Joe. For your love, your support, your jokes, jibes, and back rubs. For nicknaming me Brownstone and reading this book four hundred times. For smiling and holding me, for snuggling and wrestling, and for constantly, doggedly competing with me in everything and anything. I love you so so so much.

And then there's my business partner, Alan Picus. The king of NYC's gay nightlife universe. The head of BoiParty.com. I thank you for taking me under your wing, helping to make me a someone, and working every day to make me even bigger. Without you and your help, I wouldn't have known the world I created in these pages. I would not have wanted to know it.

Next to my editor, Chris Alexander, née Alexander X. Christopher, née X. Alexander, a man with a million names, and also one of my closest friends (now even closer since he moved from LA to NYC). While the only thing you share in common with Gulliver is the fact you both hopped on a plane and moved here on a whim, it is plain truth that this book would not exist were it not for me sitting at my computer at the beginning of National Novel Writing Month, thinking about you getting off the plane at JFK. Thanks for starting this book as friend and inspiration, and ending it by cleaning up the mess I left in my wake.

And then to my Best Amigo, Austin Helms, who made absolutely no contribution to this book at all. Thanks for the distractions, the laughter, the free drinks, the podcast partnership, the VIP section cohabitation, the trust, the Four Loko, and the inside jokes.

To the real boys whose names I brazenly kept intact, despite the departures from the characters that I created: Servando Rosario, Rowan Pierce, and Shane Mercado, thanks for letting me stick you in my fictive world.

To all of my first readers who gave me invaluable insight, harsh criticism, and free drinks when I felt like I was losing my mind: Patrick Damon, Kristin Speranza, David Calafiore, Paul Beswick, Kyle Braaten, Jeremy Ritz, and Erin Badillo.

And last, but nowhere near least, a HUGE shout-out to all of my nightlife BFFs who keep the clubs wild and memorable every night of the week, and who are there to dance with me on the floor, or secretly throw me in a cab when I get too messy: DJ Steve Sidewalk, Dougie Meyer, Justin Pope, Matthew Tharrett, Jonathan Nish, Mat Gundell, Brandon Propst, Geo Louis, Daniel R. Coda, Nathan Kelly, Kevin Ryan, Paul J. Getty, Brendan Young, Darius Rose, John Hernandez, John Marto, Jake Tidwell, Levi Dawson, Morgan McClean, Shorty, Rob Devito, Jason Hellinger, Filippo Fornasini, Griffin Nieves, Rafael Cordero, Michael Andrew Lucas, Konrad Blachowicz, Alex AJ Armani, and any of the other ten million of you I've forgotten in a moment of idiocy. Thanks for giving me a place to be at night.

Thank you, thank you, thank you. Gully and I will be back before you know it.

JL